Sexy
for the

A Collection of Short Stories

Published by Accent Press Ltd – 2006
ISBN 1905170246
Copyright © The Authors 2006
Edited by Victoria Kirwan-Taylor

Printed and bound in the UK by
Cox and Wyman Ltd, Reading, UK

Cover Design by Emma Barnes

The publisher acknowledges the financial support
of the Welsh Books Council

Acknowledgements

'Highland Fling' by Maureen Brannigan appeared in *That's Life Fast Fiction* (Australia) Spring 2004 and *Best* in April 2005. 'Pre-destination' by Bernardine Kennedy appeared in *Candis* in 2004. 'A Room With a View' by Lynne Barrett-Lee appeared in *Woman's Weekly Fiction Special* Summer 2003. 'It's My Party' by Jane Wenham-Jones appeared in *Woman* in November 2005. 'A Different Viewpoint' by Sheila Alcock appeared in *Woman's Weekly* in 2000 and *You* (South Africa) in 2002. 'Waiting for the Storm' by Karen Howeld appeared in *Peninsular* in January 2002 and *The Amethyst Review* (Canada) Winter 2001. 'Holiday Baggage' by Jane Bidder appeared in *Woman's Weekly* in 2005. 'The Naked Truth' by Della Galton appeared in *Candis* in June 2005. 'Litigation' by Sue Houghton appeared in *Woman* in December 2005. 'Saving Grace' by Jan Jones appeared in *Loving* in August 1994.

Contents

Sea, Sand and Socks
Fran Tracey

I'd been excited at first when Rob called suggesting a beach for our next rendezvous.

'And maybe the sea too, if the waves aren't too crashing.' I paused. 'And there's no jelly fish.' It had been ages since we'd met up and I felt like a kiss and a cuddle, plus extras, of course. And I'd been missing Rob, although that's not the kind of thing we talked about.

'Can't believe we haven't thought of it before. *From Here to Eternity* is one of my favourite films.' His voice sounded excited.

That was something I didn't know about Rob, I realised. His favourite films. It was only the last time we met, punting on the river, that I discovered Italian was his favourite food. The punt had reminded him of the gondolas in Venice. We'd pondered on the erotic possibilities of sharing a bowl of spaghetti and one thought had led to another. The punt rocked dangerously for the next half hour, and we got tangled in weeds at the river's edge.

'You can be Deborah Kerr, I'll be Burt Lancaster,' he said. So of course I assumed that it'd be an exotic destination. The Caribbean? Somewhere with golden sands and warm, crystal clear water lapping at our entwined feet. The Canaries would do. I'd have to try and get a couple of weeks off work. We usually did this a bit last minute, Rob and me.

'How about Norfolk?' Rob whispered. 'We had great family holidays there when I was a kid. Fantastic beaches.'

Something else I didn't know about Rob. Where he spent his childhood holidays. Why hadn't his Mum and Dad thought to take him to Barbados? I paused for a moment.

'But won't it be freezing cold?'

'Maybe. But we'll keep each other warm.' I could hear the smile in his voice. 'Where's your sense of adventure? You've never been reluctant before. It was you who suggested the pub garden in Devon.'

'Yes, and who could have predicted Morris dancers would appear at our crucial moment. The sound of their bells drowned us out, though. Did you ever get all those rose thorns out of...?'

'Got to dash,' he interrupted. 'Perkins is approaching, face like thunder. See you Saturday. Ten o'clock. King's Cross. Ticket hall.'

The phone line went dead. I was too busy at work to worry about the venue too much right then. I was engrossed in untangling some creative accounting when the phone rang again. Probably Rob with a change of heart. Telling me to book leave and meet him at Heathrow instead. Pack your bikini with the ties at the side and the easy to undo clasp, he'd say. Well he would if he knew I'd bought one for this very purpose last year.

'Sally, it's me.' My friend Nicole spoke in her best hushed tone.

'Hello me.'

'Are you free on Saturday? I've got a lawyer for you this time. Called Tim. Still, he can't help his name. Very sexy according to Liz. But then she's married to Mike so what would she know about sexy? He's worth a packet. Don't want to still be single when you hit thirty, now, do you?'

'Don't I?'

Nicole was always trying to set me up with rich and attractive losers. The kind of men who talk non-stop about their possessions and achievements. Not like Rob. He may not be as suave and sophisticated as Nicole's blind dates, but he was sexy, in a quirky, scruffy kind of way. And very bendy. And I'm hardly movie star material, just an ordinary girl with a less than ordinary hobby. And Rob never boasts, he's just kind and fun. Perfect boyfriend material, if we weren't so hooked on our current arrangement. And, yes, I did want to be single at thirty if you call the occasional erotic encounter in unusual outdoor places, with a man you've known forever but not too well, being single. I was quite happy with what Nicole would call "my situation", thank you very much.

'I think you're scared of commitment,' Nicole said smugly, not for the first time. Having my cake and eating it was what I called it. Though sometimes, just sometimes, I did wonder what Rob did on a cold Wednesday evening in November. Watched TV? Rang his mum?

'Sorry, Nicole, I'm busy this weekend.'

'Not your dirty weekend man again? Aren't you getting on a bit for all that shenanigans, Sally? Exposing yourself in multi-storey car parks. Getting caught by the police.' I wish I'd never told Nicole about Rob. Or about the police and me and Rob, in what I called the multi-storey car park misunderstanding.

'The police didn't catch us, I've told you. One of them just shone their torch in, but we kept very still on the back seat and they went away. And anyway, this time it'll be on a beach. When did you and Ben last make love on a beach?'

'Last summer, if you must know. On St.Lucia. Every day for a fortnight. And in the sea too.'

I put the phone down. I liked Nicole. I just wished she wouldn't try and organise my love life. And deep down I was a bit envious of couples who made love every day for a fortnight and still had someone to share the cleaning with. Maybe I was missing out. I might never even find out where Rob shopped, or if he bought organic.

It had all begun long ago when we were in the sixth form. Raging hormones at the end of term disco led to our first fumble. I blame 'A' level English too. All those repressed Victorian heroines like Jane Eyre and dark brooding heroes like Heathcliff. Rob wasn't so sure. He did biology and said it was definitely the hormones.

'Though I do wonder what Jane Eyre would have been like once her stays were released and she was ravished by Rochester,' he'd said.

Whatever it was, seeing Rob saunter down the corridor to double Maths on a Thursday morning made my stomach flip. And he still has that effect on me. When he rushes up to meet me at the train station, my heart flutters. Biology I guess.

The school football pitch was our first venue. Between the goalposts. Not that either of us were football fans. Quite the opposite in fact. But that's where we found ourselves after a little too much spiked punch. We were fairly timid that time. Let's say the ball didn't cross the line. Then term ended, we lived a few miles apart and didn't see each other over the summer. Somehow we never got round to it in the upper sixth. We were too chock full of teenage embarrassment.

After 'A' levels we went off to different universities, me to study Maths – well English had never been my strong point – Rob to study Economics. Our next encounter was at the first school reunion. This time we went a little further. A bit more vodka in the punch and a few years of experience at university helped fuel us. We made our way onto the roof of one of the prefab buildings at our old school and I wouldn't have been surprised if traces of asbestos were left on my backside. But it was fun. After that night we went our separate ways, promising to keep in touch. I became an accountant, Rob a salesman in a ball-bearing factory. With careers like these our main chance of having fun and thrills was through our erotic encounters. So we kept in touch, meeting every few months. It was a kind of stress relief. And we got to know each other a little bit better each time too.

'I used to spend my pocket money on superheroes comics and some kind of sherbet that blew your head off,' reminisced Rob.

So it's not as sordid as people might think. Neither of us had a significant other, and we'd agreed that if either of us met someone we would like to settle down with, the other would bow out gracefully. Sex in suburbia forever for the lucky person who found themselves in a permanent relationship. The horror of this is at least partly what made our arrangement so attractive.

I don't know what Miss Pickles, our 'A' level English teacher, would've thought if she'd known what naughtiness was inspired by our set books. She'd never thought either of us showed much flair for understanding the finer points of our nation's rich literary heritage.

"Robert Jones, would you like to share with the class what you and Sally Bredon find quite so amusing about Cleopatra and the asp," she would ask in a waspish tone.

No, Miss Pickles would not have understood. Mind you, neither of us had been much good at history either, but we managed to visit a few historic buildings, like a Scottish castle. I found being ravished on the ramparts with the promise I could pour boiling oil on my enemies (where were you when I needed you, Miss Pickles?) a real turn on.

I enjoyed dressing the part too. Long velvet dress and cape for the castle, and no knickers for authenticity of course. Floaty cotton gypsy skirt for the field of corn. But if Rob thought I'd be stripping to my bikini on the beach in Norfolk, in February, he had another think coming. He'd have to enjoy finding the real me under the many layers I'd be wearing, though he was certainly not peeling them all off.

On Saturday we made it to the beach by mid-afternoon, not long before dusk. A gale was blowing. We walked in silence. Rob casually draped his arm around my shoulder. I nestled snugly into his chest. I was cold. I wondered if we looked like those people you see on the cover of holiday brochures. Like real lovers in a real relationship. Only with lots more clothes on.

'You must've been stressed to suggest this,' I muttered. 'Is Perkins putting on the pressure?'

'Not exactly. I've been missing you. We haven't met for months.' He looked at his feet. I was a little taken aback. This was new. My stomach gambolled.

'But we often don't meet for months.'

'I know, but,' his voice faded. 'I thought this time we could talk a bit. More than just about our favourite things.' He smiled. 'We could take a different leaf from Julie Andrew's songbook next time, you know, climb every mountain, then have a quickie at the peak? Bet she and the captain never made love amongst the edelweiss. But I know you like having your back caressed, but not your toes touched, that you've read *Jane Eyre*, you understand quadratic equations, and that's about it,' Rob said, all in a rush.

'I can tell you I like the feel of warm sand between my toes and collecting exotic shells. Well, I would if I ever got the chance. Sand dunes, couch grass and biting gale force winds, that I can take or leave.' Rob pulled away from me a little.

'I thought we could be private here,' he said.

When had he ever worried about being private before? We'd made love in some pretty public places. There was the ghost train at the fair last year. And the tunnel of love. There'd been foreplay on the waltzers too. Then there was the bandstand in the park, not whilst the band was in full swing, of course.

'I'd been hoping we could stop over somewhere,' his voice faded into the wind. We'd never stopped over. Not together anyway. Not that I hadn't thought about it. Of course I had. And recently the thought occurred more often.

'I've provisionally booked us into the King's Arms, in town. Their website said it had some of the biggest four posters in England. I thought we could pretend we were back at the castle. Only indoors. And with the comfort of twenty-first century central heating.' He grinned. 'But without the dungeon, I'm afraid.'

He'd got me there. The castle had been our best encounter yet. I changed the subject, but not without a pang of fear. Was Nicole right? Was I too hooked on my fantasies? Worried that if we got to know each other too well it might all fall apart and I would never see him again?

'So where's the best spot here, then? Let's get started. And if you think I'm getting naked like in the ancient forest you can think again. A few twigs and spiders have nothing on this. No sex without socks, I'm afraid.'

'I was ten when I was here last,' he protested, 'how would I know what was the best spot?' But he led me into the dunes and shook out the tartan rug we'd bought at the castle as a souvenir in the gift shop on our way out. It still held memories. Rob was on to a winner now, and he knew it. The tartan rug always made me feel in need of a cuddle. Trouble was every time he threw it into the air the wind whipped it away. I giggled.

'Let's try without it,' I suggested. 'It's not like we're not protected by many layers of clothing, now, is it?'

Or so I thought. Silly me. I'd forgotten how sand works its way into every little crevice. But as soon as Rob kissed me the wind seemed to drop. I tugged his shirt from the waistband of his trousers and held him close to me, massaging his back. He flinched.

'Good grief, Sally, you could've warmed your hands. At least I blew into mine before tackling your bra.'

'Whose idea was Norfolk? In February?' I said sharply.

'OK, fair point. But make sure those hands of yours are good and warm before you undo my belt. You're not getting those blocks of ice into my boxers, that's for sure.'

I don't know why this time it felt different, but it did. Less rushed, more like we were a proper couple, not two people who just happened to meet to exercise their pent-up lust every few months. Well, it did until the only other person in Norfolk mad enough to leave the warmth of their home decided to let their dog off its lead in the sand dune next to us. The dog nosed its way right up to Rob's nether regions and let out a distressed yelp. Not the rabbit it had been hoping to find, obviously.

'Come on, Jake. Get a move on. I need a pint,' shouted its owner.

The dog sauntered off. It probably wasn't the first time it had stumbled across love in the dunes, but I bet it was usually rabbits involved.

Alone again, we threw the rug over ourselves for protection from the stinging rain that had just begun. We lay on our backs watching the darkening sky, sharing a companionable silence. This was new, too. Usually we made our way back to the train station fairly quickly. I looked at Rob. It was like being on our hundredth date. It was nice.

'I don't know how much longer I can carry on with this, Sally.'

My stomach flipped and I gulped. This was the moment I had been dreading. Rob had brought me here for our swansong. If he'd got a girlfriend, someone to share cleaning the bathroom with before making love in the shower, and it wasn't me, I wasn't sure now how I'd cope. I stared even harder at the sky, trying to make stars appear from behind the dense clouds.

'Apart from anything else, I'm running out of ideas of places to go.'

'Me too, to be honest,' I replied. I shuddered, not least at the thought of Nicole organising my dates from now on.

Rob squirmed in the sand a bit. I wondered if a crab had surfaced and nipped him. He looked as though he was going to say something, then thought better of it. I wanted him to speak, but dreaded what he would say. He cleared his throat.

'Maybe we could try somewhere indoors next time,' he whispered. 'Perhaps you'd like to come to my place for a change. We don't have to stick to the bed. There's a nice big kitchen table.'

His place. I didn't even know if he had a flat or a house.

'It's not a palace. Just a little terraced place in the town centre. You'd be welcome any time.'

We both looked up at the sky again, avoiding each other's gaze.

'I suppose there's no reason why I can't,' I tried to sound nonchalant. 'Next time. In a couple of months? Do you have a garden?' Please say sooner, I begged silently.

'I was wondering about sometime next week.' He turned to me and kissed my nose. 'I've even got a shed,' he added.

I didn't hesitate.

'I'd like to see you sooner, too. Maybe you can play me your favourite music.'

'Of course.' He pulled out a bottle of champagne from his rucksack, and we lingered in the dunes, making love again, slowly this time. We stayed over in The King's Arms too.

And that's what led us here. I smiled as I heard the registrar's voice say:

'And I would like to thank you all on behalf of Sally and Rob for sharing their double celebration today, their marriage and the birth of their daughter Scarlett Sandy Jones.'

No one but Nicole raised an eyebrow at Scarlett's name. I'd finally discovered Rob's favourite film is *Gone with the Wind*. We're honeymooning in North Carolina. Scarlett is coming with us, but one night we'll have a babysitter and I will wear the tightest stays and biggest crinoline imaginable, and Rob will wear a cravat. And he'll have fun finding out what good Southern girls wear under all those layers of lace and frills.

A Room With a View
Lynne Barrett-Lee

It was a miserable start to a holiday. We were practically dropping with fatigue from the flight, but the transfer – two hours with a maniac coach driver – had left our nerves shot to pieces and our legs with the shakes. And now this.

'Look! I knew it! Look out there, Elizabeth! If that's a sea view I'm a cat in a hat!'

I stepped out on to the balcony and looked. Paul was right. It wasn't a sea view at all. Just a low wall, some scrub, a cluster of dustbins, some crates and a couple of beaten-up cars.

'But you *can* see it,' I answered. 'A strip of it, anyway. Look, there, to the right. See?'

'Elizabeth, that is *not* a sea view. That is a view over the picturesque hotel back yard, and will doubtless be further enhanced during our stay by the comings and goings of lorries and dustcarts and, if we're lucky, an entertaining nocturnal tableau of young staff on mopeds, plus cats, rabid dogs and possibly donkeys.'

He stomped back inside and peeled off his jacket. It was still early morning – we'd taken a night flight – but the day already promised to be fearfully hot.

I followed him in and sat down on the bed.

'No matter,' I told him, attempting some jauntiness. 'We're here. *That's* what matters. On holiday at last. Let's have a sleep and ask the rep later. I'm sure she could help. It's probably a mistake.'

But Paul wasn't to be mollified. I could tell by his expression. He shook his head.

'No. I'm going down to sort this out now.'

I kicked off my sandals. 'But it's not even six!'

'Precisely,' he growled. And moments later, like my cheerful holiday mood, he was gone.

       *   *   *

"Lucky, lucky you!" my friend Carol had declared, when I'd told her our plans for an impromptu Spanish break. "It's just what you need. And with the children off your hands it'll be a bit like a second honeymoon, won't it?"

I'd nodded, of course. Even returned her cheerful wink, but privately, I had my doubts. It had been years since Paul and I had been away alone together. There'd been the odd weekend, when the children had been smaller and had gone to stay with their grandparents, but, even without them, they'd always dominated our thoughts. *And* our conversation, I realised wryly. We'd run out of things to talk about barely an hour into the flight. As I ferreted in my case for a night-shirt, I wondered just what sort of a holiday this would be. Paul had been irritable since we'd arrived at the airport; with the car park, the airline, the well-meaning holiday rep, but most of all, I gradually realised, with me.

And I, I had to admit, with him. I felt myself bristle as he came marching back in, minutes later.

'Don't bother with that,' he said, loftily waving a hand at the cases. 'I'm waiting for the night porter to ring. They're going to see if they can move us later on.'

I shrugged. 'It's no bother. I'm just sorting some clothes out. I'm going to shower and get my head down for a couple of hours. Anyway, "see if" isn't the same as "will" is it? I expect the place is full, now I think about it. Don't you?'

He exhaled noisily.

'But we've *paid* for a sea view. We have a right to expect it! And if we don't kick up a fuss, we won't get one, will we?' He pointed outside. 'I for one do not intend spending a fortnight looking at *that*!'

As ever, I tried to keep the peace. 'I know,' I reasoned, 'but you know what it's like. They probably made a mistake with the booking. Please don't get in a flap about it. If they can't move us, I'm sure they'll compensate us. Let's not let it spoil our holiday. You're tired. Let's get some sl…'

11

'Hrmmph! It already has!'

He swept up his sponge bag and headed for the bathroom. Weary of arguing and dead on my feet, I flopped onto the bed and fell promptly asleep.

Determined bright sun-shafts cajoled me into wakefulness mid-morning. That and the faint sound of laughter below. Paul was nowhere to be seen. In the lobby, no doubt, bemoaning our lot. He would be, I knew, just like a dog with a bone. That was his way, and it had served him well this far. I just hoped, for their sakes, that they *had* another room. Feeling refreshed but mutinous, I wandered out to the balcony, and found myself actually grinning as a dustcart drove off. Directly below me, a couple of waiters were sharing a companionable few minutes off. The pungent aroma of strong cigarettes wafted up and the sun crafted stripes on their glistening dark heads. My Spanish not extending far beyond *gracias*, I didn't have the first clue what they were saying, but as a pretty titian-haired girl passed them and waved, their appreciative comments didn't need any translation. I thought about my own sons, now long-limbed teenagers, and how short a time it seemed since Paul and I had been so ourselves.

'There you are!'

My husband, evidently in marginally better spirits, came out on to the balcony to join me.

I swung round. 'Any luck?'

He jiggled a hand. 'Hmm. Yes and no. They *are* full, so they can't move us today, but apparently there's a group leaving on Monday, so they *say* they might be able to move us then.'

'There we are then. All sorted.'

'Not necessarily. There are more booked in and it will depend on them not having been allocated sea views themselves. I shall have to keep the pressure up. The rep's due in later. I shall wait in reception and make my presence felt.'

12

He said this with his habitual world-weary but imperious air. Which went down very well at work, no doubt, but was beginning to get on my nerves.

'I was hoping we'd get down to the beach,' I protested.

'And we will,' he assured me with his first grudging half-smile of the holiday. 'You go down and grab a prime spot, and I'll follow once the room's sorted out.'

Which it wasn't, of course, and I was getting exasperated by the whole business. A good hour after I'd spread out our towels and covered myself in factor fifteen, he finally harrumphed his way across the sand. He flopped down, forehead beaded with sweat and well furrowed, oblivious to the sparkling blue vista around us, to the soft balmy breeze or the swoosh of the foam.

'Useless,' he barked. 'They're an absolute shambles!'

I kept my eyes closed and my hat brim well down. His flapping was causing a sandstorm.

'No move, then?' I asked mildly.

'Just the usual excuses. They're sorry, but *this*, and they're sorry, but *that*... apparently the only rooms with a view they'll have available are family rooms, which they won't give us.'

I rolled over on to my stomach and picked up the sun cream. 'School holidays. They're bound to have families coming in.'

'Which isn't the point. We were here first!' He pulled his T-shirt off with a scowl. His torso was already nut brown and shining. Paul always tanned easily. And didn't look anywhere near his forty-five years. Though he felt it, I knew. I pulled myself up to my knees and squeezed some suncream into my hand. If nothing else it might soothe his hunched shoulders a bit.

'Look,' I said, as he surrendered himself to my vigorous rubbing and pushed off his flip-flops, 'let's just forget about it, shall we? We have all the view we'll ever need right here five minutes walk away. We have nothing to do but enjoy ourselves, and will doubtless get a refund that'll pay for a nice dinner when we get home. OK? There.' I flipped the top back on the bottle. 'You're done.'

He looked shamefaced. 'Except now I'm going for a swim.'

But even the twin pleasures of a warm sea and a cool breeze were insufficient to keep his irritation at bay for long. We returned to our room after an evening of desultory chat and yet more hotel grievances, to the yowling of an unseen dog and the throb of engines. I slipped out to see what the cause of the noise was, and, just as Paul predicted, saw a huddle of bikes. I picked out the two waiters I'd seen earlier, astride them. They were both still in uniform, obviously having just finished their shifts. The titian-haired girl was just donning an oversized helmet.

'They'll be off soon,' I told Paul, who was tutting beside me. 'They must work long days – they were all here this morning. I expect they're off to get changed and go clubbing somewhere.'

The girl swung her leg over and climbed on the back of one of the bikes, planting a kiss on her boyfriend's cheek. I smiled wistfully as I watched them roar away.

'Why don't we go back down for a night-cap or something? It's still early.'

But Paul was back in the bedroom, his nose in a book.

'What?' He looked up, having only half heard me.

'A drink,' I repeated. 'And there's a disco as well. We could…'

His expression stopped me.

'I'm too tired,' he replied.

True to his word, Paul was indeed tired. He was asleep before I'd even undressed and snoring soon after. I looked down at his sleeping features and saw the face of someone I felt I barely knew any more. Did he feel it too? Without the glue of the children we just couldn't seem to keep things together – we were about as close as our wretched hotel room was to the sea.

But, restless in the small hours after my morning nap, I found the bed hot and claustrophobic. I got up, drank some water and headed outside. Softened by moonlight, our view was transformed, the sea flecked with spangles and the coast road a pretty ribbon of pale lemon lights. Beneath me the hotel still beavered and bustled, but quietly, as if accompanying the cicadas' high trill.

It was almost five when I saw the light of a motorbike swing into the yard. My first thought was one of dismay that Paul might hear it. I could already picture him out on the balcony, giving them yet another piece of his mind. So many pieces – so much agitation! But his snores reassured me and I was able to carry on gazing silently down. The young couple from earlier, for couple they obviously were, had got off the bike and were standing beside it. She took off the helmet and he slipped it over the handlebars. She probably, I realised, lived at the hotel – lots of the young chambermaids and waitresses did – and he must be bringing her home.

Enchanted but embarrassed, I found myself blushing as he folded her into his arms and kissed her, his hands moving tenderly over her hair. There was no frantic groping, no urgent fumbles, but it seemed they would kiss till they could kiss no longer, before he jumped on the bike and wheeled it into the darkness. She stood there and waved till the light from the headlamp was no more than a pinprick of white in the distance, then slipped silently under the awning and in. I stepped inside also, and pulled back the sheet, now saddened and melancholy and not quite sure why.

'The monastery,' Paul read, 'was built in 1287, and boasts some of the finest architecture of its time. How about it? Or how about this? The vineyard. Ah. But that excursion's Tuesday. No, today it's either the monastery or the evening barbecue. So we'll go for the monastery. Yes?'

'I'd rather spend another day on the beach,' I interrupted. 'I need to unwind. *We* need to unwind. We can do those things next week, can't we?'

Paul took a bite from his croissant and put the pamphlet down. Then swallowed and cast his eyes around the bustling restaurant.

'I didn't come all the way here to lie around doing nothing, Elizabeth. I want to see a bit of the place. If we spend all our time just lolling about we'll be –'

'Bored?' I inserted.

He looked at me, as if for signs of annoyance, which I hid.

'No,' he said. 'Not at all, it's just that I don't fancy another day –'

With me? On our own? With no kids to organise? Nothing to do but be a couple again?

'Look,' I said, feeling his discomfort and hating it, 'why don't *you* go to the monastery, and I'll go to the beach.'

'Don't be silly,' he said irritably.

'I'm not. Just realistic. We obviously have completely different agendas, so we'd be better off on our own, wouldn't we?' I drained my coffee and stood up. Something sad and perplexing was happening between us. I wasn't sure why or what on earth to do about it, I only knew that with those long years of frantic parenting behind us, we seemed to have lost each other along the way. As if to endorse it, Paul then stood also.

'It's not that. I just don't happen to want to lie on the beach,' he snapped.

'Or talk to me, swim with me, *be* with me, even. Well, that suits me fine! You can take your foul mood with you off on your coach trip.'

'Point taken,' he said flatly. 'I'll go book a seat.'

The day passed slowly, in a heat haze of torpor. I couldn't settle to my book, and felt fretful and miserable. Even swimming in the bathwater-warm crystal water did nothing to soothe my now growing unease. I should, I thought, have accompanied Paul on the excursion. Together we may have niggled and then gone through the motions, but apart if felt as if some unspoken gulf now gaped between us.

I made my way back to the hotel around teatime, showered and changed into a long dress. It was a new one – bought, rather fancifully it now seemed, specially for the occasion – but by the time I had sat on the balcony for an hour it had already become hopelessly crumpled and creased. I looked at my watch – half the evening had gone. Surely the coach should have been back by now?

'*Ola*!' called a voice. I peered over the balcony. My waiter friend, greeting his girlfriend again. Again they were kissing, again arm in arm. Again wanting nothing, it seemed, but each other. I leaned back in my chair so I didn't have to see them, all at once desperate for the way we once were. How would the two of us find our way back there? Worse, was there anything left to be found? We just didn't seem to connect any longer. We were simply co-existing along parallel tracks. I glanced down again, my mind's eye on our young selves. We'd been like that once. Could we be so again?

I went back inside, wiped my face, put on lipstick and decided to go down and track down that coach.

But I was beaten to it. I opened the door to find Paul already striding down the corridor towards me, bottle in hand and a grim expression on his face. He waggled the wine.

'Peace offering from the tour guide,' he told me. 'Flat tyre south of Nerja. And guess what? No spare.'

I stood aside to let him in. He seemed different. He was dusty and grimy and looked hot and exhausted, but beneath that, his eyes seemed to glitter.

'I'm so glad you're back,' I said. 'I've been worried about you. I –'

He was staring at me. 'Is that new?'

'What? The dress?'

17

'Yes. I don't think I've seen it. You look – well – lovely. Sort of – I don't know – nice.'

'*Nice*?' Despite myself I laughed. '*So* romantic! You should have stopped at lovely.' But then his expression changed and he dropped his eyes. He was, I realised with surprise, embarrassed. I walked over to him.

'Nice will do just fine, though,' I said quietly. 'And for what it's worth, I think you look pretty nice as well.'

He took my hand and led me out onto the balcony. My young friends had gone. No rabid dog howled at us. At long last, we had the place to ourselves.

'Ridiculous,' Paul observed, wine bottle in one hand. The other one still held mine. Tightly.

'Ridiculous what?' I asked, not sure of his meaning.

'Ridiculous us. Ridiculous *me*!' He turned round to face me. Then put down the bottle. 'I've been dreadful. I've been – well, I just haven't known what to *do* with myself. Just me and you and, well, *us*. It's felt so odd. No agenda. No kids…. Well…. I'm so sorry,' he said.

'You have nothing to be sorry for,' I answered, nodding my acknowledgement of the feeling we couldn't quite put into words. 'It's me who should be apologising. For being so pig-headed. I should have come with you today.'

'No you shouldn't. If you'd come with me I wouldn't have come to my senses.' He took my other hand, and pulled me towards him. 'I missed you so much today. I felt suddenly – I don't know – strange. Like a fish out of water, I think is the term. If you'd been there – well, that's it, isn't it? You *have* always been there. So much so that sometimes I haven't been able to see the wood for the trees…'

'Or the sea!' I finished for him.

He laughed. Properly, for the first time in ages. I snaked my arms around him and snuggled in closer. 'Phew!' I said. 'Better stop before you run out of clichés! And we don't have to do all that talking stuff. That's for grown-ups. We *could* just try kissing. It's a popular pastime round these parts, I'm told.'

18

Paul bent his head, lifted mine and then kissed me. And we kissed like we had when we'd met, all those years back. Like we'd just met again, which, in some ways, we had.

'By the way,' he said, finally. 'Just been nabbed by the porter. If you want there's a room with a proper sea view.'

I looked at Paul, framed by the coast road and buildings, the sheeny grey dustbins, the crates in the yard. And saw only the man I was just re-discovering.

'No thanks,' I answered. 'If you're not that bothered, I'm perfectly happy with the view I have here.'

Highland Fling
Maureen Brannigan

'You are kidding, Ben! You want me to sleep in a *what* on our wedding night?'

I hitched up my totally impractical Regency-style wedding dress – found at the local charity shop when I was actually looking for a funky kilt pin for Ben – and looked at my brand new husband in disbelief. All this fresh mountain air was definitely going to his head.

It was the end of a long happy day. We'd been married on top of this mountain by Ben's minister brother, Alasdair. The weather, which had been my main worry, was glorious. After the simple ceremony Ben and Alasdair had barbequed for our families and a few friends to the happy sounds of a babbling burn on this spot at the bottom of the mountain. The champagne had flowed and I couldn't imagine feeling any happier.

Our guests were on their way home, and now, when I was expecting to be whisked away to some exotic, memorable location for our honeymoon, Ben, still magnificent in his kilt, was unloading the back of his battered old Land Rover.

Seeming completely unconcerned, he whistled happily and lifted out camping paraphernalia. 'You'll have changed your mind after the first night, Roxy, my love. There's nothing quite like waking up to a bracing Highland morning. The awesome sight of a few Highland cows, herds of red deer, and frolicking spring lambs will have you as besotted with the place as I am.'

I highly doubted it. Thinking that Ben should be working for the tourist industry, I put my hands on my hips and placed my hiking boot on what I imagined was the tent. 'Have you gone completely mad? If you dare put that thing together I am divorcing you. You know I hate camping.'

Still smiling, Ben stroked my cheek and said, 'Ah, but you've never camped properly before, have you?'

He was right, of course. The only tent I'd ever been in was a pup tent we had at the bottom of my parents' garden. My memory was that we were always wet, hungry, cold, itchy and scurrying back into the warmth of the house as soon as darkness fell.

So I always had an excuse ready when I saw the "sleeping under the stars" glint in Ben's eye.

The glint was definitely there now and I'd missed the warning signs because I was so excited about our marriage and so besotted with my Mr Right. Huh!

He had the cheek to hand me a tent pole. 'I love the way your beautiful eyes sparkle when you're annoyed. Now, don't worry. I promised you the honeymoon of a lifetime – and the honeymoon of a lifetime you are going to get.'

I threw the pole as far as I could, considering the outfit I was wearing. It slid out of my silk-gloved hand and came to ground with an unremarkable thud mere feet away. Angry tears threatened and this awful squeaking noise came out of my mouth. 'Annoyed! You think this is just about being annoyed, Ben Murdoch? I'm sure you said that we would have a honeymoon to die for. Forgive me if Hawaii or Bali popped into my head – not the freezing, blustery wilds of Scotland. You – you are a complete nutter!'

Still unfazed, Ben put his strong arms around me. 'Believe me, Rox, the next week will make a convert of you. The weather is going to be perfect, and this,' he said, waving his arms around, 'this is the most romantic place on earth.'

Completely deranged. Maybe he does have a dark side after all.

Until I met Ben I never believed in love at first sight. Now look at me. We've only known each other six weeks and until today I was so sure we were right to get married so quickly.

But we have quite different ideas on lots of things. Ben is employed by the Save the Highlands people, or whatever they call themselves nowadays. He eats, drinks, dreams and breathes the Highlands. I, on the other hand, have always loathed the outdoors. All that fresh air, cow poop, nettles – and what about those blasted midges? The miracle is that we ever met at all. If anyone had told me I'd agree to a date with, never mind marry, a man whose idea of a good time is crouching in a hide, which is, if you would believe, a little wooden hut cleverly concealed, with a kind of small slit in the wall for spying on unsuspecting birds, I'd have laughed in my gin and tonic. Here Ben will sit hour after frozen hour to ensure the survival of the osprey.

In fact if my stiletto heel hadn't got caught in a manhole cover in the middle of Princes Street I'd still be dating some office Lothario. Ben, on a rare trip to the city, came swiftly to my rescue.

OK, I'll admit I was bowled over by his ruddy good looks, his complete lack of guile. Ben's chat-up line consisted of him telling me that stilettos would give me bandy legs, and that smoking was detrimental to the environment!

The men I usually hung around with at that time were metrosexuals. You know the type, patter merchants with their Prada suits, facials, high colonics, and weekend after weekend at expensive gyms and spas.

In more ways than one Ben was a breath of fresh air. After years of dating men who spent more time than me choosing hair-care products, who would break a date because their Botox injections appointment had been brought forward – Ben was a delight.

My mother loved him on sight. 'God, Roxy. Ben is the man of my dreams, never mind yours.'

From that day on Ben could do no wrong in her eyes.

But… as my pessimistic sister Cassie is fond of saying, every silver lining has a cloud. And, take it from me, if it's left up to Ben I'll see many a cloud as I emerge from his tent a broken woman, likely frozen, soaked, stung and, my worst fear, being chased by an angry stag.

Ben was holding me tighter now. Suddenly it all felt so right. I sniffed and snuggled into his jacket remembering all the great things I loved about him and resolved to make the best of the fresh air honeymoon. After all, I was with the man I adored.

Ben cradled my face in his hands. 'Come and sit down. I owe you an explanation.'

I prepared myself for the worst. He was going to tell me he was broke, or worse, had only six months to live. At this thought a great sob broke from my throat and I hurtled myself at him. 'I don't care about exotic places for now. All I want is right here. I'll learn to love these mountains if it kills me.'

Ben started to laugh. 'You are the funniest little thing. I'm only going to tell you that I had to postpone our trip for a week as Calum has broken his leg. He was to take over from me until we got back from the honeymoon.'

Relief swept over me and I wiped my face on the hem of my dress. 'You mean you're not dying?'

He laughed again and took his jacket off and put it round my shoulders. 'What am I going to do with you?'

We sat for a few moments then I said, 'Did you say we're only going to be here for a week?'

He reached down and kissed me softly. 'We'll pick up tickets to anywhere you like for two weeks when Calum's replacement gets here.'

At that moment I couldn't have cared less about going away. My heart was full.

'And that's not all,' Ben said, looking over my shoulder to a ridge of Scots pine trees. 'I want you to meet some friends of mine.'

I looked around but could see no one.

Ben pointed to where two white-crested birds sat observing us. They started to chatter to each other, 'tchip tchip tchip'.

'Roxy, I'd like to introduce you to Hector and Molly Osprey, who have just returned from their honeymoon in West Africa.'

I looked up at my wonderful husband. Right at that moment I would have happily stayed on those hills with him forever. I suddenly understood about true love... Enduring, selfless love. Hector and Molly seemed to nod in approval.

Silly Boy
Linda Michelmore

'Paul,' Shelley said in her runny honey purr, 'why don't you take off your jacket?'

'My jacket?' Paul said, as though he'd only just realised he owned one, let alone was wearing one.

'Well, yes,' Shelley leaned towards him, her lips just brushing his earlobe. 'I'm not asking you to give it away, silly boy, simply take it off. You must be awfully hot.' Shelley embellished the word "hot" with a slow caress of warm breathiness.

'Hot?' Paul said, as though the word were new to his vocabulary. He was just a tad put out that Shelley had called him a silly boy when he'd been pretty certain until that moment he was now a man, and any other place than here he would have proved it to her. But she was unnerving him, this beautiful woman with the figure of a goddess, the looks of an angel. This was her patch, not his, and her confidence was in the ascendant. 'My jacket?'

The jacket had cost Paul a fortune – or at the very least the better part of a day's pay. Linen. Designer. He'd had to ask his friend Gabriel (Gab for short – or Gab the Gob after a few drinks), who was something whizz kid with finance in the City, what the form was for lunch on the coast with a woman you'd only just met. "Linen jacket, old chap," Gabriel had said, "Ben Sherman shirt, preferably striped, crease-free chinos, toning silk socks, brogues. Easy-peasy. Oh, and get a haircut."

Ha bloody ha. Paul was a hair stylist.

Things had moved a bit fast with Shelley, but who was he to argue? Ninety-nine percent of women assumed he was gay, being a hair stylist. Paul didn't bother to put them right, normally, because it made life easier not to be chatted up all the time. Not that he hadn't had his bit of fun, and not that he hadn't chatted up a few women he'd fancied in his time either. But it had been Shelley who had chatted *him* up. Oh yes, she'd chatted him up all right. An older woman. Quite a bit older actually – and for older, read experienced. "My husband's away a lot," she'd said the first time she'd come into the salon and insisted Paul cut and coloured her hair. "New Zealand at the moment, to be exact. For months and months actually. You understand me?"

Oh yes, Paul had understood. How lucky could a bloke get? You couldn't get much further away than that, could you? So here he was, lunch not the damask-clothed, set with the best silver, table affair he'd thought it would be, but a picnic. Even if it was the biggest hamper Fortnums can provide, with champagne chilling in huge plastic boxes, which had clinked with ice cubes as Paul carried them down the narrow path. A picnic on the beach. Paul hadn't come prepared for the beach.

'Yes, your jacket, Paul. Take it off. I mean I'm feeling a bit silly in my bikini with you in your jacket. Tell you what. I'll do you a deal. You take off your jacket and I'll undo my bikini top.'

'OK, right.' Going topless wasn't likely to get you arrested for indecent exposure, was it? Well, Paul was a big boy now, wasn't he? Off came the jacket. He threw it with something approaching bravado and cringed at the thought of what sand and bird droppings and oil-covered seaweed would do to a couple of hundred quid's worth of jacket.

'That's better, much better. And if you take off your shirt, I'll…'

'I'm acclimatizing, don't rush me,' Paul said, and a nervous smile set off a tic-like twitch at the corner of his mouth.

'Be a devil,' Shelley said. She undid the buttons of Paul's shirt quicker than you can say needle and thread and slipped a hand inside Paul's shirt, slid it up towards the top of his left arm, eased the fabric down over his shoulder. With a movement smoother than satin, she then repeated the procedure with the other sleeve, until Paul was bereft of his shirt.

25

'You look, um, stunning,' Paul said, trying to clock Shelley's breasts without staring like a fourteen-year-old with a copy of Esquire. He folded his arms across his hairless chest and vowed never to ask Gab the Gob for advice ever again. This should all have been happening by candle-light at the very brightest. And here he was, with the sun giving out God knows how many kilowatts of heat and light and he was bound to get sunburn.

'Flatterer,' Shelley laughed. 'That's what I like about you, Paul, you know how to pay a woman a compliment and mean it.' She fingered her choppy-cut fringe; honey blonde no 2 – Paul knew that beyond any whisper of doubt because he'd put it on for her. 'And you can unfold your arms. This is a beach, Paul, not a Buckingham Palace garden party.'

Could he trust himself if Shelley were to massage his chest with sunscreen? Did she even do sunscreen? From where he was sitting it didn't look like it: her skin like café au lait, smooth and glowing with health and... God, but he could bonk her right here and now if only there wasn't the chance of a summons for indecent behaviour hovering in the heat-filled air.

'Sunscreen,' Shelley said. 'I use factor fifteen now because, well, my skin's darkish naturally, but at the beginning of each season I start with factor thirty.'

'Do they do a factor six hundred and eighty-five?' Paul quipped.

'Hmm,' Shelley said, 'you are a bit milky looking. Good job I like dairy!' She gave Paul's shoulder a flick of a lick, then uncapped the sunscreen. 'Roll over Beethoven. Back first, because the shoulders always catch the sun first.'

Paul rolled.

'Um, this isn't the first time you've done this, is it?' he asked. Shelley's hands seemed to be all over his back, and everywhere at the same time. He sent up a silent prayer it wasn't his front she'd decided to do first, because part of him was fast making slithery-snake patterns in the sand beneath him.

'Definitely not,' Shelley said. 'Now... turn over, very slowly. I'll do your chest next.'

Paul turned, feeling like a pig on a spit roast. He gave himself up to warm hands slithering and sliding over him. He closed his eyes and thought impure thoughts. And then, before he even realised it was happening, Shelley's fingers had unbuttoned his fly, and were easing the waistband of a hundred quid's worth of chinos down towards his feet. Somehow, she managed to slide his socks from his feet at the same time for which he thanked the god of all new lovers because what worse sight was there than a man in his boxers wearing socks? More than a few women in Paul's time had laughed at the sight, rendering him useless between the sheets.

'Cat got your tongue?' Shelley screwed the cap back on the sunscreen and slipped it into her bag. She also slipped her bikini bottoms down, hooking them over her ankles with a perfectly manicured hand – Fabulous Fuchsia nail polish; Paul's nail technician, Kelly, had applied it for her and right at that moment he thanked God for that fact because it was something to focus on and he knew if he looked up he was going to see the sleekest, smoothest, silky skin (courtesy of Paul's beauty therapist, Emma, and her Class A Brazilian treatment). Shelley added Paul's boxers to the pile of clothes on the sand.

'Is this wise?' Paul asked in a voice he wasn't sure was his own. 'I mean, isn't there some sort of law against taking all one's clothes off in public?'

'Not on a nudist beach,' Shelley told him, the tip of her tongue peeping out, sliding around the contours of her lips. 'And especially on a *private* nudist beach.'

'Ah, right, got the picture,' Paul said.

The rest, dear readers, is censored, save to say that it should be remembered that it is best not to bare skin that has never before been exposed to the sun for as long as Paul exposed his pert little bottom as he made love to Shelley, because wives – as Paul's did – tend to notice these things!

What If
Nina Tucknott

What if I'd remembered to set the clock back one hour last night? How different things would be now…

For a start, I wouldn't have seen Tom come out of that large plush hotel, his body literally wrapped around a young slip of a thing. Which means I wouldn't have had to take in those slobbering kisses, all that heavy petting. Instead, I'd have remained blissfully unaware in my little flat as I tucked into cornflakes and milk and texted him some soppy message. My usual morning ritual.

But no, I thought it was eight forty-five so I was racing along the seafront trying to get to work on time.

And then, what if those lights hadn't changed to red just at that moment? If they'd remained green I'd have missed that passionate hotel exit and would never have realised that Tom wasn't in Devon on a course at all.

But no, again, my Mini had to grind to a halt along with everybody else's and as I waited for one filter upon another to change to green, my world turned upside down.

They didn't see me of course. Far too wrapped up in each other.

She looked so young. So pretty. So perfect.

I can imagine her wedding dress; sleek and sophisticated with shoulders bare and narrowing at the waist – no wired petticoats hiding a multitude of sins. Still… mine looks absolutely stunning and I am sure even Tom will agree. Only nine weeks now to our big day…

But that's still in the future, this is now; the present. Another day altogether.

A day when my Tom looked so pleased with himself. Like the cat that got the cream. A whole saucerful judging by the way he kept licking her left earlobe. Honestly! His saliva must

28

have been trickling down her swan-like neck like nobody's business.

Just as the lights changed to green again, they shook hands with the doorman. Tom even slapped him hard on the back. And one of them said something very amusing because they all laughed heartily. There was something in their manner which screamed that they were almost bosom pals. No way was this the first time for Tom and his ladyfriend at this hotel.

In a state of shock I drove off wondering what would have happened if they'd seen me. How would Tom have reacted? Would he have stuttered and spluttered trying to come up with the perfect excuse or would he have accepted defeat there and then? Well… I'll never know because I didn't exactly stop and introduce myself…

What if I'd had the guts to do just that? To have calmly parked the car, courteously said how-do-you-do to that young thing, and to the doorman as well of course, and then boxed Tom straight on the nose. So hard that blood would have oozed.

But oh no, I was a good Catholic girl brought up nice and proper by nuns who'd taught me to behave like a lady – no common tart stuff allowed here. But boy did I feel like it!

The rest of the day passed in a blur. I sat through two meetings and took copious notes that made no sense at all. I even went to lunch with Penny and Millie and tried so hard to listen to their incessant gossiping, but failed miserably. I ate a plate of cheesy nachos and dips – my favourite – but it might just as well have been cardboard for all I noticed, or cared.

By now, my brain had become a cruel video recorder where the rewind button was automatically pressed whenever the lovebirds' film came to an end. Over and over Tom and that girl hugged, kissed and petted. And I had no way of stopping the film. Had no way of erasing it all.

Despite my inner turmoil, the day raced on. Another meeting, more hieroglyphic note-taking and then time to go home. Funny, but I really didn't feel like leaving the office at all…

But then I was given a breather. Mum called to say they'd received the proofs for the wedding invitations. Could I come over tonight as they needed me to approve them?

Of course I could. Straight away.

They were so pretty; cream and burgundy to match our outfits. One hundred and sixty-five pristine vellum cards soon to be propped against the mantelpiece or pinned on the notice board. Some maybe even destined for the fridge door; to be held in place with a jolly magnet.

And soon, of course, acceptances would be landing on mum's doormat too.

And before long, Debenhams would be dishing out wedding gift lists left, right and centre. The entries for the white square dinner service would receive a tick in the column as someone bought a plate or two, a covered vegetable dish or the huge serving platter. And the funky glassware would be snapped up too. And surely someone would give us the chocolate fondue set, and the vegetable steamer. And Auntie Joan, coffee-holic number one, would no doubt settle on the cafetiere.

But that was all still in the future. In the future which had looked so rosy until this morning, but which rosy tint was definitely beginning to fade. In fact it wasn't pink at all any more, more a dark, dark purple. Or black maybe…

And then, a little later, for my grand finale to a spectacularly crap day and to really twist that knife deep into my heart, I saw them again.

By now I was driving home along the seafront, having purposely left my mobile switched off so Tom couldn't reach me, and there they were. Not by the hotel, but instead entering that swish restaurant facing the sea. The one I've so desperately wanted to try for ages and ages but the one we can't afford...

And how lucky they were to have found a parking space so easily – just across the road. I mean just across the road? Parking in Brighton's usually nigh on impossible.

But no, Tom's red motor – his pride and joy – gleamed under the street lamp. I hastily double parked and peered inside. A bunch of red roses lay on the back seat, the hotel bill tucked underneath, while a red pashmina lay discarded on the front passenger seat.

I saw red. Well and truly.

Switching on my mobile, I had seven missed calls. All from Tom. There was even a voice mail from him: '*Hi darling, so sorry I keep missing you... but I'm late for a meeting already so I'll call you when it's finished, otherwise tomorrow... love you...*'

Meeting? Meeting my foot! This was the final straw... I pressed his number. The mobile rang loud and clear but not across the road in that posh restaurant as I'd hoped, but instead from inside the BMW. But then again, who needed a mobile when you were busy wining and dining your lover, eh...?

Continuing to see red, I returned to my car and headed back into the town centre. Debenhams was still open. I asked the shop assistant for the wedding gift list of Mr Tom Sullivan and Miss Louise Collins; the one with no ticks on it because the invitations hadn't been sent out as yet. Not that she knew that of course.

Making my purchase, I watched her place that very first tick in one of the columns – the first, but also the last.

Racing back along the seafront I was relieved to find Tom's car still there. Thank goodness! And hey... to hell with being a lady – at least now I'd be able to test the sharp carving knife I'd just bought – the one with a lifetime guarantee and the very same he's been coveting for ages.

Driving Her Crazy
Ann West

'… And when I bang the dash with my clipboard I want you to do an emergency stop.' Mandy nodded, took a gulping breath and started the car.

'Turn left out of the car park.' Mandy edged cautiously into the traffic stream and joined the queue heading for the sea.

'Take the next left.'

'Right!… I mean OK… yessir!' babbled Mandy.

'Calm down, you're doing fine so far.' She didn't believe that.

'Turn left at the next junction.' Mandy slowed down, making sure that the road was clear, before turning the corner on to the esplanade and accelerating smoothly away. She could see the sea sparkling in the sunlight over to her right, reflecting the glorious deep blue of the sky. Small boats and windsurfers darted across the waves. Children screamed with delight on the beach and paddled at the water's edge.

Lovely day for a swim, she thought, I could do with cooling…

Bang! Down went the clipboard and Mandy stomped down hard on the brake and clutch pedals to bring the car to an abrupt halt. Her foot slipped off the brake pedal, spoiling the whole manoeuvre, as the car bounded forward again.

'Sorry, my foot slipped,' she murmured, shakily.

The driving test continued, taking her through the routine of hill starts, three point turns, reversing, parking. With each exercise her confidence shrank a little more and, by the time they reached the test centre car park, she was sure she had failed. She drew to a halt and switched off the engine.

'I'm very sorry but I can't pass you,' said the examiner, handing her a printed form with a number of crosses on it. These are the points where you failed. Better luck next time.'

He offered her his hand to shake, got out of the car, and walked back into the test centre shaking his head.

'How did you get on?' asked her instructor, Ryan, as he got into the car beside her.

'Failed again. My foot slipped off the brake pedal on the emergency stop.' She hung her head miserably.

'Oh no!' he sighed, 'I really did think you would make it this time. Nerves again?' She nodded, unable to speak for a moment, uncertain what to say in the face of his obvious disappointment.

'Are you going to give up, or sign up for some more lessons?' She looked at him. Thought of her dwindling bank balance. Took a deep breath and smiled a wobbly smile.

'I think I can just about afford another set of lessons,' anxiety clouded her face, 'unless you think I'm just wasting everybody's time and will never be able to pass?' He smiled.

'Nothing of the sort. We'll get you through that test yet Mandy. I'm sure it will be fifth time lucky.'

'I do hope so.'

'You know I really am puzzled. You're a pretty good driver. Do you just go to pieces with nerves for the test?'

You don't know the half of it, she thought to herself. They arrived at the driving school and she went in to book for more lessons.

'Do you want to try a different instructor this time?' asked the receptionist kindly. 'Perhaps a change would help. We've got a new young fellow just started with us. He's ever so good-looking.' She sighed dreamily.

'Do you really think so? I'm not certain that it would help having to get used to another instructor.'

'Well, if you're sure.'

'I think so. I'm used to Ryan; I'll stick with him.'

'OK, if you say so.'

Mandy left the driving school and went to the coffee shop down on the seafront where her best friend, Liz, was waiting for her, dawdling over a large mug of latte.

Mandy bought herself a coffee and slid into the booth beside her, let out a sigh of relief, and began to sip the scalding liquid. In her mind's eye she went over the events of the afternoon. At one stage she had been convinced that she might pass the test this time. She wasn't looking forward to facing the family with the news of yet another failure. They were making her the butt of every bad driving joke they could think of. The weekly edition of *Top Gear* was a nightmare of teasing from her younger brother Paul and her father.

'Well, how did you get on then?' Liz could bear the suspense no longer. 'Did you pass?'

'I failed.'

'Not again?'

'Yeah, my foot slipped off the pedal when I did the emergency stop.'

'Oh, back luck.'

'Not according to my father, he reckons I shouldn't wear such daft high heels to drive in.'

'How did your dishy instructor take it?'

'Disappointed; what else do you expect?'

'Hey, tell you what, perhaps my brother Dave could teach you. He's just taken a job as a driving instructor.'

'Oh no! I'm quite happy with the one I go to, thanks all the same.'

'You should hear some of the stories he comes home with. Absolute hoot some of them.'

'Really?'

'Oh yes! You wouldn't believe some of the daft things that pupils get up to. He says he's had one young lady drive up onto the pavement during a lesson. Another burst into tears because she couldn't do reversing when he asked her. He reckons it's a laugh a minute. Especially when all the instructors get together at tea break and swap stories.'

'It sounds like he's really enjoying this new job.'

'Oh yes! There's only one thing he doesn't like about it.'

'What's that then?'

'Well it seems that one of the company's rules is that you're not allowed to form relationships with the clients, so it's put a damper on his chatting up the birds who come to him for lessons.'

'Goodness, how frustrating for him.'

'Well you know my brother; he's not exactly short of girlfriends.'

'That's true, they almost queue up for him outside your house.'

'He was telling me about one pupil they've got, where they're almost despairing of getting her through the test, she's failed so many times.'

'Heavens, really?'

'Really! Apparently she's failed four times; just like...' Liz trailed off and looked at her best friend, 'you,' she mouthed silently and pointed a finger at Mandy. They looked at each other in dawning horror.

'You've fallen for him,' accused Liz. Mandy nodded and sighed.

'Yes, ever since that first lesson. He's just so dishy.'

'You haven't... You haven't...' Words failed Liz as she doubled up with laughter.

'Haven't what? What are you laughing at?'

'Don't tell me you've been failing the test deliberately,' Liz gasped and tears of mirth poured down her face. 'Not even you could be that stupid, could you?' Her laughter ceased momentarily, her face creased in doubt. Mandy nodded silently, feeling wretched and silly. Then the humour of it struck her and she joined Liz in her hilarity.

'All that money on lessons!' chuckled Liz.

'All those botched tests,' Mandy mopped her streaming eyes, 'sometimes it was quite a struggle to fail, you know.' Laughter rendered them both speechless for some minutes.

'Well, you're going to have to pass next time,' said Liz when she managed to regain her breath.

'Oh, I'll probably be so nervous I'll fail again,' said Mandy airily and they both subsided into frantic giggles again.

Finally Liz sobered, wiped the tears of laughter from her eyes, took a deep breath and said seriously, 'No Mandy, next time you've got to pass.'

'But I can't. I may never see him again,' wailed Mandy.

'Oh, you idiot! That's what Dave's been telling me, your instructor is absolutely desperate for you to pass, so he can ask you out!'

Train in Time
Tina Brown

Sasha took in the smell of history as she sat on the hard, cold padded seat of the steam train, contented yet with a feeling that there was something missing in her life. She had thought this holiday alone would fill the gap but it didn't. She knew what it was that was missing. Romance. Pure and simple!

The divorce over and done with, her children now settled with partners and children of their own, she reflected on where her life was heading.

So deep in thought, Sasha jumped when a train pulled alongside hers. She saw her reflection in the window, mirroring her aging but pretty face. A quickly taken breath stuck in her throat as she saw another image through her reflection.

Three small children playing on a beach. Their hair almost as white as the fine sand they played on. Their sun-kissed skin glowed golden. Sasha gulped that half-swallowed breath as she realised that the children were herself and her two brothers many, many years ago.

The train jolted then chugged as it slowly moved along the track. The image of the children faded as her reflection disappeared and the green countryside was revealed.

She remembered those days so well now that her mind had been jolted back in time. What happened to destroy those happy carefree children? Life? Selfishness? It had been such a long time since she had spoken to her brothers. They each lived at scattered corners of the country. The yearly Christmas and birthday cards and the odd phone call was all that connected them now. Instantly Sasha decided she would visit her brothers.

The train slowed as it chugged up a hill, plumes of steam floating past her window, before entering a dark tunnel, her reflection was back. With each indentation of the tunnel wall, Sasha saw a part of her childhood through to her teenage years.

She watched as her brothers surfed and she sunbathed. Saw her young school friends join her at the beach, where they laughed and played in the years from being children to young teenagers.

The bright light from the sun almost blinded her as they exited the tunnel and she wondered what had ever happened to those friends of hers. Slowly one by one they had dwindled away to be consumed with their own lives, just as Sasha had been with hers.

Sasha took in a deep breath and thought she could detect a hint of ocean, that clean fresh smell of sea air but shook her head, knowing that she couldn't. She sighed and breathed again the stale air of the steam train.

The train slowed to pull in to another station, Sasha looked at the station sign and then flipped through her travel pamphlet to discover that her stop was the next one.

The train came to a stop and Sasha glared at a bland concrete bridge pillar that was blocking her view. The more she glared the more she could see her reflection again. This time there were no children in the image that revealed itself.

A slim young girl, fresh out of her teenage years, blossomed amongst the activity surrounding her. Groups of young people scattered on the hot sand, playing with a huge round beach ball, some playing cricket, others building sandcastles. It was summer break and Sasha wished she had a figure like that again.

Standing outside the groups was a young man. Handsome, yet not strikingly so. He wore a sad, sullen look as he watched the young Sasha. She heard a name being called from the distance and Sasha looked up towards the sullen young man. Their eyes met. For Sasha watching the image, it was like time standing still for the young couple. She felt her heart beat, felt the longing all over again. Knew precisely what the yawning gap in her life now was all about.

'Jonathan.' Sasha reached out to caress the window with her fingertips. He was being called away by his parents.

An arm snaked around young Sasha's waist. The body of a burly lifeguard caught her off guard and swung her around as he laughed and teased her, threatening to throw her into the deep blue sea.

Sasha glanced over the shoulder of her would-be husband to find nothing left of Jonathan but the imprint of his footprints in the white, hot sand.

When the image faded, Sasha realised she had been so deep in thought that the train was already pulling into her intended station.

Grabbing her handbag, she dashed along the aisle to the carriage door but as she came level with the last seat a man stood up quickly and stepped into the aisle in front of her. Sasha slammed into him hard, almost knocking the breath from her. He turned quickly and steadied her before continuing towards the door. He stopped and turned to her with a frown. It was then that Sasha saw the sea blue of his eyes. The same eyes that had been on that beach over twenty years ago. His face had aged well over the time since she'd seen him last. Physically he hadn't changed much at all.

'Sasha?'

'Jonathan?'

They spoke in unison.

The train started moving, jolting them together. Jonathan steadied her with strong hands before jumping from the carriage to the platform, holding his hand out to Sasha in invitation, stepping alongside the slow-moving carriage.

Sasha knew she only had seconds to make a decision. Continue on the train of memories or jump into the arms of fate.

Her feet barely hit the platform before Jonathan's arms wrapped round her waist and swung her around. Sasha's laugh was cut short as Jonathan kissed her in the way she had wanted him to kiss her all those years ago.

Muggee Muggee Beach
Mo McAuley

Roz kicked through the graveyard of coral. The bleached twigs crunched like bones beneath her feet. Muggee Muggee Beach – at last she was back. How she'd loved the name when she first discovered its existence. It was aboriginal, the hotel staff had informed her although they didn't know its meaning. No one ever went there because it entailed a long trail through the rainforest and a steep final descent. That had been enough to entice Roz on that hot summer day last year.

It had been the hottest day of the holiday. When she'd finally jumped down on to the searing white sand she'd wanted to cry out, but with joy rather than pain. In front of her lay an empty crescent of a bay with the rainforest hugging as close as it could get to the beach. A chatter of rainbow lorikeets swooped down from the trees – riotous, feathered jewels winging over the expanse of sand.

Stripping down to her bikini she folded her T-shirt and shorts before tucking them neatly into her rucksack. As she walked along the water's edge, the sea slapped against her ankles, teasing and tempting her into its cool blue depths. It was all hers. She was the custodian of all this beauty. She would never tell anyone how wonderful it was.

The sun was now an indefinable blur of heat in the blue sky. Up ahead, eucalyptus trees overhung the beach, creating a naturally shady area. In front of them was a cluster of rocks, half in the sand, half in the water. Roz stooped under the overhanging branches to see a slight indentation in the sand. She took out her towel, lay down and closed her eyes.

A gentle clinking sound interrupted her relaxation. She peered down the length of her legs in the direction of the noise to see a rowing boat, tied up to one of the rocks. It must have been hidden behind them because she hadn't noticed it when she arrived. But now it was in full view, firmly secured by a rope, moving in and out from the shore with the beat of the waves. The oars were inside the boat, rattling against the rowlocks.

It was irritating. There wasn't another area of shade for her to go to. She looked at the boat, the dull, flaking green and blue paint juxtaposed against the clarity of the landscape. She had an eye for colour. As the fashion editor of *Roma* magazine, it was her job to see the picturesque and the possible in everything. She had her camera with her. Decision made. She would stay a while, take some pictures and have something to eat and drink.

She lay back on the towel and ran a hand over her stomach, enjoying the flatness of her belly under her palm. It was important in her job to look good. It was equally important to stay one step ahead. And she'd been moving several steps ahead in the last few years, with two promotions and a recent move into a new unit in a fashionable area in Sydney. It had meant dumping a boyfriend but that had been no great sacrifice. She slid her hands up over the smoothness of her body – taking stock. It was also good to take stock, of your appearance, of where you were going and what you wanted out of life. That way everything ran smoothly and according to plan.

There was a sound of bare legs sloshing through shallow water and a sudden clatter of oars in the boat. She sat up. A blond-haired man, wearing a pair of wet board shorts, was standing thigh high in the sea near the boat. He threw in a hessian bag and it thudded heavily as it hit the bottom. He was about her age, perhaps a bit younger, in his early thirties. His body was tanned to a deep, golden colour, his hair bleached and stiff with sand and sun and salt water. He was a product of his environment, a sun child honed and shaped by his outdoor life. Definitely not her type.

She stood up and brushed the sand from the backs of her legs, then sauntered out from under the tree. The man looked surprised and then smiled. It was a spontaneous, accepting gesture, without question or curiosity.

41

'Hi,' he said and began to undo a thick belt around his waist. There was a knife attached to it, hidden in a leather scabbard. Her heart beat fast. She should have stayed under the tree, waiting and watching quietly until he'd gone. He threw the belt casually into the boat.

'Oysters,' he explained. 'Rock oysters.' He held up the bag and shook it. Roz heard the clatter of shells inside. She smiled with relief. 'D'you want one?' he said. 'You won't get fresher than this.'

Roz shook her head. 'No thanks, I'm vegetarian. Well, nearly.'

'Poor you!' He grinned and leaned over to get something else out of the boat. 'So I can't tempt you with this?' He held up a squid, its limp body gleaming and slimy in the sun, its tentacles long and dishevelled as they draped over his fingers.

Roz shuddered 'no way' but laughed. 'Are you a fisherman?' she asked.

He shrugged. 'I supply to the hotel but I do other things as well, build boats, help out in the art studio. Have you been to the Victor Lewis studio? It's quite a hike but well worth a visit.'

'No. I just want to lie around and relax while I'm here. I'm on rest and recuperation. To be honest, the less contact with others the better for this two weeks.'

He threw the squid back in the boat and began wading into the water to untie the rope. 'Well, I'll leave you to it then.'

Roz felt her face flush. How supercilious she'd sounded. But then she wasn't used to apologising or losing ground. She struggled to find the right words. 'I'm sorry. That sounded terrible. I didn't mean to be rude.'

'No worries.'

He waded back through the water holding the rope high and pulling the boat up onto the beach ready to climb into it. He was standing right in front of her now and she could see his eyes were blue under the fairness of the lashes and eyebrows. A flop of hair hung over his forehead.

'I understand how you feel,' he said. 'I spend a lot of time on my own. Just me, the boat, this…' He swept his arm out to indicate the landscape around him. 'I'm not a great one for crowds and noise. I escaped from all that a long time ago. Anyway, I'll leave you to your tranquility. Nice to meet you.' He turned and began to climb into the boat then stopped and looked back. 'Unless you want a lift. It's a hell of a haul back up from here. I can row you round to the hotel if you like.'

Roz felt another flush creep up her cheeks and hoped it was lost among the effects of the sun. Why should she go back? She'd only just arrived. And now she'd have the place to herself, once he'd gone. He began to push off, taking her silence to mean a negative answer.

Suddenly she wanted to be in the boat, among the dead squid and rock oysters, with the sea water at the bottom slopping around her feet. 'Wait,' she said, 'I'll just grab my stuff.' She dived under the tree and snatched up her belongings.

He held her hand as she stepped in. His was rough and strong from manual work and the nails were split. The veins up his arms stood proud as he began to row and she tried to keep her gaze from his body as he swept the boat through the water with ease. It was hypnotic – the slap of the oars, the movement of his body leaning towards her then pulling back with each rhythmical stroke. At times the sides of his feet brushed against hers and the slight contact of flesh on flesh made her shiver. His were tanned to the colour of honeyed oak and roughened to greyness underneath. Her own looked absurdly pampered, the toenails a lush gleam of purple. She shifted them to the bottom of the boat where they shared the space with not just one squid but several others, she now realised.

She thought of the boyfriend she'd abandoned a year ago. She hadn't had a relationship since then and was happy to keep it that way. Men and sex always turned out to be a complication. She could do without either.

He rowed in at the far end of the hotel beach. She climbed out, determined to do it without his help this time.

'I'm Mike, by the way.'

'Roz, Roz Jackson. The Roz is short for Rosalind.'

Mike pushed off again and began to row away. 'I'm there most days I'm afraid,' he yelled across the water. 'But I'll try not to disturb you.'

She hesitated as he started to row further down along the shore.

'Don't worry about that,' she called. 'It's fine by me.'

'I don't normally do spontaneous. It always leads to trouble and it's certainly not the way to achieve what you want,' Roz flopped back on her towel under the tree. 'In fact I can't quite believe I'm spending all this time with you.' Mike sat beside her, cross-legged, opening rock oysters with his knife.

'Stop apologising to yourself. You're feeling happy aren't you? What's wrong with that? Anyway, your life sounds terrible to me,' he said. 'I'm surprised you keep bragging about it or want to go back.'

Roz propped herself up on her elbows and looked at him in annoyance. 'I'm not bragging. Just explaining all that I have to do, to look after, the amount of responsibility I have. It's not easy. That's why I need to treat myself to decent holidays like this.'

Mike laughed. 'But you go on about how hard it all is, how stressed you always are and then you try to convince me how much you enjoy it, how much I'm missing out on. If you enjoy it so much why do you have to keep telling me over and over again? Why do you never talk about *you*, the inside you? Do you even know the real you among all this achievement?'

He poked the edge of his knife into the ridge of the oyster. Roz watched him working the tip into the unyielding crack. 'Careful,' she said, as the knife slipped for the second time and nicked his wrist. She shuddered at the sight of the thin trail of blood. He laughed and licked it away.

'Sometimes it's good to feel a bit of pain. It makes you realise you're truly alive.' At last he prised open the shell, revealing the wetness tucked inside the protective frills. He held it up for her to look. 'Don't dismiss it out of hand. Just admire its beauty.' Roz leaned closer. She felt his hair brush against hers. Goosebumps rose defensively on her flesh in spite of the heat of the day. He smelled as salty as the oyster he held in front of her, moving it this way and that so the light fell on the pearlised membrane, catching the gleam. 'Just look at that,' he said. 'Designed to please all the senses. Clever Mother Nature.' He lapped it into his mouth with an expression of ecstasy then rolled on his back hugging himself with joy. Roz smiled at his exuberance.

'Try one,' he persuaded. She shook her head. He grasped her forearm. 'Go on. Be spontaneous, Roz. Do something you'd never normally do in a million years, something that doesn't need a meeting, or a stack of phone calls or e.mails, to make you decide.'

She pulled her arm away and frowned at him. 'You're very critical of me.'

'No I'm not. It's just that the way you live feels like a performance to me. And I get the feeling you're quite capable of sabotaging any good thing that comes into your life, anything that gives you real pleasure, anything that makes you question yourself or the way you've chosen to live. I hate to think that.'

'Well, don't think about me at all, in any shape or form. I think for myself. I don't need anyone else to think for me or about me.'

'Don't you?' He turned away and began digging into another oyster. He held it out to her, his eyes twinkling with mischief. 'Come on,' he coaxed. 'I dare you. It will make you feel fantastic.' She narrowed her eyes sceptically. He tilted her chin with his fingertips. 'Come on. Close your eyes. It's important to do that the first time. Now open your mouth and relax your tongue.'

He slipped the oyster into her mouth. 'That's it, well done.' His voice was soft and encouraging. 'Now squeeze it to the top of your mouth with your tongue and just hold it there, then

45

you'll release the full flavour. Hold it, wait, wait... just savour the experience, the moment. I'm going to follow its slippery passage.' His fingers pressed gently to the base of her throat. 'Now... swallow...'

The salty freshness slipped down her throat. She waited for the gagging reflex to come but it didn't. Instead she shuddered with pleasure at the new sensation, at the unfamiliar taste and the feel of his fingers resting on her skin. His breath was warm against her cheek. Tears started behind her eyelids and she felt a panic at the unexpected emotional release. She clenched the lids tight to prevent them escaping.

'Open your eyes,' he said gently. She shook her head fiercely from side to side. 'Please. Open your eyes.' Obediently she opened them to find Mike looking at her intently. He pulled her towards him and gently placed his mouth on hers.

There was the cluster of rocks with the waves still fussing and frothing among them and the shady area under the eucalyptus trees where they'd first made love. She pulled aside the leafy curtain and her heart jumped at the sight of the indentation in the sand, the soft hollow of a body shape. The noise of metal clinking against wood made her look round. The rowing boat was tugging at its rope like a dog on a lead.

'Roz, Roz? Where've you gone? Look at this.'

Roz ducked out from under the tree. At the far end of the beach her assistant, Roger, was calling to her through a megaphone. 'It's like a bloody armada!' He gestured to the open sea. Two boats were powering through the water in the direction of the beach. Loud rock music blared into the air sending the cockatoos whirling up from the rainforest in a screeching white cloud.

A movement on the headland drew her attention away from the sight, a figure making its way over the rocks, naked apart from a pair of wet board shorts. He was carrying a couple of sacks and had a belt around his waist. She shaded her eyes against the glare as she watched, excitement and fear gradually giving way to a strange mixture of disappointment and relief as the figure drew nearer.

'Hi,' he called. 'What the hell's going on down there?' He waved a hand in the direction of the boats, now disgorging people and equipment on the shore.

'Where's Mike?' she asked and heard the catch in her voice. 'Isn't this his boat?'

'Mike? He left last year. He sold the boat to me. I took over the little arrangement he had with the hotel. Why? Did you know him?'

'Not really, well a little. Where's he gone?'

'No one seems to know. He left at the end of last summer. Hey, are you all right?'

Roz fumbled to put on her sunglasses. 'I'm fine. We're just doing a fashion shoot here. We've got permission.'

He looked down the beach to the gathering crowd of people. 'It's a bit of paradise isn't it, Muggee Muggee Beach? And normally so quiet. But I guess this kind of thing was bound to happen one day, once people got wind of it. Your foot's bleeding by the way, quite badly. It was probably the coral. It can be quite sharp. Wow! that must hurt.'

Roz looked down. Blood was seeping from her big toe. 'I didn't feel it,' she said slowly, staring down at her foot. 'I didn't feel it at all.'

He was looking at her with curiosity now. 'Well, I suppose I'd better get on,' he said at last. 'Sorry I couldn't help about Mike. Nice guy. Very at ease with himself and the world.' He waded out to untie the boat.

Roz walked down to the shoreline where they'd played, naked and sleek as seals. She dipped her foot in the water. The pain was sharp as the salt entered the wound, much sharper than she'd expected. She felt the tears start as she watched her blood swirl and twirl away into the sea.

I think I've fallen in love he'd said on the phone.

I don't think I know what love is she'd lied.

'Roz, Roz, We need you. We're lost without you!' Roger yelled to her through the megaphone.

Roz put on her sandals and stepped carefully over the fringe of broken shells and coral, only taking them off when she reached the pale cushion of sand above the debris. She held them above her head and waved them in greeting. 'I'm coming,' she called and hurried down the beach toward the waiting crowd.

The Naked Truth
Della Galton

The first time I saw Sam he was standing with one foot on a bale of hay. He had a fork in one hand, which matched the devilish look in his eyes, and his other hand was covering his modesty. Which was necessary, because he was completely naked.

So was Charlie, who was sitting on the hay bale alongside him with only a border collie pup between him and indecent exposure. Perhaps I should explain that Sam and Charlie didn't usually prance about in the altogether, well I didn't know what Sam did, but I knew for sure that Charlie didn't. He was more at home in overalls, pottering about on the dairy farm his father owned, than stripping off for a photo shoot. But this was for charity. Everyone was doing it these days.

The naked farmers' calendars sold faster than Jeanie Carter's home-made steak and kidney pies. Jeanie Carter was the landlady of the Dog and Ferret in the village and she always kept the latest farmers' calendar behind the bar.

I'd known Charlie since school. But I'd never met Sam before. He was Charlie's cousin and on leave from the army. Not technically a farmer at all, but he hadn't seemed to mind being roped in. I've always been a sucker for a man in uniform and Sam looked wonderful in his. I'd seen photographs in Charlie's back room. But I had to say he looked even better without it. He was taller than his cousin with a well-honed six-pack that made Charlie look skinny. He had short dark hair, black smiling eyes and the wickedest grin I'd ever seen. They were both grinning now as I lined up my camera to get the final shot of the day.

'Come on, Linda,' Charlie shouted, 'We're freezing our...'

'Socks off,' Sam interrupted, giving him a sharp look. 'It's all right for you, standing there in your scarf and mittens, sweetheart.'

I laughed and snapped away and then I chucked them their clothes and turned my back on them and wondered why I could scarcely breathe. After all, I was putting together the whole calendar and they weren't the first naked men I'd photographed today.

The answer to that question caught up with me as I was putting away my camera gear in the boot of my car.

'If you're not rushing off, we could take you for lunch? Or maybe you've already seen enough of us.' Sam's deep chocolate voice had a thread of humour in it and I turned, hoping I wasn't blushing.

'No, I've finished for today. And thanks, lunch would be great.'

Half of me prayed that Charlie wouldn't come along and half of me prayed that he would. I wasn't shy around men – I'd been brought up with four brothers – but there was something about Sam that scrambled my brain.

Half an hour later we were sitting in the beer-scented warmth of the Dog and Ferret with three pints and three packets of salt and vinegar crisps in front of us.

'So what do you do when you're not photographing naked men, Linda?' Sam asked, wiping froth from his mouth.

I wished he hadn't mentioned naked men. He was wearing a dark fleece now and jeans, but I couldn't stop thinking about his hairy chest and muscled biceps. He'd been stationed abroad and had obviously not kept himself too covered up because his body was lightly tanned. In comparison, Charlie, who'd just come out of an English winter, was pale from the neck down. I shook my head. I had to get a grip on myself.

'Er – weddings, corporate photography, you know for brochures and that. Whatever pays the bills.'

'But she's not getting paid for this,' Charlie said lightly. 'Are you, Linda? She's doing it for love like the rest of us.'

'That's right.'

'And what do you do in your spare time?' Sam asked, a glint of interest in his dark eyes.

'She steers clear of bozos like you,' Charlie said with an edge to his voice that made me glance at him in surprise. He was so laid back normally; did I detect a hint of jealousy directed at his handsome cousin?

Sam laughed easily. 'Back off, mate, I'm only asking.' He leaned across the table and traced a fingertip carelessly along my forearm, which caused half a dozen sparks to dart straight towards my heart. 'I'm sure Linda can speak for herself.'

His eyes held mine. I felt as though I was drowning.

'So how about you show me the sights of the village? I've got another ten days leave.'

'There aren't exactly many sights,' I heard myself say in a voice that sounded surprisingly normal.

'I'm sure that's not true.'

I was vaguely aware of Charlie shaking his head and then the scraping of chair legs on the wooden floor as he got up from the table. 'I've got work to do. I'll leave you to it. If that's all right with you, Linda?'

'Fine,' I mumbled. At that point I wouldn't have noticed if the whole world had disappeared. Actually I think it did. We stayed in the pub for the rest of the afternoon, which was something I hadn't done since I was a teenager. Then Sam said he'd walk me home because neither of us could drive.

We took a shortcut across the fields. And when Sam slipped his arm around my waist it felt perfectly natural. As though I'd known him all my life. Even the cows looked oddly beautiful, grazing peacefully in the late afternoon sunshine. The whole world looked beautiful, rose-tinted, or possibly beer-tinted, but I wasn't aware that I was grinning inanely until Sam dipped his head and said, 'Penny for them?'

'I was just thinking that I haven't had such a wonderful afternoon for ages,' I said. And a small voice in the back of my head muttered, 'definitely alcohol.' If I'd been sober I'd have come out with some flippant remark. Sam was the type of bloke who'd run a mile if he thought I was too keen.

'Me too, pet,' he said, stumbling over a hillock and looking down at me with slightly glazed eyes.

I gazed back, mesmerised. And when he put his arms around me I went willingly into his embrace. He was swaying a bit when he lowered his head to kiss me. Or perhaps that was me, but it didn't matter. This was destiny, this was meant to be. This was the most magical moment of my life. Or it would have been if we hadn't ended up stumbling and tipping over backwards on to the damp field in a tangle of arms and legs.

And if there's one thing that isn't at all conducive to romance, it's opening your eyes and finding you've fallen a hair's breadth from a particularly wet looking cow-pat and then realising that the man of your dreams hasn't been quite so lucky.

'Uggh, yuk, yeow urrr.' Or at least I think that's what he said. He was scrambling to his feet, wiping frantically at his jeans, which didn't help much, just transferred the mess to his hands.

'It'll wash off,' I said, getting up too, and hunting through my pockets for a hanky, which he snatched out of my hands without a word of thanks.

'Ugh, God, yuk, that is so disgusting.' Sam's face was screwed up into sharp lines of disgust. 'I've just remembered why I hate the countryside so much. How can you live here with all these disgusting animals?' He kicked the ground with his boot. Then he kicked it again. And I would have laughed had I not been able to see he was furious. I mean I could understand him being upset, but I thought he might be getting things a little bit out of proportion.

We walked the rest of the way home with three feet of awkwardness between us. Sam still smouldering and muttering about how hideous the countryside was, and why on earth had he bothered to waste his leave visiting it? And me, feeling a little sad because I loved living in the countryside, and for a few glorious hours I'd thought I'd found someone who was exactly on my wavelength, as well as being the most gorgeous creature I'd ever set eyes on.

I asked him if he wanted to come into my flat and get cleaned up, but he just shook his head and stomped away. The last picture I had of him was his hunched, retreating back, which was speckled ornately with bits of green. A far cry from the smiling, handsome man I'd photographed earlier that day.

I didn't see Sam again. When I next bumped into Charlie he told me he'd left to go and visit some friends in London.

'Are you OK?' he asked me, his eyes shrewd. 'Only Sam came back in a heck of a mood when I left you down the pub that time. I wondered – if – er – anything had happened between you?' Then he blushed. 'Not that you have to say. You know – if you don't want to.'

'Nothing at all happened between us,' I murmured. 'Although I did get the impression that Sam wasn't too keen on the countryside.'

'No.' Charlie looked relieved. 'He's never been that fussed, I don't think. He prefers towns and pavements and street lamps.'

And city girls with immaculate hair and make-up, I thought ruefully, wondering how on earth I'd come so close to falling for a man who was as far apart from me as a tractor from a Porsche.

When the calendar came out, all the girls in the village drooled over the cover picture of Sam and Charlie.

'Aren't they different?' Jeanie Carter said, running her finger down the centre of Sam's hairy chest. 'Was he this good looking in the flesh, Linda?'

'No,' I said, smiling. 'It's not true that cameras never lie. They're the biggest liars in the world.'

'Shame,' she muttered. 'I guess I'll have to stick to my fantasies then.'

'You don't need fantasies, woman, you've got me,' said her husband, Burt, coming into the bar and sticking out his beer belly.

'We all need fantasies,' I said, narrowing my eyes. Which is why I put a copy of the calendar on my lounge wall. There was no denying that Sam was eye-candy. But it's odd how after a while I started to look at Charlie with new eyes, too. He wasn't skinny, I decided, just a little on the lean side. And his smile was quite cute. But my perception may have changed a bit because I quite often saw him in the Dog and Ferret and we'd usually end up chatting and having a laugh.

It never went anywhere though. Well, not until a month ago when he kissed me for the first time. And that's when I realised that there are different kinds of sparks. There are embers and there are white hot, five-foot high flames. I think it shocked Charlie a bit too. We were in my lounge at the time, and when we drew apart he kept blinking and shaking his head and saying, 'Wow.'

Eloquent, it was not, but I did know how he felt because I couldn't formulate a sentence either.

Fortunately we didn't need to. We kissed again. I think we both wanted to check that the second kiss was as good as the first. It wasn't, it was better. Masses better. A lot later, when we finally prised ourselves apart, Charlie reached up and turned my calendar to face the wall.

'I hope you don't mind, but it's making me feel uncomfortable,' he said. 'Having Sam – you know – in the room with us, with – er – well nothing on.'

'I haven't noticed Sam for months,' I told him, and smiled when he blushed. 'But no, I don't mind you turning it around.' I put my arms around him and kissed him again. When we came up for air, I added idly, 'Who needs a picture, or a fantasy come to that – when the real thing is so much better?'

The Love Bug
Maggie Knutson

'Robbie, we've got to talk!' I said. 'I'm really worried about Mum and Dad!'

There, I'd said it. It hadn't been easy to pluck up the courage but this was the last day of our holiday and we needed to do something pretty quickly.

But Robbie was too busy preening his hair in front of the mirror to listen to me. If he put more gel on, he was in danger of toppling over. As it was, it looked as if he had stalagmites emerging from his scalp. Why my brother took so long to get ready was a mystery to me. Were all seventeen-year-old boys like him? I just shoved on T-shirt and shorts, slipped my feet into flip-flops, swept my hair into a ponytail and that was me done.

'I've got the love bug,' he declared, in that annoying self-absorbed way of his.

'Yeah, yeah!' I sighed. 'So who's the lucky girl?'

'Jules, and she's not a girl. She's nineteen and very much a woman!'

He was grinning like a dog that's found a juicy bone.

'And what about Rosie?' I asked, pointedly.

'Who's Rosie?'

'Just the girl you've been going out with for two years. You know, the one who goes to college with you, the one you claimed undying love for.'

'Oh her,' he replied dismissively. 'She was just a passing fancy, like Rosalind in *Romeo and Juliet*. Jules is the real thing! My Juliet! Oh, but I'm sorry little sis, you probably don't know what I'm talking about.'

I bridled at this.

'As if! Like I'm not studying it for my GCSE's, you idiot! Anyway, in the play, it was Rosalind who was older than Romeo. You've got the ages all the wrong way round.'

'Details, details! It's true love, Sis. But you wouldn't know anything about that. You've always got your head stuck in a book.'

'Boys are just a waste of time and if they're all like you then they can't be trusted either!'

'This time it's different, honest. She's everything a guy could want: tall, long blonde hair, legs up to her neck and the biggest...' Jamie stopped. He had obviously remembered that he was talking to his sister and not one of his loud-mouthed mates. 'Anyway, we're going to write when we go home and hook up at week-ends.'

'She sounds like a Barbie doll!' I replied scornfully. 'And aren't you ready yet? We're only going to the beach!'

The beach was OK if you liked that kind of thing but pouring smelly oil over your body and then frying yourself was not my idea of fun. Luckily, there were plenty of shady trees to sit under and read and also, I had discovered, an excellent place to spy on your parents.

Robbie and I walked to the edge of the sand and scanned the mass of bodies on beach beds. He was obviously looking for his latest conquest but I had more important things on my mind and as soon as I spotted Mum and Dad, I grabbed Robbie's arm.

'Robbie,' I hissed, although no one could possibly hear us above the grunts of the lads playing football and the water jets scooting over the aquamarine sea, leaving foaming patterns in their wake. 'Haven't you noticed that Mum and Dad are behaving very strangely?'

'What do you mean?' he asked, still on the look-out for his latest conquest.

'This holiday. Mum's headaches every evening. Dad going off boozing with his new-found mates.'

'What's wrong with that?' Robbie grinned. 'They *are* getting on a bit.'

I tugged his arm harder.

'But look at Mum. Does she look ill to you?'

She was making her way to the bar, looking pretty fantastic in that new skimpy black bikini of hers and keeping one eye on the bronzed, muscular bodies of the lads chasing after that silly little football. Dad was always joking that no one could believe that she had teenage kids and here she was now, acting like a sexy superstar.

'Watch her!' I urged. 'Look how she's wriggling her hips! It's obscene!'

'It's gross!' Robbie agreed. I had his full attention now.

'And Dad obviously hasn't got a clue what's going on. He always seems to be snoozing these days. Must be all those evening drinking sessions.'

We watched as Mum perched herself on a stool.

'Now look... you see that young Greek waiter... he'll come over and serve her, like he's done every day... there you are... Brandy Sour... I knew it! And then they'll have a little chat... real cosy, aren't they! See how they're laughing... and now he's passing her a piece of paper... oh no, she's kissing him on the cheek!'

'Is that his address so she can keep in touch when we get home?' Robbie sounded worried.

'It's just so like *Shirley Valentine*!' I breathed. 'You know, the film we all watched together last Christmas, when we were a *happy* family. About the bored middle-aged house-wife who has a fling with a Greek waiter.'

'I remember,' Robbie whispered back. 'Have you heard Mum talking to the kitchen wall recently?'

We both racked our brains for any memories of Mum acting strangely. Trouble was, she was always having a laugh at something or other so it was hard to know when she was being serious or not.

57

'But one thing's for sure,' Robbie said. 'We've got to do something to stop this!'

That evening we all ate together at the local taverna. Dad ordered the traditional Greek meze – dozens of scrumptious dishes that we normally polished off with no trouble. But Robbie and I were too distracted to eat. *And* Mum and Dad didn't even notice! Parents can be so selfish at times.

Even worse, Mum was so tiddly that she knocked her bag over on the way to the loo and the contents spilled out like escaped convicts. And there, amidst all the rubbish of lipsticks and sunglasses was a silky red negligee, low cut and festooned with yards of lace. Robbie and I looked at each other with horror; just when was she planning to wear that? But she merely giggled coyly and shoved everything back in with apparently no shame at all.

At the end of the meal, Mum's face took on a pained expression.

'I'm sorry, love,' she said to Dad, as if she really meant it. 'That migraine has come back. I'll just have to lie down quietly in the room. And we were having such fun, too! But don't worry about me, any of you. All I ask is that you give me a couple of hours to rest by myself.'

Poor Dad was so sweet.

'Don't worry, pet, we'll be fine. I'll pop off to the bar and the kids can meet up with their pals at the café. That's OK with you two, isn't it?' he asked.

'Yeah, fine, Pops,' we lied. But we had other plans.

'We'll give Mum fifteen minutes and then we'll confront her,' Robbie declared as we pretended to walk to the local café.

'And what about the luscious Jules?' I asked.

'Don't you think saving our family is more important?' he declared, and then added, mischievously, 'Anyway, I can always see her later.'

As we tiptoed nervously to the door of our apartment, it was just as we feared: low, lovey-dovey voices and the provocative flickering of a candle winking at us from under the ill-fitting door.

Very gently, Robbie turned his key.

'Now we'll give that Greek waiter what for!' he mouthed. And then he flung the door wide open and shouted: 'Just what do you think you are doing with our mother!'

'Robbie!' It was Dad's voice! He was wearing a pair of Snoopy boxer shorts and had a red rose poised between his teeth.

'Megan!' It was Mum! And she was wearing the red negligee. She looked fantastic and *very* happy. They were in each other's arms and frozen, tableau like, in what appeared to be a long, passionate embrace. They obviously still had the love bug!

Robbie and I talked like never before on the plane the next day.

'Why couldn't they just tell us that they wanted some space?' I complained.

'Dad said it was more fun being secretive. More spicy. Who'd have thought it of them!' he chuckled.

'How puerile!' I groaned, 'But I guess you have to admire them for their play acting: the pretend headaches and the pretend drinking friends. They should go on the stage, those two.'

'And the famous letter!' Robbie teased me.

'How was I to know it was the address of a lingerie shop the waiter's girlfriend had passed on?' I pouted. 'What did Mum say? "I felt like giving your dad an extra treat on our last night!" If only they hadn't laughed so much,' I added, blushing again at my mistake. 'I felt like a prize idiot!'

'Don't worry, Sis,' Robbie's tone was softer now. 'As Shakespeare once said: "All's well that ends well!" And aren't you glad that Mum and Dad are still crazy about each other. Gives us hope for when we're that age!'

'Which reminds me,' I said. 'What about the radiant Jules?'

'Oh, her!' Robbie breezed. 'Turned out she wasn't so wonderful after all. When I eventually found her last night, she'd hitched up with another guy. Can you believe it! Anyway, I've got the sweet Rosie waiting for me.'

I *was* going to say something suitably caustic in reply, but I'd just noticed one of the guys from the beach sitting opposite and, for some strange reason, I had to do a double take. Blond hair, beautifully tanned, faded blue jeans, white T-shirt. Very presentable! And, as if he was reading my thoughts, he turned and gave a shy smile. Hazel eyes, nice teeth. I gave a little smile back, surreptitiously tucked my book away and considered taking my hair out of its ponytail. Mum and Dad were still cuddling up to each other in the seats in front; Robbie was dreaming about his Rosie; perhaps this love bug thing was infectious!

Candystripes
Christine Emberson

'A beach hut!' Sally exclaimed.

'They're very exclusive you know, Charles Saatchi paid seventy-five thousand for his one.'

'But it's a shed,' Sally continued.

'No, they're Victorian, they used them for their bathing machines you know,' Rebecca replied smugly.

'Alright, a Victorian shed!'

Rebecca laughed at her and carefully folded the letter she had moments before waved enthusiastically at Sally. She had inherited a beach hut from her grandfather. It had been in the family for years and she recalled fondly as a child visiting it, with its linoleum floor, and camping gas stove to make tea. 'Well I've got one, and it's going to be beautiful, I'm thinking blue and white candystripes and I'm having a name plaque made for the door.'

Sally raised her eyebrows. 'OK, what's it to be – "Shangri-La" or "Dunroamin"?'

'No, actually I'm going to call it "Manderlay".'

The reality of "Manderlay" was exactly what Sally said it would be, a shed, and a dilapidated one at that. Rebecca stood yards away, her feet gently sinking into the warm sand, clutching her newly engraved sign. She took in the sight and could not help but feel a little demoralised. Sandwiched between two beautiful dwellings was a ramshackle excuse for a beach hut. It had not seen a lick of paint for years, and whereas the others stood proudly in a row, bordering on cuteness with their regimented dimensions and tasteful pastel colours, Rebecca's inheritance appeared to cast a dark shadow on the picturesque beach. She sighed heavily; her inheritance had most definitely turned into hard work.

61

It was a slow process rubbing down the wood, but Rebecca was determined to be thorough and make a good job of it. She frequently walked the length of the beach taking in details of all the other beach huts, chopping and changing her mind on colour schemes. One in particular took her eye, not that it was as appealing as some of the others, more that it was distinct. Painted white with a pale green door, it had a small traditional brass bell that the wind caught frequently. Rebecca found herself listening out for the bell if the breeze picked up as she worked. It was the height of the season and more and more owners were arriving to open their huts. Rebecca met her neighbours and laughed at herself for being relieved they were "nice" people.

'It's not as if I'm going to live in it but I was so pleased to see they were normal people.' She later relayed to Sally.

'Well, not many axe murderers own beach huts, I guess.' Sally retorted.

'Oh, you know what I mean.'

'No nice hunky men owning one then?'

'No sign yet!' Rebecca laughed and found herself thinking of the hut with the bell. 'Actually there is one hut, but it seems permanently empty. I had been thinking it must belong to someone who lives a distance away, maybe a doctor or lawyer who just uses it as a bolthole when his job is too stressful.'

'It probably belongs to a family with six kids who can't afford to get away.' Sally said laughingly.

'No, I asked the neighbours, I was sort of right; they said it belongs to an old chap in London, only visits twice a year. Isn't that a waste?'

'Criminal!' Sally replied sarcastically as she picked up Rebecca's tea mug. 'Staying for another or are you too busy painting the Forth Bridge?'

'I've only been painting for two days.' Rebecca retorted.

'Really? you've been talking about it for ten.'

Rebecca grabbed the tea towel and flicked it at Sally. 'I don't know why I keep you as a friend, you're wicked to me.'

'Because I'm the only one that listens to you and your mad romantic ideas.'

By the end of the week Rebecca had made impressive progress, she had opted for her original choice of pale blue and white candy stripes and she was delighted with the result. Frequently she stood back to admire her handiwork and relished the thought of spending her first day in her beach hut without working.

'You missed a bit!' A voice reverberated up the beach.

Rebecca swung round quickly trying to pinpoint its direction. The sun was full in her face; she squinted painfully.

'Here.' The voice was closer and finally she could see a man walking towards her. He waved. She noticed how easily he walked barefoot on the hot sand. Within seconds he faced her. He smiled broadly at her with perfect white teeth. *Dentist?* Rebecca wondered immediately.

'Have I missed a bit?' Rebecca asked coyly.

'No, well I don't think so. It's just one of those silly things people say, isn't it?'

His voice was deep and smooth, he ran his fingers through his hair, the muscles in his upper arms flexed gently. *Fitness instructor?*

'Yes... I suppose people do say typical silly things.' Rebecca could feel herself blushing gently. 'I'm Rebecca.' She added quickly, surprising herself and offering her hand for him to shake.

He took it firmly. 'James Etherington. Very nice to meet you.'

Lawyer – with that name and handshake, maybe?

Rebecca found herself staring at him. He smiled and winked slowly at her.

'I've got the beach hut along there, the white one.'

'With the bell?' Rebecca asked quickly.

'Yes the bell, you noticed that?'

63

She nodded, feeling herself embarrassed again under his gaze.

'Yes, the hut used to belong to my parents but I've sort of inherited now, came down earlier in the year to do it up. It used to look as bad as yours.'

Rebecca threw him a scornful look.

'Well I can see you haven't quite finished, I'm sure it's improving daily.' He was grinning widely at her. 'Yes, as kids, my brother and I spent all our holidays down here.'

'And the bell?' Rebecca asked, her curiosity getting the better of her.

'The bell was rung to call us back for lunch.'

Rebecca imagined two boys jumping around in the waves, dashing back as the bell was sounded for sandy jam sandwiches.

'Actually, talking of lunch, fancy joining me?' He spoke confidently and indicated towards his beach hut.

'Well... I'm painting and...' Rebecca stammered.

'Look, I'm here for a few days, have lunch with me and because I can see you adhere to a tight working schedule, I'll make up time and help you with the painting.'

Rebecca smiled at him. She just could not refuse an offer like that, nor the fact that the more she gazed at him, the more attractive he appeared. *Property developer?*

James's beach hut was finished to perfection. Two wicker chairs with an abundance of cushions had been set out. A small table had been laid with bread and cheese and a bunch of grapes lay between two white china plates. It all looked very precise and Rebecca found herself pinching a grape just to see whether they were real. James produced a bottle of wine and glasses and poured without asking.

'So Rebecca, it's "Manderlay" then is it?'

'How do you know?'

'Ah ha!' He tapped his nose mischievously then added, 'Actually I saw the sign resting against the door the other day.'

'This is the first time I've seen you here and…'

'You've been looking for me?' he asked with a subtle mocking tone.

'No, its just I've met virtually everyone and I was told… anyway it doesn't matter. This is lovely cheese.' She was glad to try and change the subject.

'Yes it is!' He was definitely laughing at her now.

'Come on, eat up. We've got painting to do.' She suddenly announced, standing and brushing the crumbs from her paint-splattered shorts.

'You're a hard task master, I like an assertive woman,' he said flirtingly.

Rebecca stepped out of his beach hut into the glaring sun. *Salesman* definitely!

With the two of them working on the beach hut, within hours the progress was staggering. They chatted, a little stiltedly at first, keeping to safe subjects, the weather and the colour schemes of the other beach huts. But as the afternoon wore on Rebecca found herself laughing easily with him, he mimicked the other owners and relayed wonderful stories of their visiting habits. By teatime she threw her paintbrush back into the pot with a satisfied grin on her face.

'I reckon that just about does it.' She stretched and stood with her hands on her hips. Her "Manderlay" was finished – all it needed was the sign.

'Thank you for your help.' It somehow seemed a formal and final thing to say after all the chat and laughter they had shared.

'You're welcome.' James said, adding his paintbrush to hers. 'I'll be seeing you then.' He turned to go.

'Yes… I'll be here…' Rebecca added feebly.

'Think you'll find you've forgotten something.'

'Really?' She asked a little too enthusiastically.

'The inside! Last time I checked it out it still looked like a builder's hut. Reckon I had better come back tomorrow and make a start on that.'

Rebecca laughed at him as he sauntered along the beach. Suddenly she called out to him and asked, 'What do you do?'

'Haven't you guessed yet?'

Rebecca arrived at her beach hut before James the following morning and was attempting to clear out the debris from inside. For such a small space it had accumulated an awful lot of rubbish. He tapped gently on the opened door.

'Anyone at home?'

'Come in, if you can get in,' she said a little wearily.

'Good morning to you too!' Without hesitation he stood before her and kissed her gently on the cheek.

Flustered, Rebecca grabbed the nearest box and thrust it into his arms. 'Take that outside will you?' He turned and went obediently. Rebecca could feel herself panic. She had questioned the events of the previous day over and over in her head. She had relayed every moment to Sally who, in her own imitable way, had pointed out to Rebecca that sexy good-looking men do not just arrive on your beach hut doorstep and offer to help you out. Well, that being a valid point, Rebecca decided she wasn't going to turn him away. Not only was he doing a sterling job, he was amazing to watch too.

'You're a tax collector?' Rebecca tried.

'Wrong.'

'You're an escaped convict on the run?'

James didn't reply immediately and Rebecca caught his arm to check his reaction.

'No, but had you worried!' he sniggered at her.

'Vet?'

'No, animals hate me.'

'I'm going to give up soon.' She threw some papers at him.

'No you won't, I'm not going to give in and tell you so you'll keep trying. I can see you're a woman who goes after what she wants.'

'A psycho-analyst, or whatever they're called?'

James laughed loudly.

'A chef?' Rebecca secretly hoped this was going to be true, she had images of him cooking up a feast on the beach, salmon in foil to rival Jamie Oliver's.

'No.' He sidled up next to her and pinched her waist gently. 'Having fun?'

Rebecca grinned. She was having fun, a lot more than she ever thought possible. 'Yes I am.' She could feel his hand hadn't moved from her waist and instinctively she moved closer to him. Her face was level with his. She imagined kissing him, and, as if reading her mind, his head dipped gently towards her. His kiss was light at first and then suddenly intensified. Rebecca succumbed to him and allowed him to draw her towards him. Unexpectedly he pulled away.

'I'm sorry, I shouldn't have… I mean…' he flustered.

Rebecca smiled, she'd not seen him lost for words before.

'I'm glad you did.'

'Really?'

'Yes, I like you.' She couldn't imagine why he didn't realise and then added, 'I don't know much about you or what you do, but I like you… a lot.'

James punched the air. 'See, I knew my hard work would pay off! In fact there's something I need to do, I won't be long, give me an hour.'

Rebecca shrugged. 'What hard work? You're running away!' She shouted after him as he set off at speed along the beach.

It was truly a beautiful evening; the sun was setting in wondrous tones of orange and yellow. Rebecca sat inside her beach hut looking out through the open door listening to the waves lapping up on to the beach, it had been a busy day and she was feeling sleepy. Suddenly, punctuating the peacefulness, Rebecca heard the loud ringing of a bell, relentlessly it went on. She stepped out of the beach hut, it was nearly dark, James was just visible standing outside his beach hut waving to her. She wandered towards him.

'Bit late for lunch isn't it?' she asked casually.

'Actually it's dinner.' He said proudly, producing a pizza box from behind his back.

Rebecca giggled at him as she reached up with her hand and silenced the bell that was still tinkling gently.

James pushed open the beach hut door, it was lit throughout with white candles and there, propped on every surface, were paintings, some still on canvases, some framed. Rebecca stepped into the hut; her shadow jumping in the candlelight. Picking up one painting after another she took in the detail, they were magnificent. Each one depicting a different beach hut, against a different sky, the colours and hues were captured and intensified perfectly.

'You're an artist.' Rebecca said breathlessly, looking at him.

'Actually my love,' he walked towards her, wrapping his arms around her firmly. 'I think you'll find I'm a painter of beach huts!'

I've Been Expecting You
Kelly Florentia

Don't you just hate it when you ask a guest what they'd like to drink and they say, "anything"? What exactly does that mean, a cold drink? A hot one? Alcohol?

'Oh, whatever you're having,' says my guest. Well, actually I wasn't planning on having anything until you turned up, I want to say but I don't.

'Coffee then?' I offer. She nods politely.

When I return with the drinks I find her holding a framed photograph of David and me, staring at it mesmerised.

'That was a long time ago,' I say, placing the tray down on the coffee table. I think I've startled her a bit. Her blue eyes widen a tad and she looks a bit flushed.

'I'm sorry,' she begins, 'I hope you don't mind.'

'Be my guest, I've got more if you're interested?'

'No, I mean about me dropping in on you like this?' Now she is blushing. I do mind actually, I would've preferred a phone call first just to prepare myself. Not that I need to tidy up or anything. The good thing about working from home is flexibility and I get all the housework out of the way first thing.

'I don't usually do this sort of thing,' she continues, giving me a weak smile from those plump, red lips, the lips that have been kissing David for the last two months.

She's a lot different from what I expected. Quite tall and very slim with a short, spiky, boyish kind of hairstyle and very feminine elf-like features. Not his usual blonde, buxom type at all, perhaps I should feel threatened but I don't.

She sits with her legs together sipping her coffee. My eye catches her black pointed shoes that peek at the flare of her pinstriped power suit. Hmm… probably *Manolo's* I'd say, fine leather, stylish. Shoes are my weakness, you see. David says

I'm worse than Imelda Marcos but at least my obsession is confined to shoes.

'So, it's nice to meet you at last,' I say, with a hint of sarcasm. Well, she is the reason why my husband is never home. I watch her over my coffee cup.

'Yeah,' she looks uncomfortable, which gives me impish satisfaction. 'I've been meaning to drop in for ages.' I'm not surprised. David's new secretaries have a habit of developing this urge.

'Really?' I say, in overdone amazement, 'that's nice.' I wonder how long it will take her to confess? After all I presume that's the reason for her visit, spill the beans on their affair in an effort to get me to leave David, but she's wasting her time.

'It's just nice to put a face to the voice,' she says, with a smile. I help David run his successful and expanding small business, book-keeping, a bit of admin, you know, that sort of thing. I get to speak to most of his staff on a daily basis, particularly his secretary.

We talk for a while, about work, holidays, hobbies. She tells me she's a keen photographer and I'm impressed.

'What are your subjects? Children? Weddings?'

'Nah, I'm much more adventurous than that.' She gives me a wide grin then puts her coffee cup on the table and takes an A4 envelope from her briefcase.

'Anyway, we need you to look at these,' she hands me the envelope, 'I wanted to make sure you received it.'

'Oh,' I frown, David didn't mention any papers needing signing. 'Shall I open it now?' Why did I just say that? Ask *her* for permission?

'If you like.' She glances at her diamond-encrusted watch, no doubt a gift from David. He's got a habit of showering women with lavish gifts but makes sure he's always in control. Most of our assets are in his sole name.

"Tax purposes, honey," he'd said, "What's mine is yours." This despite the fact that I'd set the business up with my personal savings, but love is blind, isn't it?

'Look, I'd better go,' she stands up abruptly. She looks irritable, nervous.

'I've gotta get back to the office before David leaves.'

At the front door, she hesitates.

'Tracey, did you know about us?'

Well of course I knew, and about the others before her. It used to hurt… a lot in the beginning. A constant ache in the pit of my stomach, but the ache faded and now all I feel is numb.

'I'm sorry, Tracey, I thought I was in love with him.' And with a blank expression I shake my head and say,
'More fool you.'

She nods thoughtfully, then adds,

'I want you to know that I didn't mean to hurt you.'

She wants my forgiveness too? I don't think so.

She knew he was a married man. I don't answer. 'He'll never divorce you, Tracey? He's told me so.' Yes, I was aware of that, but only because I'd want what's mine.

'Thanks for bringing this over, Chantel.' I say, finally. She looks at me, confused, and then, with a little sigh, she shakes her head slowly before heading off into the afternoon.

I close the door behind me and tear open the envelope. The sound of '*yesss*' escapes from my lips as a rush of satisfaction shoots through my entire body. I flick through the glossy eight by tens of David, hair all over the place, with a young, buxom blonde in the back seat of his BMW.

'Nice shot, Chantel, you should take this up professionally,' I whisper to myself. There's a yellow note attached that says, 'Once a cheat, always a cheat – see you in court – I hope. I'll back you all the way.' And signed simply Chantel.

Images of *Jimmy Choo*'s, in full range and colours, float in a heavenly manner before me, glistening under spotlights.

I look at my reflection in the mirror and smile before I pick up the phone and dial my solicitor's number.

'Darling… it's me. I've got all the proof I need, now, let's take him to the cleaners.'

Elaine
Colette McCormick

The sun danced on the gloss of Elaine's long chestnut hair. I'd never realised before how pretty her hair was. No, not pretty. Beautiful, Elaine's hair was beautiful. It was a long, thick, shiny rope that hung to a place in between her shoulder-blades. It was the sort of hair that you want to weave between both hands during love-making. Elaine's hair needed hands rather than mere fingers running through it.

From my own almost prostrate position on the sand I watched her as she prepared herself for another day lying in the sun. It would be our sixth day of lying almost naked next to each other.

How would I describe Elaine? Pretty? I suppose she was. But like her hair, that word did not do her justice. She was beyond pretty, though I had never realised it until that day as I watched her strip off her T-shirt to reveal a tiny blue bikini. Like her hair, Elaine was beautiful.

Her slender arms lifted the T-shirt high above her head and her hair, momentarily encased within it, exploded as she pulled the garment free and tossed it casually onto the sand.

With her back to me, I noticed how slender her shoulders were. It looked like her shoulder-blades could perforate the delicate skin. Strange how I'd never noticed that before.

My eyes followed the natural curve of her body down to her waist. What I had previously considered a small waist I now realised was tiny. Was it really that small yesterday?

From the inward curve of her waist flowed the outward curve of her buttocks. Round melon-shaped mounds of flesh encased in blue Lycra. As she crouched down to straighten the towel that she was going to lie on, the Lycra disappeared between the mounds and there they were in all their glory just inches from my face. The skin was stretched taut and silky smooth and I wanted to touch it.

Totally unaware of my attention, Elaine pirouetted on the balls of her feet so that where her buttocks had been now were her breasts. Her tiny nipples erect in their Lycra prison, as her breasts swung gently first this way, then that as Elaine twisted herself around.

I struggled to breathe with the anticipation of what was coming next.

Elaine sat back on her heels and stretched her arms behind her. Out of the corner of my eye I admired the flatness of her stomach.

Turning over onto my side under the pretext of straightening my own towel, my eyes rested for a moment on the mound that nestled where her legs reached her body. I was tempted to brush the few hairs that had escaped back to their brothers but the temptation to delve even further into that heavenly place would have been one temptation too many.

Slowly my eyes moved up to the glory that had been revealed. With her bikini top cast aside, Elaine's breasts roamed free. Tanned from five days being caressed by the sun, they were magnificent, round and pert with nipples the colour of sherry.

Slowly she lowered herself onto the towel and, resting her head on her folded arms, she looked at me with her green eyes. The twinkle in those eyes and the smile on her peony lips told me that she was perfectly aware of what she was doing and the effect that it was having on me. How could it be otherwise?

'Will you do my back?' Her voice seemed huskier than normal.

I plucked the suntan lotion from where it rested in the sand. The bottle felt warm in my hand. Flicking the top open with my thumb nail I turned the bottle on its head and squeezed. A trail of thick white liquid dropped onto Elaine's back and she flinched ever so slightly.

'It's cold,' she murmured.

I looked around, it was still early and there was no one within a hundred yards of us. I threw my knee over Elaine's back and rested myself on her buttocks. For a moment I did nothing, I just looked at her. She squirmed slightly underneath me and I was prompted into action. Slowly I moved the lotion up her spine and then outwards. Using first my finger tips and then my thumbs I made small round movements. Tiny ridges of flesh formed and then disappeared with each circle. Then, starting just above her hips, with my hands flat using the V between by fingers and thumb, I pushed. One slow movement from her hips to her shoulders. Then I did it again, and again. Each time my fingers brushed the curve of her breasts as they lay squashed beneath her.

She giggled, 'Stop it.'

I poured some of the liquid into my hand and then rubbed my hands together. Then laying them flat on her back I pushed until they reached the base of her neck. With my fingers resting on her collar bone I used my thumbs to massage the fleshy mounds at the top of her back. Again she squirmed but this time it was with pleasure. She lifted one of her arms and used it to move her hair out of the way. Her long fingernails, painted the same colour as her lips, gently scratched the surface on their journey but barely left a mark. As she replaced her arm she adjusted ever so slightly so that more of her shoulders were exposed to my hands.

I took the hint and used my thumbs to move from her neck along the ridge to her shoulders. Gradually the white film was disappearing into her skin, leaving it almost translucent.

Placing my hands on the towel at either side of her head I rested my weight on them and leaned forward. As my face got closer to Elaine I could smell her perfume. It was the one I bought her, the one I always bought her, the only one she ever wore. As I brushed my lips against her skin I could taste a hint of the lotion that I had spread on her. That didn't matter. I kissed her again and again lightly along the length of her shoulders like tiny butterflies resting briefly before flying away.

74

When I saw her face she was smiling.

'I love you,' she whispered without opening her eyes.

And that's when I knew that with Elaine by my side I could do anything and be anything. I was the luckiest man alive.

A Helping Hand
Jill Steeples

'What the...?' I stopped in the kitchen doorway, too shocked even to scream. It isn't every day you go down to breakfast to find a strange man sitting at your pine table.

'Hello, Sally.' He said nonchalantly, flashing a smile that might have graced a toothpaste ad. 'I'm Michael.'

'Michael?' I ventured, pulling my dressing gown tight.

He nodded, before returning to his bowl of Honey Nut Haloes.

'Your Guardian Angel?' He munched. 'You gave me a call.'

It was too early in the morning for me. I rubbed my eyes and peered closer.

'Oh, I get it,' I said, cottoning on. 'This is some kind of wind-up. Rob's put you up to this.' It was the sort of thing my brother would do.

'Er, no. Saturday night, remember? You were in a bit of a state and asked for my help.'

It was all coming back to me. Another evening spent alone with only a bottle of Pinot Grigio for company, I'd been flicking through the TV channels when I came across the programme on angels. I'd watched spellbound as it told how we all have one. Apparently, we only need ask and they'll be happy to put in an appearance to offer some friendly comfort and guidance.

Well, if anyone was in need of a bit of divine intervention, it was me. Life had been dreary to say the least. I'd been made redundant, was flat broke and had forgotten what it was like to have a member of the opposite sex show any interest in me. That's if you discount the bad-tempered man next door, but his wasn't the type of interest you'd want to encourage. He'd been

76

round again, having a rant in my direction about some parcel of his that I'd supposedly purloined.

Still, if things didn't improve soon, there was every chance I'd be waving goodbye to my cosy little flat, and the irritating next-door neighbour.

So, I'd muted the sound and taken a deep breath.

"Hello," I'd faltered, "if you're there, Guardian Angel, I wondered, maybe, if you weren't too busy, you could point me in the right direction. Show me the light so to speak."

And then I'd taken another sip of wine and launched into a long spiel about my pitiful existence. The lack of funds, my sorry social life and my expanding waistline on account of all the comfort eating I'd been indulging in. And once I'd started I couldn't stop. Really, it was quite therapeutic getting the whole thing off my chest. It ended with me plea-bargaining with my imaginary friend. I'd willingly forgo the face and figure of Angelina Jolie, if only I could have the chance of a fulfilling job and a decent good-looking man to share my life with. It wasn't a lot to ask, was it?

Now, I felt myself blush as I looked across at Michael. Was he really heaven sent? He certainly looked the part. Blond, spiky hair, intense blue eyes and a well-defined physique that rippled beneath the whitest of T-shirts and the coolest of denim jeans. I was beginning to think my prayers had been answered.

As if reading my thoughts, he smiled and shook his head.

'When you ignored the feather, I thought I'd better pop in.'

Oh yes, the feather! According to the show, if you found a feather it meant your Angel had visited and left his calling card. Admittedly, on the Sunday morning I'd spotted one on the floor, but it was a manky looking specimen, all grey and moth-eaten, and I hadn't given it another thought before sucking it up in the vacuum. After all, I'd changed the duvet cover the day before.

'That was you?' I stuttered.

Michael grinned.

'It was to let you know I'm here.' His voice took on a dreamy quality. 'That you're on the right track and I'll be there to guide you, every step of the way.'

I looked across at the celestial vision of loveliness, disappointment swelling in my chest.

'Is that it?' I asked. 'You go to all the trouble of turning up and all you can do is offer a few meaningless platitudes? I don't mean to sound ungrateful, but that's the kind of thing my mother says. I was hoping for something a little more tangible. Like a job? Or a man? Or a figure to die for?'

'I thought we'd negotiated on the figure.' Michael cackled in a rather un-angelic fashion. 'A man and a job, I might be able to fix, but a new body? I can't perform miracles you know.'

'Of course, I'm sorry,' I muttered, chastised. The last thing I wanted to do was upset him. 'It's just I'm finding all this a little strange. But please, if you can do whatever it is you do, I'd be ever so grateful.'

'That's the thing, Sally. I can only gently steer you in the right direction. Your life's partner is out there waiting and the perfect job is around the corner.'

'It is? He is?' That was news to me. Well, wherever they were, they were doing a pretty good job of keeping themselves hidden.

I'd scoured the local papers for a job, filled in reams of application forms and attended dozens of interviews with only a bruised ego to show for my efforts. And as for finding Mr Right, I tried everything possible. Speed dating, singles nights at the local wine bar and newspaper advertisements. All they'd netted me was a series of Mr Wrongs.

'Sometimes, when we look too hard, we fail to see that which is under our nose.'

I nodded sagely in agreement, wondering if all Angels spoke in clichés.

'Right, well that's good to know,' I said, thinking I should really get dressed and start job-hunting if Michael wasn't going to come up with the goods. 'I'll keep on keeping on. Let's hope

I'm not a grey and aged spinster before I meet the man of my dreams. Or the flat gets re-possessed in the meantime.'

'That won't happen, Sally,' Michael smiled. 'Let me help you before I go. Shouldn't really, goes against the commandments, but, hey, no point being an Angel if you can't pull a few strings every now and then.' He paused, his blue eyes twinkling mischievously. 'Philip,' he tapped his nose and gave a knowing wink. 'The rest, Sally, is up to you.'

'Philip,' I repeated. 'Who's Philip?'

Michael raised his eyebrows heavenwards.

'Oh, I see,' I said, becoming excited. 'That's him! Philip. The man for me. But I don't know any Philips. Not unless you mean the grouch next door,' I snorted, as a picture of the guy's exasperated face came to my mind.

Michael smiled wryly.

'Oh no,' I stuttered, apprehension flooding my veins, 'absolutely no way, not him, purleease?' Michael folded his arms and nodded, enjoying the revelation.

'You have got to be kidding,' I spluttered. Trust me to end up with an angel who not only had a warped sense of humour, but was a bad judge of character too.

Philip was the ranting neighbour-from-hell, the one lacking in any neighbourly attributes. I suppose we'd got off to a bad start the day I moved in. I was having trouble negotiating the gears on the hire van, when I accidentally hit reverse instead of first and lurched into the shiny convertible behind. Really, the way he went off at me, you would have thought I'd planned the whole thing.

And then there was that nonsense over the wheelie bins. As if I was the sort of person who would go around pinching other people's dustbins. It was just a misunderstanding. Had I known it was his bin I would never have plastered it in that floral PVC cover.

My Guardian Angel had got it all wrong. My life's partner couldn't be the scowling, ill-mannered and petulant man next door.

'I'm sorry, Michael, there must be some mistake.'

'No mistake, Sally. And I'm sorry too, but I've got to fly,' he got up from the table, casting me a heavenly look.

'But, Michael.' I pleaded, before the ringing of the doorbell interrupted me.

I raced to the door, flinging it open impatiently. 'Yes,' I snapped. 'Oh my,' I stopped to catch my breath, 'have your ears been burning?'

Philip stood on my doorstop, a familiar look of disdain on his face.

'Sorry?' he said, looking confused. 'No, it's about that parcel. I've checked with the courier company. They assure me it was delivered. Two weeks ago? Signed for by you?'

I stared into Philip's enquiring face, an overwhelming sense of dread filling my stomach. There had been a delivery, that much I could remember, but surely I must have popped it round to him earlier. Hadn't I?

'Are you OK?' he asked, peering into my face, 'you look awfully pale.'

Actually, I was feeling pretty terrible. Must have been something to do with my blood sugar levels. Well that and the shock of finding an Angel in my kitchen. Oh, and the sudden realisation that the man standing opposite me might be... no, this day was getting worse by the moment. And, even more pressingly, what had I done with the wretched parcel? I was in dire need of a caffeine fix.

'Fine, I think,' I gasped before my legs wobbled beneath me.

'Uh oh, come on,' he said, guiding me back into the kitchen. 'Let's make you a cup of tea. Have you had breakfast?'

Phil parked me on the seat vacated by Michael who, true to his word, had flown. Maybe I'd imagined the whole thing, I wondered. The stresses in my life were obviously affecting me more than I'd realised.

I tried to gather my senses, watching as Phil busied himself in my kitchen, opening and closing cupboards, finding teabags and popping bread into the toaster, his concerned gaze checking on me as he worked.

'Actually,' he said, running a J-cloth across the kitchen table, 'I've been meaning to catch you for a while.'

I swallowed hard, wondering what this latest complaint might be.

'I wanted to apologise for that first time we met, er… when you hit my car?'

I flinched and nodded.

'I think I probably over-reacted. Boys and their toys, you know what it's like.' He smiled, looking sheepish, and our eyes locked together in friendship.

'Apology accepted.' I said, grinning.

In fact, I don't know why I hadn't noticed before, but Phil was rather good-looking. Not in an over-obvious way, like Michael, but in an understated, charming manner. The mop of brown unruly hair, intelligent eyes and smattering of freckles gave him an endearing, boyish look. And when he wasn't scowling he was positively dishy.

When, after my reviving cuppa, I managed to retrieve his parcel from its hiding place, the cupboard under the stairs, he didn't seem too put out by my forgetfulness, just vaguely amused.

And if I disregarded the frantic racing of my heart, I was feeling much better after my funny turn. I looked over at him, feeling myself redden at the sight of his kindly brown eyes and endearing dimples either side of his mouth.

'Are you job-hunting?' he asked, picking up the paper from the table, sending a white feather fluttering in the air in the process.

I looked at the earmarked page, my eyes settling on the advertisement ringed in silver.

'Yes,' I said smiling, without needing to look closer, 'I've a feeling that's the perfect one.'

It wasn't the time to tell Phil I'd met the perfect man too. I had it on good authority he'd be finding that out for himself pretty soon.

Holiday Baggage
Sophie King

That was it, I told myself as I checked my case in at the airport. No more blind dates ! Not even one teeny, weeny one. This holiday was going to be a fresh start. If my sister Sharon wanted me to make up a foursome on the beach, that was too bad. All I wanted was some sun and time to myself something I badly needed after the past year.

'Come on, Jenny,' Sharon, who'd checked in before me, said impatiently. 'We've got two whole hours of sightseeing before we board the plane. What are you waiting for?'

Sightseeing, in my sister's book, was spotting any man over 5ft 11 without a wedding ring on his left hand.

I shook my head firmly. 'Sorry Sharon, but we've been through this before. I'm not here to find a boyfriend. I'm here to find me.'

Sharon eyed me quizzically. 'You've been reading too many self-help books. Find yourself, indeed! You're standing right here in Departures, just in front of a gorgeous guy who is giving you the once-over even though you're blindly ignoring him. Too late, he's gone.'

See what I mean? Sharon was incorrigible and I was beginning to wonder why I'd agreed to go on holiday with her in the first place. As sisters, we were like chalk and cheese. She was the go-getter and I was... well I'm not sure. Sometimes I'm daring enough to do things that even Sharon wouldn't do and, sometimes, I just want to wrap myself up in a cocoon and be on my own.

Maybe that's why Peter had left. "I don't understand you," he'd said on more than one occasion. Well, I didn't understand him, either. Or, to be precise, I didn't understand how he could be seeing someone else and going out with me at the same time.

My friends all rallied round with sympathy hugs and cries of "He wasn't good enough for you". But it was Sharon who told me that, at my age, I'd better pull myself together and find someone else. And that's how the blind dates started.

Don't ask me why I agreed but even though Sharon is younger than me by a good five years, she's always been streets ahead in that department. "I've got the perfect man," she announced one day over the phone. "He's tall, single and not as boring as Peter was. He wants to meet you, too. I said you were free after work tonight."

Well, I didn't want to offend the poor chap, especially as he shared Sharon's office and might, as she told me firmly, make life very difficult for her if I turned him down. But the date was a complete disaster. I mean, would you go out with a man who bred hamsters for a hobby and still lived with his mother at thirty-five? I might have tried a bit harder if he hadn't proceeded to tell me, all through dinner, about the breeding habits of hamsters. Believe me, you don't want to know.

Sharon's next blind date wasn't much better. I'm a simple girl at heart: not fussy, you understand. I enjoy going out to the cinema and parties but I also like to curl up in a chair with a good book and a glass of wine. Dennis, whose sister-in-law's friend worked out with Sharon at the gym (not my favourite place) didn't have time to read and preferred to watch the telly instead of forking out good money at the cinema when the film would be available on video in a few month's time.

In fact, that's why Sharon and I were here at the airport, right now. We were walking to the cinema when we happened to pass the travel agent. And there, slap-bang in the window, was such a good last-minute deal to Menorca that you'd have to have been as boring as Peter (Sharon's words) to have ignored it.

Somehow, I managed to wangle a week off from my boss and Sharon (who was very good at wangling all sorts of things with hers) went ahead and booked before I could change my mind. 'One rule,' I said firmly. 'This is not a man-hunting exercise. This is a break away from that sort of thing. If you find someone, fine. But don't ask him to bring a mate along.'

'Fair enough,' said Sharon airily but, by the time we landed at Menorca, I began to think I should have got her to sign a pre-holiday deal. 'Oooh, look at him,' she said, pointing to a tall dark man in shorts at the front of the passport queue. 'He's gorgeous! And he's on his own, too. No he's not. Damn. Where did she come from?'

'The loo actually,' I pointed out. 'Isn't a man allowed to stand on his own for two seconds before you get your telescopic vision into him?'

'Only trying to help,' said Sharon, pretending to be hurt. I gave her a sisterly squeeze. 'I don't need to worry, you know,' she pointed out. 'I've got years ahead to find someone. But people like you need a helping hand. Hey, look at that one. With his mates around him. He's looking at us too... Jenny, where are you going?'

I was almost dragging her by the hand towards the luggage carousel. 'To get our cases and stop you making a fool of yourself. Honestly, he could hear you.'

'So what? He'll know we're free too.'

I heaved my navy blue suitcase off the belt. 'You might be. But I'm here to ...'

'Read all those boring books you've got inside that thing,' finished my sister.

Exactly. I couldn't wait to unpack my new Sebastian Faulks and lie down with him on a sunbed. Except that by the time we got to our room, I discovered Sebastian wasn't there.

'I don't believe it,' I cried, staring into my suitcase on the hotel bed. 'I've got the wrong bag.'

'You can't have,' said Sharon, opening hers. 'Mine's all right. And we put them on at the same time.'

I pulled out a pair of blue and red swimming trunks with a forty-inch waist label.

'Suits you,' giggled Sharon. 'They'll get you noticed all right.'

By this time, I was going all hot and cold, trying to remember what I'd packed and what might now have gone for ever. At least six expensive thick paperbacks which I'd been dying to read. A nearly-new bottle of Chanel No. 5 which Mum had given me for my birthday. A travelling alarm clock. A brand-new bikini which had taken several hours to find (am I the only woman whose bottom has very little in common with her top?). And a pair of flat sandals because I meant it about finding myself. I intended to explore the area, which would have been difficult in the more elegant shoes I had travelled in.

Instead, I had the following items in front of me. The swimming trunks (enough said). A travelling clock. Six thick blokey action-type books, including two by Robert Harris, whom I'd never read. A blank sketch pad. A rather nice cable green jersey. A pair of trainers size 11. Several T-shirts and shorts, none of which were folded particularly neatly. One of those cheap disposable cameras. A tennis racquet. And a magnetic draughts set.

There was more, as Sharon pointed out, but that's as far as we got because I stopped her delving any deeper. 'Spoil-sport,' she said. 'Don't you see? It's our ideal opportunity to see how blokes tick. This one's definitely on his own; if he'd had a wife, she'd have folded those T-shirts.'

I neglected to point out that my own hadn't been folded either. Peter had been a stickler for tidiness which had been another bone of contention between us. He'd also owned a very expensive camera which he would fiddle with for hours before finally getting round to taking a picture. Pushing this thought to the back of my mind, I rang the hotel rep who said she'd do what she could to track down my missing suitcase.

'Is there a name on the one you've got?' she asked.

Naturally, I'd already checked but the piece of flimsy string hanging from the handle suggested the label had been pulled off. I only hoped the same hadn't happened to mine.

By the second day of our holiday, there was still no sign of my missing suitcase and Sharon was getting very fed up with lending me her clothes – especially as all that hassle over Peter meant that my newly-slimmed legs looked better in her designer shorts than her own did. By the third day, I was wondering why I'd never met Robert Harris before or another action-packed author whose cover I had previously ignored in bookshops.

'Do you think you ought to be reading someone else's books?' asked Sharon.

I pointed out that as the rep still hadn't been to collect the suitcase (no wonder this was a cheap, no-frills holiday), I might as well make use of it. The green sweater even came in handy one evening when it got chilly and I rather liked the manly smell on it which was distinctly familiar in an odd sort of way. The tennis racquet also gave me ideas. Well, I wouldn't have borrowed it except that the hotel was charging a ridiculous amount to hire theirs. Besides, my suitcase owner's racquet was far less superior than the one in my own missing suitcase. Blast, that's another thing I'd forgotten was in there.

'It's a bit like Cinderella, isn't it?' I said, over a crystal-blue cocktail after a blissfully hot day by the pool.

'What do you mean?' asked Sharon crossly. She still hadn't found someone nice and there were only three days left.

'Well,' I giggled (partly on account of the said crystal-blue cocktail), 'I quite like the look of my suitcase owner from his contents. And if he's got mine, and likes the look of me, we could be a match.'

Sharon eyed me sardonically. 'Thought you didn't believe in blind dates and, by the way, watch you don't splash my dress with your drink. It's dry clean only.'

I bought myself a pair of flat sandals from a local shop to go on my walks (the size 11 trainers would have dwarfed me). And, by the end of the holiday, I had it all worked out. I'd chuck in my job, which reminded me too much of Peter (his company often liaised with mine) and I'd put Peter down to experience. I'd start doing things for myself like learning to paint. That sketch pad had given me an idea. And no, I didn't borrow it. I just bought myself my own from the hotel shop.

'Not bad,' said Sharon, surprised. 'You were always good at art at school. Remember?'

I got out the sketch pad again at the airport when there was a five hour delay. I certainly had enough subjects to choose from, with hordes of holidaymakers sprawled over plastic chairs, waiting for their flights to be called.

'That's good,' said a small boy with a floppy brown fringe and a green cable knit jumper. 'My dad likes to draw too but he lost his sketch pad when his suitcase went missing. He's just gone to find out about it now. My name's Ben, by the way.'

I looked up. 'Was the suitcase navy blue?'

The small boy nodded seriously.

Sharon gave me one of her warning looks. It said 'Married'.

Just my luck to find the one blind date I couldn't have.

'He got someone else's suitcase instead,' said my new friend. 'A lady's. Well we think it was a lady even though her bikini bottom was much bigger than her top. He read all her books, though I said he shouldn't. We didn't touch her perfume because that was girly but we did play with her Scrabble. He said it was fair deals because someone else had our draughts board. I like games, don't you?'

'No,' said Sharon firmly, no doubt thinking of all the evenings I had beaten her with the small boy's draughts set. 'Is this your dad?'

A gorgeous, tall, handsome man was approaching us, with the same kind of floppy fringe as his son's. In his hand, he had a navy blue suitcase. He looked at the identical one by my side.

'Your son tells me that you lost your case on the way out,' I said. 'Me too. Do you read Robert Harris, by any chance?'

The man smiled. It was a rather nice boyish crinkly smile. 'I rather like Sebastian Faulks now. And I'd forgotten how much I enjoyed Scrabble.'

And that was how I met Peter. Pity about the name. But as I kept telling Sharon, the two couldn't have been more different. He'd had a bad experience too; Ben's mother had been rather like the original Peter when it came to telling the truth. They'd been divorced for a couple of years now. But he had an amicable arrangement with her over Ben, which was why he took him on holiday.

The following summer, I bought a large bright orange suitcase which couldn't possibly belong to anyone else. Well, it could actually. It could belong to Peter because, in fact, I bought two. They were reduced, which was, as Sharon said, quite understandable, in view of the garish colour. Still, at least it made sure that no one else could take them by mistake. I wouldn't like to think of anyone else getting their hands on my new man.

'Do you think,' asked Ben curiously, after we'd checked in our bags, 'that if someone took my case by mistake, I might find a holiday friend like you and Dad did?'

We were still chuckling over that one as we stood in Departures, when I suddenly saw him. He'd put on a bit of weight and he'd got rid of the glasses but that expensive camera round his neck was a dead give-away.

'It's Peter,' I said horrified, looking the other way in case he saw me.

My own Peter put his arm around me. He looked worried and, for a moment, exactly like the little boy who was standing next to us. 'You don't feel anything for him any more, do you?'

'Absolutely not,' I said firmly and truthfully. 'As far as I'm concerned, he's merely old baggage.'

Swimming
Lauren McCrossan

Swimming. Just the sight of that word on my school timetable was enough to bring me out in verrucas. Over my formative years I must have invented thousands of reasons why I could not possibly throw my Lycra-clad puppy fat into the yellowed school pool. I was sick; I was asthmatic; I had my period (whispered anxiously to Sister Mary Swimming Gala who put the fear of God into those who could not do the two hundred metre freestyle); I was dangerously allergic to chlorine; I was now a Muslim; I was contagious; I was not waterproof. You have to admit I was inventive but, desperate times and all that. I even went so far as to break my wrist on the first lap of a backstroke race. This was unintentional but proved an efficient way to get me out of a record-breaking six weeks swimming in a row.

To some I was an anti-swimming hero. Of course there were those more fishy among us who actually seemed to enjoy parading around in a navy regulation Speedo swimsuit in front of their peers. Those with gorgeous legs right up to their think bubbles. Those who had been taking secret butterfly lessons from the age of two and could tread water for several hours non-stop without even taking a breath. And those who were just too thick to realise what a state they looked a) getting in and out of the pool b) while floundering *in* the pool; and c) for the rest of the day with their frizzy hair and acid-peeled raw skin.

I just could not see the attraction. Even before hurling oneself into the lukewarm, stinking water there were the changing rooms to contend with. Ill-fitting curtains that exposed my pasty whiter-than-white skin and left my nosier classmates with snow-blindness. The pools of off-colour, tepid water settling in the cracks of the floor tiles that seemed to magnetically attract socks and pants, which made for an

90

uncomfortably damp or knickerless afternoon in Double Science. Then there was the swimsuit, selected by nuns for heaven's sake. If Pamela Anderson had been allowed a bit of input then maybe we would have had a chance, but nuns choosing beachwear? Hope, Hell and spuds in a saggy Lycra sack are the words that spring to mind.

If the suit was not bad enough then, oh yes, there was always the compulsory swimming cap to look forward to. Bearable if you had a well-proportioned head, neat boyish hair and the features of an elfin supermodel. As for me, I had wild curly hair that simply refused to be clamped any closer than a foot from my head. No matter how much talc I poured into the damn hat, it still ripped out half my follicles and I invariably emerged looking like the dome-headed plastic man from the Play-Doh Barber Shop.

Through the warm footbath we were then ushered, avoiding the floating used plaster and the discarded verruca sock. All the time praying to the Patron Saint of Feet that our toes would not fall off before we reached the relative hygiene of the chlorinated pool that had been urinated in by at least three classes that morning. Next came the humiliation of being put into groups. I, needless to say, was always in the slow class. Resigned to doing widths clinging to a battered blue float in the hope that one day I would be promoted to the dizzy heights of doggy paddle, I could only gaze up at the water babies in the deep end, performing synchronised somersaults off a three hundred foot diving board and not even making a splash. Not that I wanted to *be* them. I simply wanted one of them to physically demonstrate the school myth that a belly flop from a great height could split a person in half. We could then all go home and forget the whole silly business while the pool was dredged and subsequently closed down.

When my expert excuses did not get me out of swimming, I did give it my best shot. I wasn't proud of being a failure in armbands. But the truth was, swimming and I existed in different dimensions and never the twain shall meet, as they say. Where others floated happily, I sank. I also wheezed, flapped my pubescent bingo wings with little effect, splashed rather a lot and almost drowned on several occasions. Funnily enough, as I lay there on the bottom like a brick wondering whether my time was up, not a single hero in pyjamas dived down to drag me to the surface. I always knew that exercise was pointless.

"Jane, you useless lump," shrieked Sister Mary Swimming Gala as they pumped water from my failing lungs, "you simply must learn to swim. It could save your life one day."

Now even at the tender age of thirteen I could see the irony in that statement.

School taught me many things, but mostly that swimming was best left to those with very big shoulders who loved getting up at 4am to stare at a line on the bottom of a pool; and marine mammals. After all, if we humans were supposed to live in water we would have been born with gills and fins and hair resistant to frizz and skin that does not bloat up like a dead cow's if you unfortunately happen to drown. Whereat I reach the crux of the issue: drowning. A very unpleasant by-product of a rather unpleasant activity. I blame Sister Mary Swimming Gala for my irrationally intense fear of coming to a watery end. I think it was the time she saw me take a bite of Battenberg in the changing rooms just before swimming.

"Jesus, Mary and all the saints, girl, are you trying to kill yourself? Eating less than an hour before swimming? You'll surely drown."

I was thereafter terrified that one fatal Salt and Vinegar Disco too many consumed within the one-hour watershed would plummet me to the bottom of the pool like a descending submarine. Even the fear that my watch was slow and I had finished my Wham bar with only fifty-eight minutes till pool time gave me a stitch so chronic doggy paddling became a physical impossibility. I did not want to drown. I had seen it on *Jaws* and it did not look pretty. Admittedly the shark the size of a Volkswagen camper van gnawing off the poor swimmers' legs made it worse (which, by the way, is a fantastic reason not to swim in open water) but even the drowning without the shark looked like a bad thing. If the threat of drowning was the only logical reason they could give me for learning to swim in the first place then surely the most sensible thing to do was stay out of the water altogether. No go water. No drown. Simple.

When I hit my thirties there were times when I bowed to peer pressure and attempted to learn to swim. Usually around New Year when I found making a resolution to learn to swim was a great way of avoiding resolving to go on a diet or to stop buying shoes. I once joined an adult swimming group, which was run alongside the Toddler Tadpoles and, basically, consisted of myself and other usually respectable adult individuals being humiliated by three-year-old mermaids who thought swimming underwater was a bit of a lark. I even tried aqua-aerobics for about half an hour until I realised the water resistance was intended to make the exercise harder. Why would anyone want it to be *harder* for goodness' sake? So, yes, I did try but there comes a time in every girl's life when she has to realise that she is never going to be a ballerina/marry a prince/be a Hollywood starlet and, in my case, effortlessly cruise the fast lane of my local pool and emerge from the water looking like Ursula Andress in that Bond movie.

Even when my well-intentioned friends tried their best to convince me swimming is a necessary part of life, I resisted.

"But, Jane, what if you need it one day?";

"What if you want to take an adventure holiday?";

"What if you fall through ice?";

"What if you accidentally topple off the top deck of a cross-Channel ferry?";

"What if a tidal wave hits Hampshire?";

"What if your plane crashes into the sea?"

Quite frankly if a plane I am on were to crash into the sea I am sure I will be obliterated into a million pieces and swimming will be the least of my worries. As for adventure holidays; kayaking the Atlantic, surfing twenty-foot waves in a skin-tight rubber suit and throwing myself over a waterfall in a raft full of lunatics sounded about as much fun to me as bungee jumping into the outside lane of the M25 at rush hour, without a rope. I would take my holidays in land-locked cities thank you very much.

You see, deep down I knew I was right. Obviously I realised I could not avoid water for ever but I was reconciled to the fact that I was just not born to be a swimmer. How pleasant it was after all the years of being treated like a freak for not wanting to play water polo at the beach or hurl myself down a vertical plastic air-conditioning pipe expertly renamed a "water flume", that I was proved right. Not learning to swim was the best decision I could ever have made. I was however wrong to have been so afraid of drowning. The drowning part of it wasn't that bad. But the swimming, yes, I was right all along. After all, if I had been able to swim I would never have met him.

Ironically it was the Battenberg that did it. I had completely forgotten about entering the competition on the packet until I heard the news. Two weeks in Hawaii courtesy of a pink and yellow marzipan cake. An attempt, I think, to make Battenberg sexier. Now I may have been afraid of drowning but even that was not enough to make me not want to go to Hawaii. Front crawl may have been beyond me but I was not a total idiot. My most recent boyfriend had left me two weeks before. He had an unhealthy obsession with jet-skis so it would never have worked but I can safely say it was the equally unhealthy obsession with other men's wives that was more influential in our break-up. I was single, miserable and lost. I needed a holiday and, although two weeks on Sunset Beach where the waves are bigger than a stack of double decker buses would not have been my first choice, it was sunny and it was free. I even bought a bikini for the first time in my life.

I am not sea savvy, nor do I pretend to be, so I kept my distance for the first few days. On day five, due to a case of very hot feet, I dipped my toes in. It was warm and pleasant but immersing myself deeper than my swollen ankles was the last thing on my mind. In fact, if the hunk in trunks from Idaho had not asked me to take his photograph, I would never have turned my back on the ten-foot shorebreak. I would not have been shouting – "Say cheese" – as a whole herd of white horses chased by an entire safari of white man-eating tigers and a few white rhino for good measure galloped up behind me and came crashing down on my head. How was I supposed to know about tidal movements? Or that the lulls in the swells in Hawaii are often broken by shorebreaks that could consume your average bungalow? I never saw it coming. Largely because I was distracted by the incredible dimensions of my Idaho Adonis. Who, incidentally, should have been ashamed of himself for shrieking – "Oh man, my camera!" – as I was dragged into the ocean by one of the most violent waves on earth.

I have heard people say they didn't know which way was up when they were hit by a wave. I will add to that by saying I could not even remember what "up" was by the time the first wave had finished cartwheeling my head repeatedly into the sand. The second wave then sucked me out to sea for a bit of fun, while the third attempted to turn me inside out and spit my bones onto the beach like bits of broken driftwood. It was terrifying for what felt like an hour, then it became exhausting and then, strangely, I relaxed about the whole thing. I was drowning and there was nothing I could do about it. The swim police who had badgered me my whole life would, of course, say "I told you so" but then I wouldn't be around to hear them. Perhaps I should have learned to butterfly my way out of such sticky situations but it was too late; this was where it all ended. I would no longer be afraid of drowning – a) because I had in fact drowned, which was admittedly a shame; but b) because I had faced my fear head-on and realised it wasn't something that should have stopped me doing things in my life. They say you drown on a high and, as the moment became an aquamarine acid trip, I believed them. So when the beautiful merman dived down to save me I thought I was dead. The acid trip had climaxed and I was about to die in the clutches of an incredible imaginary being.

Suddenly I was on the beach. A crowd of anxious faces peered down at me. Would you believe it, a couple of tourists were even capturing the drama on camcorder in the hope a digital TV show would later pay them for the clip? His soft, salty lips were pressed against mine. His slim hands were on my bare chest. He was the most stunning man I had ever seen. I am proud to say that for someone plucked from a watery grave, I was surprisingly lucid. I even had the sense to keep my breathing secret a little longer than necessary just to prolong the kiss. My merman was real. He was a Hawaiian lifeguard with a two-for-the-price-of-one six-pack. He surfed death-defying waves for breakfast and swam oceans before dinner. He had been an Olympian. He was a natural waterman. He was my antithesis. Yet the moment he held me in his arms, I felt as if I had come home.

We met up the next day. He looked exactly the same as he had when he brought me back to life. His halo was no less radiant and he was no less breathtaking. I had made a supreme effort to look anything but similar to the wreck of a human with seaweed hair he had been forced to dredge up from the depths. And he liked me. He found me interesting. The fact I was an alien to all things aquatic was fascinating to him. We were from different worlds and we had so much to learn from each other. Although more than a single ocean divided us, we were falling in love and that was something altogether more powerful than waves the size of skyscrapers.

We later married in a simple ceremony on Sunset Beach. The ocean remained respectfully calm and the way we met was an amusing story recounted throughout the day. Naturally I was asked whether I was going to learn to swim but, as I told them, if I had been a swimmer we would never have met so why upset the status quo? Besides, with my personal lifeguard by my side, what was the point?

In the end, though, I gave in to the whole swimming thing. Enough to partake in a bit of skinny-dipping in the ocean outside our beach. This time there were no yellowed swimming pools, no follicle-stripping hats and no shrieking nuns. There was just a man who loved me for the fact I sank every time I touched water. If he was my rock, I was his brick but he floated my boat and my body soon followed.

Bitches and Blind Dates
Rosemarie Rose

'Hi, Megan!' said a familiar voice when I answered the phone.

It was a shock; I'd expected it to be my mother. I opened my mouth to speak but nothing came out.

'Megan, darling, are you there? It's Lucy. How are things?'

By "things" Lucy, my so-called best friend, was referring to my lately-acquired singledom. After Jeff's latest fling, with yet another leggy, top-heavy babe he'd spotted from the window of our beachside cottage, I'd had enough. Depressingly, apart from Mum's, the flow of concerned calls from everyone had trickled to a halt after a mere three days. The ensuing silence had been devastating, so I suppose my response, once I'd found my voice, was inevitable.

'Lucy who?' I asked, oozing sarcasm.

To give Lucy her due, she did raise an embarrassed laugh before trotting out a string of platitudes like *tempus fugit,* as well as twisting a few to suit. 'Time on your own's a great healer, Megan,' she trilled.

I stifled a scream. Jeff and I had tried to make a go of it for almost twenty years. It was hardly the end of a frivolous relationship, so why on earth would Lucy assume I craved solitude after such a catastrophic event?

I was about to tell her what a stupid, insensitive cow she was when she asked if I'd like to drop in for dinner sometime.

I thought of all those solitary meals and empty evenings; the telly, a box of Kleenex and Mick the cat my only companions. I'd given up on music when the mournful sound of Radiohead had superglued itself to the CD player. (The cathartic works of the Stones and other favourite rock bands had somehow become invisible in my grief-stricken state.) I hadn't even found the strength to drag myself out for my customary walks along the beach.

My anger drained away. She should have asked before, but what the heck. Cringe-making gratitude rose to my lips. 'I'd love to, Luce. How about tomorrow night?'

'Um, tomorrow's tricky – Phil and I are entertaining. Which is why I'm ringing, actually. I need a favour.'

I'd known Lucy for ten years. When her sentences ended on a rising syllable, an annoying habit she'd picked up from Australian soaps, it was time for serious loin-girding.

Lucy surpassed herself. She and Phil were planning dinner for Jeff and *Tiffany*. Tiffany, Tiffany, Tiffany. So *that* was the bitch's name. Not that it mattered; Jeff would replace her soon enough.

'I knew you wouldn't mind us feeding Jeff occasionally. You don't, do you.' It was a statement not a question. 'I mean, we're Jeff's friends too, and men on their own, well, they don't look after themselves, do they, and Jeff can't cook, so we've had him over a few times...' Lucy rushed on, taking as much heed of my smashed feelings as a herd of stampeding bulls. 'Anyway, Phil's had one of his clearouts – you know how he hates mess – and he's chucked out Jeff's number by mistake...' She trailed off and I thought she'd picked up on the venomous vibes I was lasering through the ether. But no. 'Sorry, Megan – I was looking for a pen. When you're ready.'

Oh, I was ready. Boy, was I ready. Instead of obliging the expectant Lucy with Jeff's number, I poured forth a string of accusations and expletives, the last of which began with eff and ended with off, and slammed down the phone.

It rang again almost immediately. 'You sow!' Lucy's voice shook with anger. 'No wonder Jeff prefers the company of other women! Even little old me!'

The world tilted on its axis. Lucy? Jeff had slept with *Lucy*...?

'Remember that IT course you went on last year...?'

I put down the phone like a woman in a trance. I stood there, unable to move or think, till the phone rang again.

'Megan. Darling. I'm sorry, I shouldn't have said that – I promised myself I'd never tell. But you were being so horrible…'

I moved the receiver from my ear and stared at it in disbelief. *I* was being horrible…? I dropped it back into place, somehow got my feet to plant themselves one in front of the other, and headed for the fridge.

An hour later I'd run out of Kleenex and polished off the first bottle of chardonnay. I was uncorking the second when the local weekly paper arrived. I'm not normally a great believer in fate, but it hit the mat and curled open at the Lonely Hearts page. I decided there and then it was high time I forgot about Jeff and found myself an appreciative man. No way, though, was I answering any ads. Oh no. *I'd* be the one who did the picking and choosing.

Feeling more alive than I had in weeks, I dusted down a Stones CD, returned the wine to the fridge, and fetched pen and paper.

A bulging package arrived from the newspaper's office two weeks later. Sifting through the thirty-plus replies was a mixed experience. Some were sad enough to make me cry. And others sounded warning bells. I discarded mature gent with large bank balance and private yacht. Out too went gorgeous hunk (photo enclosed). Serial killers, both. Well, why else would a multi-millionaire and a George Clooney look-alike cruise the Lonely Hearts columns? Anyway, I'd married a gorgeous hunk and look where that had got me.

I took a deep breath and picked up the phone. Within half-an-hour I had three dates for the following week.

No.1 sounded promising: six feet tall, dark hair, and a music-lover to boot. We'd arranged to meet in a wine bar overlooking the bay. I pushed open the door with a shaking hand and glanced around the candle-lit interior, hoping I didn't look as terrified as I felt. My date clearly hadn't arrived – a short bald man at the bar was the only solitary male in sight – so I settled myself in a squishy leather sofa near the door.

The man at the bar eyed my legs appreciatively. Flattering, yes, but I didn't want him thinking I was available. Frances Fyfield's *Blind Date* was my chosen method of identification, so I quickly took the book from my bag, convinced it would keep marauding wolves at bay.

Seconds later my heart sank. From the corner of my eye I saw the short bald man moving towards me. Then an awful thought occurred to me…

It couldn't be.

I glanced up and he held out his hand and grinned. 'Hello, Megan.'

It was.

Now there's nothing wrong with short. And bald can be sexy. Liars, however, don't turn me on. But there was nothing to go home for. A couple of drinks wouldn't hurt. I stood up to shake his proffered hand, my modest height of five-and-a-half feet dwarfing him, and hoped "music-lover" wasn't another lie.

It wasn't, but it was misleading. The blues band Blodwyn Pig was his first love. And his second and his third. You get the picture. Conversation soon dried up. When he pinned me against the sofa cushions and slid a hand up my thigh, I hastily invented a life-threatening disease for Mick the cat that required hourly medication and called a cab.

My hopes for No.2 were high. His handwriting was beautiful; bold and artistic. And his rich, deep phone voice had almost reduced me to jelly. As he spoke, my mind had plunged into my knickers. I'd imagined myself posing on the purple satin sheet that no doubt graced the day bed in his cliff-top studio, while he – dark, brooding and very naked – immortalised me in oils or marble…

But my imagination had run away with me.

He lived ten miles away, so we'd arranged to meet midway, outside a village pub. When we swapped car descriptions I was surprised to hear he drove a red saloon. I'd pictured him in something less ordinary: an ageing sports car with wire wheels, perhaps; or a battered Morris Minor, paint-spattered Jackson Pollock style.

I slowed as I reached the village. Parked outside the Smugglers' Arms was a red saloon which couldn't possibly be his. The go-faster stripe and forest of spotlights shrieked "boy racer". I drove to the end of the village and turned the car around for another pass. This time I had a clear view of the driver: a lad about half my age with volcanic scarlet spots.

It couldn't be…

He leaned through his window, waving wildly.

It was.

Horrified, I put my foot down. A minute later he roared up behind me, air-horns blaring, lights blazing. After a reckless race through miles of darkening countryside I lost him at a level-crossing. The barriers were coming down fast, but it was my only chance of escape.

I decided to cancel No.3 that night, but Mum phoned, before I'd plucked up courage, to check how things had gone. I filled her in on both disastrous dates, then told her all about Lucy's confession.

Mum was incredulous. 'Never! Whatever was Jeff thinking? You're far prettier than her!'

I smiled through my tears. Good old Mum.

'I should have guessed,' she mused. 'Her eyes are too close together. A sure sign of treachery, your Gran always said. Well I never. I don't know what that nice Phil sees in her. If I was twenty years younger…'

I laughed. Phil was definitely her type: a bit of a smoothie with looks most women would kill for. Although I preferred the rugged sort, I could see the attraction.

'Megan, chick, don't let her spoil the rest of your life. You go. You never know – it might be third time lucky.'

No.3 and I had arranged to meet in The Ship. Too touristy for my liking, but convenient for both of us. I bought a drink and, ducking under plastic seaweed looped along every beam, made my way to a window seat overlooking the beach. While Jamie Cullum crooned in the background, I swallowed half a glass of Dutch courage then looked around. The season was almost over. Apart from a group of women chatting by a fireplace, and a middle-aged couple growling at one another across a table, the place was deserted.

Then I saw him, tucked away in one of the booths designed to look like beach-huts. He was gorgeous: grey-blond floppy hair and striking pale-blue eyes. He looked at the door, then at his watch and frowned. He was clearly waiting for someone. Me. It had to be. Heart hammering with excitement, I dragged Frances Fyfield's *Blind Date* from my bag for the second time that week and coughed loudly. He glanced up and our eyes met. I tentatively waved the book with a nervous grin. His eyebrows shot up in surprise and he suppressed a smile. Then he shook his head apologetically, poured a glass of wine from a cooler on the table and resumed his watch on the door.

Red-faced, I crept to the bar and ordered another drink from the tittering barman, who'd witnessed the whole scene. I gave him what I hoped was a withering look and returned to my seat.

The women ordered fresh drinks and sat down to study menus. The middle-aged couple had stopped growling and sat in stone-faced silence. Jamie Cullum was now singing the same song that had heralded my arrival. I checked my watch: No.3 was forty-five minutes late.

A young couple arrived, bronzed surfer bodies clad in ripped denim, sun-bleached hair cascading over their shoulders. I realised to my utter dismay that if Jeff and I had been blessed, our offspring would have been a similar age.

'Yo!' said the barman, hi-fiving them. 'Good to see you – it's dead in here tonight. Apart from...' He lowered his voice and his friends began to giggle, casting curious glances at me and Beach-hut Blond. I feigned indifference and pretended to read my book.

Chairs scraped on floorboards and the middle-aged couple left, he with an arm around her waist, she with her head on his shoulder. I smiled. A crowd of lively young men swarmed in. I glanced at my watch again; I'd definitely been stood up.

As I prepared to leave, Beach-hut Blond appeared beside me. 'Amazing!' he said, brandishing a copy of Frances Fyfield's *Blind Date*. 'Two people on a blind date in the same bar, the same small town, and both choose the same book as identification. Amazing!'

I looked blankly at his handsome face and sapphire eyes. Then light dawned: Beach-hut Blond and No.3 were one and the same. This was his way of turning women to putty in his hands.

'Yes,' I spat. 'Amazing!' I snatched up my bag, resisting a strong urge to hit him over the head with it. 'Your other blind dates may fall into your bed in gratitude when you eventually deign to reveal your identity, but not this one!'

I rushed outside, fumbling in my bag for my mobile.

'Hey! What was *that* all about?'

Had he no shame…? I whirled around. 'Don't play the innocent with me,' I snapped, hands on hips. 'Your next line, after you'd asked my name, would doubtless have been that you couldn't believe I was *your* blind date – too beautiful by half. Hah! Well, let me tell you, mister, there's no way I'm falling for that one!'

'But it's nothing like that. Let me explain –'

'There's nothing to explain! Go away or I'll call the police!'

He backed off. 'I'm sorry, I'm sorry. And I'll happily go, but before I do at least let me have my say.'

'For heaven's sake,' I groaned, more weary now than angry. 'OK. Say what you have to say, but make it quick.'

'Look, I came over to commiserate because we'd both clearly been stood up. I thought we could finish my bottle of wine together –'

'You expect me to believe that?'

'Hey! You said you'd listen!'

'Yes, but that doesn't mean I have to believe you, does it?'

He ran a hand through his hair in exasperation. 'Look, I don't even fancy you. Couldn't *ever* fancy you –'

'What...? Oh great! First, you go out of your way to turn me into a soft touch, by letting me think I've been stood up, and then you close in for the kill. And now, just because I've sussed your little game, you get nasty and insult me!'

He grabbed my arm and pulled me roughly towards him. 'For the last time – *you are not my blind date!* Not unless you're in disguise and your name's Luke!'

We stared at one another in stunned silence. After what seemed an eternity he spoke.

'Sorry – I'm hurting you.' He gently released my arm. 'But now do you understand?'

I realised my mouth was hanging open. I closed it, then opened it again. 'Oh shit... Oh shit oh God I'm sorry...'

My face must have been a picture. He snorted with sudden laughter and couldn't stop. It was contagious. I joined in and we laughed until we cried, clutching each other for support.

'I'm so sorry,' I finally managed to gasp. 'You must think I'm a total bitch. Let me buy you a drink.'

'No, please. An understandable mistake. Let *me* buy *you* one.'

'Absolutely not.' And I marched him back into The Ship and ordered a bottle of wine, to the continuing amusement of the barman and his friends.

I never did find out what happened to No.3. Just as well, really. Richard – aka Beach-hut Blond – pointed out that dating on the rebound was rarely a good idea. Better to keep away from men for a while, he said. Which I did, apart from Richard, who soon became my greatest friend. We discovered we had more in common than crime fiction and being stood up. Like the Rolling Stones and cats. We even had similar jobs in IT.

One morning, as we sipped coffee over the Sunday papers in the Starfish Café, Lucy's husband Phil came in. I hadn't seen him since Lucy and I fell out.

It was a mutual case of love at first sight. I'd always wondered about Phil, ever since I'd found a friend of Jeff's fighting him off in the garden at one of our parties.

Richard's asked me to be Best Woman and I've bought a gorgeous cream silk dress for the occasion. Lucy's been invited, but it seems unlikely she'll ever get over it. Despite everything, I feel quite sorry for her; I know how she must feel. Perhaps I'll give her a call, poor bitch.

Sea Blue Eyes
Zoë Griffin

The old Chinese woman sitting next to me in the audience scowls and shakes her head gravely. I gasp and grip the arms of my chair.

We are watching a poker tournament at the Grimaldi Forum in Monaco. There are two players left in the game, the last community card has just been dealt and the audience is waiting for the players to make their final bets.

My best friend Jack is one of the remaining contestants. His opponent is a small Chinese man, who has fewer chips and seems to be more affected by the stress.

Jack coolly glances at the pair of cards in his hand, then at the cards on the table, before he focuses his gaze on the Chinese man and looks him up and down. The Chinese man's hands are shaking and he is staring at the table to avoid making eye contact.

Jack explained all about eye contact on the flight from London.

"Rosie, listen," he said. "Since you're going to be watching, you might as well understand what's going on."

I did my best to pay attention. I learned that he would be playing a type of poker called no-limit Texas Hold Em, and that the point of the game was to work out what cards your opponent had and bet accordingly. I learned that putting on a "poker face" was what you did when you attempted to keep your face expressionless so that your opponent could not work out what cards you had in your hand. Most importantly, I learned some of the tactics that Jack used to guess his opponent's cards.

"If I stare at someone long enough then they'll meet my gaze eventually," he told me confidently. "The eyes are the key, Rosie. They betray what you are thinking."

Jack shifted his six foot four inch frame in the seat and turned to face me. I giggled nervously as he attempted to demonstrate on me by grabbing my chin with his huge hands and forcing me to look into his deep blue eyes.

"I know you've been thinking about Kevin," he said seriously.

I stopped laughing. Kevin was my ex-fiancé, and he had broken my heart. I hated talking about him.

The poker tournament is no laughing matter either. The atmosphere in the audience is tense, as the players are yet to make their bets. Jack is clearly in no mood to rush. With his blue eyes narrowed to the size of rice grains, he stares at the Chinese man and holds his gaze for what seems like an eternity. The Chinese man sits rigid in his seat, looking at the table, but he starts to shift around slightly as Jack holds his glare.

'Keep looking at him, keep looking at him,' I urge Jack silently. 'He'll crack eventually.'

I blush as I remember how I cracked on the plane.

"How dare you," I shouted at him. "How dare you? YOU wanted me to come with you to Monaco to watch you play poker. YOU promised that you would help me forget about Kevin the creep during this weekend break. Now YOU'RE bringing him up again. I don't want to think about him. I want to lie on the beach on my own but instead I'm here with you. So you'd better start appreciating me."

Jack waited for me to stop shouting.

"Finished yet?" he asked eventually.

"Not really," I told him, "but I'm not going to say anything else because I don't want to talk to you."

I curled up in my seat and put an eye-mask over my face to avoid looking at him. I had been thinking about Kevin but I didn't want Jack to know that.

In the auditorium again, I notice the lady next to me shifting in her seat. I turn my attention back to the stage and see that her husband has gone all-in and pushed all his chips into the centre.

The old Chinese lady puts her head in her hands and I empathise with her. It's all or nothing now. One of the men on stage will win and the other will go home empty-handed, full of disappointment. I feel like I am used to being left disappointed by men. My ex-fiancé promised me the world when he proposed, but I soon learned that he was all talk and no action. All my friends and family, especially Jack, tell me that I should forget about him and move on, but I can't seem to get him out of my head. Jack knows that and it really irritates him.

When I took off my eye-mask at the end of the flight, Jack was staring out of the window. I leaned on his shoulder to get a better view of the clear blue sea, lush green vegetation and white stone villas as the plane slowly descended towards the airstrip.

Jack sighed.

"I'm sorry," I tried to apologise.

Jack turned to face me again. He looked into my eyes.

"You know that you will be sorry if you keep thinking about Kevin."

"I, er, I, wasn't. Really, I wasn't." I lied.

I smiled brightly and tried to make it look like I hadn't been crying when I was wearing the blindfold. I tried to pretend that my eyes hadn't filled up when I thought back to the sad day last month when I'd called off my wedding after receiving a phone call from a woman from Kevin's work. One minute, my mother had been on the line talking about wedding preparations. The next minute, the phone had rung again and Kevin's mistress had informed me that he had been having an affair. I had confronted him later that evening and he did not deny it.

Jack had been there to pick up the pieces. He had dried my tears and promised me that things would work out.

'I'm so lucky to have a friend like you,' I think to myself as I look at him on stage again. 'Please be lucky too,'

Jack decides to match the Chinese player's bet and an excited murmur reverberates around the audience as we wait for the players to show their cards. The people around me are shifting around excitedly in their seats, but the Chinese woman is strangely quiet. She is rubbing her eyes with her hands and I bet that she is crying. I start to feel sorry for her again until I catch a glimpse of her wedding ring as she moves her hands up and down. My sympathy turns to envy and I start to think again about my Kevin, my ex-fiancé.

Jack has done his best to cheer me up, but thoughts and memories of Kevin keep playing through my mind. On our first night in Monaco, Jack and I had dinner in our hotel restaurant.

It was candlelit and full of couples and everyone else seemed so happy in the romantic ambience.

"Would you please stop staring at everyone?" Jack pleaded with me. "It's not going to make you feel any better."

"How would you know?" I replied. "You've never been engaged."

A flicker of hurt passed across Jack's face and I felt guilty. He had split up with his own girlfriend shortly after I had finished with Kevin. They hadn't been as close as Kevin and I, and he always clammed up when I asked him why he broke up with her.

"OK," he murmured sarcastically, sighing heavily.

He looked down at the plate of food in front of him. I followed his gaze and then looked at my own meal, but my appetite had disappeared. I speared a piece of broccoli with my fork and lifted it towards my mouth, but I didn't fancy it.

"I just want someone to share my life with," I said, slamming my fork down on the plate. "It still hurts to learn that I'm a lousy judge of character."

Jack grabbed my arm and looked at me. "It's not worth getting angry," he told me calmly, in the way that a teacher would restrain a naughty child.

Up on stage he is equally calm. He does not even react when the Chinese man reveals his hand of two Queens, two threes and a King. Instead, he coolly looks at the cards in front of him, preparing the audience for his own final showdown.

Another ripple of noise reverberates round the audience as we anticipate Jack's hand. It is all too much for the Chinese lady next to me, who has taken her hands away from her face and is slouched down in her chair, looking at the floor. It looks as if she wants to curl up and die and I start to feel sorry for her again.

She has almond shaped black eyes, sleek black hair with a twinge of grey and is elegantly dressed in designer label clothes. Even though we are sitting in the VIP section of the auditorium, it is cramped and dark and she looks somewhat out of place. I wonder what else she has done during her time in Monaco.

Jack and I both got up late on our first morning. I was feeling fragile after my emotional outburst over dinner the night before, and the hotel bed was warm and snug. I could have stayed in it all day, but Jack had other ideas.

"Come on, it's lunch time," he shouted suddenly, jumping out of his bed, leaping over to mine and snatching my bedclothes back. "Let's go to Lavrotto beach. This is our only day off. It's poker tomorrow and then we fly home."

I got up reluctantly and shuffled towards the bathroom. When I emerged, Jack was shoving some swimming trunks into a small bag.

"I'm ready," he told me, waiting by the door. "Hurry up."

It took me a while to get myself organised. "Suntan lotion, bikini, towel, insect repellent, windbreaker, water bottle…What am I forgetting?" I asked.

Jack laughed and grabbed my hand. "You're forgetting your sense of fun," he said. "Let's go."

We sunbathed until our skin tingled and cooled off in the sea. Little children watched open-mouthed as we had a water fight. We walked back to the hotel along the cliff and ate homemade ice creams on a bench in front of the Prince's palace.

"Have you enjoyed yourself?" Jack asked me, biting off the bottom of his cone. "Yes, thanks," I told him, licking up a healthy dollop of chocolate chip ice cream. "It's been a while since I've done this."

Jack sucked some ice cream from the bottom of his cone. "You don't have to do what other people tell you, you know."

I smiled, as I looked at him trying to eat his strawberry ice cream before it melted and escaped from the end that he'd bitten off.

"I'm not," I said. "Now that I don't have Kevin, I have no excuse for not visiting the beach more often."

"But," I added. "I'd like to point out that Kevin never stopped me from going to the beach. It's just that it wasn't very much fun putting up with his moaning about getting sand in his crevices."

Jack shoved the last of his ice cream in his mouth and gave me a sceptical look. I matched his gaze but the glare from his blue eyes was too intense and I started to blush.

"Yeah right," he said, taking my arm. "Come on slow coach. Let's go back."

I look at Jack on stage and realise that it's almost time to go back for good. The weekend has passed so quickly. I wish that Jack and I had booked a longer holiday. I hope that Jack will invite me on holiday again. I pray that we will get to spend more time together now Kevin is no longer in my life.

Jack puts down his cards. He has two Kings, two threes and a Queen and he has won. Next to me, the old Chinese lady starts to cry. I cry too. Big sobs rock my body. I cry about the end of my relationship with Kevin. I cry about the end of the poker tournament, which signals the end of my holiday with Jack. It's all over. Jack has won.

Somebody turns round to hug me. I snivel into their shoulder. Somebody else comes over and takes me in their arms. Before I know it, there is a whole group of us hugging and laughing and crying all at once.

Then I hear Jack's voice.

'Where's Rosie?' He shouts. 'Rosie! Rosie!'

I stop snivelling.

'Rosie,' he asks, nervously. 'Are you still here?'

I try to find my voice.

'Jack?'

Jack dives in the group and is greeted by hugs all round. After a few minutes, he suddenly grabs my hand and whisks me out of the melee and towards the front of the stage. There is a huge trophy on a table next to the poker table, and beside that there is a shiny gold envelope with "£50,000" printed on it in big black print.

'Do you see this money?' he asks. I nod.

'I know of a way to spend some of it. I'm going to take you on another holiday.'

I stare into the distance, not trusting myself to speak or look at him.

'I think that we should go to the beach again soon. Just you and me.'

He grabs my chin and turns my head to face him.

'I know you'd like that, wouldn't you?' he said kindly. 'And I'd like to make you happy.'

'You deserve better than Kevin, Rosie. I can make you happy. Do you want that?'

I look into his big blue eyes. 'Good,' he says, reading my thoughts yet again.

It's My Party…
Jane Wenham-Jones

I smile brightly at Sarah as I sing, to show her I don't mean it.

'You'd better not,' Sarah says.

I won't, I tell myself fiercely. I take another large swig of white wine and begin to polish glasses with gusto. Sarah has arranged this gathering for me, has hung the wine bar we run together with dozens of shiny balloons, invited all our regulars and friends to come and share my night. She has done it to cheer me, to give me a good time. And a good time I must have. Even if I can't stop thinking about my last birthday and who was there then…

I give Sarah another manic grin. She comes round behind the bar and takes the cloth from me. 'You're not supposed to be working,' she says. 'Let Kate do it.' She nods at the pretty young student who works for us and then tucks her arm in mine. 'Come and socialise – enjoy being the boss.'

The boss! It still feels odd. It's three months since we bought the bar, three months since my life turned upside down. I've got a new job, a new home in the flat upstairs, a whole new social life down here. And no Paul…

But I don't want to think about him. I move through my friends, kissing cheeks, taking cards, exchanging witticisms about crows' feet. I offer them drinks, feeling their warm arms around my shoulders as I thank them for coming, trying and trying not to let my mind wander…

I know that all along I've been waiting for him to come in. Waiting for him to push open the door, walk across the stripped pine floor and place his long sensitive fingers on the bar. He'll smile at Sarah the way he smiles at all women – as if they are the most special creature on earth – push back his dark curly hair, order a cold beer in his low sensual voice, look around to see who else might be frequenting this new trendy winebar he's heard had been bought by two women. Knowing that one of them is me…

I've hoped he would. My heart twists when I think of how we ended. One minute we were so happy, the next… I shake my head at the memory. It was the wine bottle next to the bed I noticed first…

The door opens and I jump. Robert and Lyn come towards me with a brightly-wrapped present. 'Wow! You look great!' Lyn hugs me, saying with the bluntness I usually love her for: 'Got over him now, then?'

'Of course!' My smile is fixed. I feel my eyes sliding towards the entrance. I turn to kiss Robert, looking round at the throng of bright, attractive people drinking wine, eating canapés. I close my mind to the image of Paul's dark good looks and muscular arms. Arms round someone else.

'I heard his fling didn't last…' Lyn is looking at me hard.

My stomach flips over. It was only the once. He'd had too much to drink and I was the one who wouldn't be forgiving. He did say we should talk, and now there are so many things I wish I'd said…

'So I told him about tonight,' Lyn adds.

I hear Sarah's intake of breath. 'It's her birthday…' she says sharply.

'He'd remembered,' says Lyn. And her eyes swivel to the door.

Mine do too and my heart jerks and for a split second he's startled too. Then I see his face light up as he strides towards me. This is the moment I've been longing for.

'Carrie!' Paul breathes out my name on a long luxurious sigh. 'You look lovely,' he says. 'Happy Birthday.'

I smile, stomach fluttering as I move behind the bar once more, take up the cloth and begin to polish one of our biggest, most beautiful glasses. I'm trying to be cool and calm. I breathe deeply. I don't want to squeak. 'What can I get you?'

His deep green eyes meet mine. He's giving me that look. 'What do you recommend?'

I bend down – glad I'm wearing my most flattering, bottom-slimming jeans – and open the bar fridge. 'This is my favourite.'

I pull out a heavy bottle, run a finger down the beads of moisture clinging to the sides, pour a generous measure into the long-stemmed glass. 'Crisp and dry,' I tell him, 'with a lingering after-taste.'

It's the same wine they were drinking when I caught them together. A Sauvignon Blanc. Very nice stuff.

He leans forward eagerly, his lips parting slightly as he holds out his hand. But I raise the glass to my own lips and sip. 'Mmm.'

His smile goes crooked.

'Lyn's given me a wonderful present,' I say chirpily, 'bringing you here.' I drink a little more wine. 'There's so much I want to say to you.'

He looks uncertainly from me to the glass.

'Oh, you're not having any,' I tell him, seeing his confusion. I bring my face up close to his and speak as seductively as I can. 'You're not having anything to drink at all.'

I run my tongue around my lips, savouring the coldness, the dry taste and watch his eyes widen. 'Do you know why?' I ask him, softly.

He shakes his head soundlessly but hope lights his face and I smile.

I don't know what's in the silver-papered package that Lyn handed me earlier but she has indeed given me a precious gift. I suddenly know what to do and I feel free and happy in a way I haven't done for such a long time.

I look at Paul through lowered lashes, with promise in my eyes. 'You can't have any alcohol,' I say, my voice husky with pleasure, 'because…' I pause. I've always had a fantasy about being able to say these words and who better to than Paul at this perfect moment? I lean forward to give him the full benefit of my cleavage.

116

'You're barred.'

Paul's mouth drops open.

I smile sweetly. 'It's my party,' I remind him. 'And I'll do what I want to…'

Fancy That
Lorraine Winter

Debbie put down the travel brochures and sighed loudly as she leaned back. Another hot day and she was stuck indoors. Normally, on a day like this, she'd have been in the garden sunbathing, but she couldn't face the stench.

She wiped the beads of perspiration from her forehead. Damn! It was her garden too. If she couldn't bask in the sunshine in her own garden without having to pinch her nostrils, the least Dan could do was take her away for their anniversary. And if anyone deserved a Caribbean cruise on a luxury liner, she did. After what she'd had to put up with. How many other women her age had to share their husband with a coop of foul smelling, attention-seeking pigeons? Pigeons, for heaven's sake!

And to think she'd made do with a weekend in Brighton for thier honeymoon seven years ago and economy breaks every year since, so they could save for a nice home. Ironically a home with a garden... A garden perfect for a pigeon loft, according to Dan. It didn't matter if it was no longer perfect for his wife though, did it?

But despite her best efforts, she couldn't stifle a smile at the memory of their honeymoon, even if it was ironic. It was only in Brighton – a cramped room in a budget hotel. But that hadn't mattered. The sun had disappeared behind heavy black clouds and was cold for the time of year. Perfect honeymoon weather! So they'd been confined to their room with a 'Do not disturb' sign on the door...

Oh, the memory of thier lovemaking then. He only had eyes for her. And Dan was all *she'd* ever wanted or needed. Years later, he could still set her pulse racing. But it seemed the only type of racing Dan was interested in these days was pigeon racing. In fact, he was totally obsessed.

Yes, she needed that cruise. Needed to get away from those damn birds and so did Dan, although he'd take a bit of convincing. And where better to escape to than the warm seductive Caribbean islands with their white sandy beaches and palm trees swaying in the breeze? She breathed in deeply, closing her eyes and imagining the scene.

On the ship, there'd be just her and Dan gazing into each other's eyes over cocktails and romantic dinners. Well, there'd be the other passengers and crew, of course, but Debbie felt sure if she could just get Dan away from those pigeons for a couple of weeks, they could relive their honeymoon all over again. She felt a frisson of excitement tingle all the way down her spine. Once she'd won him back, she'd make sure he never lost interest again.

She looked out to where he stood. He was gazing at his beloved specimens in undisguised adoration. To think that a few years ago, she was the only bird in his life! Debbie shook her head hopelessly as she watched him. Why hadn't she seen it before? Pigeon fanciers, they called themselves. Face it, Debs. He fancies those birds more than he fancies you…

"You're going to keep what?" she'd gasped, when he first told her.

"Pigeons. Birds. You know."

"I *know* what they are," she'd snapped. "But what on earth do you want to *keep* them for? And *where* exactly are you planning to keep them?" She'd looked around her, aghast, picturing a huge cage in the corner of the room. She'd seen parrots in cages. Huh. Knowing what she knew now, a couple of birds in a cage sounded like bliss.

He'd laughed nervously. "In a loft in the garden, of course." He'd seen the look of horror on her face and had guessed what was going through her mind. "Don't worry. Bert says racing pigeons rarely do their droppings in their own garden." He'd tried to smile reassuringly. "And they'll be cleaned out regularly, I promise."

The thought of bird mess on her washing had been her first dread, it was true. That was before she'd discovered the smell, that overwhelming pong on hot days... Yuk! It hung in the air, enveloping everything within a fifty-foot radius, even if they had just been cleaned out. She almost retched at the thought of it. Then there was the incessant cooing. Enough to drive any sane person round the twist. She'd stood there open-mouthed, speechless for what seemed like ages, while she tried to get her head around it.

"Pigeons. You want to keep pigeons! Next you'll be putting on a cloth cap and lighting up a pipe. Dan, you're 30, not 70!"

"You've got the wrong idea, Debs. Pigeon racing's a sophisticated sport these days. It attracts all ages and types, from plumbers to bank managers. Even women race pigeons these days."

"Do they now? Well, fancy that!" She'd replied, sarcastically. Who was he trying to kid? Women had more sense, surely. OK, She had to concede, pigeons possessed a homing instinct that was pretty amazing, but, as far as Debbie was concerned now – a real drawback. The flipping birds kept coming back from all over the place.

"You'd be surprised." Dan had continued, his voice spilling over with boyish enthusiasm. "*And* there's a fortune waiting to be made into the bargain. Just wait and see," he'd added, imploring her with those big, brown eyes of his that could make her heart flip over.

So she'd put up with the nuisance and waited... but her patience had run out. Not only was there no sign of any big winnings but she was getting pretty fed-up with all the attention he gave them instead of her. Rivals of the human variety, she reckoned she could handle – but pigeons...

Debbie sighed deeply as she watched him caress one of his birds with all the tenderness usually reserved for a lover, in other words that he used to lavish on her. Then he moved his lips towards the side of its head. Whispering sweet nothings?

As if that wasn't enough, he lovingly planted a kiss firmly on the bird's beak before putting it in the basket. Then he picked up another one and repeated the process.

Debbie looked away. It was too much to bear! What a waste of a tasty male. She grimaced at the irony of it and, worse, the implication. If she was being realistic, it didn't look as if it would be easy to part Dan from his precious pigeons.

Soon afterwards, he came into the house, whistling softly. 'Might be late home tonight Debs. There'll have been loads of entries for an important race like today's.' He patted her bottom affectionately or was it absentmindedly? 'What about rustling up something special for dinner?'

He didn't appear to notice Debbie's mood. Nor the brochures showing cruise liners and Caribbean beaches. Well, when did he ever notice *her* lately? Or anything she was interested in? Maybe if she was to wear one of those feather boa things and start cooing to him, she'd grab his attention?

'Put a bottle of wine in the fridge. You never know. Might have something to celebrate,' he said, eyes smiling at her but his mind definitely elsewhere, Debbie thought, resignedly.

Then he pecked her cheek and was gone. Was that all she was worth? A quick peck on the cheek. Compared to the affection he showered on his birds. Well, she could think of a few things she'd like to celebrate. An idea formed in her mind and Debbie set to work. She'd give Dan a special meal all right. She'd have plenty of time to prepare it. He'd be at the club for hours.

Dan arrived home breathless and animated. Now she was having niggling doubts about how much they really were suited. I mean, to come home from a pigeon club meeting looking excited? She shook her head despairingly. Never mind. She'd had a pretty lively afternoon herself.

'Just in time.' Debbie put on her best smile. 'Coq au vin special enough?'

Dan nodded absentmindedly. He carefully put his pigeon clock on the side along with an envelope. Then he sat down at the table and poured himself and Debbie a glass of wine, before taking a mouthful of the dish she'd served up.

'You'll never guess what, Debs. You know those two chequered hens that raced today?' he gushed.

Couldn't he talk of anything else? 'Don't tell me, they've laid an egg each.'

'Nope. That's next – breeding them,' he beamed proudly, oblivious as usual to her mood. 'Better than that. I knew they were good but I didn't know how...' He paused and licked his lips.

Debbie glowered at him. She was sick of bird talk.

'Mmmm,. Hey Debs, not bad. Not bad at all.' He raised his fork to his mouth again. 'Delicious, in fact. Didn't know you could cook like this.'

Dan savoured another mouthful. 'Oh yes. I was saying. I'd a hunch about today's race. And they haven't let me down. Those little beauties have just scooped first and second prize out of thousands. You know what that means, don't you?'

She'd a good idea. More attention for them and less for her. But she said nothing.

'Loadsamoney! And not just today's winnings. They're worth a fortune now. I've already been asked to enter them in the Show next week.' Dan carried on in between mouthfuls. He reached for her hand. 'Look, Debbie. I know it must seem like I eat, sleep and breathe pigeons half the time.'

She could only stare at him. He was looking at her with a dreamy expression on his face.

'Remember our honeymoon in Brighton?' he smiled, his brown eyes crinkling at the corners. 'I reckon we could re-create it, but push the boat out, so to speak, for our anniversary...' He grinned, leaning over to kiss her but Debbie didn't move towards him. Winning that race had gone to his head. He was almost his old self... It was what she wanted. She should have been pleased... but why now? Why wait till now?

Her lips felt parched and she could feel the colour drain from her face.

'Hey, wake up.' He laughed. 'Thanks to Rosie and Jenny...

'Rosie and Jenny?' Debbie echoed faintly. Who the heck were Rosie and Jenny and what did they have to do with Dan's pigeons winning the race?

'Yep. Thanks to those two gorgeous hen birds who won us the big one, *we* are going to cruise the islands of the Caribbean.' He looked over at the coffee table where the brochures still lay scattered. 'We'll book a nice cosy cabin.' He winked at her. 'It will be like Brighton, except with loads more style. And we'll make sure we get one with a balcony. What do you say we snuggle up on the sofa after dinner and decide which islands we should...'

Debbie sat bolt upright. 'You don't mean... Not the pigeons in the basket?' she interrupted, her voice thin and rasping. Please – not the pigeons in the basket!

'Yes. My little blue chequers.' His eyes shone with pure admiration.

Debbie froze. She thought she was going to be sick. Dan's fork was poised at his lips. Eat, sleep and breathe pigeons? Little did he know.

Dan was tucking into her dream cruise...

123

Endless Possibilities
Dawn Wingfield

He'd become "poor Rob" at work. Pam, the secretary, had given him a cook book entitled "Easy Meals for One" and a mug inscribed "Endless Possibilities." The mug in particular deeply depressed Rob. He didn't for a minute believe the possibilities in his own life were endless; he believed that he was a boring, sad old git, just as Karen had said when she walked out two years ago.

As he drove home that dreary, November night, depression had settled on Rob's shoulders like a dark, heavy cloak. He yearned for something different, a life peppered with good times and love. And then he saw the poster, pasted in the window of Clark's Travel Agency. A man with nice but fairly ordinary looks was strolling on a golden beach with a woman in a red bikini. Rob parked the car and stared. I want that, he'd thought. I want sand beneath my toes and foreign skies over my head. I want a woman who'll hold my hand and think she's in heaven. "Come to California," the poster beckoned. As if mesmerised, Rob went into the travel agent's and booked himself two weeks in San Diego, at the Royal Palisades Hotel.

And here he was, one week into his dream holiday, rubbing a dollop of sunscreen into the pudgy flesh of his stomach and wondering if he'd made a huge mistake. His nose had gone all red and tender yesterday and started to peel; he'd had to switch to a sunscreen with a higher factor. In spite of the foreign skies and beautiful location he was still just Rob, a very ordinary, slightly overweight assistant bank manager from Finchley.

'I'm hungry,' the little boy a few feet away from him whined.

'Honey, it's not even eleven,' the boy's mother said.

The travel clerk hadn't thought to mention that the beaches of San Diego would be crowded with small children at this time of year, enjoying a lengthy break from school.

Suddenly, his face was hit by a spray of gritty sand. Rob sat up and looked around, blinking.

'Oh, no – I am *so* sorry,' the mother of the hungry little boy said, rushing over. 'Tyler, you need to be careful with that ball! I'm really, really sorry – did any get in your eyes?'

Rob removed his brand new sunglasses. 'I'm OK. No harm done.'

'You're sure?' She kneeled next to his towel, a woman in her thirties with brown curls.

'I'll live,' Rob chuckled.

'You're English.'

'Yes.'

'I've always wanted to go there – all that history, the countryside, the castles – it's such a special place.'

'There aren't any castles in Finchley, where I'm from,' Rob said, and then stopped. Why couldn't he have said something more positive? Agreed with her, or asked her where she was from?

'I'm Emily Young,' she said, and offered her hand, smiling.

Rob noticed she had typical American teeth, very white and straight. He kept his lips together as he smiled back at her. 'Robert Sidley. Rob,' he said, taking her small, soft hand in his.

'Is this your first time in the States?'

'It is, yes.'

'Rob, may I take you to lunch? To compensate for my son chucking sand in your face?' Emily asked.

'Oh,' Rob stuttered. 'That isn't, um, necessary…'

'But I'd like to,' Emily said.

'Oh. Well then, alright,' he agreed nervously, unused to women asking him for lunch, but not wanting to argue. She did seem rather nice.

Tyler had gone off to dabble at the water's edge with some children. His mother called to him. 'Time for lunch! Rob here is coming with us.'

'OK!' Tyler said, coming over with his bucket and spade; a little boy with white blond hair and no front teeth.

Rob smiled, feeling a twinge of nervousness; he often felt slightly uneasy around children. Then Tyler grinned at him, and Rob began to gather up his towel, book and sunscreen, the little knot of tension disappearing. He followed Emily and Tyler to a restaurant she promised made wonderful sandwiches. It was as easy as that.

Easy was a good word to describe being with Emily. When Rob dithered over the menu, she recommended the grilled chicken sandwich. It was perfect. She talked a lot, but she also asked questions, and when Rob answered, she leaned forward, nodding and listening to his answers.

'Yes, I do like my job,' he said. 'I'm good at it and I enjoy meeting people. It's just that since my divorce, everything's felt... different. As if I'm just doing the same things over and over, but nothing has any meaning.' He flushed and looked at his plate. Why was he saying all this? He didn't even know this woman.

'I realised last year that I might very well go completely bonkers if all I had to look forward to was managing Dunkin Donuts for the rest of my life,' Emily said quietly. 'I'm trying to get my real estate license.'

'Well done,' Rob said.

She looked pleased, meeting his gaze and then glancing quickly away. Tyler asked for more ketchup. And then Rob began to panic. Should he ask her to dinner this evening? Did Emily expect it? Did he *want* to see her again? Yes, he thought, watching her tuck a chestnut curl behind one ear. Yes, I do. There was Tyler though; she might not be able to get away. Maybe she just considered this to be a friendly lunch, a one-off thing...

'Is everything OK?' Emily asked, looking at him as she swallowed her last mouthful of sandwich.

Rob nodded and smiled faintly. He couldn't do it, he thought dully.

'Finished, buddy?' Emily dabbed a smear of ketchup from Tyler's chin. She picked up her beach bag and reached for her son's hand. Rob had a sudden, awful vision of them saying goodbye and walking off in separate directions.

'Wait,' he blurted, more loudly than he meant to.

Emily blinked at him.

He cleared his throat. 'I was just wondering. Would you be free for dinner tonight? It's fine if you can't make it. I just thought that, if neither of us have plans, we might as well –'

'I'd love to,' she said. 'My hotel has a babysitting service, so Tyler will be all taken care of.'

They arranged a time and a place, and Rob returned to his hotel, astonished at himself.

Emily discarded her green batik skirt and vest top for black cotton pants and a loose white shirt, then stared critically at her reflection. She looked as if she had a job interview rather than a date. Dragging off the black trousers and flinging them aside, she pulled on a pair of pink polka-dotted capri pants and took another hopeful look at herself, then cringed. Oh Lord, she thought – I look like a clown.

Biting her lip and glancing at the time, Emily pulled on the green outfit again. After all, he'd already seen the jiggly flesh at the top of her arms this afternoon, and it hadn't seemed to bother him then.

On the way out of the hotel she peeked through the glass panel of the playroom. There was a story time in progress, and Tyler was listening, absorbed. Emily took a deep breath, and stepped out into the balmy night.

It had been years since she'd been on a proper date. Her hometown in Rutherford, Iowa, wasn't exactly bursting at the seams with tasty male specimens. Cops and distracted, chubby husbands were the only men who ever seemed to come into Dunkin Donuts and Emily told herself she didn't care; her affair with Tyler's dad had been a disaster, and she hardly needed the distraction of more dates, promises, sex and heartbreak in her life. She needed to provide for her son, and get her real estate license. Tonight didn't count as a real date. It was just dinner with an attractive man who sounded as if he'd stepped out of a Masterpiece Theatre production. She couldn't believe she'd just come out and asked him to lunch this afternoon. It was as if she was on vacation from being herself for a while, free from her normal, careful self.

Emily smiled when she saw him standing outside the seafood restaurant they'd agreed on. He was wearing dark pants and a clean white shirt. He'd nicked himself shaving; there was a tiny scrap of toilet paper on his chin. When he saw her, his eyes widened. 'You look lovely,' he said, in his heart-melting British accent.

Emily felt lovely at that moment. She forgot she was an exhausted single mum who worked in a donut shop and clipped coupons to save money. On impulse, she kissed Rob's cheek and removed the toilet paper from his chin. He blushed and thanked her. 'No problem,' she said.

They ate coconut shrimp and drank margaritas. They talked about novels, politics, pets, food and their families. The conversation, the smiles, the looks they shared, were like a slow dance that brought them closer with each step.

The next day they took Tyler to the San Diego Zoo, traipsing between elephants, zebras and gorillas in the ninety degree heat. When Emily told Tyler that, no, they couldn't go back and see the lions for a third time, her son flung himself to the ground and began to shriek. She knelt beside him, hot with embarrassment, and made soothing sounds. This doesn't matter, she thought; it doesn't matter what Rob thinks. We're only together for a few days.

Suddenly, Rob knelt beside her and leaned over Tyler. 'How about a quick look in the gift shop?' he coaxed. 'I bet they have lions in there.'

Tyler's sobs subsided. Emily watched as he took Rob's hand and they trotted off to the gift store. People probably think we're a family, she thought.

'I'm sorry about Tyler's behaviour this afternoon,' Emily said later that evening.

They'd had steak and champagne for dinner and were walking on the beach. The ocean was shushing gently, sparkling beneath a silver crescent of moon hanging in the sky like a jewel. I feel like I've known this man for ever, Emily thought.

'Don't apologise,' Rob said. 'He's five years old. Life is pretty hard when you're five – don't you remember?'

'It was nice of you to buy him that fluffy lion,' she said.

They walked along in silence for a few moments, and then he took her hand. Happiness rushed through Emily, and at the same time her mood became tinged with sadness. Everyone knew about holiday romances. They were like hothouse flowers, budding and blooming in a swooning rush of colour and fragrance, only to die a few weeks later.

Rob stopped walking. He turned her towards him, bent his head, and kissed her lips. Emily's toes curled in ecstasy as she wrapped her arms blissfully around his neck. He was perfect, this man; funny, gentle and good. She completely forgot that Rob could only be a holiday romance, a quick, one-off fling.

Emily remembered two hours later, when she was curled against Rob in his king-size hotel bed. He had made love to her as if she was the most exquisite woman in the world. Their kisses had been fevered at first, but then Rob had loved her with a deliberate thoroughness she was still tingling from.

Abruptly, she sat up and reached for her clothes.

'Emily?' he muttered sleepily.

'I have to go,' she said.

'But it's early…'

'I need to scoop up Tyler and put him to bed.' She dragged on her T-shirt.

'I think you're amazing,' he said.

She didn't answer. What was the point? He was amazing too, but she was never going to see him again after this vacation was over.

Rob suddenly sat up and began to get dressed himself.

'What are you doing?' Emily looked at him.

'You don't think I'm going to let you walk back on your own, do you?' he said.

She bit her lip. If she didn't know better, she'd have thought she was falling in love.

'What shall we do tomorrow?' he asked, as they walked down the street.

'I don't know.' Emily shook her head. 'Look – maybe we should give this a break.'

'A break?' Rob sounded dismayed. 'But we've only got another four days.'

'Exactly. I don't want the next four days to turn into one long goodbye.'

'We'll see each other again after this holiday,' he said confidently. 'I've always wanted to visit Iowa.'

A burst of laughter escaped her. 'You liar, Rob!'

They reached her hotel, and Emily turned to him. 'This is lovely, but we both know it can't last. We don't even know each other, not really.'

'I know you,' he said. 'I know you drive a rusty red Honda Civic and prefer your hotdogs without mustard and have given up trying to straighten your hair. I know you love it when you wake up in the morning and find it's snowed during the night. Now, may I see you tomorrow?'

Tears blurred Emily's vision. She nodded and hurriedly turned away.

There was a pile of post waiting for him on the mat. Rob stepped over it, wearily laid down his suitcase and rubbed at his face. He'd been flying all night. It was early morning in Finchley, a dull, drizzly morning. Emily and California were half a world away. He went to put the kettle on.

When he'd told her he'd call her, she had placed a finger on his lips and shaken her head. Rob put a teabag into his "Endless Possibilities" mug and smiled, finally believing the words. The kettle whistled and he poured boiling water into the mug, deciding to skip his usual two teaspoons of sugar. Then he picked up the phone and punched in a long series of numbers, waited, and heard ringing.

'Hello?' A guarded, hopeful voice greeted him.

'It's me.'

He heard a deep intake of breath.

'Oh, Emily,' Rob said. 'You didn't think I'd let a little thing like the Atlantic come between us, did you?'

Across the ocean, Emily began to cry.

Bunny Love
Rosie Harris

Nicola was quite breathless by the time she'd climbed to the headland. The carrying cage with Pye in it seemed to have doubled in weight since she'd left the car park a few hundred feet below.

She stood there for a moment, staring out to sea, drinking in the wild beauty of the coastline around Cardigan Bay and the air of peacefulness all around her. This was exactly what she had hoped to find, she thought, as she undid the cage door leaving Pye free to find her own way out.

She waited until the plump brown and white rabbit had hopped around for a few minutes, made certain that it was safe for her to roam if she wanted to do so. Then flung herself down on the sheep-cropped turf, kicked off her shoes and closed her eyes shutting out the brilliance of the mid-morning sun.

It was the first time she had felt relaxed since arriving in Aberystwyth. What was to have been an enjoyable few days chilling out had so far been more problematic than dealing with a class of fifteen-year-olds.

Jumping into her car and driving away from the London suburbs had seemed to be the perfect antidote to stress, until she had arrived at the small private hotel where she was planning to stay.

'If you had taken the trouble to read our brochure then you would have been fully aware that pets are not allowed,' Mrs Markham, the frosty-voiced owner told her sharply. 'Whatever it is you have in that cage you most certainly cannot bring it in here.'

'It's my pet rabbit and she's called Pye,' Nicola told her sweetly. 'She will be no trouble. She's perfectly tame and well trained. At home I let her run around quite freely in my flat, but

I'll keep her in the cage while we are staying with you if that is what you wish me to do.'

'I thought I made it quite clear that you can't bring your rabbit or its cage inside my premises,' Mrs Markham retorted. 'You'll have to lock it up in your car or something.'

'I can't possibly do that!'

They'd argued for almost half an hour, but Mrs Markham remained adamant. In the end, Nicola fed Pye, changed her drinking water, played with her for half an hour and then reluctantly had done as Mrs Markham had dictated. She coaxed Pye back into her travelling cage and locked it back inside her car even though she was far from happy with such an arrangement.

Nicola was up early next morning after a fairly restless night that had been interspersed with ugly nightmares about what might be happening to Pye.

She dashed out to check on her even before she sat down to her own breakfast. To her relief Pye seemed to be all right apart from the fact that she was gnawing at the edges of her cage and seemed to be rather agitated because she'd been shut up for such a long time.

Nicola took the rabbit out of the cage, stroked and petted her and then placed her back in the cage again and locked it back inside the car. 'Give me half an hour to grab some food and I'll take you for a run,' she promised.

The minute she'd finished her breakfast she'd driven to the headland. Now, she was trying to work out what to do next. Should she stay, knowing that Pye would have to spend her nights locked in the car, or should she turn round and go straight back home.

As she felt the warm sun beating down she felt reluctant to abandon her short holiday. She needed this break, it had been a long hard term and there were still another six weeks to go before they broke up for the summer holidays.

As she mulled over the problem she felt the pad of little feet walking up her chest and then the tickle of soft fur as the

133

rabbit rubbed its nose into her neck. She opened her eyes and stared into those of the rabbit.

'What do you want?'

Pye nuzzled her neck then skittered down towards her feet and gently nipped at Nicola's big toe.

'You think it's play time, I suppose,' Nicola murmured. She fastened on the special harness. 'Come on, we'll go for a walk.'

Having explored the headland, Nicola flopped back down on the soft springy turf again, yawned and closed her eyes. 'Amuse yourself for ten minutes, Pye and then we'll go back to the car and I'll collect my case and we'll set off back home. No point in staying here if that miserable Mrs Markham refuses to allow you to come into my room with me, now is there?'

Pye nipped her ear in agreement then hopped off to sample a fresh tuft of grass and Nicola sank into a blissful snooze.

A few minutes later she was rudely awakened by an angry male voice demanding, 'Is this *your* rabbit?'

Startled from the land of dreams, Nicola sat bolt upright and stared up at the figure dressed in jeans and a T-shirt who was towering over her, holding Pye by the scruff.

'What the devil do you think you are doing,' she gasped, horrified. 'Give her here this minute.'

Scrambling to her feet Nicola clutched at Pye only to be rewarded by a sharp pair of teeth nipping her forearm and making her yelp.

'What did you expect, grabbing at the poor little thing like that?' he said censoriously. 'Someone like you shouldn't be allowed to keep a rabbit.'

'Give her here and mind your own business,' Nicola snapped. She was still feeling only half awake and resented both his criticism and his manner. Even now, when she was up on her feet, she still found that she had to look up to meet his brilliant blue gaze and it annoyed her because she felt it put her at a disadvantage.

'Please hand Pye over to me this minute,' she said in the tone of voice she usually reserved for sixth formers who'd transgressed.

'What are you planning to do with her?' he asked, holding on to the rabbit and stroking it soothingly.

Nicola bristled. 'I really don't now what business it is of yours. Are you an undercover agent for the RSPCA by any chance?'

'No, I'm not, but I am a rabbit lover and I don't intend to see this little bundle of fur being ill-treated...'

'Ill-treated? What the devil are you on about!'

'I suspect that you brought this rabbit up here with the idea of abandoning it.'

'What!' It was Nicola's turn to give a steely blue stare.

'Well, why else would you be lying there half asleep and leaving your rabbit loose in a place like this?'

'I was giving Pye the opportunity to have a play and a spot of exercise before we set off to drive back to Hertfordshire, if you must know. She's been shut up in her cage ever since we left home yesterday.'

'You came all the way from Hertfordshire to Aberystwyth yesterday and now you are planning to drive straight back again?' he exclaimed in astonishment.

'It's not my idea, I can tell you,' Nicola assured him. 'It's all the fault of Mrs Markham, the owner of the Private Hotel I'm booked into. She won't allow Pye inside the building. Last night she made me lock her out in my car all night. Poor Pye. Anything at all could have happened to her. She could have been eaten by a fox, kidnapped, taken hostage, absolutely anything.

'Bit drastic on your landlady's part, isn't it?' he frowned.

'She seems to be against all pets. I could understand if Pye was a Rottweiler, or even an Alsatian, but a rabbit! I ask you!'

'And is that why you are in such a rush to go home?'

'What else can I do? I've been looking forward to this holiday break so much, but I can't let her sleep out in the car for a second night, now can I?'

He looked thoughtful as he went on stroking Pye's thick fur. 'You could book in somewhere else.'

'Not possible at such short notice at this time of the year.'

'No, I suppose not,' he agreed. 'Would you stay on longer if it wasn't for this problem about Pye?'

'Of course I would! I've been looking forward to coming here all term.'

'Can I suggest a solution?' he asked tentatively. He hesitated. 'You mightn't like it,' he warned, still stroking Pye even though she was now settled quite contentedly in his arms.

'Go on.'

'Let Pye stay with me. I've got a rabbit of my own so I know how to take care of her, she'd be well looked after,' he assured her.

Nicola looked stunned. 'It's very good of you, but I'm not sure. She's certainly taken to you,' she admitted reluctantly, 'but she likes a lot of attention and she's used to me being the one to handle her.'

'You can come and see where she will be staying and you can visit her as often as you wish and stay with her as long as you like when you do.'

Nicola looked at him uncertainly.

He smiled back at her. 'I know we haven't been introduced, but I mean what I say and I'm not trying to steal her. Why don't you both come and meet my rabbit and if Stu and your Pye approve of each other then that will help to set your mind at ease. I'm John, by the way. And you are?'

'Nicola!' She held out a hand and felt it encompassed in a firm warm handshake.

'Come on then, before I change my mind,' she agreed impetuously.

'Shall I pop Pye into her cage?'

'Yes please; mind she doesn't nip you.'

With John carrying the cage they set off back to the car park and he directed her which way to go to his flat. Nicola was impressed by the spacious garden and also by the roomy cage and excellent run that John had for his own rabbit. On the way there he'd told her all about Stuart, or Stu as he preferred to call him.

'He looks more like a hare than a rabbit,' Nicola exclaimed when she first saw his rabbit.

'Yes, well he's a rare breed, that's why he looks so different,' John explained. 'We'll put Pye's cage alongside his and let them get used to each other first,' he suggested, 'and then she can use the run as well if she wants to. While they do that we'll go indoors and I'll make you a coffee, or you can have a cold drink if you prefer.'

Half an hour later they found that the rabbits had taken to each other and were almost as friendly as they were with each other.

'Well, I think she'll be much safer here than hopping around on a headland where she could end up falling off the edge on to the cliffs below, or even straight into the sea if the tide is in, don't you?' John said.

'Don't talk rubbish. Pye's not stupid, she'd know better than to do something like that.'

'Would she? She's been to the seaside before, has she?'

Nicola shook her head. He was probably right; it was something she hadn't thought about before.

'Not here, she hasn't.' Nicola admitted evasively. 'It's the first time I've been here myself, as a matter of fact.'

'Really! Then can I offer my services as a first-class guide so that you see all the local beauty spots, go to all the best places and enjoy every minute you are here?'

'That's a tall order! Why should you bother to do all that?'

'Because I love the place and I feel I'd like to show you all the best spots so that you love it as much as I do, and then you and Pye will come back again.'

The next three days passed in a whirlwind of new experiences and unexpected entertainment. It wasn't only the heart-stopping scenery of Strumble Head, the delightful out-of-the-way country pubs and cafes in the Plynlimon mountain region John took her to, or the strolls along the promenade and beach. It was much more than that. It was John's company.

They went dancing, water skiing and even messed around in the rock pools as the tide receded. She'd never ridden a horse in her life before, but with John by her side she'd found it exhilarating to trot along the darkly dappled sand.

Nicola found that so many new experiences, with such a warm and friendly companion, opened up feelings that had become deeply hidden or pushed aside while she'd been determined not to deviate from the career path she'd set herself. It was like drawing back a heavy curtain and revealing an entirely new world.

Up until now, she'd had no time for close friendships, certainly not for any that bordered on romance, because she'd made her career her first priority. Now twenty-five and Head of Department at one of the biggest schools in the south of England, she decided she had achieved the height of her ambition... for the moment.

She certainly hadn't been looking for romance when she'd decided on Aberystwyth for her half-term break, merely a change of scenery and a chance to chill out and plan her future career.

Thanks to Pye it looked as if fate had taken a hand. It was now a very different kind of future she was looking forward to when she and Pye came back later in the summer to stay with John and Stu for rather longer than a few days.

Life's Illusion
Catrin Collier

Esme Morris didn't enjoy social evenings in the yacht club. It was her duty as Captain's wife to attend every function, but Roy invariably deserted her the moment they walked through the door, generally to attend to one of his mistresses. Women her sister and the other wives in Traceport enjoyed telling her about and she found difficult to ignore – even for her children's sake. But this time Roy hadn't even escorted her.

Fearful of being late and upsetting him, she'd taken a taxi, only to find he hadn't arrived. Nervous at the thought of Roy turning up and berating her because she'd misunderstood his instructions, she tried to make herself useful behind the bar. Experience had taught her that time passed quickly if she was busy. And serving drinks gave her no time to exchange anything other than simple pleasantries and offered fewer opportunities to irritate Roy with her inappropriate remarks.

She was exhausted by eleven o'clock when a shortage of glasses drove her into the kitchen. She was still washing them at two in the morning when the vice-captain called a halt to the evening. She shouted goodnight to him as he left, then looked around. There were only a few young bloods left. There was no sign of her daughters, her husband, or her son. She went to the door and looked outside. Seeing no cars she recognised, she returned to the kitchen.

'Have you seen Roy, Piers or the girls?' she asked the steward.

'I'm sorry, Mrs Morris, I haven't,' she answered.

'I'd better call a taxi.'

'They take an age to arrive at this hour.' The kitchen hand cum barman, John Chin, a young and striking, blond, half Chinese boy emerged from behind the dishwasher he was attempting to fix. He rinsed his hands under the tap. 'I've

139

finished here apart from this machine and it needs a professional's touch. So, I'll take you home, Mrs Morris.'

'Really, it's no problem,' Esme protested in embarrassment. 'I'll ring for a taxi.'

'My boat's moored outside. It's half an hour by car but only ten minutes down the creek. You do have a landing stage at your house, don't you?'

'Yes, but . . . '

'I thought I'd seen one when I sailed past.'

'If you're sure I won't be taking you out of your way,' Esme capitulated.

'You won't be.' John said goodnight to the steward and escorted Esme out of the club and down the path to the dock and his tender. 'There's a blanket in a plastic bag under that seat if you're cold.'

'Thank you,' Esme shook it out. 'It's been a glorious day but now night's fallen, there's a definite chill in the air.' She was almost garrulous when it came to discussing the weather. It was the only topic Roy never accused her of botching.

'Just look at that sky. Did you ever see anything like it?'

Esme looked beyond John's shadowy figure to the infinite expanse of deep, dark velvet night sky punctured by a million starlights. 'Not for a long time because I haven't really looked at it.'

'It makes me feel very small, and glad to be alive.' John's voice carried softly over the water. 'Think of all the people who've lived here and seen what we're seeing now.'

'They might not have had boats, so they wouldn't have had the same view.'

'You couldn't live on this creek without a boat.'

'Not if they wanted to fish,' she agreed.

'Never mind fish, they would have needed them for dreaming.' John steered out, into the wider channel. 'Someone told me you were an artist.'

'Did they? How strange.'

'You did go to Art College?' he checked.

'I never finished the course. I had to give it up when I married Roy.' She spoke as though it was a natural progression of events.

'Do you paint?'

'No. Painting's messy. You need a studio. And we've never had space for one.'

John sought and failed to find a trace of irony in her voice. Roy Morris owned a six thousand square foot modern mansion, luxurious even by creek standards, and that was without the servants' annex, separate leisure complex, outdoor pool, pool-house, bank of garages, gazebo and two-bedroomed guest house. Even if Roy considered painting too messy for the house he could easily have built a studio for his wife in the grounds.

'When did you leave Art College?'

'Twenty-seven years ago. I was only eighteen. I didn't even finish the first year.'

'That's a lot of years not to paint.'

'I don't have much free time. My husband entertains a great deal. He needs a full time hostess.'

'I've joined Traceport Art Society.'

'What's it like? I've often thought of joining.' Esme's voice showed the first real signs of animation.

'Why don't you come with me and find out? We're exhibiting in the old Town Hall gallery next week.'

'Anything of yours?'

'If I'm lucky enough to get something accepted by the hanging committee.'

'If you don't mind being seen with someone old enough to be your mother, I would like to come,' she answered hesitantly.

'I'm not working next Tuesday. I'll meet you in the wine bar next door at twelve so we can eat first.'

'You don't have to do that.'

'It would be my pleasure.'

'I'll have to pay for my own meal,' she qualified.

'If that's the only way you'll come.'

141

'Thank you. You've given me something to look forward to.'

He was touched by the sincerity in her voice.

'There's our jetty.'

He slowed the boat. Holding on to the dock with one hand, he offered her the other. 'Until Tuesday.'

'Wouldn't you rather take a girl your own age?'

'I invited you, Mrs Morris.'

'I'm not a charity case, Mr Chin.'

'I didn't think you were, and please, call me John.'

'I'm Esme, and thank you for bringing me home. Until next week.'

It was absurd. She had grey hairs, she was old enough to be a grandmother, but a surge of excitement quickened her step and set her pulse racing as she ran up the bank into the floodlit garden.

'Sorry I'm late.' Esme rushed into the wine bar at twelve-thirty. She was wearing a pleated skirt, classic blouse and tweed jacket. Middle-aged county clothes that Roy had picked out for her. She had a wardrobe full of similar garments and very little else.

'Would you like a drink?' John lifted his almost empty wine glass.

'I shouldn't in the middle of the day.'

'Are you driving?'

'No, that's why I'm late. My daughter's car was the only one in the garage and it wouldn't start. That's probably why she took mine.'

'White wine?' he asked.

'Perhaps just a small glass.'

John pointed to the menu chalked on a board. 'I can recommend the ploughman's.'

'Ploughman's will be fine.'

He ordered the food and carried their drinks to a secluded booth. Feeling like an adulteress, Esme sat opposite him.

'Do you have to be back early?' he asked.

'No, the children – I must stop calling them that – my son is twenty-three and my twin daughters are twenty, are going on to a party after college, and Roy's working late.'

As John had seen Roy Morris enter the Harbour View Hotel with a woman when he'd berthed on the quayside, he doubted it, but said nothing. Their food arrived and they began to eat. He sensed that she wouldn't begin the conversation, so he did.

'What sort of painting did you do, traditional or modern?'

'I wasn't in college long enough to develop a style. But I liked oils and watercolours although they're very different techniques. The creek somehow seems to lend itself to broad washes of colour…' embarrassed because she suspected that she was talking too much, she changed the subject. 'What about you?'

'I just dabble, sketches, pastels, the odd watercolour. I didn't study art at college. My family thought accountancy would be more useful. But I joined the college art society. The trouble with living in the creek is it's so picturesque it ruins any pretence I have to an artistic soul. Instead of creating, I sit and stare.'

'I've spent the last twenty-seven years sitting and staring without once picking up a brush.'

He touched his glass to hers. 'Shall we drink to artistic action?'

'Please.' She risked a smile. 'This is a marvellous treat. I haven't talked art in years.'

Awed, Esme stood in the centre of the gallery and whispered to John, 'Every single painting is wonderful.'

'Aspiring artists should have some pretensions to discernment,' an elderly "dragon" from the Traceport Art Society snapped from the volunteer's desk where she was straining to listen in on John and Esme's conversation.

John wasted a smile on her. 'We're trying.'

'I would never have thought of painting anything like this.' Esme admired an oil. 'It's exactly how I imagine a Roman villa

143

would have looked, and these are delicious,' she exclaimed at two pencil sketches of a Persian kitten at play.

'Seeing this exhibition with you is like seeing it for the first time,' he murmured, too low for the dragon to hear.

'John, please – you have to see this.' She stared mesmerised by a painting of the creek. 'The artist has captured the essence of the creek in winter. Those skeletal trees, the water, you can sense the coldness, and those buds on the branches, the bulbs poking up through the dead leaves, poised, yet holding back, waiting for spring... ' she turned her rapt, excited face to his. 'And that tree. It's the only touch of green but the green is ivy.'

'The tree is hollow and dead, the ivy a parasite. What you see is an illusion of life.'

'You painted this?' she guessed.

'Guilty,' he conceded diffidently.

'It's brilliant. Are there any others of yours here?'

'He's done well to get one painting into the exhibition, Mrs Morris, considering he's only been here for two months,' the officer informed her tartly.

'Can anyone join the society?'

'Be delighted to have you,' the woman barked. 'We can always do with new blood.'

'Really?' Esme looked from John to the old woman as though someone had just given her Christmas.

'That was the most wonderful afternoon, thank you.' Esme floated out of the gallery in a haze of creativity. 'If only I had somewhere to paint where I wouldn't have to worry about making a mess. I could work in oils – pastels – watercolours –'

'What would you start with?'

'Sketches. Isn't that what all beginners start with?' she asked anxiously.

'But you're not a beginner.'

'After looking at the exhibits I don't see how I can possibly call myself anything else. I feel like buying a sketch book and some pencils right now.'

'Then, let's do just that.' He led the way to Traceport's only artists' suppliers. Once through the door Esme was like a sugar-starved child unleashed in a sweet shop. She fingered the pads of rich white and creamy paper, ran her fingers along the clean smooth lines of the pencils, drooled over boxes of pastels and oils, and, while she was lost in admiration, John bought half a dozen sketch books of varying sizes, sets of soft and hard-leaded pencils, and a box of pastels. By the time Esme had made her choice and was walking to the counter with a single sketchpad and two pencils, his purchases had been parcelled. He presented them to her.

'A thank you for your company.'

'I couldn't possibly take anything from you. Not after you've been kind enough to take me to the exhibition...'

He took the sketch book and pencils from her hands, laid them on the counter, and led her out of the shop. 'If there's no room for you to work in your house, there's always my yacht.'

'The *Freedom*?'

'You know her?'

'I've seen it berthed in Smugglers Creek.'

'I'm lucky the Commander allowed me to drop anchor there, it's a beautiful spot.'

'It's a beautiful boat.' She remembered Roy's comment the first time he'd spotted it. "A toy that only the idle rich would buy." Roy had been consumed by jealousy the moment he'd set eyes on the *Freedom*'s sleek lines.

'I only have her on loan for a year. And I meant what I said about you using it as a studio. I'm working more or less full time in the club, so if you want to board her any time, feel free. I've an easel, paints and some other things in the cabin. The deck has excellent vantage points, if you want to sketch the birds, and there's a marvellous view from the bow.'

'Your painting?'

'Yes.'

'After seeing your masterpiece I wouldn't dare tackle it.'

'You will. You've an artist's eye, and now you've been bitten by the bug again nothing will stop you.'

She held out her hand. 'Thank you. It's been a wonderful day.'

'It still could be. It's only four o'clock. Why don't you come out to the boat with me?'

'I couldn't...'

'You said no one's waiting for you. I'll drop you back at your landing whenever you like. You do want to see the *Freedom*?' he added persuasively.

She looked at him for a moment. He was a beautiful boy, and younger than her own son. But that didn't prevent her from following him into his boat.

'And this is the bathroom.' John swung open the door on a fully fitted bathroom. No stainless steel cubicle the size of a broom cupboard with a shower head poised over the toilet, like all the other yachts Esme had seen. The suite was white fibreglass, the panelling mahogany, the fittings polished brass.

'Pure luxury.'

They walked back on deck and leaned over the rail. A kingfisher swooped low over the water. While she watched it, John pulled the pin from her hair and it tumbled to her shoulders. She turned and looked at him.

'Did anyone ever tell you how beautiful you look with your hair loose?'

'John, I'm...'

He silenced her with a kiss. Whether it was the wine she'd drunk at lunch, the warmth of the sun, sheer spring madness, or simply happiness at seeing and talking art again, she neither knew nor cared. For the first time since she'd said "I do" twenty-seven years before, she forgot Roy, her children, her sensible and tedious life – everything except the sensation of John's lips on hers.

Sliding her hands around his back, she held him close, rejoicing in the feel of his heart beating against hers, returning his

146

embrace with a fervour she would have never have believed herself capable of.

His hands tenderly cupped her face; he drew back and looked into her eyes. All capacity for thought fled. She reached out and stroked his cheek. His fingers explored her hair, her lips, the texture of her skin, almost as though he were committing a tangible portrait to memory.

His eyes, almond shaped, velvet dark, held hers in thrall as he slowly unbuttoned his shirt. She brushed her fingers over the skin on his chest, soft, supple, smooth and golden. Their hands met, fingers interlocked.

Her blouse joined his shirt on the deck. They clung to one another kissing, stroking, caressing. His touch was light, barely perceptible, but it sent shudders down her spine. Holding her, he guided her into the cabin. She was vaguely aware of doors opening and closing. Of a stateroom with a bed. Moments later she was in his arms beneath the covers.

Roy had never made love to her the way John did: slowly, infinitely slowly, and unhurriedly, until her whole being ached for consummation. Then, all pretence at gentleness fled as passion burned, exhausting, consuming. The submission and subservience Roy had ingrained in her died when she clawed savagely at John's naked back, forcing him closer until they fused into one warm, fervent being. When his body finally pierced hers, she cried out. A harsh primitive cry of pure, intense emotion.

What should have been culmination was the onset of a reckless, heedless state where nothing mattered except fulfilment of the need John had engendered in her. It was a long time before either of them closed their eyes or lay peaceful and sated in one another's arms.

'Good afternoon.'

Esme looked up sleepily. John was standing over her in a black silk kimono, a bowl of grapes and two glasses in his hands.

'If you make room, I'll feed you champagne and grapes.'

147

'That sounds delicious. I've never had champagne in bed before.'

'I felt like celebrating.' He gave her a glass and slipped a grape into her mouth. It was ice cold. He replaced it with another. Kissing her, he bit through the grape, taking half into his own mouth.

'Champagne, grapes and sex in the afternoon. Could this be decadence?' she asked.

'That depends,' he sat beside her and kissed her, 'on how you view decadence.'

'I love your sense of occasion.'

'A compliment freely given without an apology for taking up my time?' he teased.

'Thank you,' she wrapped her arms around him and laid her head on his chest.

'It is me who should be thanking you.' He kissed her once more before pulling the sheet back and tickling her toes. She tried to cover herself.

'I want to look at you. You're beautiful. All beautiful.'

'I'm old.'

'Age doesn't destroy beauty; it enhances it, as it does antiques and fine wine.' He pulled her to her feet. 'Let's swim. I want to remember every second of this afternoon and I won't if we sleep any more.'

'I have no costume.'

'The lady's naked in my arms and she's worried about a costume?'

'Someone might see us.'

'No one comes here at this time of day. The genteel people of the creek are all taking tea.'

'Grapes and champagne?'

'Tea and cucumber sandwiches. Hurry up; I want to see if it's possible to make love underwater.'

The sea was freezing but they were both laughing when John helped Esme back on to the boat.

She looked at the water on the deck.

'We're making a mess.'

'You're being a housewife again. It will dry.' He pushed her inside and down to the bathroom, leading her into the shower, he turned it full on. The first jet was icy cold, and for a split second the shock sent her senses reeling. She suddenly saw herself through impartial eyes. She was married. There had only ever been Roy. No one before and no one after – until now. A few conversations, the shared experience of an art exhibition, that was all that lay between her and a boy half her age, and here she was cavorting naked with him, when she had always been shy of her body, even with her husband.

John pulled her closer and shut the cubicle door. The sound shattered the illusion and, with it, her guilt. He reached for the sponge and soap and began to wash her. Her back, her arms, her breasts. She picked up the shampoo and squirted it over both their heads, massaging his scalp along with her own.

He tried to tickle her, but not for long, their needs were too urgent for prolonged foreplay. Finally, they spilt out of the cubicle into the bathroom. John opened a cupboard and took out two towels, wrapping the larger of the two around both of them.

'John . . . '

'I forbid you to say anything serious.' He'd sensed that her bubble of happiness was about to burst. 'Tomorrow? You'll come tomorrow? In the morning. I don't have to go to work until midday.'

'I shouldn't.'

'Please try,' he urged. 'There's not much happiness around. I know. I've been looking for it. We have to hold on to this while we can.'

'I'll be here.' She went to the door. 'My clothes are in the bedroom.'

'I'll make coffee and bring it out on deck after I've dressed.'

Esme pulled on her boring middle-aged clothes and resolved to buy herself some jeans. She took her precious parcel of art materials and went on deck. Smugglers Creek was her favourite

149

spar off Farcreek. The entrance cut back sharply from the estuary, and the mouth, overhung with willow and beech trees, was impossible to see in summer unless you knew it was there. And few who lived outside the creek dared navigate Smugglers Creek passage. Its sandbanks and rocks were notorious – rocks that according to legend had been dragged and dropped there by ancestral Farcreeks who resented the interference of the excise men in their enterprises.

Esme looked over the rail. The rising tide lapped against the *Freedom*'s hull, the scuttle of crabs over rocks mingled with the cries of gulls as they circled out to sea, and while she listened, she studied the lush spring greenery, looking for the tree John had painted. She smiled when she found it. He had painted a dead hulk wreathed in ivy, creating an illusion of life where there was none.

She opened the parcel, and lifted out the smallest of the pads of paper and a soft pencil. The first sketch she attempted was of the tree with its ivy cladding. But one of its branches was bearing small yellow flowers and they suddenly seemed very significant.

Some Like It Hot
Ginny Swart

'You didn't wash up before you went to work,' accused Verity, her severe little face crunched in disapproval. 'It's your week on duty and you know I hate coming back to a dirty kitchen.'

Penny gritted her teeth. 'I didn't have time but I stacked them in the sink, didn't I? I know it's my turn, I'll do all the dishes after supper.'

Her fussy flatmate was driving her mad. She didn't like Penny's music, she disapproved of Penny's boyfriends and she was irritated by Penny's undies drying over the shower rail. And she wasn't shy about saying so, loudly and often.

'If only she'd move out!' groaned Penny to her mate Jill at work. 'I must have been insane to take her as a flatmate.'

'Well, why did you?' asked Jill. 'I could have told you it wouldn't work.'

'I felt sorry for her, I suppose, she said she was stuck for a place to stay for a few weeks. And I thought someone to help with the rent would be good for a while. But it's been four months now, and she won't leave. She keeps paying her share but just smiles vaguely when I ask her to find somewhere else.'

'Well, how about moving out yourself? Leave her to it!'

'No way! I was incredibly lucky to find that flat in the first place and I'll never get anything as good. The rooms are huge, it's got loads of built-in cupboards and that great view over the park. Plus I can walk to work. No, *she's* got to go. And soon.'

'Does the Domestic Goddess know about your new evening job?'

'Good heavens no.' Penny giggled. 'She thinks all dancing's sinful and if she knew I was moonlighting at The Cabana Club as a dancer...! I've told her I'm taking French lessons twice a week but she's starting to wonder why I only get home at two am. Not that it's any of her business.'

Penny could barely get by on what she earned as a record clerk in an insurance company but her casual job as a dancer in the nightclub had earned her a nice little nest egg, which she hoped would grow to be a deposit on her first car by the end of the year.

'Doesn't she have any boyfriends herself?'

'No, but she's so prissy, no one I know would want to date her.'

That evening after tea, Penny was about to tackle the washing-up when the phone rang.

'Hi babe, I'm picking you up in ten minutes, be ready!' said Mike. 'One of the lads is off to the States tomorrow so we've just decided to throw him a party at the Club.'

Mike was a good-looking guy who dressed head-to-toe in black leather, danced like a demon and rode a Harley, all plusses in Penny's book.

'I'm ready already!' she grinned. 'I'll wait for you downstairs.'

She didn't want a repeat performance from Verity, who had opened the door to him last time, taken one look at his multi-coloured tattoos and locked herself in the bathroom.

'Where do you think you're going?' asked Verity suspiciously, as she watched Penny fling on her briefest mini and spray her hair with glitter. 'What about the dishes? And the kitchen floor needs a good mopping. We'll have cockroaches if you don't clean up properly.'

Her piercing whine followed Penny down the stairs.

'I'll do it tomorrow before work!' shouted Penny and slammed the door.

If only Verity would stop sweating the small stuff and get a life.

But to her surprise, the next week Verity said primly, 'I'm entertaining a friend this evening. Will you be in?'

'No, it's Tuesday, my – er – French lesson,' said Penny. 'I'll be out till late. Who's the lucky guy?'

'Just someone I met at work. His name's Charles.'

'Well, that's great, Verity, have fun. I'll see you tomorrow and you can give me all the juicy details.'

'Juicy details? What sort of a girl do you think I am? He's just coming for supper. I'm making him cottage pie, I make a very good one.'

'I'm sure you do,' said Penny.

Onstage that evening, as she wiggled seductively in time to "Can't get you out of my head", she wondered what sort of man was enjoying her flatmate's cottage pie. Wouldn't it be marvellous if Verity could win his heart by wooing his stomach with her home cooking? She might get married and move out. Naah, pigs might fly.

But a vision of her beautiful flat, with no Verity fingering the mantelpiece to check for dust, almost caused Penny to miss her cue for sashaying down amongst the audience.

The men loved that bit. She chucked them under their chins and gazed into their eyes, and perched temptingly on the laps of the younger, better-looking ones.

It also meant she was up close and could gracefully receive the notes they tucked into the top of her very brief bustiere.

Some nights she made more in tips than she earned all week at the office.

'So? Did you have a good time? Did Charles enjoy your cottage pie?'

'Very nice, thank you,' said Verity. 'Yes, I think he liked it, he asked for seconds.'

'Seconds, eh? Always a good sign,' teased Penny. 'And after supper?'

'After supper we listened to a Schubert symphony on the radio and then he went home,' she said. But she had a secretive look in her eye that Penny hadn't seen before. Something was definitely stirring there.

Penny became aware that twice a week Verity was entertaining someone. There were tell-tale signs of a male presence – the seat up in the loo, or a single bottle of beer in the bin along with Verity's empty carton of orange juice.

'How are you and Charles getting on, then?' she asked after some weeks, to distract Verity from the fact she'd forgotten to put out the rubbish that morning.

'Um – actually, we're getting engaged.'

'That's wonderful! Congratulations!'

Verity allowed a small, smug smile to cross her thin lips. 'By the way, I meant to tell you, that runny cheese you bought was smelling so strong I had to throw it out.'

'My lovely Camembert? You threw it – oh never mind.' Penny was so pleased, she could forgive her flatmate anything. 'When are you planning to marry?'

'Quite soon, actually, in September. Charles doesn't want a long engagement, so I'll be moving out at the end of August. Sorry about that, you'll have to find another flatmate.'

Two months! She'd only have to put up with Verity for another sixty days! She could handle that.

'So when am I going to meet this man of yours?'

'One of these days. But I don't expect you and Charles will get on at all. He's quite old-fashioned and has very definite ideas about women's behaviour. And he wouldn't approve of your taste in clothes or music or anything.'

Honestly, thought Penny irritably, what planet is she living on if she thinks wearing minis and riding pillion on a motorbike adds up to bad behaviour?

'I certainly don't want to risk upsetting Charles,' she said coolly. 'So I shouldn't suggest Mike and I make up a foursome with you two to celebrate, then?'

'Certainly not, thank you.' Verity gave a shudder.

'Only another week to go!' exulted Penny. 'I swear she's getting worse. Today she told me I should iron the drying-up cloths before I put them in the drawer! I really pity that fiancé of hers when he finds out what a dragon he's married.'

'He probably thinks ironing dishcloths is a good quality in a woman,' giggled Jill. 'So, are you going to have a farewell party for her?'

'Of course, but after she's gone! We'll have the mother of all rave-ups.'

That night the Cabana Club was packed, with a large, noisy group of men seated in front. It looked like a celebration of some sort and they kept calling raucously for more drinks, except for one podgy middle-aged man who nursed his beer and watched his friends with an uncertain smile on his lips.

Poor guy, thought Penny, watching from behind the curtain of the tiny stage, he's really not enjoying himself. Let's see if I can help.

She fluffed out her curly blonde wig, wet her lips and shimmied onstage in her silky white pleated dress, the perfect Marilyn Monroe look-alike.

The record started playing and she mimed the words, pouting and flirting and looking straight at Fat Man, singing for him alone.

'I wanna be loved by you, just you…'

She pointed directly at him and winked.

'Just you, and nobody else but you…'

She licked her lips sexily and slowly flounced down the steps, swinging her hips just as Marilyn had done in *Some Like it Hot*.

Fat Man was certainly feeling the heat, wiping his forehead with a clean white handkerchief and grinning foolishly at her.

'I couldn't aspi-iiire
To anything hii-iigher
Than be filled with desii-iire…
To make you my own…'

He's loving it, she thought. May as well give him a night to remember. It looks as though the party might be in his honour. Maybe he's had a promotion or something.

155

'Boop-boop-ee doo!'

She sat on his lap and smiled into his eyes, smoothing his sparse hair and running her fingers provocatively around his ear and under his double chin. He stared at her in fascination while his mates hooted and banged the table and she pinched his cheek before slowly rising and returning to the stage. Then she shimmied for the last time, pointing her finger at Fat Man and gave him a last slow pout before disappearing behind the curtain. The audience shrieked and whistled.

'Nice one, Penny,' said the manager. 'They loved you.'

'Thanks.'

'Excuse me, dahlings... my fans are waiting.'

Penny stood aside as the man billed as The Red Hot Chilli Pepper minced past her on to the stage, amidst a roar of applause, in his impossibly high heels and glittering gown. This drag queen had been a favourite at the Cabana Club for weeks and Penny couldn't resist watching him again.

'If I hadn't been told Chilli Pepper was a guy, I'd never have guessed,' she said. 'He's excellent.'

'He's so convincing he gets fan mail from men, would you believe it?' said the manager. 'They even send him flowers.'

Verity had been packing her things for the past fortnight but the following evening, when Penny came back from the office, she found her savagely ripping open the boxes. Her face was red and puffy from crying.

'Verity! What on earth's the matter? What's happened?'

'It's Charles! We're not getting married any more!'

'What?' Penny's heart sank with a hollow thud. 'Why ever not?'

'Charles met someone else! He says he's in love for the first time in his life! He says he realises he never really loved me at all – the pig!' She collapsed in a heap on the floor, sobbing.

'Oh Verity, sweetie, I'm so sorry.' She hugged her awkwardly. 'Who's this other woman? Someone from work?'

'No. He met her at his stag party last night. They took him off to a horrible night-club and he's fallen for some cheap tart he met there.'

Penny went cold. With a horrible certainty she knew what was coming. Of course – Fat Man had to have been Charles. And he'd fallen for *her!* Or rather, he'd fallen for Marilyn Monroe.

'He says he's seen how exciting a real woman can be. He says she's glamorous and sexy and uninhibited and she's everything I'm not.'

Oh this is too awful, thought Penny. What on earth am I going to say to her?

Verity's voice rose into a wail of outrage. 'And she's called Chilli Pepper! What sort of a name is *that*?'

Then she wiped her eyes and started taking her clothes out of the boxes with a sigh.

'I suppose I won't be leaving after all, Penny, so you'll be pleased to know you'll be spared all the trouble of finding another flatmate.'

Supermarket Sweep
Gerry Savill

There must be a better way to spend Saturday evening than pushing a trolley full of goods she didn't even want around in the hope that someone just as pathetic as her would chat her up. The "in place" to meet unattached males, the magazine had said. Well, Jan had been circling this supermarket for two hours now, her feet ached and she just wanted to go home. As for the unattached males, well this evening had been the same as the previous four Saturday evenings she had spent here – a dead loss date-wise.

She had become adapt, however, at trolley reading. There was a definite art to analysing the owner of the contents of a trolley. Single meals, wine, books, chocolates were OK. Budgie food, bulk buying of fags and booze and anything connected to babies were out. As was anything that looked like it could possibly be being bought for an elderly parent, especially a mother. The last chap that Jan had been dating lived with his mother and his idea of a romantic tryst was his battered old Ford Fiesta. Jan had decided very quickly that a grope in a car, while trying to perform all sorts of contortions to avoid the steering wheel, was definitely out at her age. What she wanted now was comfort – all forms of transport were out (luxury yachts and private planes the exception of course).

Jan had even mastered the art of looking into the trolley without being too conspicuous (or hoped she had). However, there was always the dilemma of whether or not to put on her glasses. Vanity versus seeing clearly. Did she want to mistake Preparation H for toothpaste? Clear eyesight usually won for Jan. If, and currently it seemed a big if, she was going to meet someone then they had to accept her, faults and all.

Just do your shopping late on a Saturday night, the article had stated and the place would be crawling with unattached, good-looking males just dying to meet her. Why she read, or believed, this drivel she didn't understand. Or rather she did. She had been single now for two years. She had never been lucky enough (or was that unlucky enough) to have been married but she had lived with someone for 10 years. She missed that companionship. Avenues for meeting men who were unattached, like-minded and, let's tell the truth, of a similar age were few and far between. She had unsuccessfully tried evening classes – although she had made several lovely garden pots and was coming along great with First Year Spanish. She was also fed up with "office romances", although how the word romance ever came to be associated with a quick one up against the filing cabinet or on the boss's desk with a stapler stuck to your bum she would never know.

Tonight had gone much the same way as the previous Saturday. She put a select choice of goods in her trolley, and then wandered around hoping that Mr Right just happened to pop in to top up his store cupboard. Tonight's offerings were the usual mix. The first trolley had looked promising; single portion meals, four cans of lager, rolls and various cheeses plus other unassuming goods. Jan had put a nice smile on her face and glanced at the owner. It wasn't that she had objections to older men but old enough to be her grandfather? She made her escape through the dairy section.

A very nice looking, probably slightly too young, man became a contender for trolley number two. But after a minute it was obvious that he had never been in a supermarket before and didn't know where anything was so had obviously been sent by the wife to get something. This was confirmed by the jumbo pack of nappies that he slung into his trolley. Strike two.

A third prospect came into view. Maybe it would be third time lucky. He was pleasant to look at, nicely dressed (maybe too nice for shopping) and the contents of his trolley were not alarming. In fact they were too perfect. The ultimate shopping trolley full of just the right type of groceries. The romantic CD, very expensive bottle of wine, selection of delicacies from the deli, luxurious bubble bath, designer shirt, cologne – everything the magazine would recommend for the perfect partner. Jan became very smug. He had obviously been reading the same articles as her. How did she know this? Well, apart from the cologne, her trolley was an exact match.

Instead of the cologne however, Jan had opted for the sexy undies. This week she had chosen the very risqué red bra and thong set. Not that she had any intention of buying it – why anyone would want to wear something that was as uncomfortable as cheese wire up their backside she couldn't imagine. No, she just gave the selected choice of the week a jaunt round the supermarket for a couple of hours before putting it back on its hanger. Of course, the items that she really needed; toothpaste, dental floss and corn plasters, were hidden under strategically placed items.

At this point a very good-looking man rounded the corner into the aisle she was in. He was much too young for her, but no harm window shopping. He had a quick glance into her trolley and smiled at her. No, it wasn't a smile; it was a smirk, and, yes, now he was laughing. That did it for Jan. What did she think she was doing? She might as well have a huge sign on her head "Desperate for a date – line up here". Why was she so intent on finding a partner anyway? She had a good job, loads of friends with whom she went out when she wanted, several great holidays a year. Now she came to think of it, when would she even find the time to see anyone? She would have to give up going to the gym or to classes, or miss seeing her mates. It would be a relief not to have to get tarted up to the nines just because she was seeing someone whose idea of a good time was going down the local for a game of darts and a pie on the way home. No more being plucked and waxed to within an inch of your life in case your current beau suffered a heart attack at the sight of a stray leg hair.

For Jan this was a turning point – no men, just me. She started to put back the goods that she had hand picked for her trolley. The red underwear went back first, to be replaced by some lovely, comfortable pink fluffy slippers. She decided to keep the wine and other goodies she had selected – why not? she deserved them. Back went the romantic CD to be replaced by the latest thriller by her favourite author.

As she waited in the queue to be served, she noticed her trolley being eyed up by the only remaining eligible male left in the shop. He didn't look impressed at the pink slippers but she didn't care. She felt as though a weight had been lifted off her shoulders as she walked out of the entrance. Until the alarm bell sounded. Everyone turned to look at her. So, as well as being one of those saddos who did their shopping on a Saturday to look for dates, they probably also thought she was a shoplifter. This day just got better and better.

The assistant manager approached her. Not that Jan was interested now, but he had the loveliest smile she had seen for a long time.

'Oh look, the tag on your slippers didn't get removed', he told her as he took the offending tag off. She was very grateful at that moment that she hadn't bought the red thong.

'Well at least you've livened up my Saturday night. Could have been down the pub with my mates but us single men always get caught for the weekend shifts,' he joked, flashing that beautiful smile at her.

'Hmm', Jan thought, 'I'm sure I could miss the odd night out with my friends. And why do I need to learn Spanish…?'

Litigation
Sue Houghton

I sensed her approaching, despite the fact I was looking in the opposite direction and my mind was occupied with more important issues; like had I the willpower to ditch my usual burger/cola/sticky bun, for a salad and diet shake?

'A few moments of your time, sir,' came the voice over my left shoulder. 'Have you had an accident in the last three years?'

I did a ninety-degree turn to avoid confrontation. Congratulations Stevie, your SGR is fully functional and operational. SGR? That's Sales Git Radar. It's like my brain's finely tuned in to their clipboard wavelength or something. Spaniels trained to sniff out drugs at airports have less success than I do.

This gift had developed over the six years I'd taken the lunchtime stroll between my office and the sandwich shop. Except I wasn't so much strolling that day as dashing from beneath shop canopies. It had been tipping down for days.

I turned up the collar of my jacket and braved the rain once more.

'Sir?' She was right beside me now.

I kept my head down. I usually favour the non-eye contact method of avoidance, but this pesky critter had learned that a carefully placed prod in the neck with the prongs of an umbrella was an effective way of gaining a person's attention.

I waved a dismissive hand, but still didn't turn to make eye contact. Odds favoured her being some crone wearing too much make-up, the smell of cheap perfume clinging to her corporate suit.

The burger lunch beckoned and I quickened my step, but she was persistent.

'Five minutes can change your life, sir.'

I was just thinking they should issue shoppers with taser guns, when a lorry thundered past sending a sheet of dirty rainwater my way. I sidestepped, lost my balance and collided with my pursuer.

Her ballpoint pen found its way up my left nostril about a nano-second before my face made contact with her breasts.

I was acutely aware – maybe my senses were heightened by the damage inflicted by the Parker Rollerball – that these were not the breasts of a crone.

'Jeez! What the...!' The breasts heaved. 'Get off me, you... you... Stevie?'

'Lily?' To be precise, Lily my ex-fiancée, whose heart I so cruelly broke when I screwed her best friend, Steph, in the spare bedroom while she and her mother were downstairs icing the wedding cake.

'Blimey, Lily. What are you doing here?' I'd moved fifty miles away after we broke up. What was she doing in my town?

'You,' she said. It hung there between us, neither a question nor an accusation, but strangely threatening.

'Lily.'

'Stop saying my name. I hate you saying my name.' She was hopping on one foot, the heel of a shoe hanging off. A ladder snaked up her stocking. Lily always wore the finest denier. The ones with the deliciously sexy lace tops. Oh come on... It's the sort of detail men notice.

'Sorry,' I said.

She glared at me, her eyes less like Bambi than I remembered. I suddenly knew what it felt like to be a newborn springbok cornered by a hungry hyena. I saw a documentary about hyenas recently. Their incredibly strong jaws and digestive tracts can dispose of entire corpses, including bones, hide, and hair. I had the feeling Lily was capable of doing the same to me.

'How are you?' I asked. 'Long time, no see.'

'Six years, no see,' she spat back.

'Has it been that long? Well, well. Time flies, doesn't it?'

'When you're enjoying yourself? Been having a ball have you? Good. No, really, that's great. I'm pleased. Because while you've been having a ball, I've been picking up the pieces.'

'Blimey, Lily, you can't still be mad.' It was a stupid remark considering she was waving the broken heel menacingly in the direction of my flies. I held my hands aloft and shrugged in an "I'm-a-loser" fashion. 'Listen, Lily. You're obviously upset. Not to mention wet. Let me buy you coffee.'

She glared at me again. 'You screw my best friend, my matron of honour, no less, then walk out on the eve of our wedding day never to make contact again and now you want to buy me coffee?'

I chanced my trump card. 'And shoes?'

'Why did you do it?' Lily shot the question at close range as we sat on bar stools in Starbucks. Her hair, caught up loosely on top of her head, had gone all springy with the damp and her cheeks were flushed. I'd forgotten how beautiful she was.

I traced my finger in the froth on my coffee. 'I was scared.'

'Of my father?'

That went without saying. It was he who'd come up the stairs to use the bathroom and caught Steph and me at it. Believe me, fear doesn't cover it.

'I mean, I was scared of the whole wedding / commitment thing,' I said.

'You think I wasn't?'

'You were having second thoughts too?'

'Difference is, you reached out for my matron of honour instead of me.'

'It wasn't like that.'

It was exactly like that. Lily had been wrapped up in the wedding plans for months. Where once we used to spend our weekends having a laugh, watching movies, or going bowling, we'd spend them discussing seating plans and how many glasses per head you could get out of thirty bottles of Pimms.

Lily offered me the amaretto biscuit from her saucer, just as she used to do. She hated anything almond. She even left the marzipan off the wedding cake as I recall.

'Steph told me it was her who made a move on you, not the other way around,' she said.

It was true. That night I'd wanted to talk out my feelings with Lily, suggest we cool it a bit, but couldn't bring myself to do it. Steph offered me a shoulder to cry on and I'd been weak. I took full responsibility.

'Does it matter who made the first move?'

'It might have, back then.'

I hadn't hung around to find out. I'd bolted that same night without any explanation. Packed my bags and moved north.

'Would you have forgiven me if I'd stayed?' I asked.

She shrugged and her hair gave up its struggle and tumbled about her shoulders. My heart boomeranged.

'Probably not.' She handed me her napkin and gestured. 'You have a nose bleed.'

'Oh, thanks.'

'No need to thank me,' she smiled. 'I've wanted to inflict injury on you for a long time. You're going to have a black eye too if I'm lucky.'

'You can certainly bear a grudge.'

She fixed me with doe eyes. 'I like to think so.'

'Is the score settled now?'

She nodded and drained her cup. 'The rain's stopped. I have to be going.'

'Wait here, I'll go buy you some shoes.'

'No. My car's parked around the corner.' She slid both shoes into her bag and jumped off the barstool. 'I have a spare pair in the boot.'

'But you can't walk through the streets without any shoes.'

'Don't tell me what to do, Stevie.'

'No, sorry.'

I held open the door for her to step outside. For the first time in days, the sun broke through the clouds.

'So, I might see you around,' I said.

She juggled her clipboard and umbrella. 'I expect so.'

'OK, well, bye Lily. Have a nice life.'

'You too.'

I reached awkwardly to kiss her cheek, letting my face linger beside hers to breathe in the soft warmth of her perfume. I noticed she closed her eyes.

'Be seeing you, then,' I whispered. 'Take care.'

With treacle feet I walked away. I stopped a few paces on, pretending to look in a shop window to gather my thoughts. A leaflet fluttered by my face, dropped into the rainwater in the gutter and floated towards me.

Have you had an accident? Call Litigation Help For A No Win, No Fee Claim.

I felt a trickle of blood run from my nose. I turned to see Lily disappearing into the crowd. I remembered her words earlier, *"Five minutes can change your life."*

'I think I have a claim for personal injury,' I said, when I caught up with her. 'But I'd be willing to settle out of court.'

'What do you propose?'

'Instalments for the rest of my life?'

'I think that would be acceptable,' she said, smiling.

I reached for her, gathered her in my arms and kissed her.

drifted by more practical matters took over, like taking the children off her hands for a few hours to give her a break.

Several doors away the blue and white striped hut belonged to the Beachams, it had plastic curtains hanging in the doorway that whipped about in the wind so much that half the streamers had shredded off over the years, a bit like George's receding hairline. They always turned up at weekends with their tiny dog Molly and spent many hours beachcombing, come rain or shine, looking for drift wood and shells to turn into works of art, which always ended up looking like piles of old rubbish. George and Rita took their turn with the children, buying them arm-bands, teaching them to swim, playing cricket and hunting for crabs in rocky pools, loving the children as if they were their own.

The sisters Elsie and Jessica, were also very fond of Sara and her children, they had known her when she was a child and had come to the huts with her own parents. They had watched her grow into a lovely woman who'd married her darling man, then had the children and who should have lived happily ever after.

Elsie and Jessica, who'd been promoted to Aunties, always had a good stash of nice goodies for the children and kind hearts for Sara, who always looked so sad and lost. They knitted jumpers for the children and introduced their nice nephew Peter, who tried very hard to melt Sara's heart. The Beachams' gormless son also tried his best to win her over, but she just wasn't remotely interested in anyone.

George and Rosie from London had a large family and had dragged many a male relative down to their hut during the past summers, hoping she would take a fancy to one of them. The only one Sara had ever bothered to talk to was the painter who decorated George and Rosie's hut. She thought he'd painted it so tastefully with the white picket fence half way up, intertwined with pale blue flowers on Wedgwood blue walls. He was seventy if he was a day and bald as a coot.

As the summers drifted past without excitement, other owners came and went, they stopped for a chat, discussed the weather, washed the huts. Then, midweek in July, a rumour started that hut number ten, with its dull flaky blue paintwork, was up for sale. The owners had decided to move abroad for the sun. It became apparent that it had been sold when a stranger turned up and started to paint the hut a wild mix of lilac and turquoise. Well, it nearly caused world war three and an angry deputation of owners marched up demanding that he stick to the tradition of blue and white. They did not handle it very diplomatically and the owner ended up telling them all to clear off, ending the shouting match they had started with him. Everyone was up in arms about his uncooperative attitude and so he was sent to Coventry, which made him dig in his heels even more.

George threatened to knock his block off, Rosie had to drag the silly old fool away, the stranger was so well built he could have done George a mortal damage. A petition to the council and a letter about traditions sent to the local paper made no difference. Sara's children thought the hut was really pretty, so did she come to that, but she had to be firm and forbid the children to have any contact with the man, trying to explain the need for old traditions and loyalty towards their old friends' feelings.

She felt very cross with the children later in the week, when she noticed they had wandered further down the beach and were totally engrossed by a giant red dragon stunt kite being manoeuvred by the new owner. The dragon spiralled and twisted through the air, skimming the waves and dancing above the children's heads as they stood open-mouthed in wonder.

As she started to march down the beach to reclaim the children, Sara couldn't help noticing the man's powerful back and arm muscles as he grappled with the double control cords and braced his sturdy legs to stop himself from being dragged along the beach. Feeling rather flustered, she used a sharper tone in her voice than she meant to as she called to the children, making him glance at her with a dark, brooding look. The children called her a spoilsport as she marched them back up the beach, dragging their feet and sulking. Tom, her oldest son argued, 'He's really nice Mum, we don't care about the hut's stupid colour, he was interesting. He flies kites in competitions and he was going to show us how to do it. He knows all about aerodynamics and stuff like that.'

Sara felt a bit mean inflicting adult issues on the children, so she relented and allowed them to watch the man the following week, as long as they didn't talk to him. As she sat outside the hut most afternoons, the wonderful Red Dragon was airborne for hours at a time and her eyes kept straying to the man's powerful body, his tanned muscles rippling as he battled with the wind to keep the kite under control. It always drew a crowd of spectators, she even saw old Ben, the children's fishing teacher and friend, watching. His hut was navy blue with a white anchor on the door, he was pretending to keep an eye on the children when in fact he was enthralled with the kite himself.

The watching crowd had roared with laughter on the day the Beachams had been taking Molly for a walk. As they strolled nonchalantly past the Red Dragon, Molly noticed it zooming above her beloved children's heads and erupted into frenzied barking as she dived in front of them to save them. The kite man knew Sara had been watching him and with a subtle turn he made the Dragon race across the sky towards her as if to attack her. Startled, she started to move out of the way, but it reared up and began to shake its giant red head in her direction and jiggle its tail end suggestively.

Sara pretended not to notice and looked away in case he saw how flushed she was. Later in the week, when she went shopping in town, she noticed big posters everywhere advertising "The Kite Flying Championships" being held a few days later at the next seaside resort, a few miles further along the coast. It looked fun, the advert showed a funfair, with line dancing , a pop group, pony rides and other attractions beside

170

the kites. The children would have loved to go and watch but Sara flinched when she saw how much the entrance fee and the fairground rides cost, unfortunately it was way beyond her budget.

She wouldn't admit it to herself but she'd have liked to watch the Red Dragon taking part in the competition. Well, its owner at least! Later that evening, Tom ran back to their hut with a small box kite, 'Mum,' he yelled, 'the man with the kite is called Ryan, he said I can have this kite and he'll teach me to fly it, if you say it's OK, and also can we go and watch the kite flying championships on Saturday?' Sara smiled at him, he was growing up fast.

She ruffled his hair, saying 'Yes to the first part, if you don't make a nuisance of yourself, but I'm sorry darling, we just haven't got enough money to spare for the Kite Championships. I must admit, I'd like to go there for the day myself but it's rather awkward. I also have to take sides over the blue and white hut argument and give my support to the other owners.'

As he leapt back down the beach to fly his kite, Sara's heart shifted, he looked so much like his father at times. She suddenly felt very lonely.

When the two smaller children came back for their tea without Tom, she started to walk down the beach to find him. She felt shy as she saw Tom talking to Ryan, the pair of them were huddled together deep in conversation and she didn't like to go any further as she felt herself redden.

'Tom, tea's ready.' She yelled and saw them both slap hands in a high five, then Tom jumped up and ran towards her, his face alive with happiness.

'What have you been up to?' she asked.

'Nothing,' he replied grinning as he lugged his kite back to the hut, turning to wave to Ryan, who put his thumbs up.

'What were you two talking about?'

'Nothing' he said, not looking at her face as he fiddled with his kite.

'You aren't really supposed to be talking to him at all, are you?' she said

'Well,' he replied, 'he had to tell me how to fly the kite and anyway he's really cool, he's a pilot and flies airplanes to other countries.'

Next morning the children were over-excited and champing at the bit to get to the beach quickly. Tom rushed Sara as she was packing some lunch and almost dragged her along the sea front as they made their way to the beach huts for the day. When they neared the steps leading down to the sand they saw that Ryan had parked his big van on the top of the seawall and was waiting for them, leaning casually against the bonnet. As they got closer Sara felt all of a quiver and didn't know what to say, her heart had begun thumping loudly, she'd forgotten how to flirt. The children had run and dived on Ryan, tugging and giggling as he shoved one under each arm and walked over to her, smiling his best smile.

'Please,' he asked nicely, looking deep into her eyes, 'would you and the children come to The Kite Championships with me? You can be my lucky mascots, we promise to behave, don't we kids?'

'Yes,' all three shouted as he waved some official tickets in front of her nose.

Sara's lips trembled, 'I would love to,' she said. 'But I truly can't, the other hut owners have really cared for us over the years and I must take their side over the hut.'

Tom was laughing, 'Look Mum look, you don't have to,' he shouted. She turned her head, her eyes following his finger as he pointed towards the row of huts.

There in front of hut number ten she saw a big cardboard sign saying 'Wet Paint.' Her heart missed a beat with delight as she gazed at Ryan's hut, it looked wonderful. The new paint job glistened in the sun. Blue walls, white trim, big white hearts on the side panels and a smaller one on the front door.

Sara squealed with pleasure and, laughing out loud, yelled, 'Let's go then.'

She felt his strength as he lifted her up into the van and when she saw him wink at the children, she realised the little devils had known about his plans all along. Sara suddenly knew she was going to be watching a lot of kite flying in the future.

Pre-destination
Bernardine Kennedy

As the 767 lumbered down the runway, I silently cursed my sister long and hard. Rachel knew full well how much I hated flying but it hadn't stopped her pleading for me to personally transport myself, and also her designer wedding outfit, to Florida. Despite three divorces in quick succession, each and every one because Rachel had "got bored", she was about to tie the knot again, this time on a hotel beach in Florida to her new prince charming, a hunk called John whom she had only just met.

I, meanwhile, had only got to kiss a selection of toads.

Although more than a little envious of her success with the opposite sex, I also disapproved of the way she discarded her men as soon as the next eligible one dropped by.

I was also disappointed with myself for allowing my slightly older and much more gregarious sister to once again railroad me into being her dogsbody.

"Please sweetie," she had cried down the phone, "I really, really want you there, you can be my attendant, I can't imagine having a wedding without you, you've been to the others!"

The big catch followed mere seconds after I had predictably caved in.

"I've just thought of something! If you're coming anyway, could you just pop down to London en route from jolly old Manchester and pick up the outfit I've ordered from Harvey Nicks? You could bring it with you, pleeeaaase?"

Of course, Rachel, anything you say, Rachel! I may be soft but I'm not silly and I knew that the outfit was the reason I was being invited, but still I couldn't bring myself to say no to her, hence my presence on board the big silver bird.

As the plane continued to thunder along, its vast wheels rumbling and vibrating, I screwed up my eyes and gripped the

The Blue and White Bathing Huts
Brenda Robb

With time-defying elegance the row of ten Victorian beach huts stood facing seaward in a neat sentinel row, a vision in blue and white. In the past, tradition had laid down rules that the huts could only be decorated in any shade of blue and white. The owners, all liking to be different, had come up with original, varying paint schemes and the huts looked striking against the seawall. This year the elderly sisters, Elsie and Jessica Ward, had opted for the sedate look, white walls, with a dark blue trim. They only came to the huts on nice warm days and sat facing the waves in their deck chairs, each wearing a matching floppy sun hat while they carried on with their eternal knitting. A kettle bubbled away inside their hut on a tiny primus stove, always at the ready for tea for any visitors who came calling.

Next door to them was Sara, widowed with three small children, their hut was painted by her husband before he had been killed in a car crash. He'd lovingly decorated it with the children in mind, a fluffy cloud-dotted pale blue sky on the top, with a row of pretty blue cresting waves underneath. A sprinkling of wonderful life-like sea creatures completed the pretty scene. Sara's fingers never failed to trace some of them on each visit to the hut, wistfully recalling the happy times they'd spent giggling together inside the hut on hot sultry nights before the children came along. Sadness would then overtake her as she remembered his laughter at the babies' antics once they started arriving every other year. Her wonderful Paul had made everyone laugh and his tragic death had affected every one in the huts very badly. It was like being in an exclusive club to be the owner of a bathing hut and the other owners took Sara and the children under their wings after the tragedy. At first it was kind words of comfort, tissues and listening, then as time armrests in anticipation of the sickening soaring up towards heaven, the roar that I couldn't help thinking was the precursor to aerial annihilation.

'Are you OK there? Phobia about flying?' the words came from my co-passenger who had settled into his seat at the last minute, by which time I'd already been palpitating so I hadn't taken any notice.

'Yep,' I muttered nervously without looking, 'it's just the going up and going down, I'll be OK once we're on the straight.'

I heaved a sigh of relief as the aircraft levelled off and slowly opened my eyes to sneak a glance at my neighbour, only to be confronted by a huge pair of navy blue eyes that were beaming concern straight at me from under a sun-bleached floppy fringe.

Then the eyes crinkled and he smiled. I smiled back.

He smiled wider. So did I.

He flashed a set of perfectly capped and whitened teeth. I grinned and kept my own slightly crooked and unbleached set hidden behind my tightly clamped lips.

Sinking back into the squishy chocolate leather seat, I could instantly picture in my mind a whole ten hours, elbow to elbow with a visual sex god, stretching out in front of me. For once, I felt gratitude towards my wayward sister who, with no conscience whatsoever about bribery, had insisted on paying for an upgrade from the DVT zone to the hallowed ground of leg room that was business class.

Ten hours? Huh! It seemed like a mere ten minutes before we were circling Miami and as the descent began he took my hand and squeezed it gently while I closed my eyes and totted up a mental CV from the information I had gleaned en route.

Justin Hamble. Aged thirty-five, financial wheeler-dealer in the city, high income, divorced, no kids, apartment in trendy Islington.

As for me, well I'm ashamed to confess that I just opened my mouth and the lies flowed out. I didn't want to admit to being a humble receptionist in a hairdressing salon in Manchester, so I just hinted darkly about 'confidential business in Key West' and changed the subject mysteriously.

When I told him I was driving down through the Keys to Key West, Justin immediately countered that, although he had business in Miami, purely by coincidence he had two free days beforehand.

'I could come along for the ride, keep you company, then fly back up to Miami. It'll give us a chance to get to know each other, we could take a slow drive and maybe stop and recharge our batteries en route...' His cool velvet voice washed over me sensuously.

'Sounds good to me,' I replied nonchalantly.

'Ooooh Yeeessss,' my hormones screamed silently.

From plane to parking lot his hand nestled protectively in the small of my back.

I savoured the sun, sea and waving palms that stretched out before us as the bright red convertible sucked up the miles down Highway One, but mostly I savoured the gorgeous Justin sitting dangerously close beside me.

How could this be happening to me? What was I doing? I was the original Minnie Mouse, gawky, insecure and frightened of my own shadow, while the lovely, lively Rachel took life by its throat and tried to strangle it enthusiastically. Admittedly a little too enthusiastically sometimes, but at least she didn't hide in the corner and blush. Yet there I was, flirting and smiling like an old pro.

'Turn off just here, there's a great little place tucked away,' Justin's smile was full on as he leaned close and pointed, 'we can have lunch by the sea. You'll just love it here.'

To my delight I soon discovered that Justin's 'great little place' was a luxurious five-star resort on its own Key that jutted appealingly out into the blue-green waters of the Bay of Mexico.

We strolled along the beach holding hands, sipped cocktails with our feet in the calm waters of the Bay and exchanged morsels of seafood from our over-piled plates.

Slowly but surely, I was seduced not only by the scents and sounds of the balmy Floridian atmosphere, but also by thoughts of the delectable Justin.

Padding across the bleached blond sand, I knew without a word being spoken exactly what would happen when we got back to the hotel. In fact it felt so inevitable that I wasn't even put out when I found out that Justin had already booked us into a suite.

A luxury suite, of course.

The inevitability of it actually added to the anticipation and it seemed perfectly natural when, along with a couple of lethal banana cocktails, we eventually retired to the voile-draped four poster with a sea view and made love into the night to the hum of enormous ceiling fans.

'Far more romantic than air-conditioning,' Justin murmured as he pulled me gently over to the bed, whispering sweet nothings seductively.

Because I hadn't been prepared for any sort of romantic encounter I wasn't equipped for unbridled passion so had no choice but to strip off completely and hide my reliable, but distinctly unsexy, mismatched underwear well out of sight.

My natural inhibitions had miraculously sunk without trace the moment we had stepped out of the airport and into the sexy convertible and, despite the lack of clothes to hide my body's faults and failings, everything came together perfectly.

I truly thought I'd died and gone to heaven!

We were fast and furious in bed, rampant in the shower and slow and gentle on the balcony, which, fortunately, was on the tenth floor.

The next day, tired but sated, we carried on down the highway to my destination of Key West and booked ourselves onto a touristy sightseeing bus, but the only sight I was interested in was right alongside me with his arm laid loosely across my shoulders.

'I have to fly back to Miami tonight, things to do tomorrow I'm afraid,' Justin sighed as we stood hand in hand in Mallory Square at sunset watching the orange globe sink gracefully into the sea. 'But I'll call you once we're home, maybe we can meet up in London sometime?'

The lively crowd clapped and cheered as the sun disappeared from sight and I felt an embarrassing prickle of tears starting up behind my eyes. Not at the awesome sunset but at the realisation that Justin was about to disappear also.

He still hadn't given me a contact address and what had started as a miniscule niggle of doubt in the back of my mind, suddenly grew arms and legs and started to run.

'Give me your address then and I'll send you a postcard from Key West,' I laughed maniacally, trying not to sound desperate.

Justin smiled and leaned forward to plant a kiss on my nose.

'No need, I've seen it all with you and the memory of it will stay in my mind forever. I've had a great time...' he sighed and put his head on one side, 'but now business calls me back, I'll phone...'

With a casual wave of his now familiar sexy hands he strode off into the crowd and was gone. Just like that.

Swamped by the crowds, I stretched and peered as I tried to catch another glimpse, but it was too late, along with the setting sun Justin had disappeared.

Desolately I wandered back to the car and, after a quiet sniffle, negotiated my way to the trendy hotel that my sister had chosen to be her latest wedding venue. Predictably Rachel was waiting for me, looking as gorgeous as ever, all long tanned limbs, tousled blonde hair and bursting with self-righteous indignation.

'Where the hell have you been? I was worried sick, I'm getting married tomorrow and you go and disappear with my outfit. Let me see it now, I want to check it's OK.'

Her hand reached out and she snatched my suitcase handle from me with the ferocity of a street mugger.

'Nice to see you too, Rachel, and yes, thank you I'm fine…' I snapped sarcastically and then relented, after all I was very late. 'I'm sorry, something came up but your dress is OK, it's at the bottom of the case wrapped in tissue paper, it's fine, I promise…'

'That's OK then,' her mercurial smile flashed back as she grabbed my arm and dragged me off through the buzzing reception area of the hotel, 'we're all in the bar having a pre-wedding celebration. Minnie I'm so excited, this really is IT for me. The big one.'

'John darling,' she waved frantically across the room, 'better late than never, come and meet my baby sister, she's here at last.'

Her fiancé stood up and smiled. Tall and handsome with a floppy blonde fringe and familiar navy blue eyes that instantly clouded over with fear!

Rachel smiled. 'Minnie, this is John, my husband to be, isn't he just the most gorgeous man in the whole wide world?'

Suddenly I felt sick and faint.

Looking Justin in the eye, I held out my hand and smiled grimly. 'So you're John the wonderboy. You don't look like a John,' I put my forefinger up to my lips. 'No, no, you look more like a…' I hesitated, 'I've got it, you look much more like a Justin!'

He looked at his feet and reluctantly took my proffered hand.

'Mmmm,' he mumbled.

Rachel looked from one to the other, grinning widely.

'Minnie, you're a scream, he doesn't look like a Justin at all! Now, come and sit with me and I'll tell you all about it. You'll never guess where we first met, it was on a flight to

Miami last month, we both knew right away, it must have been fate.'

'More like pre-destination I think Rachel,' I sighed, 'I've a strange feeling you two truly deserve each other.'

Cleaning Up After Clive
Elaine Everest

Cari wiped the fresh blood from the knife, cursing her husband as she did so. Never had she felt so let down and betrayed. As a lifelong vegetarian she abhorred what she'd done. Never mind the ethical reasons, she just hated the smell and touch of dead flesh.

'Damn Clive, I'll never forgive him for this, he's let me down once too often,' she muttered as she swished the mop in the bucket and savagely slapped it back on to the blood-stained floor. After mopping and scrubbing for ages she stood back and nodded to herself.

'That'll do, no one will be able to tell what happened in here tonight. Now, what else is on my list? Hmm, ring my boss and let him know I won't be going into work for the next few days. Luckily I'm due some leave; I can really do with it after what I've been through!'

Glancing at the clock, she shrieked to herself, 'My God, I should be at the hairdressers, what am I thinking? After talking Tracy into a last minute appointment for a complete style and colour change, I could at least be on time!' She grabbed her coat and dashed out the door.

Inside the house only the stringent odour of the freshly bleached floor and the hum of a large chest freezer, as icy fingers reached into the fleshy contents, hinted at the fact that Cari had been there at all that morning.

Several hours later, Cari bustled back into the kitchen, arms full of bags labelled with logos from the most expensive boutique in town. Her long blonde locks were now styled into a short cap of bubbly chestnut curls. Dumping her bags down, she lifted the heavy freezer lid to check its contents. Poking the packages with a long manicured finger she shuddered with

181

disgust before kicking off the fast freeze button with the tip of her new stylish shoes.

Bending to check she hadn't scuffed them, she smiled to herself. 'I enjoyed this morning, and Clive paid for it all!'

The telephone rang as she peered at her new image in the mirror on the wall.

'Cari, it's Mummy, is Clive there?' It was Clive's dreadful mother.

'Hello Mrs P. no, Clive's not here, he had to pop out for a while. Can I give him a message?'

'No dear, I just wondered how the little surprise was coming along?' she giggled coyly. 'You know how I love to be surprised.'

She shuddered at her mother-in-law's simpering words. 'Whatever do you mean Mrs P.?'

'Clive said he thought you were planning something special for my birthday?'

'Oh yes, don't we always?' Cari replied, a smile on her face showing her relief. Every year Clive's mother insisted on a surprise birthday party. Her husband had produced the most elaborate theme parties. Since his death Clive had been expected to continue the family tradition. Mrs P. of course hinted weeks beforehand as to what the theme should be. She would make a grand entrance in a ridiculous costume and lord it over her cronies for the evening. Visions of her mother-in-law dressed as Shirley Temple still had her gagging after the Hollywood Stars party from the previous year.

Yesterday's surprise delivery from Mrs. P. had sent her over the edge. She hadn't stopped to draw breath since, to make sure this birthday would be one that her mother-in-law would certainly remember.

She thought for a moment that Mrs P. knew what she'd been up to, but how could she? Cari always believed she was a witch, perhaps that was the answer!

'Look, Mrs P. I hate to appear rude but I've got a million things to do.'

'Perhaps you could ask Clive to ring me dear?' Mrs P. sounded miffed.

'Of course I will,' Cari purred back, best not to get on the wrong side of her now she thought, as she put down the phone.

That's all she needed, Mrs P. interfering at the wrong moment. In the five years she'd known Clive his mother had been a thorn in her side. Cari had lost count of the number of times she'd been told that Clive had been destined for 'better things.' The better thing in Mummy's eyes would have meant being married to anyone but Cari. Preferably a meek obedient girl who would have pandered to Mrs P.'s imagined illnesses and funny ways. The meek young thing would also have to have come from the landed gentry, something she had hoped to marry into herself.

Cari had quickly cottoned on to her mother-in-law's little schemes and had weaned Clive away from Mummy and her clinging arms. Now, all her carefully nurtured plans would have been for nothing if 'Mummy' turned up too soon.

Checking the answer-phone, she found a message from the travel agent, the hotel she'd requested was booked along with all the travel documents for the last minute journey. All she had to do was to pop into the agency on her way to the airport. Everything was ready.

Clinking her champagne glass against Clive's, Cari gazed into his eyes. The restaurant overlooking the moonlit beach was the perfect setting. She smiled with satisfaction. 'Do you like your surprise, dear?'

'It's perfect, what more could a man want than his beautiful wife, a lovely meal and the prospect of a few days away from it all revisiting our honeymoon hotel.' Clive swallowed his champagne and looked at his watch. 'About now someone else is in for a surprise!'

'Oh Clive, I hope I haven't been too hard on your mother but these silly whims of hers have got to stop. This year seemed the ideal time to do it.'

'You'll never stop surprising me, Cari,' he took her hand and kissed her fingertips. How you managed it all in twenty-four hours astounds me. I'm stuck in Paris at the conference, leaving you to make all the preparations, no wonder you flipped. I don't know how you did it, booking a last-minute flight, sorting out Mother and spending your birthday money. Did I say how fantastic the "new you" looks by the way?'

'Yes, but you can tell me again, later when we're alone. I did worry that you wouldn't go along with my plan. I just couldn't spend another year pandering to your mother when it was my birthday as well. Just sending you a note telling you to meet me at the airport seemed a bit risky. But this year will be the last one we spend as a couple. Next year there will be the three of us. I just wanted to spend some quality time alone with you.'

Clive reached out and gently touched her stomach. 'I still can't believe it, mother will be livid, she hates the thought of being a grandmother.'

'She'll be even more livid when she bursts into our lounge in thirty minutes from now expecting a Calamity Jane birthday party. All she's going to find is the side of beef she sent me yesterday for the barbecue, neatly chopped and stored in our freezer. Oh, and a Happy Birthday Granny card on the kitchen table!'

Lili Marlene
Jeannie Johnson

'She is always there. Look at her, trying to appear as though she is waiting for a sweetheart when in fact... Lili, my darling, we know why you are there, we know what you are.'

Hans made a crude sign and grinned down at the darkening street below where the woman, who they had christened Lili Marlene after their favourite marching song, stood beneath the lamplight across the road from the main gate.

Johan was less condemning. 'She does what she has to do. I admire her.'

Winter was breathing frost over the windowpanes and the cobbles were slick with the first fall of snow. Her coat collar was turned up, hiding most of her face, but her eyes shone. Even from this distance he could tell they were not quite brown, but hazel, a warmer colour in his estimation.

The cold easterly that penetrated ill-fitting doors and stung exposed faces chose that moment to tug at her collar. For a brief moment Johan glimpsed more of her pale sad face and saw even more of it when a soldier passed on his way back to barracks. Smiling, she turned down the swiftly bundled up collar.

Like a rose opening in summer; first her face, and later...

'I hear she does not charge very much,' said Hans as he picked the last crumbs of their evening meal from his jacket.

'How would you know?'

Hans laughed. 'I have women falling at my feet. Why would I need to pay?'

Johan shook his head and watched as Lili and her customer walked away, probably to some warm doorway, their coupling melting into the darkening night.

Hans rubbed at his stomach. 'God, I'm still hungry. Do you want that?'

He pointed to the last crust of bread and the stiff rind of a Bavarian cheese Johan had left on his plate.

'Help yourself.'

His breath misted the window. His finger made a squeaking sound on the glass as he drew a curvaceous female form in the dewy wetness.

'Is that a picture of what you think she looks like?' asked Hans, spraying crumbs against his comrade's cheek as he scrutinised the damply fading outline. 'You know. Without her clothes.'

'I can dream, and anyway, it isn't just about her body; she's a comfort. Even you must admit that.'

'Comfort? Yes! Something warm and cuddly to dream about, but that is all you can do my friend; dream of what she's got hidden beneath that warm winter coat.'

'It's a Wehrmacht overcoat. Did you notice?'

Hans shook his head as he swigged back the last of the coffee, grimaced at the taste, then belched. 'Can't say I did.'

'I don't believe you. You *pretend* not to notice or to care. But you do. Deep down you do. You're as affected by the sight of her as I am.'

Hans laughed. 'Wouldn't mind bedding her, but you're talking like a lovesick fool. Now where's the sense in that?'

Johan shrugged and bent to push what was left of the firewood into the gaping mouth of the potbellied stove that must have been years old in the Great War, let alone in this one.

'In a way I am. She brightens my nights, my days too as far as that goes.'

Hans sniggered. 'But only from afar, my friend.'

Johan didn't answer. Although the windows were ill-fitting, jolted by the incessant bombing, he would bear the draught if it meant another glimpse of Lili. Hans wasn't far wrong about his feelings for the girl. He often imagined strolling arm in arm with her, enjoying her voice, her smell and the touch of her hand. Fantasies helped keep the fear at bay.

Hans played his harmonica for a few minutes while Johan settled himself in a chair and read a few pages of a bible given him by the padre attached to the barracks.

"For your comfort, my son."

Flicking through the pages, he came across half a dozen well-remembered passages, and although he tried to read them, his thoughts kept wandering.

He only became aware that Hans had crossed the room and stood at the window when he began playing Lili Marlene. The words that had started as a poem back in 1915 ran through his mind.

Underneath the lamplight, by the barrack gate,
Darling, I remember the way you used to wait,

The haunting refrain lured him to the window in time to see a shadow fall across the frozen snow. She was back!

The snow had stopped falling and it must have got a little warmer because she emerged out from her coat collar, her face upturned to the lamplight. She stood very still, looking in their direction.

Hans stopped playing. 'She's quite good-looking, if you like that type,' he said.

'She can see us,' said Johan.

Hans moved so that more of his body filled the frame. 'Do you think so?'

Johan waved. She waved back.

'Well, I'll be damned,' said Hans sounding totally surprised. 'She does see us.'

He waved too. Again she waved back.

A questioning look crossed his face. 'Do you think she can hear us?'

'I doubt it,' said Johan who was finding it impossible to tear his eyes away from her face. His heart was pounding against his ribs, the blood coursing through his veins and warming a body that had got used to cold and deprivation. If only he could go down to her. If only he wasn't confined to barracks.

'Lili! Lili!' shouted Hans and banged on the window, grappled with the catch and flung it open.

Both men squeezed their arms between the bars.

'She hears us,' said Johan.

He turned his eyes to his blond-haired friend. Some bigwig in the SS hierarchy had once declared him the epitome of Aryan masculinity. That wasn't what they called him now.

Johan sighed. 'I think I'm falling in love with her.'

Hans eyed him quizzically. 'How can you say that? You don't even know her.' Abruptly he turned his gaze back to the girl, his expression inscrutable, as though he was unmoved by Johan's words.

'She's got the most beautiful face I am ever likely to see again, and you have to agree, my friend, I might never see another woman ever again.'

'You sound like an actor in a Greek tragedy.' Hans's voice was firm and brave, but Johan knew he was as scared as he was. Hans went on. 'I refuse to be moved by her. She is pleasant enough to look at, and that is all. Not that it matters much.' He spat in the direction of the stove, his sputum sizzling on the hot iron surface. 'She's either married or got the pox. That's what I think.'

'She might be married and hungry like everyone else.' Johan's voice was soft and he looked at her as though he really knew her, had shared her life and shared her bed. 'Widowed perhaps? And as for being diseased... well... she's like hundreds of women in this city, thousands all over Germany; trying to survive by any means she can. That's what war does to a woman. That's what it does to everyone.'

Hans made a mocking sound. Unseen by Johan, his eyes betrayed what he truly felt, but he must be strong. He must continue to act as though their being here was a mistake, a joke on someone's part, at worse a misunderstanding of the circumstances. He began to play Lili Marlene. The woman beneath the streetlight began tapping her foot in time with the music.

'I think that coat belonged to her husband or her lover,' Johan said softly. 'He probably died on the Russian front. Yes. That's it. He was killed on the Russian front and has left her with four hungry mouths to feed.'

Hans stopped playing and sneered. 'How do you know that?'

Johan shook his head. 'I don't *know* that, I'm simply guessing; trying to form some picture of her life, to know who she really is.'

'She's a whore!'

'No matter. She helps me cope with what I am facing and if I should ever leave here, I will do my best to seek her out and take care of her.'

Hans returned to being his dismissive self. 'We know who she is; she's a whore.'

Johan clenched his jaw and counted to ten. There were times when Hans simply refused to see anything except hard facts. He'd met dozens like him, stiff military types afraid of declaring their true feelings in front of brother soldiers.

'She hasn't always been a whore! It's the war that's changed her like it has all of us. We above all others should know that. It changed me! It changed you!'

Hans looked taken aback, the blue eyes blinking as though Johan had slapped his cheek with the proverbial gauntlet. He appeared to recover. 'And now we must face the consequences. We disobeyed orders. One part of me is ashamed of that...'

Johan's eyes glowed with anger. 'And the other part?'

Hans shrugged, but refused to meet his gaze. 'It sickened me.'

It had become his habit to block out the memories of that fateful day when they had allowed – actually *allowed* a family to escape a goods train headed for Auschwitz. They had pretended not to see them run off into the adjoining forest, but someone had. They'd been reported. It didn't matter that they'd only just returned from the Russian front where Hans had won himself the coveted Iron Cross. Nothing mattered to some people except that they hadn't been cruel enough.

Forget it! What was the point of remembering? Self-destructive. Just self-destructive.

When Johan turned his gaze back to Lili, she was on the arm of an army corporal. He fancied she glanced up at him before she walked off as if to say, '*This is business. I have to survive. But I'll come back to you. I promise I'll come back to you.*'

Hans slapped at his shoulder. 'Now there's a shame! Your sweetheart is gone, but there's no need to worry. It won't take long. She will be back very soon.'

The glass shook in its frame as he shut the window.

Johan thrust his hands into his pockets and sat down, a faraway look in his eyes.

Hans picked up his harmonica. Again the same marching tune, the lyrics unsung but snatched from the air; favourite lines singing in their minds.

… Soldier boys are marching…

… you hold me tight…

…we say goodnight…

I love you still, I always will,

My Lili of the lamplight, my own Lili Marlene.

The sudden wail of air-raid sirens preceded the dowsing of lights. No one bothered to open the locked door and take them down to the shelters, not that they expected them to. There was no time nowadays and who cared about two prisoners waiting for court-martial?

Johan reopened the window, his eyes searching the darkness where she usually stood.

'I'm going to write to her,' he blurted. 'I'm going to tell her what she means to me.'

Hans laughed. 'You're quite ridiculous!'

Johan spun round on him, his eyes blazing. 'Still the man of iron, eh Hans? Still the unswerving loyalty to Fuehrer and Fatherland!'

Hans was visibly shaken. 'No need to get so emotional.'

A little moonlight filtered through a fringe of ragged grey clouds silvering the black shapes of American bombers.

Johan dragged the table and a chair over to the window in order to get the best of what light there was, found a piece of paper and a pencil and began to write.

Hans avoided looking at him. Cloaked in darkness he closed his eyes and prayed, all the fear he'd held in now pulsing in sweaty drops through his skin.

'I've written her a note,' Johan said once he'd finished. 'I'm going to ask Otto to give it to her. I'm sure he will. If not... if I do not return... will you?'

'Can I read it?'

'I'd rather you didn't. I'll leave it here. Promise not to peek?'

Annoyed by Johan's demand Hans threw himself onto the bed. 'You're a bloody idiot.'

Satisfied with what he'd done and still thinking of Lili, Johan lay down on his own bed and closed his eyes. In his dreams the war was over and he was with Lili, the girl who had given him the strength to get through this – if he got through it.

In the morning the time they had dreaded finally came. Both were called together to face the charges brought against them. It had been Johan's intention to give their guard the letter, but it was not Otto who came for them but a surly young officer of the SS who had few words for men he regarded as traitors.

The haggard face of the SS major they stood before was totally at odds with his neatly pressed uniform. Weary of war, though afraid to admit it, he carried out his orders like a clock marking time. Eventually it would stop and so would everything else.

'Examples must be made... but one example will be enough.' He looked directly at Hans. 'A man awarded the Iron Cross can be forgiven.' He turned sharply back to Johan. There was no need to say anything else.

Stunned and shaken, Hans was back in the room he'd shared with Johan when the shot rang out. He'd been ordered to pack his kitbag and make ready to leave. He was too shocked to feel elated, too sad and angry that Johan was dead.

The day dragged on. He sat on the bed, too numb to move. Through the open window came the sound of sporadic firing and buildings crumbling to dust. Night was falling.

Sensing a fluttering of movement, he drew closer. A figure stood beneath the lamplight, coat collar turned up around her face. His heart skipped a beat. He was alive, and Lili, the girl who had given him hope, though he'd never admitted it, was standing underneath the lamplight. He had never shown his feelings as Johan had, mainly because it had seemed so futile; what was the point? The immediate danger was now past. She was his – if he so wished.

About to dash out, he remembered his harmonica, and then Johan's note. He picked up both.

The night air prickled his face with the promise of a sharp frost, but he didn't care. Never had he felt so alive and so grateful. Lili had given him strength; it seemed only right that he should thank her.

'Lili?'

Letting the collar fall from her face, she turned round. 'I'll be Lili if you like, darling.' The woman facing him was at least forty years of age and showing all the ravages of a hard-lived life.

Hans gulped. Surely there was some mistake. Surely they hadn't been so far away that they could mistake her features for anything but handsome? 'I'm sorry,' he said falteringly. 'I thought you were someone else.'

She made a dismissive sound and turned away.

Not knowing what else to do, he walked around the block, climbing over rubble that was once proud buildings. Close to half an hour later he was rounding the corner that would bring him back opposite the barrack gates.

Disappointed and confused, he pulled his harmonica out of his pocket and began to play his favourite marching song, his feet stepping out in time with the music.

Keeping his eyes lowered he played *Lili Marlene*, bits of cracked pavement and people's feet passing beneath his gaze.

It wasn't until he heard a woman singing that he realised he was back where he had started from.

Taking his lips from the harmonica, he raised his eyes expecting to see the same woman he'd seen earlier.

She carried on singing.

He stared. His spirits soared. A different woman. Lili. The real Lili.

"... *my own Lili Marlene.*"

She smiled. 'I heard you playing and I saw you and your friend waving at the window. I used to hum when you played. It made me feel I was not alone and that someone cared.'

Although her face was pale as porcelain, she still struck him as being beautiful.

'We felt like that too. My friend left you this,' he said and handed her the note.

She looked surprised. 'For me?'

He nodded whilst marvelling at the blueness of her eyes and the long fingers unfolding the letter.

She read it quickly. 'Where is he now?'

'Gone.'

'I heard a shot. Did they shoot him?'

'He was an honourable man. He didn't deserve it.'

Her expression turned grim. 'None of us deserve this.' She waved carelessly at their bleak surroundings.

Hans's curiosity overwhelmed him. 'What did my friend write?'

'Didn't you read it?'

'No. It was private.'

He couldn't drag his gaze from her eyes, her hair, the clear softness of her skin. It had been easy to be contemptuous when viewing her from afar. But not now. Not close up.

'He told me he understood why I was doing what I do. It appears he even knew something of my history. He guessed that my husband was killed in Russia.'

Hans could hardly believe his ears. 'And you have four children?'

She laughed. 'No. Only one.'

'I apologise.'

'No need to.'

Her expression turned serious. 'It is sad that your friend is dead. He said he would look after me.'

'Then I will look after you. First, I will take you for coffee.'

'There is no coffee.'

He took some marks from his pocket. 'Take these.'

'Shall we...'

'I want nothing in exchange.'

She hung her head and brushed her fingers across her right eye. 'You're very kind.'

He'd never viewed himself as kind. Her description moved him, but he couldn't let his feelings show – not yet.

He slid the harmonica across his lips. 'Sing for me. Sing *Lili Marlene*.'

'For you?'

'For me. And for my friend.'

Caves
Linda Povey

'Drach means dragon,' Darren said, reading from his guide book. 'The Caves of Drach are the Caves of the Dragon.'

Alice suppressed a yawn. The journey to the famous caves of Majorca was proving longer than she'd thought. They'd had to get up early after a late night. It would help if she could have a little nap. But it seemed Darren wasn't going to let her do that.

'The underground lake reaches a depth of 46 feet.'

Any minute now he's going to start talking about stalagmites and stalactites, thought Alice.

'The stalactites...' began Darren. 'Do you know the difference between stalag...'

'You told us all in the bar last night, remember?'

Darren smiled, 'Oh, yes, sorry.'

'Actually, I think I'll try and kip for a bit. You go on reading to yourself.'

Alice closed her eyes as the Spanish coach driver sped along. She was on her honeymoon. She should be having the time of her life, and she wasn't. The truth of it was, Darren was beginning to get on her nerves. She thought of Pete and her heart pounded.

The couple they'd met up with the night before were about their age and the four of them were getting merry over jugs of Sangria. Then Alice got up to go to the loo and Pete did the same. They got lost on their way back to the hotel bar and found themselves by the pool. Pete grabbed hold of her and began kissing her. They'd ended up making love on one of the sunbeds.

What a risk to take! Anyone could have seen them. And they had to be quick, or they'd have been missed. But that just added to the thrill. When they got back, Darren was giving

195

Helen a potted history of the island. Helen's eyes looked a little glazed over. Alice had thought it was the Sangria, now she wasn't so sure.

'Here we are then.'

Alice opened her eyes. From the dryness of her mouth, she knew she must have slept.

'Enjoy your little snooze?'

'Mm. We're here, you say?'

'Yes, exciting, isn't it?'

Exciting, thought Alice, you don't know the meaning of the word. Stop it! she told herself at once. Just try and enjoy the day. Then, as they entered the caves, she remembered the touch of Pete's hands on her skin and shivered.

'Bit cool for you is it? Here.' Darren took off his jumper and placed it over Alice's shoulders.

He'd brought an array of camera equipment with him and was soon snapping and videoing everything in sight. Everything except me, Alice noted.

'These caves are amazing,' he said into the microphone of the camcorder. 'You just have to marvel at the shapes that centuries of dripping water have produced.'

As they went deeper in, Darren added his own personal commentary to that of the guide. 'Of course, Alice, Majorca's riddled with caves. There's another group not far from here called the Cuevas de Hams. Cuevas is caves in Spanish, you know.'

'Yes, I did know,' said Alice irritably. 'I'm missing what the guide's telling us with you talking.'

Darren gave her a hurt look and Alice felt ashamed of herself. She linked arms with him and said, 'Help me over this slippery bit, will you?'

They'd reached the underground lake and the guide was giving them a few statistics which Darren was disputing.

'Forty-six feet deep, are you sure about that?' he shouted out.

'Sh, sh,' hissed Alice. 'Of course he's right. You told me yourself earlier on.'

The light in the caves gradually dimmed and then there was total darkness. Alice felt an arm around her and imagined it was Pete's. Pools of light appearing over the lake revealed it to be Darren's, of course.

'Scared, were you?' he asked.

'Not at all,' said Alice, shaking him off.

The lights came from three vessels, slowly gliding into view as a string orchestra began playing. The effect should have been romantic and magical, but all Alice could think of was the touch of Pete's lips on hers. She wished he was here instead of Darren.

'It's a pity Helen and Pete both suffer from claustrophobia. They'd have loved this,' said Darren, as if picking up on her thoughts.

'It's not their fault,' Alice snapped. She had a sudden mental picture of Pete and Helen together on the boat trip they'd decided to go on instead, and felt an irrational pang of jealousy.

As they made their way back to the entrance, Darren held up his camera and asked Alice, 'Do you want to be in on this one?'

Since he hadn't taken a single photo of her yet, Alice thought she might. Facing him, she struck what she thought was a sexy model pose.

'No, no, go over there. Pretend to be looking at that.' Darren pointed to an unusual rock formation in a far corner.

Alice walked off in a huff. There was no way she was going to be an incidental in one of his pictures.

'What a wonderful experience that was,' Darren remarked as they made their journey back to the hotel.

'Huh, huh,' said Alice.

Pete and Helen were waiting for them as the coach arrived. Helen's smile of pleasure when she saw Darren told Alice that the glazed expression last night must have been due to the Sangria.

As for herself, she was delighted to see Pete again. And the look of happiness on her husband's face told her he felt exactly the same.

Sex Versus Chocolate
Dawn Hudd

Juliet slowly uncurled the wrapper from the chocolate, and delicately placed it on her tongue. She savoured the smooth velvety feel as it melted and slid down her throat. Sitting back with a sigh she surveyed the mountain of wrappers on the sofa. That was the last one.

Chocolate – expensive, handmade and preferably a gift from someone special – was to Juliet an almost orgasmic experience. But, unlike good sex, which left you with a warm, contented glow, all Juliet felt after a chocolate binge was guilt and ten pounds heavier. With another sigh, she heaved herself up and gathered the colourful wrappers. She tossed them into the waste bin and picked up the box. Empty. Just like my love life, she thought. Unfortunately, chocolate instead of sex for the last six months had had a disastrous effect on Juliet's waistline.

'I've got to do something about it, Liz,' wailed Juliet the next day. The two friends had met up for their weekly treat at Carlo's Coffee Shop.

'What? The weight or the lack of a fella?' asked Liz.

'Both, really, but without a man in my life all I do is eat.'

'And when you're in love all you do is go doe-eyed and forget the food,' added Liz. 'But look at the last three. Joe was a disaster. He trashed your car, flooded your house and almost killed your mum's cat…'

'… with the vacuum cleaner. I know. He was a bit clumsy, but he was really sweet. I just couldn't afford to keep him around – and he wasn't exactly The One, was he?'

'Heaven help you, you could do better than him.'

'I know. And Pete. Well Pete, he just got irritating. Always going on about my size. Always wanting me to lose just a bit more. He had to go.'

'Especially when he suggested the boob job,' Liz smiled.

'And he wanted *me* to pay for it,' Juliet reddened as she remembered how he'd made the suggestion, loudly, at her mother's birthday party. 'But Steve…'

'Look, Juliet,' said Liz, taking her friend's hand, 'some things are best left in the memory bag, eh? Don't drag it out again and upset yourself.'

'Steve never told me he was married,' said Juliet firmly.

'Separated. But I thought we weren't going to talk about him.' Liz stood up and took a note out of her purse. She dropped it onto the table for the coffee and pastries they'd just devoured and announced, 'Get your coat, girl, we're going shopping.'

Two hours later they sat in Liz's kitchen nursing a low calorie hot chocolate. The table was covered in magazines.

'When you said we were going shopping, I thought you meant for clothes. Or shoes.' Juliet picked up the closest magazine. 'Slimming World? Weight Watchers?'

'Look, Juliet, I might not be able to improve your sex life, but I can help you do something about your weight. Or at least help you to feel better about yourself.' She opened a copy of Dieters Delight. 'Did you know you can still have chocolate on this diet?'

After three full weeks of dieting Juliet was back in Liz's kitchen.

'It's not working, is it?' Liz plonked a cup of coffee in front of Juliet. 'What's the problem? I really thought you'd feel better if you lost a bit of weight.'

'You're right. I just don't have the incentive. It's a man I need, not a diet.'

'You can't rely on love for weight-loss,' said Liz. 'What happens if you never meet anyone else? You'll end up one of those people they have to hoist out through the bedroom window!'

'Don't,' Juliet looked hurt.

'I'm sorry. I was only trying to help, but as long as you compare every man in the street to Steve you won't get close enough to anyone to fall in love. Oh, Juliet,' sighed Liz, 'why did you let him go?'

'He lied to me,' spat Juliet.

'He neglected to tell you he had baggage. That's not the same.'

Juliet stared at Liz, who changed the topic.

'So, if you can't lose weight with the mags, how *are* you going to do it?' asked Liz.

'There's a local slimming club listed in here. I thought I'd give it a go. Maybe if other people are watching me it might spur me on a bit.'

'That's a great idea,' said Liz. 'I could come with you.'

Juliet looked at her skinny friend and laughed. 'I don't think so! No, I'll be OK on my own. It's only down the road in Browning Street. I might even know some of the people already, it's so local.'

'If you're sure?'

'Yep. Look, there's even a choice of times for the classes. I can go to the second one on Thursday, straight after work.' Juliet ripped the page out of the magazine and put it in her bag. 'Yes. That's what I'll do.'

Juliet took a deep breath and got out of the car. She'd managed to get reasonably close to the church hall where the class was being held, but it was a couple of minutes walk. She never was good at going alone to new places, but skinny Liz would have looked daft coming with her.

As she turned into Browning Street the stragglers from the previous class were leaving. Juliet's heart did a flutter as she caught sight of the back of one of them as he turned the corner. No, it couldn't have been him. The shoulders were too broad, and Steve never wore black. It was just the colour of his hair that had caught her off-guard. And Steve was, always had been, slim. No. He wouldn't have been at a slimming club.

The class was just as she had imagined it would be. Mostly women, mostly middle-aged, and mostly overweight. It was a slimming class, after all. Noone there was hugely obese, and there were two or three that obviously had either lost the weight or never needed to in the first place and were using it as a social club. Juliet filled in her details on the form she'd been given at the door and joined the line to be weighed.

Juliet felt encouraged to find that she was only eight pounds over her ideal weight.

'People with low self-esteem often have a different perception of their body image to those around them,' offered Cara, the club leader. 'I'd be delighted to have you as a member if you really want to lose that half stone,' she continued, 'but it shouldn't take you long. How about I sign you up just for the three month trial and see how you go? What's your worst calorie habit?'

Juliet had the decency to look suitably guilty as she replied, 'I just can't resist chocolate.'

'Chocolate is a comfort food. It increases the levels of serotonin in the brain, which is what gives you that feel-good factor,' lectured Cara. 'You need to find out what triggers the craving and avoid it.' She handed Juliet a diet sheet.

'At least it's getting you out and meeting people,' said Liz as Juliet told her about the class.

'I suppose so. I'll give it till the end of the three month trial.'

'Good,' said Liz, and made them a fresh coffee.

The next Thursday, Juliet was early. She managed to park her car just a few yards from the church hall and was able to watch the previous class as they ambled out, some looking glum and some smiling. You can tell the losers from the gainers, she thought. Suddenly she ducked down in the seat. It *was* him! Steve. It had been six months, but he was unmistakable – even if he had put on what looked like two stone. And, she realised, he looked miserable. He turned in the opposite direction without even glancing down the road, and within a minute he had gone.

Shaken, Juliet joined the weigh-in line.

'Well,' said Carla, 'No loss, but no gain. Exactly the same.'

The class went by without Juliet noticing, and soon she was home. She reached for the bar of chocolate in the fridge, but for some strange reason she suddenly didn't feel like eating it.

Saturday, at Carlo's, Juliet turned down the raspberry Danish that Liz offered.

'It must be love!' exclaimed Liz. 'Come on, spill.'

'No,' said Juliet with a grim face. 'Far from it. Remind me. Why did I dump Steve?'

'You said, and I quote, I can't trust somebody who can't be honest from the start.'

'But he was married, and he didn't tell me.'

'He'd been separated for more than a year; he was waiting for a divorce, and there were no kids.'

'He didn't tell me for seven months, and he wouldn't have then if we hadn't seen his ex in the shopping centre. Was I wrong?'

'I don't know. Hey, what's brought all this on?'

'Dieting makes me depressed, I suppose.' Juliet sipped at her skinny latte and changed the subject.

The following week Juliet arrived with fifteen minutes to spare. This time she didn't duck when the class came out. She watched a dozen or more class members stroll out, but with just five minutes to spare before her own class began, there was no sign of him. She was about to get out of the car when the hall door opened. He was there, and this time he turned towards her. Juliet gasped at the look of shock on his face as he turned away and walked in the opposite direction. With shaking hands she started the car and drove home.

'I knew something had happened, you sly thing,' exclaimed Liz at their next meeting.

'The trouble,' said Juliet 'is that I don't know now if what I miss most is Steve or chocolate. I just didn't realise.'

'It might not be too late.'

'It's been six months. And I dumped him, remember?' Juliet sat clutching a cold coffee. 'He ran a mile when he saw me. And he's bound to have someone else by now.'

'He hasn't.'

Juliet looked at her friend, shocked. 'What do you mean?'

'I mean I asked around. He's single. And has been for a very long time. Tom, you remember his mate, Tom? Well, I bumped into him a while back. And Steve is still *very* single.'

This would be her last class, Juliet decided as she arrived deliberately early, managing to park her car in almost exactly the same position as the previous week. He's going to think I'm stalking him, she thought. If he turns up at all.

With five minutes to go before he ought to walk out of the door, Juliet's heart was hammering. She started the car to go home, but sat there with the engine idling. Then she saw him as he walked around the corner. He hadn't been to his class.

This was a mistake. Juliet started to pull out, and then stopped. What was he carrying? She watched as he ran towards her car, the paper round the flowers flapping as he went, and the carrier bag knocking against his legs. She wound down her window. It was a moment before she could speak.

'Steve. I...'

'Um. Juliet,' he interrupted. 'I was, um, I was wondering if you'd like these.' He pushed the flowers through the open window.

'Pink carnations!'

'Still your favourites?' he asked.

'Yes,' whispered Juliet.

'Oh,' he looked awkward, but rummaged around in the carrier. 'And I got you these. Thought you looked as if you could do with them.' This time he smiled as he handed her a box. 'Can we talk?'

Hours later, as she lay in bed, she mused on her favourite subjects. Which was best? Sex or chocolate? She couldn't decide, and as Steve leaned across and popped one of the deliciously creamy, expensive, handmade chocolates that he'd bought her into her mouth, she realised – there was no need to choose. Both together, please.

La Formicaria
Penny Feeny

Once upon a time La Formicaria had been a boathouse. Now its timbers were quietly rotting and ants filed regularly through cracks in the wood. They even marched across the sleeping faces of the girls crammed into two small bedrooms. The girls had been warned not to let a crumb drop, but often they forgot and took their siesta among the debris of fruit cores and nibbled *biscotti*. Frequently they woke screaming at the tip-toeing of a thousand tiny feet and had to comb ants out of each other's hair.

La Formicaria lurched above the water at the far end of the harbour. The crescent of pink and gold stuccoed villas swelled in style and splendour as it curved along the shore. Like the yachts that nudged each other's moorings with wet noses, the most lavish were to be found towards the town. The Hotel Marina, with its canopied entrance and wrought-iron balconies, commanded a prime location. It was not widely known that its summer staff had been herded out to the former boathouse to free up beds for high season.

The girls were young, foreign, and still naive enough to view everything that happened to them as an adventure. In skimpy vests and shorts they would lean over the salt-whitened rails of the creaking veranda, their cigarette smoke spiralling upwards, and spy on the yacht people. They had been warned against the veranda too, liable at any moment to crumble into the sea, but they enjoyed the view and the sensation of a life lived precariously.

The yacht people did not sleep in infested beds. They had crew to set their sails and order their provisions and pour their cocktails, clinking with ice. Yacht people, it seemed, had very little to do except stretch out on sun loungers by day and dress up at night for dinner and dancing in the Hotel Marina. There was only one exception: one woman who sought the shade at all cost, and the girls called her, after the name of her boat, Helen of Troy.

Helen of Troy's face was nearly always hidden under a wide-brimmed straw hat. Only at breakfast, when the sun was still gentle, did she leave it off. She would sit drinking orange juice, her freckled arms pale and bare, while her husband stood behind her and brushed her long red hair with slow, even strokes. Every morning without fail she would sit and sip and he would brush and finally pin the coils of hair to the top of her head.

Later, the yacht would glide out of the mouth of the bay, its mast tilting so close the girls could almost reach out to touch it. Sometimes Helen lay on deck, under the broad shadow of a white umbrella; sometimes they watched her step onto the quay, her arms and legs decorously covered, and disappear into a café or a taxi. Shopping, they sighed, and wondered if it was ever possible to be bored with such wealth.

They looked out for her too, when they were on their evening shift at the Marina, clearing tables and washing dishes. Helen and her husband would always sit in the same spot by the window, where they could watch their boat rocking on the black water, glittering with reflected lights. Helen's hair was piled high and delicate strands of gold cascaded from her ears and around her neck. She stayed mostly silent; he was the expansive one, talking rapidly and earnestly, his agitated hands coming regularly to rest over hers, as if to say: she is mine.

Daniel, blessed with easy charm and boyish looks, was a drifter. He had drifted in and out of La Formicaria so many times that the girls had let him have a key. He was a comfort when the latest affair had failed and, with his guitar, he was company on a night off or during a long hot sleepy afternoon. He left his belongings for days on end in a corner of their basement, a room so dim and lapped by water that risking ants upstairs seemed preferable.

The girls rarely entered the basement. They guessed he entertained women there – they could hear soft voices or the chords of his guitar – but as he gave them money from time to time for the privilege and as their accommodation was provided free, they did not complain. The discovery, early one evening, of a single long gold earring glinting on the stairs was cause for speculation, but Daniel wasn't telling. He smiled and shrugged when they teased him about his fancy girlfriend, as if there might well be others.

That night at dinner, Helen of Troy wore a pair of gold hoops that swung languidly as she gazed out of the window, her hand passive beneath her husband's. The night after, she wore a flash of emeralds, then a cluster of opals and aquamarines. The girls kept tally and grew inquisitive. They rooted around in dark corners when Daniel was out and finally found the hoard collected in an old shoe box: carefully wrought swirls of gold, tear-drops of pearl and jade, the glitter of crystal.

They watched Helen stepping ashore most mornings now, escaping the tedium of another fishing trip. She could often be glimpsed ordering a cappuccino or mailing postcards, but they never found out how she managed to slip unseen into their very own basement. They supposed she indulged her passion with Daniel through the siesta, while they slept exhausted from early shifts and late night skivvying. They pictured her long creamy limbs spread across the rotten floorboards, wearing only a gold chain around her neck, her flaming locks loosened, her make-up kissed off. Afterwards he would smuggle her into a taxi for the short distance back to the yacht, her booty secreted for a rainy day.

Once the girls had envied the experience of yachting life, of tax exile, of being cosseted by quantities of money and admiration. Now, as they rubbed suncream into each other's blistered shoulders and shrieked at finding spiders in their shoes, they began to notice Helen's impatience with the hair-brushing ritual at breakfast, the frantic wandering of her glance at dinner. They even began to feel sorry for her.

The slim figure walking along the quayside with a slight swagger was not one they recognised, until she turned onto the gangway. With her elfin crop and lack of jewellery, she looked like a teenage boy. Sharing the binoculars, leaning perilously over the veranda rail, the girls watched an explosion take place on the Helen of Troy. The husband, dark and effortlessly suntanned, throwing up his hands, yelling in horror. The wife, pale, handing over a bundle: a thick coil of fiery hair. Snatches of fury skimmed across the ripples of the bay. Even the other yacht people, so studiously self-regarding, now craned their necks in curiosity.

For a few moments the girls believed that Helen would shrug off her husband's outrage and return to dry land to follow Daniel, her shorn head high, her hands empty. But when he began to sob, when his threats turned to pleading, she drew him instead below deck, away from enquiring eyes. On the wooden table, catching hints of gold from the sun, lay the abandoned plait.

The couple did not eat dinner in the hotel that night. Quite early the next morning, as the girls were bundling soiled laundry into wicker baskets, the yacht slipped its moorings and, because there was no breeze, motored noisily out towards the open sea.

When Daniel returned for his possessions in the basement, disappointed after empty hours of waiting at the bus station, he was already too late. The girls had spent a pleasant afternoon sifting through the contents of the shoebox, sharing out the spoils.

Life's a Beach
Kelly Rose Bradford

I have a sign above my monitor at work. It says *Life's a Bitch*.
Sarah in accounts gave it to me after Dan and I split up. I stared
hard at it as Julie nattered on at me over our partition.

'So, are you up for it, then?' I heard her ask, her nasal tones
finally penetrating into my reverie.

'Up for what?'

'The Beach Party, stupid,' she rolled her eyes and flicked
her hair back like a character on an American kids TV show. I
see a lot of them now I'm on my own. There have been nights
when Nickelodeon has been my saviour.

'Which beach?' My geography wasn't great, but even I
knew that, here in central London, getting the sand between
your toes usually involved a couple of hours stuck on the
motorway.

Julie dropped a flier on to my desk.

'Tonight. We're all going. Meet you in the wine bar
opposite at eight? We can get changed in the loos there.'

Get changed? I read the flier with a wrinkled nose and
furrowed brow:

> *Hot Summer Nights At Ocean's night-club.*
> *Join us for some Sex on the Beach, Sea Breezes and much*
> *more.*
> *Have some Fun in the Sun at Oceans*
> *Bring Your Bikini and a towel!*
> *10pm –2am.*

Good Grief! I was thirty-five years old. I hadn't been in a night-
club in years. And I didn't even own a bikini. Well, actually, I
did. Left over from my honeymoon fifteen years ago. It was
pink with a white tropical print on it. And what's more it was

209

packed away in my loft, where it could stay for all eternity as far as I was concerned.

'I don't think so,' I muttered, flicking the flier back over the partition.

'Why not? You won't be out of place or anything. There's always lots of older women there.'

Julie dropped the paper back on my desk and sashayed off, her thin legs wobbling dangerously in her frighteningly high heels. Lots of older women there! The cheeky young minx. Oh to be eighteeen and single and have the world at your feet. Sure beat being thirty-five and single with the world's weight bearing on your shoulders.

I looked at the advert again. What the hell, I thought.

'OK,' I called after Julie, 'I'll be there.'

One of the best things about working in London is having everything on your doorstep. And that includes the miracle that is the Drop-In Beauty Centre just across the road from my office.

I'd struggle to pluck my eyebrows, shave my legs and slap some make-up on in under an hour at home, but thanks to the Drop-In Centre I am waxed, buffed and polished in less than sixty minutes.

I've never really been a big fan of fake tan – I don't see the attraction of the Dale Winton-esque polished mahogany look, but my therapist has done a fab job. Despite having to work on a cellulite ridden canvas. I have been airbrushed a discreet shade of walnut. My entire body is smooth and hair-free – well, not entirely hair-free. What I do have left has been styled into what they call a landing strip. Not that I intend to have anything landing in that region, you understand, but, frankly, my thigh-brows and tummy beard were getting too much even for me to stomach, let alone complete strangers in a night club.

I've even gone as far as to have a manicure and pedicure with a French finish on both.

'Crikey!' said Julie when I re-emerged in the office.

*   *   *

As a precaution I've bought a new bikini. A black halter neck with high cut pants and a matching black sarong with tassels and beads. I didn't know if the old one in the loft would still fit fifteen years on. Nothing else does from that period in my life. Without even trying, I've lost a stone since Dan had left me. I should have got rid of him years ago. Where WeightWatchers and Slimming World had failed, Dan had succeeded in spectacular fashion – not only have I lost the fifteen stone of ugly fat that was him, I've also shifted fourteen pounds of my own. And as I twirl in front of my mirror at home, I have to admit I look good for a thirty-five year old 'older woman'.

She was twenty, the girl he left me for. Reed thin, blonde hair extensions and boobs pushed up under her chin. She walked with the strange gait of a catwalk model; kind of leaning backwards with a jutting hip thrust forward. He said he'd fallen in love with her without realising it, he didn't know how it had happened. I didn't care how it had happened. I just wanted to know why. What had I done? Wasn't I pretty enough, sexy enough, thin enough, young enough? But of course it wasn't me. It was him. He was sorry, apparently. So very sorry.

It gave me a blast of confidence thinking about him and her. Thinking about the night he'd told me. How frumpy and worn I'd felt, sitting there in my nightie waiting for him to come home, having pulled back the curtain and peered out every time a car had stopped outside. Desperately hoping he'd just been delayed at work, whilst the little jumping feelings in my tummy and the dull ache in my heart tried to tell me the truth.

Looking at myself in the mirror, all tanned and lithe, eyes bright and teeth white against a sheeny brown face, the anger and the hurt made me all the more determined to go and enjoy myself.

We wore regular clothes over our bikinis and converged on the wine bar at eight. Several glasses later we felt brave enough to scuttle, giggling, to the Ladies where we stripped off our

211

suits, tied on sarongs and pulled our winter coats back on before running across the road to the club.

'I've had a bikini wax!' confided Fiona from sales before shrieking with laughter.

'So have I!' I squealed.

'Oh my God – did you have an American or Brazilian?'

'Er, I don't know – an Airport I think – I've got a landing strip!'

Everyone screamed with laughter.

'I've gone all the way!' Fiona admitted, 'the whole lot. I felt like a turkey being plucked for Christmas. She was ever so nice though, the woman who did it. She was telling me all about her herbaceous borders!'

'Hers or yours?' demanded Jackie-the-temp.

We were nearly hysterical as we joined the queue outside the club. Despite the weather, some girls were parading up and down the line in their bikinis and no coat. I wondered where they were keeping their lipstick and powder compacts.

That's when I saw her. Doing her strange back-tilting walk, wearing what looked like a thin leather belt strategically wrapped around her extremities. I looked out for Dan but he was nowhere to be seen. I almost wanted to bump into him, looking as good as I did.

Once in the club we ditched our coats and self-consciously loitered round the bar. The place was heaving. The music was so loud I could feel the beat of it pounding in my chest and head.

We ordered cocktails and stood sipping them, taking in all the glistening bodies around us. She was at the end of the room with her back to me, chatting to a young guy in surfer shorts. Long short trousers, my mum would call them. She stood with her legs slightly apart, one hand on her hip, the other constantly twiddling and playing with her hair extensions. Although I couldn't hear her, her body language said it all. But the guy didn't seem to be paying any attention, he was staring right over her shoulder as she wittered on. I smiled with amusement.

When he smiled back I realised it was me he was watching. Well, I looked behind me first to make sure. But it was. He said something to her and walked over in my direction. She turned round, a haughty expression on her (orange) face. Then she saw it was me and the look turned to pure venom.

'Can I get you a drink?' he joined me at the bar. He was young. *Very* young. Late teens or early twenties.

'Thanks,' I smiled, 'Sex on the Beach,' I said, looking straight into his eyes. He was smooth and golden brown, with thick black hair, closely cut, a full mouth and tip-tilting nose. I didn't know if it was him or the effects of my intimate waxing giving me the strange tingling sensation in the depths of my bikini.

My work-mates stared wide-eyed as we took our drinks to a private booth in the corner.

'What's your name?' I asked him.

'Alex,' he said, 'and yours?'

'Rosie,' I replied. I desperately wanted to ask him how old he was, but knew I couldn't without being asked the question back. He sat close to me, our thighs touching. He stared at my face the whole time I was talking. I hadn't been in this kind of situation for a long time. Over twenty years in fact. A realisation hit me. I was at least fifteen years older than him. He was a young man out on the tiles for a good time. He didn't want a relationship with me. He hadn't been staring at me because I was the woman of his dreams who he wanted to take home to mother and marry. He had bought me a drink and steered me to a private booth because at that moment in time he fancied what he saw, the fake tanned body, the carefully straightened, shiny hair, the perfectly made-up face. He liked what he saw and he wanted a piece of it and nothing more. He didn't care that my name was Rosie, that I was thirty-five and worked for a firm of accountants. He didn't want to know that my fave meal was spaghetti bolognese and that I had a cat called Carrie.

I allowed myself to push up closer to him and smile coyly as I put my straw between my lips.

And as he didn't care, neither did I. How old he was, what he did, who he was. I put my drink down and put my hand on his thigh.

'Nice shorts,' I said, my eyes still planted firmly on his and with a smile that made my intentions clear.

He moved nearer and his mouth met mine. Cool and menthol from whatever concoction he'd been drinking. I let my hands run over his shoulders and back, through his hair and across his thighs, while his fingers snaked under the back strap of my bikini.

We moved on to the dance floor, where he danced close to me, his body pushing up against mine with an urgency I hadn't felt in a long time.

The girls were agog. Julie gave me the thumbs up, Jackie a wink, and Fiona whispered 'You dirty mare!' in my ear as she danced past me.

She was stood at the bar. I caught a couple of glimpses of her as we did our thing under the hot lights and pumping music. But I knew she was watching me, so I didn't need to watch her. We danced and kissed and caressed all night. At two a.m. I didn't want to let him go.

'Night-cap?' I suggested. He came back to my flat. For such a young man he knew the geography of a bikini inside and out. What he lacked in age, he made up for in technique and creativity, taking me on a physical adventure of the type I'd previously assumed only existed in the minds of the script writers on Sex and the City.

He left before I woke.

I lay in my bed and stretched luxuriously. It was only seven a.m. but I felt more awake and more alive than I had done in a very long time. My body ached with life and exhilaration.

On my bedside table there was a scrap of paper. It said "Alex, 652-5643. Call me. Please!"

I tore it in to tiny pieces and threw it in the bin.

Life's a Bitch said the familiar sign above my desk as I sauntered jovially into work that morning. I took a marker out of my pen pot and made a quick alteration.

Life's a Beach it says now.

Ace's Angels
Heather Lister

To be honest, I'd never have crashed my bike if I hadn't been totally mesmerised by Adrian's bum. But then again, if I'd had any kind of self-control none of this would have happened.

I don't remember which of us thought of forming a women's biker gang in the first place, but everyone agreed it was a great idea. Flushed with triumph after getting our licences, we all wanted to polish our skills and become safer and bolder. And who better to lead us than Adrian – Ace, as everyone called him – the instructor who'd got us through our tests? Ace was unassuming, not much to look at, and without a patronising bone in his body – an honorary woman in our eyes. Well, almost. The other thing I don't remember is the first time I realised that his leather-clad bottom was truly something else.

And soon Ace's Angels were born. We'd meet in town and practise slow manoeuvres and driving in traffic, all very sensible and responsible, and then at regular intervals we'd go out on the open road and let rip.

The day of the crash dawned sunny and cloudless. I looked out of the window and knew it was going to be hot – one of those days when it's brilliant once you're out on the bike, but you begrudge the whole business of struggling into leather trousers, jacket, boots and gauntlets to start with. It's necessary though, because, as Ace sternly observes, you can leave an awful lot of your skin on the road if you're not properly dressed when you come off a bike at high speed.

We met in Tesco's car park as usual. We were a motley crew that morning – all ages, shapes and sizes. There was Pamela, ex-Head of my local Primary School, who'd celebrated her retirement by upgrading from a scooter to a big touring bike. She was talking to Danielle, a tiny, diffident French

216

student given to wild gesticulations. There was raven-haired Dana, mother of five boys, with a leprechaun on her handlebars. There was Sarah, a tall, Jamaican forty-something librarian, who was laughing with middle-aged Gert, who worked at the chemist's and who was the jealous guardian of our first aid box. There was shy, sexy Ramona, who used to work in a massage parlour. And there was me – plain Jane Farmer – nurse and biker, 28, single and loving it most of the time. Seven of us, plus Ace – not a bad turn-out.

Ace was sitting on the wall, his long legs dangling. 'We'll stick together over the Severn Bridge,' he said, 'and then we can spread out a bit going up Bryn Mawr to the Devil's Elbow. Dana – can you be back marker to start with? By popular request, we'll meet at the Rooster Café at the top.'

There were murmurs of approval – this was a favourite run.

'Special focus on this ride,' continued Ace, 'watch your road positioning.'

'What's your favourite position then, darling?' asked Gert, with a dirty chuckle.

'The one where I can see danger coming, love,' returned Ace, and earned another cackle from Gert. We were all in high spirits. Good old Ace.

We got out of the city as quickly as possible, roaring over the bridge across the gleaming Severn estuary and up into the green Welsh hills. At first Ramona was leading the group. I tried to get myself into the best position, right behind Ace, but Pamela beat me to it, so at the start of the run I was treated to a view of her less lovely posterior. In my mirror I could see Danielle behind me, jockeying for position. She'd always made it clear, even in her halting English, that she appreciated our instructor's particular charms.

We all did, as a matter of fact. Sometimes during a long trip a rider has to stand up for a second or two, to allow the circulation to return to the buttocks. Whenever Ace did this, a communal sigh went through the group.

We remained fairly bunched together over the bridge, riding sedately until we began the long, tortuous route up to the Rooster Café. This was a beautiful road – broad and smooth, winding steeply upwards. The forest dropped away on the left, and the trees met high over our heads, like a cool, green cathedral.

Ace opened his throttle and forged into the lead. I am a fast rider, and I was soon right behind him. Gradually we drew away from the rest of the group, powering up the hill, getting into the rhythm of the curves. Soon there was nothing in my head but the roar of the bikes and keeping Ace in sight.

Then – the Devil's Elbow itself!

Ace leaned hard into the long, right-hand bend. He took it like a racer, shifting his weight across the saddle, his knee almost grazing the tarmac. Then, to my wonder and delight, he straightened the bike, stood up on his foot-pegs, and *wiggled.*

Have mercy! Hardly out of the bend myself, I was fixated by his gorgeous backside – two perfect spheres above the arch of his braced thighs. I must have lost concentration for a second – that's all. It was enough. I touched the gravel at the edge of the road, and felt my back wheel slide from underneath me. The bike went sideways into a low stone wall and I came off in style, cart-wheeling into the forest.

I felt myself falling, as if in a dream, and turning as I fell. Somewhere in my mind I prepared to die. All my senses alerted, I felt each thump as my body struck the ground at sickening intervals, and I heard the whipping and scratching of brambles against my leathers, as the green canopy of the trees spun madly around me.

All kinds of thoughts fly through your head when you believe your last moment has arrived. I had time to think of my parents, getting on a bit now, in Stoke-on-Trent, and Mr Webb, my favourite patient. I thought about my children – how I rather wished I had some. I thought of Ace. Finally I hit the ground for the last time, rolled across a clearing and thudded against the trunk of a beech tree, which knocked all the breath out of my body.

There was silence. Through my visor I could see the forest floor close to my face, teeming with life. I discovered I was still breathing. I waited a few moments and then began to move slowly. First my arms and legs – then, very gingerly, my neck and back. I sat up, leaning against the tree, and took off my helmet. I was alive. Hot, bewildered and aching, but alive. I breathed more deeply, smelling the bracken and the damp leaves. The sun was on my face, and somewhere a bird was singing. Life was suddenly very sweet indeed. I groped for my mobile. No signal.

Then I heard footsteps rapidly coming closer, and Ace appeared at the edge of the clearing. He had taken off his helmet, and he was breathing hard. Moving quickly across the grass, he dropped to his knees in front of me without a word, scrutinising my face as though he'd never seen me before.

'I'm alive,' I croaked.

He touched me with his fingertips, as though I were something most rare and precious.

'So you are,' he said.

We were very still, very close. I looked at him and wondered why I had ever found him ordinary. His eyes were fierce and profoundly blue. His fair hair, standing up in spikes where he'd pulled off his helmet, was like living sunshine. He was laughing with relief. I was laughing too, when suddenly he took my face between his hands, and kissed me. Warm life flooded through my body. I slipped my hands inside his open jacket and felt the heat of him through his T-shirt, the hard muscles in his arms, his pounding heart.

I desired him, and felt his desire. We drew apart again, hesitating, only half-believing. There was a long moment, while his gaze burned into mine. Then we fell upon each other, and the silence was suddenly filled with the zipping of zips, the popping of fasteners and the ripping of Velcro, as we tore off our clothes. We made love furiously, amongst the crushed ferns and the butterflies, with the dappled sun on our skins and the breeze shaking the summer leaves. We tumbled over and over, holding each other, tangled together. I knew in that moment I was in love with life, and in love with Ace. And at last we lay still in each other's arms, gazing into one another's eyes.

'When did you *know?*' asked Ace.

For a second, I thought of telling him I had harboured a deep and abiding passion for him for months – it didn't seem right to say I'd only been admiring his bum. But I couldn't lie.

'I knew I loved you the moment I somersaulted off that bike, and thought I was going to die,' I said.

Ace nodded gravely. 'Yes,' he said. 'Same here.' And then, after a pause, 'Life is *very* good.'

'It's getting better all the time,' I observed.

It was then that a new sound broke into our consciousness. Ace frowned, his finger to his lips. We could both hear it – a distant crackling and crashing through the undergrowth, a thunder of boots, voices raised in alarm. Ace and I looked at each other, startled. We did not need to speak our thoughts.

As I said, it takes a long time to get dressed in motorcycle leathers – especially if a person has been perspiring, and her garments are strewn about in a forest clearing. And the approaching noises were unmistakable now. It was the rest of Ace's Angels, God bless them, hurtling down through the forest to our rescue.

Trawler Trash
Phil Trenfield

The brown envelope landed on the mat with a final thud. Erica emerged from the kitchen clutching a cup of tea and bent down to retrieve the mail. She knew what it contained before she even opened it.

Her divorce was final. She was now a divorcee, back on the market, single!

She read the letter one more time, her eyes blurry with tears. One broke away, trickled down her cheek and landed on the letter, making the ink run. She tutted.

What did it matter? she thought.

She knew what her best friend Sophie would be saying. "You've binned him, now bin the letter and move on." Erica placed it back in the envelope and was putting it in the drawer with her other important paperwork when the phone rang.

Sophie was on the other end of the line.

'I'm fine, Sophie. Yes, it's final. No, I'm not dancing around in my knickers. I'm feeling quite sad and alone actually. There's really no need. Hello. Hello?'

Erica looked at the phone, realising that Sophie had hung up. About to make her way to the bathroom, expecting Sophie's imminent arrival, she looked around her kitchen. Piles of pizza boxes, empty packets of crisps and chocolate wrappers stared back at her. She'd been comfort-eating for the past two weeks and had become best friends with any company that delivered food. Putting the empty wrappers inside one of the pizza boxes, she piled them up and carried them outside to the wheelie bin. Erica considered cleaning the rest of the kitchen but her brain told her she wasn't in the mood.

Forty-five minutes later the doorbell rang. Erica could see Sophie's face squashed up against the glass, like a burglar checking for signs of life before breaking in.

'Thank God, I thought you might have killed yourself,' Sophie blurted out as she stormed into the house.

'But you spoke to me less than an hour ago. You're the crazy one.'

'So my shrink keeps telling me. Well, I've come to get you out of this house and away from your life for the weekend,' Sophie announced.

'I don't know if I'm ready Soph, I think I need more time to get settled.'

'What in? Sheltered housing?' Sophie laughed. 'You and twit-face separated ten months ago, you are now divorced and a free, sexy agent. So we are going away and that's final!'

'Where?' Erica asked, still unsure.

'I'll tell you in the car. Now go and pack for fun, frolics, sea and, hopefully, sex.'

Reluctantly Erica went upstairs to pack a weekend bag. In the car she found out their destination.

'St Ives?' Erica repeated after a minute.

'Yes, St Ives, It's the perfect place for fun.' Sophie replied firmly, fiddling with the radio.

'Where did you hear that?' Erica asked. 'I thought it was where old people went to get in the queue for heaven.'

'Rubbish. Now be quiet, I'm trying to concentrate,' Sophie snapped. 'You know I've only just passed my test.'

The next few hours were torture for Erica as Sophie nervously said everything before she did it, for reassurance.

'Right, check mirror, signal and manoeuvre.'

After what seemed like days in the car they finally arrived.

'Here we are,' Sophie said, turning the engine off. 'I hope they've got a bar.'

'I hope they've got valium,' Erica replied, forcing a smile as she climbed out of the car.

'Now, the hotel is just cheap and cheerful,' Sophie stated.

'Sunny View,' Erica said, one eyebrow raised. 'It sounds like a retirement home.'

'Well, I've had my eye on your house for years and I've decided this is the best place for you,' Sophie replied, giggling. 'Now stop whingeing and let's go in.'

An elderly man who was reading the paper met them at the front desk.

'Aft'noon. What can I do for you? he asked, closing the paper.

'We have a reservation under the name of Carson,' Sophie replied.

'Right, fill your details in on this card and I'll get your keys sorted.' After they had filled in the card, he showed them to their room. The noise of the key turning in the lock failed to mask his noisy flatulence. Sophie sniggered. Erica didn't.

'Such a classy joint you've chosen for us here, Soph. How many stars has it got?' she asked, smirking. Quite undaunted by what had just happened, the old man shoved the door open and walked in.

'Now, breakfast is served from 7am until 9am in the dining room downstairs. Enjoy your stay.' He handed the key to Sophie and walked out.

They looked around the room. Two single beds, one against each wall, with candlewick bedspreads. One chest of drawers, one wardrobe and a pedal bin.

'I'd say this place would be lucky to get one star,' Sophie said, 'but we won't be in here much anyway so let's not worry.'

'Right, shall we go and explore?' Erica replied.

The girls left the hotel and made their way down the street towards the beach. They passed an ice-cream seller, parked in his van. The wind was blowing and the sky was full of dark, menacing clouds.

'I wonder if we'll find any sexy blokes while we're here?' Sophie said, scanning the street.

'Not at this precise moment I hope, because this wind is ruining my hair," Erica replied with her hands on her head, trying to keep her hair in place.

Sophie tutted and kept marching forward. The girls arrived at the beach and started laughing as they saw a middle-aged man trying to change under a towel.

'I don't know why he's bothering, it's not exactly swimming weather,' Sophie spluttered, still laughing.

'I think I'm going to go over to the rock pools and look for crabs,' Erica said, not really listening.

'I don't think you've got them, it's probably just because you shave,' Sophie replied looking serious, then bursting out laughing.

Erica rolled her eyes and made her way along the beach, leaving Sophie still cackling at the poor man getting changed. She wanted some time alone with her thoughts, all crammed inside her head, searching for attention. Almost like a classroom of needy children.

Reaching the end of the beach she sat down on a rock and burst into tears. Hot and salty, they trickled down her face. She watched the progress of a trawler making its way back to the shore and was surprised when the fisherman waved at her. Making an effort, she waved back. After a few minutes she stood and walked back to where Sophie was sitting.

'Are you all right?' Sophie asked.

'I'm fine, just needed to let something out.'

'Like the old man in our hotel?' Sophie replied smirking.

'No. Something else, Soph, but I'm OK now,' Erica said, forcing a smile.

'I have an idea. Let's go and get some fish and chips.'

'Now, that's the best idea you've had all year,' Erica replied, linking arms with Sophie.

The girls found a fish and chip shop and decided to eat them sitting on the wall outside.

'Why do they always taste better when you eat them outside the shop?' Erica asked.

'That's just the way it is. They're really good, but not for the figure! But who cares?' Sophie replied, with a mouthful of chips.

The girls sauntered back to the hotel. As they walked in they heard music and laughter. Through the door frame they saw a small bar at the end of the lounge.

'Drink?' Erica asked.

'Well, it would be rude not to,' Sophie said with a cheeky grin. The girls ordered their drinks and sat down by the window.

'Thanks.' Erica said, touching Sophie's arm.

'For what?'

'For making me come here. I needed to get out of that house,' Erica replied sighing.

'A toast to getting out of that house and out of that marriage,' Sophie said, lifting her glass.

As they were about to leave, a group of fisherman walked in, one of them smiled and winked at Erica. She smiled back and began to blush.

'Do you need to tell me something?' Sophie asked, eyebrows raised.

'When I went for my walk on the beach, a trawler went past and he waved to me.'

'He's pretty darn cute,' Sophie said.

'I'll say,' Erica replied, going red again.

'Go and ask him if you can suck on his Fisherman's Friend.' Sophie said, giggling.

'Filthy.'

'I was talking about the sweets. That's your dirty mind,' Sophie replied. 'Don't look now but I think he's coming over here.'

The man started walking over. He was wearing jeans and a plain white T-shirt. He had dirty blonde hair and a chiselled face.

'Hi, I'm Danny. Can I buy you a drink?'

'Hello, my name's Erica and this is Sophie. That'd be great thanks. A gin and tonic.'

'Same for me please,' Sophie piped up.

Danny looked as if to say I just meant your friend, but nodded and walked to the bar. After a few more drinks, the girls were suitably tipsy.

'So, you gonna ask her out?' Sophie blurted out.

'I'm thinking about it,' Danny replied calmly. 'Would you like to?' he asked Erica.

Sophie dug Erica in the ribs.

'Ouch. Yes, I would like that very much,' she replied, clutching her drink for moral support.

'How's tomorrow at 8 o'clock?' He looked at her with hopeful eyes.

'Perfect.'

Danny rejoined the other fishermen and the girls eventually headed up to their room.

The following evening, Erica was panic-stricken.

'Breathe, breathe, breathe,' Sophie said, searching for a paper bag. 'It's only a date.'

'Yes, but it's the first date I've had in about seven years,' Erica replied between gasps.

Finally she calmed down and an hour later was waiting outside the hotel for Danny to pick her up. Every little noise made her jump. She felt like a whole nature reserve was flying and crawling around her stomach, never mind just butterflies. Twenty minutes later she was still waiting. Sophie came out of the front door to go for a walk.

'Where the hell is he?' she asked.

'If I knew that I wouldn't still be standing here,' Erica replied.

'Why don't you call him?'

'I can't. We didn't exchange numbers,' Erica said.

Realising he wasn't coming, she stormed angrily back towards the hotel. Eyes blurred with humiliation, she didn't notice the step in the path. Suddenly her inner feelings were mirrored in reality as she tripped, flying through the air and landing in a jumbled heap. 'Owwwwwww!'

'Oh God! are you alright?' Sophie asked, shocked.

'I don't know. I don't think I can walk.' Erica replied, trying to put weight on her foot.

'I'd better get you to casualty,' Sophie said, excited by the thought of all those eligible doctors.

On the drive to the hospital Erica was nursing her pride, what there was left of it, after being stood up. It wasn't just her ankle that hurt. Thankfully, the casualty department was almost empty when they arrived.

'The doctor won't be long,' assured the girl behind the desk, so they waited until they were summoned in to a cubicle. Erica did a double take as her eyes took in the blond hair and chiselled features of the doctor.

'Erica? Is that you?'

Danny the fisherman was wearing a white coat, a stethoscope around his neck.

'Danny. What are you doing here?' She asked, not sure whether or not to hit him for standing her up.

'Unfortunately I got called in as they are short-staffed. I am so sorry I couldn't meet you tonight. I tried ringing the hotel but no one answered.'

'I thought you were a fisherman,' Erica said, confused.

'That's my dad's boat,' he said, grinning and showing a perfect set of teeth. 'I help out on my days off.'

'Ding, ding, jackpot. A doctor!' Sophie blurted out.

'Sophie, go and make yourself useful and clean out the bedpans,' Erica said, scowling.

Sophie retreated from the cubicle but lingered behind the curtain.

'So you didn't stand me up, then?'

'Christ, no. I was gutted I couldn't come and meet you.'

Erica hobbled a step closer to him and looked deep into his dark brown eyes.

'I was gutted you didn't come and meet me, too,' she said, tilting her head slightly.

Danny responded by tilting his head and moving in to kiss her.

227

'Yessssss.' Sophie cheered.

'Excuse me. Do you need to see a doctor?' The receptionist had just finished dealing with another patient and had her pen poised over some forms.

'No, I'm here with my friend and I think she's getting all the medicine she needs,' Sophie said, smiling.

Reference for Romance
Jackie Winter

'You want a reference for Jack?' Bewildered, Tessa stared at the phone. 'Jack Hughes? My ex-boyfriend?'

'That's right,' agreed the stranger, who'd introduced herself as Bianca. 'I want to find out if he's worth bothering with.'

'Worth bothering with?' Tessa stammered.

'I fancy him rotten,' came the crisp reply, 'but if Jack Hughes plays Jack the lad, I'm not wasting my time on him.'

'I see,' said Tessa. Which was stretching the truth by a long way. 'So who told you about me?'

'He did, of course.' Jack's would-be girlfriend was getting impatient. 'I asked for references about his relationship track record and he gave me your phone number.'

Cheek! thought Tessa. Was this Jack's way of telling her she meant nothing to him any more? That he was ready to move on?

'I'll meet you,' she said. 'Where and when?'

They decided on the following evening at a local pub. Putting the phone down, Tessa frowned. Exactly what was this all about?

Arriving at the pub early, she chose a table with a good view of the door. Bianca sounded a very self-assured young woman. Tessa wanted a few moments to size up the opposition.

It arrived promptly, in the form of a sleek redhead, smartly dressed in a black suit, high heels and white silk shirt. Obviously Bianca had come straight from the office. Her satisfied expression suggested she might well have emerged triumphant from some high-powered meeting. Tessa could imagine her kicking aside a few male colleagues, still grovelling around on the floor, picking up the pieces of their wounded egos. Not Jack's usual type, she thought, glancing down at her comfortable jeans and favourite woolly jumper. But... she sighed, maybe he'd changed.

'You must be Tessa.' Bianca plonked a bottle of mineral water next to Tessa's half of lager. 'Thanks for coming. Let's get down to it, shall we? Why did you dump Jack?'

Tessa gasped. Talk about not wasting words! But was there really likely to be much girlie talk with this alarming young woman?

'It didn't happen like that,' she said. 'He wanted commitment and I wasn't sure.'

'Not going to hang around for ever, is he?' said Bianca. 'I can't stand ditherers, myself.' She frowned. 'So Jack's not afraid of a serious relationship. Does that make him warm and caring or a wimp looking for some mug to wash his socks?'

Tessa smiled. 'You evidently haven't met his mother,' she said, silently apologising to kind Mrs Hughes.

Bianca's green eyes narrowed. 'What's his mum like?' she snapped.

'Jack's an only child.' Tessa shrugged. 'The son she thought she'd never have.'

'Molly-coddled.' Bianca nodded. 'I get the picture. What about money?'

'Money?' Tess stared at her.

'Has he got plenty of it?' Bianca studied her scarlet fingernails. 'Is he generous?' Her lips tightened. 'Or does he make a habit of forgetting his credit card?'

'We didn't have expensive tastes,' said Tessa. 'The curry house or local Italian suited us fine. And when I paid my way, it was because I wanted to,' she added.

Bianca looked down her elegant nose. 'A cheapskate.' She smiled, condescendingly. 'You probably deserve better. I know I do. He sounds a dead loss.'

'Not worth lowering your standards for,' agreed Tessa.

'It might be worth stringing him along, just for a decent holiday,' mused Bianca. 'After all, he works for a travel company.'

'We spent a fortnight in a tent on Dartmoor last year,' Tessa told her. 'Running an adventure camp for under twelves. Great fun.'

Bianca winced. Draining her water, she got up to go. Then hesitated. The faintest flush coloured her exquisitely made-up face.

'What's he like in bed?' she murmured.

'Tender. Thoughtful.' Tessa sighed, dreamily. 'Imaginative. Plenty of stamina…'

'Worth a one-night stand then?' suggested Bianca.

Tessa laughed. 'One night with Jack won't be nearly enough,' she promised. 'You'll be longing for more. Lots more.'

Bianca paled. 'Not my type,' she gulped. 'I like to be in control.'

'I'd never have guessed,' said Tessa.

'I can do without messy, emotional complications.' Bianca shivered. 'I'll be off. Nice talking to you.'

And she was gone. Tessa heaved a sigh of relief and polished off her drink. She was looking forward to something quite a lot stronger. Ten minutes with Bianca was enough to have anyone reaching for the bottle. Then she noticed a familiar face peering cautiously around the door.

'Jack!' She stared. 'What on earth are you doing here?'

'Are you on your own?' He looked poised for flight.

'Yes. If it's Bianca you're worried about, she's gone.' Tessa glared at him. 'You've got a cheek, roping me in for support when you're trying to pull a new girlfriend.'

He glared back. 'You've got it all wrong. Bianca decided she liked the look of me.' He shuddered. 'You've no idea how determined she can be.'

231

'I think I can imagine.' Tessa did a bit of shuddering herself.

'Can I get you a drink?' he asked. 'Your usual? Half of lager?'

'Don't be such a cheapskate.' Tessa grinned. 'Vodka and tonic, please.'

Jack slouched off to the bar, looking confused. Tessa knew how he felt. Bianca had a lot to answer for.

'Why are you here?' Five minutes later, she had another go at getting some answers.

'I felt guilty, landing you in it,' he admitted. 'Bossy Bianca's pretty scary.'

'I coped,' Tessa assured him. 'What was all the reference stuff about?'

'That was her crackpot idea,' said Jack. 'So I thought – aha, I'll give her Tessa's phone number. I hoped I could rely on you to have her running for cover.'

'No problem,' agreed Tessa. 'You're much too nice for her.'

Jack reached for her hand. 'And I was rather hoping you might be missing me.'

'I must have been mad to let you go,' she murmured.

'Not too late.' He put his arm around her. 'Shall I book that fortnight in Barbados? We couldn't find a more romantic place to discuss our future.'

'My bikini's as good as packed.' Tessa snuggled up. 'Remind me to take a pen.'

'A pen?' Jack looked puzzled.

Tessa grinned. 'Mustn't forget to write Bianca a postcard.'

Waiting for the Storm
Karen Howeld

Aunt Connie sits outside on the veranda, her rocking-chair crunching on grit as she frets back and forth. She stares intently at the swelling clouds as they mass over the Caribbean and assesses the approaching hurricane with her all-knowing eyes, just as she did when Beth was misbehaving as a child. Her face glistens with sweat, seems thinner, more wrinkled than Beth remembers.

Beth leans forward and clasps Connie's hands, which are crossed in her lap like a woman at prayer. 'You want pineapple juice?'

'No, honey,' Connie replies eventually.

They're silent until they hear the sound of Abe in his truck, returning from St John's. Beth leans over the wooden balcony to watch her cousin.

He brakes so hard that the wide planks of wood balancing precariously in the back threaten to tumble out. He jumps out of the cab and unloads the planks two at a time. 'They're saying on the radio it's gonna be a big wind, Ma.'

Connie glances at the horizon then turns back to Abe. 'Last time de sky went so black it's like de devil come down. Dat's what your father always say.'

She smiles but it doesn't ease the dull pain Beth sees in her eyes. Beth knows, from when Mama died seventeen years back, how grief swallows you up so whole that you forget things, behave like you're someone else while the "real" you is in hiding. Connie had said the Good Lord had wanted to take Mama, it was nature at work. But Beth also knows that Connie and Abe won't want to talk to her about their grief at Wilbert's death. She came back to Antigua to see her uncle but was only in time for his funeral. She's not seen any of them in four years

233

and the rhythm of their voices is a familiar song she's not heard for far too long.

Abe comes up on to the veranda, lines up one of the planks against the slatted-glass window of the front room and holds it in place with one hand while hammering nails with the other to fix it down.

Beth hopes it will prove strong enough to protect the glass from the heaviest winds. She hovers on the veranda, wanting to be involved. 'Can I help?'

Abe doesn't reply. He hammers furiously, slogging until his T-shirt becomes transparent with sweat and he strips it off his body. It really gets to her, his sullen manner, as though he doesn't give a damn that she's here. She knows that's not true. She caught his reflection in a window yesterday and he was staring at her.

She doesn't want to show how hurt she feels at his ignoring her yet again, so goes to sit with Connie. All the time she's surreptitiously storing his every detail in her hungry mind. She claims the graceful patterns his straining muscles etch on his bare back, the way his cut-off jeans hug his hips. He sure has filled out in the time she's been in London, "seein' places", as Connie put it.

Beth senses Connie's eyes on her so she tilts her face to the yellow-black sky. Here in Antigua, they were lucky if they got through a season without at least one hurricane watch. As a child she and Abe used to play and lark around on the veranda while Mama, Connie and Wilbert cleared the back yard and muttered at the sky. That'd been when all five of them lived here. Four rooms with a corrugated iron roof and a loo in the unfenced back yard. Once the clapperboard walls had been the same azure tone as the sea but the paint had flaked off over the years and they had turned the colour of the stagnant water in the ghetto's open sewer. Connie and her mama were sisters. Mama was the eldest but she never married, told Beth her father went back to St Kitts before she was born. Beth was nine when Mama died, and Connie and Wilbert looked after her like she was one of their own. Connie was always hugging and kissing her, as though to make up for Mama. Uncle Wilbert sat in his comfy chair out front having a smoke with the taxi guys, ranting about Old Man Bird screwing up the country. Then he'd see her and squeeze her tight until she wriggled free, giggling as she went.

The hammering stops and Abe walks round the veranda, wiping his hands on the flanks of his jeans. 'All done.'

'Will it be long before the storm?' Beth asks Connie.

'An hour, maybe. Only the good Lord knows that.'

The lyrical way she says it stabs bittersweet at Beth's heart; sounding just like Mama. It's like Mama's still here, yet she's not. Beth shakes away her memories because they remind her how lonely, how alone, she's felt in London. She is amazed she forced herself to stay away from here so long. She wants to slip back into her family life like it was another skin, but it doesn't fit right and it hurts that she doesn't know why.

Aunt Connie's eyes narrow. 'You OK, honey?'

Beth snaps out of the chair.

Speaking to her directly for the first time since he arrived at the house, Abe says, 'Where you goin'?'

'Down the cove.'

Connie gestures with a stubby finger. 'Stay here. De storm's comin' in fast.'

'I'll be fine.' Beth stalks off down the veranda steps to the stony path.

'Beth!' Abe shouts. 'Come back!'

She doesn't stop but hears his expletive followed by running footsteps. The warm breeze is picking up momentum, breathing its veiled threats of worse to come.

'Why d'you take no notice, Bethnee?'

Beth doesn't bother to answer. She's thrilled he used his childhood nickname for her, and she's got what she wants – to have Abe on his own. They're walking close enough that it's clear they know each other well, but with a certain perceptible distance dividing them. Once they're on the beach she kicks off

235

her sandals. He waits for her. He's watching her. She can sense it. Deliberately, she unbuttons her denim shirt to reveal a skimpy sports top and toned midriff. Her skin prickles with awareness like she's got a heat rash.

They walk along the beach. Beth takes baby steps, lets each of her toes sink deep into the damp sand along the shoreline.

'You never wrote me in London,' she accuses.

He shrugs, not looking at her.

'Stupid of me to hope you would, considerin' you didn't come to the airport when I left. Uncle Wilbert looked all over for you, real angry he was.'

'I know. He was sore 'bout that for weeks after,' Abe admits.

'Aunt Connie was in a strange mood too, like she was unhappy and relieved all at the same time.' It was Connie who'd urged her to go in the first place, had given her the ticket to London for her eighteenth birthday, along with what little money was left from Mama. Said Mama wanted her to go places. Leaving home had hurt, more than Beth is willing to let on. She'd felt she wasn't wanted anymore, and she'd never been able to work out why, nor could she face coming back without reason. Wilbert's illness had given her that, but she'd been too late to see him.

'This place hasn't changed, not since we were last here.' She looks pointedly at Abe and knows he remembers, too. It was the day after her birthday and they were smoking a spliff under the shade of manchaneel trees at the far end of the cove.

"You gonna go to London?" he'd asked, lacing his fingers with hers.

"I guess." Connie had been so insistent that Beth had taken the ticket. "You could come with me."

"Don't have de money." He'd nuzzled her neck. "Besides, Ma won't be happy, 'specially if she sees us like this."

"It don't matter we're cousins."

"De church don't like it neither."

She'd looped her arm with his. She does that again now, caresses the tough yet vulnerable skin of his inner forearm.

'Don't!' He jerks away like he's been stung.

'Why not?' She runs her fingers along his unshaved jaw, guides his hand to her naked waist.

'Beth! Just stop! You don't understand.'

'Too right I don't. One minute we're hangin' round together, the next you don't wanna know me.'

'It weren't like that, Beth.' His voice is as heavy as the growl of the increasing wind.

'Yeah, right,' she retorts sarcastically. 'How's Dionne?'

'How d'you know about her?'

'Connie wrote me. Thought she was gonna get a daughter-in-law.'

'Man, she got no right.'

'So, what's she like, your Dionne?' In a masochistic way she wants to know, wants to guess how she matches up to her.

'Don't matter, she's not on the scene no more.'

'Why d'you finish things?'

He sighs. 'Long story.'

'She cheat on you?' By the look on his face she's guessed right. 'I wouldn't put up with that.'

Abe shakes his head. 'You've changed, Bethnee. There's something different 'bout you.'

'I'm not some silly girl any more.' In London, she'd grown another skin.

'I'd noticed,' he retorts dryly. His eyes drift to her bare midriff then rip away.

They reach the end of the cove where the sea sucks at the smooth underbelly of rocks. She perches next to Abe on the rocks, runs the tips of her fingers along the jagged edges. 'So, why you been ignoring me since I got back?'

'I got stuff to do for Pop.'

'But you won't let me help you. Won't let me near you.'

'I don't...'

'Let me help.' She takes his callused hand, sandwiches it between her own, draws it to her lips.

He snatches his hand away, breathes like a man who's run miles. 'Don't do this, Bethnee.'

'Why?' she pleads.

'I don't want to talk about it.'

'What are you runnin' from?'

'Bethnee…' He scrambles off the rocks.

'Tell me.'

'Pop.' He looks despairingly up at the sky, looking for guidance. 'Who d'you think your father was?'

Everything's black, wearing the coat of death and the devil.

'I don't believe you.' She runs down the beach, away from him, but he chases and catches her easily.

'I didn't want to tell you.' Rain carves down his tormented face. He stretches out his hand to her.

'Don't touch me,' she warns, sickened at how badly she'd wanted him to do just that only a few moments ago.

'You know I'm telling the truth, else you wouldn't freak out at me being near you.'

She puts her T-shirt back on. She's shivering, despite the heat. The strong winds punch her in the gut.

'Listen to me, Beth, we're goin' back to the house, it's getting dangerous out here.'

'Not until you tell me what you know.' She's rooted still, hands on hips.

'Bethnee!'

'Tell me!'

'All right, but only if you start walkin' with me.'

They walk, heads bowed. The wind tosses her braids loose from their tie.

'So?' she demands.

He sighs, scrubs at his forehead. 'I overheard Ma and Pop talkin'. De day after your birthday, it was. Ma was saying she'd promised your Mama they'd take care of you but there'd been enough sins committed in this house and she didn't want no more. You and me were misbehavin' and she wanted to put a stop to it before de devil got his way.' Abe wipes the rain out of his eyes. 'I didn't cotton on until Pop said there was no need to break us up, to send you away. He wanted to tell you he was your pop. Ma went mad, said she wouldn't be able to hold her head high again.'

Beth feels tears prick at her eyes, swipes at them with her hand. 'Why didn't you tell me then?'

'Couldn't face it. That's why I never said goodbye.'

'You should have told me. All of them should have. I'm going to ask Connie.'

'No, don't.' Abe grabs hold of her wrists. 'If they'd wanted us to know they'd have said something. Secrets should stay secret.'

'Not this one.' She snatches her arms free and runs to the house, hardly able to see for the rain stabbing at her eyes.

The howling wind is a demented animal, scavenging round the house. Beth sits in the corner of the front room and Abe is next to Connie in the rocking chair. All the time she's aware of Abe's eyes on her like a scared cat's: bright, frenetic.

'You two only got back here just in time,' Connie reprimands.

Beth doesn't give a damn right now. Thoughts race in her mind with the same intensity as the wind. She wants to know everything. It had never occurred to her to wonder about her father. She'd taken what Mama had said for granted. Connie and Mama were so close, she can't imagine them keeping secrets from one another. When did Connie find out about Mama and Wilbert? Were they sure she was his daughter? She had her Mama's wide girth, smooth skin, but nothing she could see of Wilbert's. And there were few similarities between her and Abe. How could she look so different from her brother?

Suddenly the wind takes one God almighty breath, then roars. Tree roots crack, the power fails. Beth ducks, burrowing her head in defenceless arms. Seconds tick by, one... two... three. Rain pounds the back of her neck. Abe swears and she follows his gaze. The hurricane has ripped a sheet of the roofing right off and through the hole she can see the wind, actually *see* it, like a ball of tangled string, white and furious.

Connie lights a kerosene lamp and the flame throws out enough colour to see the damage. 'Can it be repaired?'

Abe grabs a chair and cranes his neck. 'We'll have to wait 'til the eye passes over, get it done in the lull before the winds twist back for a second shot.'

'You sure it's safe, boy?' Aunt Connie takes his hand. 'It don't matter about de rain, de things in here will dry out.'

'We'll have up to an hour, Ma. For now, we'll go into the bedroom.'

The lull, when it comes, is a pocket of eerie silence, a false sense of security. Abe and Beth stretch a sheet of heavy plastic across the gaping hole and secure it into place any which way they can. All the time Beth concentrates fiercely on the physical task, her eyes fixed on the roof, trying not to flinch when their hands brush together in their haste to get the job done quickly. Her arms ache from the effort. 'Do you think it'll hold?'

Abe stares at her pointedly. 'Maybe, maybe not. If the storm wants to tear us apart then it will.'

They sit in the front room again, dark with misshapen shadows. Aunt Connie pours juice and talks about arrangements for Uncle Wilbert's funeral. She wants Beth and Abe to walk with her in a cortege up to the church graveyard, then he's going to be buried next to Beth's mama.

'Why is Pop going next to her?' Abe demands.

''Cos when de Good Lord takes me I want to be next to my husband and my sister. My family. Surely you understand, boy?'

Beth knows he doesn't understand, and that Connie has forgiven Mama. Abe catches her eye, pleads silently with his hands, willing her to stay quiet.

The plastic sheeting bucks under the pressure of the wind and the hurricane twists back with even greater ferocity. Suddenly Beth can't take anymore. Connie must guess because she grabs hold of Beth's clammy hand and it's like they're thirteen years back and Beth's a kid again, standing by Mama's grave with the only family she has.

'The Good Lord'll look after us.' Connie's voice drifts away then comes back stronger, full of certainty. 'It's just nature at work, honey.'

Sex on the Beach
Ruth Joseph

My darling. I'm sitting here in the place where our relationship began – an old deserted beach hut overlooking the sea on the Gower coast. It's where we promised we'd return to when we'd finally organised our lives. The weather is cold now and there's no heating, so I've filled the beach hut with cushions and soft blankets and, in a large basket to the side of one of the weather-beaten wooden seats, lies a picnic; waiting. I spent hours planning what to bring and all the time a voice inside kept telling me that the whole thing was hopeless and that you wouldn't return. In the basket there are homemade granary rolls and a really good eighteen-month Pecorino cheese from the cheese-shop – like the one you enjoyed last time we were together. And I've made a rich carrot and lentil soup and some lemon curd tarts with my own lemon curd. All this food; like a party with no guests. But I can't believe, no, I won't believe, that you won't come.

Do you remember how we met? It was in the summer: one of those rare hot days with the water barely moving, only the occasional ripple on the surface as if it was a length of blue shimmering silk, just sheared off the bolt. I was sitting on my own by a clump of rocks, forcing myself to concentrate on a book while trying to make sense of the recent events that pained like an open wound. Eventually I put down my book, realising that I had read the same paragraph five times, and poured a glass of water, placing it close to a new sun-hat – a large straw arrangement; the crown decorated with a chiffon scarf which made me feel elegant and important, bought on my way here in a "sod it moment" – retail therapy to defy the growing knot of hurt that twisted, growing inside my stomach.

Suddenly, the peace was shattered by the panic shouts of a man's voice.

"Domino! Domino! Come here! No!"

Before I'd realised, a large Labrador dog with his fur in tight sticky strands from a recent dip bounced over to me, slapping my legs with a combination of wet sand and brine. Then he licked my face, knocked over my water, and picked up my straw hat, chasing away with it across the damp sand and finally dumping it into the sea. The dog's owner ran over to me.

"What can I say? I'm so, so sorry. I'll pay. Oh Lord was it new? I just can't believe it. He's only a pup and I just let him off for the first time, to enjoy the water for a second. I never imagined he'd do all this damage."

I looked at this man, slightly older than me, maybe forty, and at a set of blue sparkling eyes; then I gazed out at the sea-shore where an animated black dog was playing with my straw hat and burst into tears.

"Oh please, I feel so bad. I'm sure we'll be able to get another hat."

"No, no, it's not that," I said feeling pathetically female. "It's everything."

"Sorry?"

"Oh, just my life right now, and the hat – oh, what the hell!"

By this time, Domino had returned back to his owner with the hat scrunched in his mouth. A straggle of bladder-wrack clung to the chiffony tie.

"Listen, I feel awful. You will let me pay, won't you? Better still, would you have dinner with me?"

I have to be clear about this. I'd never dated a stranger before. I had friends who enjoyed the frisson of a secret affair; some positively thrived on clandestine relationships and would relish telling me all the details at work or later over a few drinks. And it wasn't that I hadn't had offers. But up until now I'd been happy to be the faithful partner to someone, I thought, equally committed, with a shared mortgage, joint gym membership and even a few pooled investments. That was until a few hours ago, when I'd discovered that Mark had been playing away. The reason I'd come to the beach; to think out my life.

"Have dinner? With you?"

"Look, I promise, all above board. No silly stuff. I'd just like the chance to apologise properly to you. Please let me say sorry?"

I looked at this man, tanned, dark, greying a little, with a ready smile.

"Look, you say where. We'll meet there if you like. What do you say?"

"Well, yes, yes, OK. How about Mario's in the High Street at eight?"

"Great,' he smiled. 'Come on now Domino. You need a bath."

He turned back. "Please be there. Yes?"

As he walked away there was a buzz in my heart I'd not felt for a while. That evening I took trouble with my appearance and chose the better underwear – the set that arrived in a scented box with tiny beads of fragrance. I bathed, put on stockings and suspenders, my six-inch red stilettos, a long black silk skirt and matching camisole that clung to my curves. As I left, I glanced quickly at my reflection. *You look good, girl,* I thought, trying to blot out the hurt that at times was overwhelming me.

Dinner at Mario's was perfect and by the end of the evening, I wanted to see more of Jake. I slipped into his old Saab convertible, admiring its classic looks.

"Shall we go for a drive?"

I nodded.

Jake drove to the beach and down a pebble track. The car rolled to a stop. In front of us was a derelict beach hut. I kept thinking that this was a typical scene that happens after a woman has been let down by her man – to go with someone on the rebound. Even the setting was classically forming part of the action. A sarcastic voice inside shouted:

Yeh, yeh, a full moon, velvet black sky, loads of stars; yet in the car, next to me, seemed to be a really kind guy.

I heard myself saying, "Let's explore, shall we?"

Jake pushed open the door of the beach hut.

"Must be a faulty lock," he said.

Feeling like intruders, we walked into the tiny space.

"Just a minute," said Jake and returned from the car with a large blanket, which he laid on the floor. He pushed the door and held it open with a large washed pebble. Then he gestured to me and we sat on the blanket with the vision of the moon on the water reflected in a thousand silvered ripples.

"It's so beautiful," I said. I looked across at Jake. I knew he wanted me and I wanted him, but I wanted to delay the moment. He slipped his arm around my shoulders and I could hear the beat of his heart so close to me. Then he looked at me questioning, yes? He cupped my chin with a cool hand and I answered, "yes". He slipped the fine strap of my camisole off my shoulder and kissed my waiting skin and, again, I answered, "yes".

Afterwards we lay together and talked, sharing our lives. Outside, the tired moon relinquished its hold on the night and gave way to a rising sun and we watched the morning arrive with gold on the water and a mass of seagulls dipping and swirling around a returning fishing boat.

"Breakfast?" he said.

"I'll have to change, but yes, yes please."

He drove me home to slip on my favourite pale blue denims and a soft pink sweater and we sat outside the Harbour Moon pub and dipped chunks of buttered toast into fried eggs, with hot coffee on the side.

But then he took his wallet out of his inside jacket pocket and showed me pictures that belonged to another life. A woman smiling and two children – a little girl with her hair in bunches, about five years old and an older boy with his two front teeth missing. They were laughing together. I was acutely jealous and felt wounded again. I couldn't believe that I had been conned twice by two men who promised love but just used my body.

"You don't understand," he said. "I'm showing you these because I want to be honest with you. What I had with Sally is over. It's been over for years. I've been lazy. I needed that push to make the final break."

"But your children. Surely they will be hurt?"

"I suspect that living in a family of moods and rows and, at best, indifference is doing them no good at all. Nonetheless to do the thing right by them is going to take time. I want to see them financially secure and make sure that they still know that I love them. So can we say that in six month's time we will meet again at the beach hut and that we will be ready to be with each other?" He stared into my eyes.

"Please will you wait for me? Can you wait for me?"

I nodded, unable to speak.

Looking out of the open door of the beach hut, the sea throws itself at the sky with a white-topped grey, angry horizon. There are very few people on the beach except those that enjoy taking their dogs out in the winter. Only a couple of Labradors barking loudly with excitement and their owners, braving the icy wind. We said lunch. Jokingly I promised to bring it. "I'll make soup," I'd said. "It'll be freezing." I resist the urge to look at my watch again, but I've looked so many times in the last hour. It's almost two. I've been a fool. I should have realised that he wouldn't come. But some good has emerged from our meeting. At least coming across Jake has made me take stock of my life and I can start alone now. All the shared investments with Mark have gone; he's moved out and I've taken time to create a space that is mine, new curtains, certainly a new bed after what had happened.

Two o'clock. He can't be coming. I feel desperately sad. I had hoped…

'Vicky! I'm so sorry I'm late. I had to get someone to look after Domino and at the last minute… Why are you crying? Aren't you pleased to see me?'

A Different Viewpoint
Sheila Alcock

I've a problem with men. When one of them so much as smiles at me, I scowl and think of Richard. The man who was the love of my life, and whose smile could send me into meltdown faster than butter on a hot muffin.

That's the moment I freeze. I'm desperate to forget Richard and the memory of him with my best friend. I want to dump my memories of our time together into a bin marked "not wanted", but I can't. Instead, I snub any guy who's rash enough to put himself in the firing line.

'You should get out more,' said my sister.

'I'm always out,' I snapped.

'I mean, you should meet more people,' she persisted. 'And what are you doing about a holiday this year?'

'Haven't thought,' I said.

She frowned, with an expression I'd noticed more and more recently. A "what am I going to do about you?" sort of look.

'You can't spend your whole life going backwards,' she muttered.

'Well, if it makes you happy, you'll be pleased to know I'm thinking of going on a holiday course,' I admitted. I'm fond of Lizzie, and hate to see her worried.

I was rewarded with a smile of relief.

'That's great,' she sighed. 'What's the course?'

'Photography techniques,' I said.

I could see she was already wondering if there'd be any eligible men going along, but I stopped her before she framed the question out loud.

'So that's settled. And now it's time I got back to the office,' I said briskly, making my escape before she had time to go into interrogation mode.

I left for the holiday a week later, arriving at the hotel in a thunderstorm, which culminated in a dramatic streak of lightning, just as I rushed through the double doors.

'Wow. Some entrance!'

He was smiling as he came forward to help me with my camera strap, which had got caught up on the door handle. Just for a moment, I had time to notice grey-green eyes under black brows, but then, as usual, Richard got in the way.

'I can manage,' I said frostily.

He looked startled. Then, as I began to mumble something in a sort of apology, he turned brick red with embarrassment and hurried away.

I hated myself.

I stayed in my room that evening. There was supposed to be a get together in the bar, for course members to meet each other, but I chickened out, so I didn't come across him again until breakfast, when I discovered he was the course tutor.

'Good morning everyone. My name's Chris, and today we'll be working on the portrait photograph, so I need to split you all into pairs,' he announced.

There was a flurry of activity, and, as if by magic, everyone had a partner. Everyone except me, that is. While I'd been brooding in my room, the rest of the course members had met up and made friends. I was left standing alone. Odd one out, as usual.

Chris looked around desperately, then made up his mind.

'Right, well, I'll be your partner for this exercise,' he said abruptly.

We took photographs of each other inside the hotel, with flashguns and reflectors, then outside in the gardens, using natural sunlight. When they were developed, the pictures I took of Chris showed a closed expression and a frown between the eyebrows. As for the ones he took of me, well, I'd never realised until then that I could look so hostile.

Things got better after that. There were some great people on the course. There was also a guy who reminded me of

249

Richard so much, I nearly choked whenever I saw him. After a while though, I couldn't help noticing how much he needed to chat up every female in sight, and it opened my eyes. I suppose I should have thanked him. Told him what a cure he was for an inferiority complex the size of the Eiffel Tower. I didn't though. Instead, I began to enjoy myself. We explored glorious gardens, turned snap-happy over bridges and lakes, and in the evenings, we made our way to the bar and talked half the night. I'd forgotten all those new horizons. Taking pictures of people and things made me aware of myself as a subject, and I wished I'd seen myself as clearly before I snapped at Chris on that first day.

'Today, we'll be looking at the difference a polarised filter can make,' Chris announced when we'd arrived at our destination by the river. 'Choose a subject. A boat, a tree, or those ducks over there. Now rotate the filter on your lens until you get the desired effect, and if that doesn't work, try changing your viewpoint.'

It was as if I'd discovered the meaning of life. I began to laugh, and he looked at me properly for the first time since I'd been so rude to him.

'What's the joke?' he said, clicking away in my direction.

'Oh, it was just something you said about viewpoints,' I muttered.

The rest of the group wandered off to find suitable subjects, and we were left behind on the river bank.

It was hot. There was the occasional plop of a fish breaking the surface. We stood beneath a willow trailing its leaves in the water, and Chris stared at me with a bemused expression.

'It's a wonderful day,' I smiled.

'Getting better by the minute,' he agreed.

On our last night, we compared our first photographs with the ones we'd taken later in the week. Even Chris was persuaded to put his prints on the table along with the rest of them. I blushed as I saw the first one he took of me, tight-lipped, looking into the camera as if I wanted to smash it.

'Try these,' Chris grinned, and produced another set. They were a revelation.

'These are fantastic,' I said, amazed. I was in a sunlit world, leaning against a tree, smiling like someone with a wonderful secret, at peace with the world.

He moved closer, grabbing my hand.

His touch was electric. I wanted to stay like that, holding hands for ever. I thought, fleetingly, of Richard, but the image blurred and was gone. Finally filtered out, I thought happily.

I forced myself back to the present, and the business in hand, reluctantly producing the shots I'd taken that day.

'These are very good.' He sounded impressed.

He was watching me, waiting for me to say something.

'You've learned a lot in a week,' he persisted. 'And when you smile, you blow me away,' he added, moving closer.

'Amazing what a week can do,' I said, leaning in his direction. I found myself laughing, disbelieving, and drowning in those grey-green eyes.

'You said it yourself. If something doesn't work, you just have to try a change of viewpoint.'

Mad About the Moustache
Jan Wright

When I'd said I'd walk Gran's dog while she was in hospital, all I'd had in mind was a quick once around the block in the early morning sunshine before work.

"But Lucy, the castle is the only place you can let Cleo off the lead. I've always taken her there," Gran had said. And, as she was in such a flap about her operation, I didn't like to add to her stress by arguing.

Which was why, despite the English summer leaving great puddles of mud everywhere, I was dutifully trudging my way around some old ruins at seven in the morning. Patches of fog were still lingering, making the stones look eerie in the muffled silence. I gathered from Gran lots of walkers came here, just not at this ridiculously early hour. I was halfway round the castle when I heard another dog. Then, out of the mist, walked a moustache.

Well, it didn't walk on its own, there was a man attached to it. Not that it was possible to look at anything other than the thick black hair that drooped below his nose. In fact, it wasn't until we'd passed that I realised I couldn't remember anything else about him. Not his height or what he'd been wearing, only that he reminded me of some Mexican bandit in those old Hollywood movies – sinister, but very, very sexy.

I saw him again the next morning and tried to take in other details. Trouble was, he smiled at me as he hurried past. At least I think it was a smile, all I really saw was this black mass move on his face. It was fascinating.

When I called at the hospital to see Gran that evening, I asked her about him. She shook her head. "No Lucy, I've never met anyone at the castle with a thick moustache, not unless you count old Mabel," she chuckled. She then started telling me about her operation, so I had to stop thinking about Pedro for a while.

Which wasn't easy, because the guy kept invading my thoughts. I'd named him Pedro when I'd decided he was a bank robber; although on the way home from the hospital I started fantasising about him being an international spy. This was probably an indication of how very sad and boring my life was at that moment in time, but I didn't like to dwell on that too much!

The next morning, I was up extra early so I could do my hair, apply some make-up and dress much more smartly for my walk. Not my best idea as it turned out. It started raining the moment I arrived at the castle. That fine, misty summer rain that somehow manages to soak you completely. I must have looked like a drowned rat by the time I saw Pedro, but that didn't stop him speaking. Even if it was only to say, 'Lousy weather,' as he jogged past.

Ooh, you should have seen what that did to his upper lip. It was no good, I was smitten. I spent the rest of the walk imagining that moustache slowly brushing across my naked body as Pedro tortured me with his passionate kisses. It certainly took my mind off being so wet, even if such thoughts were making me damp in other places!

I'd always fancied trying a man with a beard, but guys my age hardly ever grow them. The closest I'd got was dating a guy while I was at university. He was in Media Studies and thought his designer stubble gave him the right image. It gave me a rash. After a month my cheeks, neck and other more delicate places were so sore that I'd had to tell him it was the sandpaper or me. And guess what, the self-centred, vain cretin chose the stubble!

Pedro's moustache wasn't anything like that, at least not in my over-active imagination. I'd decided it had a silky smooth texture that merely tickled in the most delightful way. Trouble was, I had the feeling my imagination was the closest I was likely to get to Pedro unless I did something drastic. Gran didn't intend staying in hospital for ever.

A week later, and I'd only managed to get him to say hello and comment on the weather. Gran was home and ready to resume walking Cleo so, if I wanted to get up-close and personal with that moustache, it was now or never. So I came up with a plan.

As soon as I caught sight of his dog, I called Cleo to me. Then it was just a matter of keeping her close, so it would look like I'd tripped over her. Pedro was getting nearer, and I gave a little scream as I started a delicate, graceful fall to my knees. Or that was how it was supposed to happen. Cleo thought I was playing and pounced on me, which pushed me off balance and down into the old moat. I landed with a splash, in the filthy water that lay at the bottom.

'Are you OK down there?' my hero yelled, as he carefully climbed down the steep side.

I'd certainly got his attention. 'I've twisted my ankle,' I said truthfully, as I attempted to stand up. Trying not to cover his jacket in anything too disgusting, I let him help me out of the moat. I felt such an idiot. Especially as that moustache looked even sexier just inches away from me.

I had a feeling Pedro wasn't used to damsels in distress, but somehow he managed to get both dogs and me back to the road. It took several not-so-subtle hints from me, to get him to offer to drive me home – but then I suppose I was dripping smelly mud everywhere.

By the time we got to my place and he helped me out, he'd told me his name was Marvin, which was a terrible shock because I thought only paranoid androids were called that! But it didn't discourage me from saying that I'd like to buy him a drink somewhen, to thank him for his kindness.

'I'll be down The Wishing Well about eight tonight, if your ankle's up to it,' he said, before wiping the muck off the passenger's seat and driving off.

Yesss! I had a date with Pedro. Well, a sort of a date. OK, it was just a drink with Marvin – but whatever his name was, he still had that wonderful moustache.

My ankle didn't hurt at all by the time I finished showering, but that could have been the adrenalin pounding through my veins. The day at work dragged, but, after a frantic dash home to give myself maximum time to look my best, I arrived at The Wishing Well at eight-thirty.

Pedro was standing at the bar with a group of yobbish-looking guys, and suddenly I wasn't so sure this was a good idea. I hesitated slightly, which was when he noticed me. I saw him say something to his friends, who all laughed. Then he walked towards me.

I spent the rest of the evening sitting in the corner listening to Marvin tell me all about his job. Far from being a spy or a bank robber, he actually worked in the plumbing section of the local DIY store. I suppose I was disappointed, but I was still mesmerised by the moving moustache as he told crass jokes about plastic U-bends and ball cocks.

He introduced me to his mates just before closing time. 'You're not thinking of kissing that porcupine are ya, Lucy?' one of them asked.

Then they all started on about how ridiculous he looked, and how they'd been telling him for ages that he'd never get a girl unless he shaved it off.

'I think it's sexy,' I said. Which caused the whole drunken bunch to fall about laughing.

'Do you see much of your mates?' I asked Marvin as he walked me home.

'Yeah, quite a bit. But Alex is getting married in a month, so I guess the old gang is about to break up.'

Now that was encouraging, but not as encouraging as our first kiss. Whilst Marvin was far from how I'd imagined Pedro, his moustache was everything I'd dreamed it would be. It was hard to be happy with just feeling those soft hairs on my face, but, as Marvin had already asked to see me again the following evening, I figured I could wait a little longer to experience the moustache in more intimate places.

A week later and I was still mad about the moustache. Just a glimpse of it made me go weak at the knees.

'But you can't date a moron, just because you like his facial hair,' my best friend kept telling me.

'Marvin isn't a moron,' I protested. 'He may be a little educationally challenged, but that doesn't make him a bad person.'

'It doesn't make him interesting to be with either,' she pointed out.

Gran didn't like him either. 'He's a waste of space, and I'm sure his dog has given Cleo fleas,' she proclaimed over tea and fruitcake.

But it didn't matter to me. I was besotted. When his kisses made me this happy, who cared about conversation? But I was a little concerned about the things Marvin's mates were saying. Especially Alex's bride-to-be, who was insisting that Marvin have a shave before the big day. 'I don't want that great fat black caterpillar crawling under your nose in my wedding photos,' she insisted. Seems Marvin hadn't had the moustache when they'd asked him to be best man.

But I was confident Marvin wouldn't get rid of it; not with the way I worshipped the thing. Then, the day before the wedding, a terrible thing happened. I called round and found him… barefaced!

'What have you done?' I cried.

'It wasn't me,' he muttered, rubbing his lip. 'We all went out last night and I got plastered. I woke up this morning and found my mates had shaved half of it off. So I had to get rid of the other half.'

'I thought it was supposed to be the best man's job to play tricks on the groom – not the other way round,' I said. Trust Marvin to get it wrong.

'Don't worry Lucy, it won't take me long to grow it again,' he said. But that wasn't the point; I'd now seen how dull and boring his face looked without it. OK, it did go perfectly with his dull and boring personality, but that didn't make me feel any better.

I didn't stay round his place very long that evening, but I couldn't just ditch him the moment the moustache was gone. It would have made me seem such a shallow, heartless person. Which possibly I was – but I didn't want other people to know that!

Which was why, the next day, I found myself attending Alex's wedding. It was beautiful and sunny, and I wore a pale mauve chiffon dress that Marvin obviously hated. Looking embarrassed to be seen with me, he wandered off to chat with his scruffy idiot friends.

I was over-dressed and out of place, and didn't know what to do as I stood in the registry office hallway waiting for the bride and groom. A barrage of rude comments and wolf-whistles heralded their arrival, and I looked around hoping that no one I knew would spot me with this rabble.

It wasn't that I was a snob, well not normally, but suddenly I longed to be as far away as possible. I was looking for an escape route, when I saw the man of my dreams walking towards me. 'I'm Alexander Pickering, the registrar. You must be the bride,' he said, offering me his hand.

My heart almost stopped as I took it. It was cool and smooth, and I could have held on to it for ever. But slowly my senses returned and I muttered, 'Umm no… the bride is the one over there in the black denim jeans.'

'Oops, sorry!' he laughed, before whispering, 'I guess I'm used to her being the most beautiful woman in the room. Still, I'm rather pleased you aren't getting married in five minutes.' His eyes twinkled, and I felt myself blush. Which no doubt meant that my mauve dress now clashed horribly with my red face.

The next half hour passed in a kind of misty haze. I sat on the edge of my seat not listening to the vows or looking at the happy couple, I certainly didn't pay any attention to Marvin. I was away in fantasyland doing all sorts of wild and wonderful things with the incredibly gorgeous, well-spoken Alexander. Who, I was pleased to note, kept glancing over and smiling at me.

Finally the marriage ceremony finished, and everyone dashed outside. Everyone but Alexander and me. 'You're not joining them?' he asked.

I shook my head. I figured it would be a little insensitive to be in the wedding photos, being as I was just about to ditch the best man.

'So, what are you going to do now?' he continued.

If it was all the same with him, I rather fancied finding out if that gorgeous, sexy beard of his felt as soft and erotic against my skin as I imagined. Of course, I didn't say that. 'I'm not sure what I'm going to do,' I said, flashing him a smile. 'Have you any suggestions?'

He did, and very good ones they were too.

Which meant I now knew that his beard was everything I'd ever dreamed a beard would be, with the added bonus of it being attached to a great guy this time. Ah, what more could a girl ask for?

Well… possibly a foreign accent. But that's a whole other fantasy, and one we probably shouldn't go into just at the moment!

Love Will Find a Way
Dee Williams

Jenny smiled at her mother who was singing along with the Rod Stewart C.D. she had bought her for Christmas.

'Taking a chance on love,' trilled Shirley Gates slightly off-key.

Jenny looked at her mother. 'Would you take a chance on love again, Mum?'

'I would if the right man come along.'

Jenny knew her mother had plenty of love to give if only Mr Right would come along. Things hadn't been easy since her dad, John Gates, had left them for some over-painted, silicone-boobed tart. What was wrong with her father, was it the male menopause? The divorce had been hard on her mother and even after five years she was still afraid to let her feelings show.

'Mum, I'll be going out this afternoon. Emma wants me to go shopping with her. She had some money for her birthday and she can't wait to spend it.'

'That's fine. I've got to cut the grass. It don't take long in this weather to grow.' Shirley sighed. 'I wish I had a nice young man to come and cut the grass.'

Jenny laughed. 'So do I. I wouldn't be going out if he was dishy, I can tell you.'

'You find your own blokes.'

'If only.'

Shirley looked at her daughter. 'D'you know, I reckon we're destined to spend the rest of our lives together like a couple of old maids.'

'Good God, I hope not.'

'Well, you're all of twenty and still haven't got a bloke.'

'I'm fussy, that's all.'

'Aren't we all?'

Jenny was fifteen when her father left them, at first she was a bit of a rebel but when she realised what the divorce had done to her mother she settled down. Now they were very close.

That afternoon when Jenny met Emma she told her about that morning's conversation with her mother. 'I wish I could find a bloke for her. Although she don't say it, I know she's very lonely.'

'It's a shame, she's still attractive and she looks after herself.'

'She'd be pleased to hear you say that. She's not bad at all for her age and she's got good legs.'

As they walked along, suddenly Emma said. 'What about a lonely hearts club, speed dating, or what if we went on the internet for her?'

'Can't see her taking kindly to any of that.'

'I'm sure we could find someone for her,' said Emma, warming to the idea. 'What about those ads in the local paper? That way perhaps we could go along and vet him when she meets her man.'

'I can't see my mum doing that.'

'Well, I reckon it's worth a try.'

For the rest of the afternoon that thought filled Jenny's mind. Should she have a word with her mother about it?

On Friday when she was looking through the local paper, she turned to the Friendship Page.

There were plenty of men looking for women, and some looking for men. One or two caught her eye, but the one that really sent her searching for paper and pencil was:

"Widower. Late forties. Non Smoker. Own house and car. WLTM lady for eating out. Theatre. Holidays and walking."

Jenny wrote down the number to phone and his personal number.

'Mum, I'm just going round to Emma's,' she called out.

'Don't be too long,' said her mother. 'Remember I'll be going to the club later.'

Jenny picked up her bag and left. If her mother was going to a mixed club she would have been happier, but as it was for women and most of them were, in Jenny's estimation, old, her mother shouldn't mind if she was late or missed a night.

'You phone.'

'No, you, after all it's your mum.'

Jenny tentatively picked up her mobile and dialled the contact number. 'It's ringing. It's an answering machine.'

Emma came close to her friend and together they listened to the instructions.

'Quick, get a pen,' said Jenny.

Emma handed her a pen. 'I would like to meet you. I am forty-two, reasonably good-looking and my phone number is –' she reeled off her mobile number. She put the phone down as if she'd been scalded. 'Oh Emm, what have I done?'

Emma giggled. 'You ain't done nothing yet.'

'But what if he phones back?'

'Then you'll have to make a date for your mum.'

'But what will she say?'

'Probably have a good laugh about it. Remember she don't have to go.'

'But he's got my mobile number.' Jenny was beginning to panic. 'What if he's a dirty old man that plays on vulnerable women?'

'The only way you're going to find that out is to go and meet him. That's if he phones back. He might have had a load of replies.'

As Jenny walked home she was worried. Should she tell her mum? On second thoughts she wouldn't say anything till, and if, he phoned.

Two days later, Jenny was round at Emma's when her phone rang.

'Yes, that's right.' Jenny waved her hands furiously at her friend. 'That would be fine. I'll see you at eight then.'

'Was that him?'

Jenny nodded. 'I'm meeting him, or me mum is, at the King's Head at eight.'

'When?'

'Tomorrow night.'

'How will you know him?'

'He said he has white hair and he'll be sitting at a table in the window.'

'This is so exciting.'

'But will my mum think so?'

Emma shrugged.

As Jenny walked home she felt very apprehensive. What had she done? What if her mum wouldn't go along? Well she'd find out soon enough.

Her mother was sitting watching television when Jenny walked in. 'All right, love?' she asked, as her daughter plonked herself next to her.

'Mum. What would you say if I told you I've got you a date?'

'What?'

'I've got you a date for tomorrow night.'

'Where?'

'At the King's Head.'

'What? You expect me to go along to that sleazy pub to meet a bloke I don't know? You must be raving mad. How did you get round to doing this?'

Jenny took the remote control and turned the sound right down. 'You see, I'm worried about you. I want you to go out again and have fun, not be stuck in here most evenings. I want you to meet people.'

'I meet enough people all day.'

'I know. But sitting at a checkout in a supermarket all day ain't exactly a thrill a minute.'

'I don't know, it can have its moments. Anyway, how did this all come about?'

Jenny went into great detail about how it happened.

'And he wants to meet me?'

'Yes, but don't worry, me and Emma will be there.'

'Don't you think he'll worry about three women all turning up together?'

'We won't be with you, we'll be sitting watching, making sure nothing happens.'

'What's his name?'

'Ted. So you're going to go?'

'No. Course not.' Shirley shifted her seat and took back the remote.

'Mum, he's got my phone number. What if he phones me back?'

'Then you'll just have to change your number.'

'But Mum.'

'You got yourself into this, so you can get yourself out of it.'

'I only did it for you.'

'I know. But I'm not going on any blind date.'

'But Mum,' said Jenny once again. 'Just come along. He might be very nice.'

'And he might be some old man who wants a home and someone to wait on him hand and foot.'

'Oh, there's no pleasing you. I'm going to bed.' She stormed out of the room, leaving her mother speechless.

The following evening Jenny and Emma made their way to the King's Head. Jenny had decided to go and apologise to the man and explain about her mother.

'D'you think he'll be annoyed?' asked Emma.

'I would think so.'

'Are you worried about meeting him?'

'Course I am.' Jenny pushed open the pub door and looked round. 'That looks like him,' she whispered to Emma.

'Well, go on then.'

Jenny went up to a white-haired man who was sitting in a window seat. 'Excuse me. But you wouldn't be Ted, by any chance, would you?'

He looked up, surprised. 'Yes, but you can't possibly be Shirley.'

'No. Shirley's my mum.'

'So what's she doing sending her daughter along, she got cold feet?'

Jenny looked down. 'I was going to tell you that she wasn't well, but that wouldn't be true. You see this was all my idea and, well, she wouldn't come.'

He finished his drink. 'Do you think I would go to all that trouble to put an ad in only for a slip of a girl to try and make a fool of me?'

'No. No I didn't. It's just that my mum is so lonely and I thought she should meet someone who sounded nice.'

He looked at her. 'I see.'

'You all right dad?' A tall good-looking young man came up to them. 'Is this that Shirley?'

'No. This is her daughter.'

'So where's Shirley?'

'My mum wouldn't come.'

'You've got a bloody cheek setting my dad up like this.'

'No. No it wasn't like that. You see I thought she would. I am very, very sorry.' Jenny stood up. 'I'd better go.' She walked over to Emma. 'Well, I really mucked that up.'

'I can see that.'

'Come on, let's go and tell mum that he seemed a decent man.' Jenny was disappointed that she hadn't found a man for her mum.

Two weeks later Jenny was in the reference library when some one who was sitting at the opposite table whispered:

'Have you answered any adverts lately?'

'Sorry?' said Jenny.

'You was in the pub a couple of weeks ago.'

'Yes, that's right. Who are you?'

'I'm a friend of Mark's.'

'Who's Mark?'

'Ted's son. I went with Mark, he was there to make sure the lady he was meeting was all right.'

'So, did you both have a good laugh about it?'

'No, we didn't. In fact we both admired you for looking out for your mum.'

'Thanks.'

'Mark was going to phone you but his dad had deleted your number. Wait till I tell him I've seen you again.'

'Why?'

'He quite fancied you.'

'Good for him.'

'But on second thoughts I ain't gonna tell him.'

'Please yourself. I ain't worried one way or another.'

'What you reading?' he asked.

'It's a reference book for my evening classes.'

'What you studying?'

'Journalism. What about you?'

'Horticulture.'

'That sounds interesting.'

'It is.'

'My mum loves gardening.'

'It's a bit more than just gardening. What's your name?'

'Why?'

'I'd like to take you out.'

He certainly had something, in a good-looking, rugged kind of way. 'Where?'

'Anywhere you fancy.'

'Me and my mate Emma go to Freda's on a Friday. We could meet you there.'

He smiled. 'You and Emma? Do you always play it safe?'

'What d'you mean?'

'Always take a friend along for safety.'

'No.'

'Right. I'll see you there about eight.' He closed his book and picked up the notes he'd been writing.

Jenny watched him walk away. He was rather nice. She smiled. She had been trying to get her mum fixed up and now it seemed that if things worked out right, not only had she found someone to help her mum in the garden, but she had found herself a bloke. She closed her book. She was very, very impressed with herself.

Saving Grace
Jan Jones

Grace pelted down the cliff path, her slim flip-flopped feet slipping on the loose sand. 'Taz!' she shouted at the top of her voice. 'Taz!'

At the next turn she skidded hazardously and found herself sliding towards the railings. 'Aargh!' she yelled, fetching up hard against a young man in a black T-shirt and tight denim jeans.

The owner of the clothes gasped as the breath was knocked out of him. His professional name was Oliver Catterick and for twenty uneventful minutes he had been staring glumly at the beach, the sea and the pier. In the past ten seconds, however, he'd been crashed into first by a lunatic Labrador and then by this harum-scarum girl. His rib-cage was now rather better acquainted with the shape of the railings than it had any wish to be.

'Oh lord! Sorry.' Grace pushed a tangle of wind-blown hair out of her eyes. 'It's these stupid shoes. Are you all right?'

'Possibly.' Oliver straightened up, inhaling cautiously. Everything still seemed to work. He pointed down the path. 'If you're chasing a dog, he went that way.'

Grace grinned. 'Thanks.' She made to charge off again, then peered back at him. 'Excuse me, are you Oliver Catterick? From the Pier Theatre?'

Oliver turned red.

Her voice rose. 'You are! Gosh, how wonderful. You look different in normal clothes and without the stage make-up, but I recognised you because of your picture in the programme. My name's Grace.'

Oliver's reply was snatched away by a strong gust of wind.

'Pardon?' shouted Grace.

Oliver began to feel foolish. He couldn't continue being broody and doomed with an eager fan screaming questions at him. A flash of black caught the corner of his eye. 'Your dog!' he said, and set off at a circumspect lope down the path.

They reached the bottom, floundering in the deep, soft sand of the beach. Grace took hold of his arm to steady herself while she shook her flip-flops out. Oliver was glad of the halt. He was out of breath and his knees didn't feel as if they belonged to him. Maybe he should exercise more.

Grace was chattering on. 'Taz is terrible. He pretends he doesn't know where we're heading, then as soon as we get to the top of the cliff, he slips his collar and off he goes.' She grinned up at Oliver with her plain, open face. 'Come on, he'll be this way.'

For no real reason, Oliver walked alongside her. At least it was sheltered from the wind down here. He peeked surreptitiously sideways. She wasn't as young as he'd first thought. Early twenties probably, but lithe of body and as natural in disposition as a child. She certainly made a refreshing change from the super-charged artificiality of his working life.

'Sorry for blurting out all that about recognising you, but you were so wonderful in the show, I couldn't help myself.'

'Wonderful?' Oliver stopped abruptly and looked back with bitter loathing towards the theatre on the pier.

'But you were!' cried Grace.

'Hmph.' Oliver strode on along the beach where the going was firmer.

Grace had to half-run to catch up with him. 'What's the matter?'

'Nothing,' he ground out.

'Look, would you –' Grace was really running now '– would you mind autographing my programme?'

'Christ!' The expletive burst from Oliver. Then, as he stared down at Grace's rounded eyes and the "o" of her mouth, the professional in him reasserted itself. 'Yes, yes of course I will. Bring it round to the stage door some time.'

To his surprise, she reached up a hand and touched his cheek. 'You're a really nice man, d'you know that? Would you like a cup of tea?'

'Er –' Bewildered, Oliver followed her to a group of beach huts set amongst the dunes. At the foot of one lay a panting black Labrador, tongue lolling, eyes unabashed.

'Hello, horrible,' said Grace. 'Apologise to the nice man this instant.'

Taz rolled over on to his back.

'No shame, you see? He says you can rub his tummy if you want. If you're a doggy person, that is.'

'I used to be.' Oliver sat on the wooden steps and accepted Taz's invitation. He found he rather liked the approving look on Grace's face. He rather liked her legs too, now he was at eye level with them. She evidently spent a good deal of time walking her dog.

She fished a key out of her shorts and unlocked the door. From inside the beach hut she brought a drinking bowl and a container of water. Taz scrambled upright, gulping it down with a total lack of anything which might be described as table manners.

Oliver prudently moved a couple of steps higher. From the assortment of stuff inside the hut (some of it looked to have been there for years), he deduced Grace must be local. He didn't envy her that. It was the end of summer and already the weather was beginning to have bouts of unpredictability. Oh, it was pleasant enough here in the sun, but he wouldn't like to be around during a winter gale with the sea slate-grey and whipped into lashing fury.

Grace was making restful domestic noises behind him. He watched the holiday-makers on the sands: kids digging holes and building castles, mums knitting, dads dozing under their newspapers. Time slipped by. He looked up, surprisingly relaxed, to find Grace turning off the camping stove, sitting down at the top of the steps and handing him a steaming mug of tea. She'd kicked off her flip-flops and had finger-combed her tangled hair. She'd also discarded her overshirt. The small, neat mounds of her breasts, delectably suntanned, showed clearly under her strappy top.

'I'm sorry if I upset you before. You looked as though you might run for ever.'

Oliver looked away from her enticing body. 'I considered it,' he admitted.

'Why?' asked Grace.

He didn't meet her eyes. 'Because I'm not a wonderful actor. I'm adequate, that's all. I'm twenty-six years old, I'm playing second lead in a second-rate end-of-the-pier show and I'm never likely to do better. And we close next week and I haven't got any more work lined up until a possible panto at Christmas. Which I'll only get because of my singing voice.'

'So?'

Oliver twisted to face her. 'So it isn't exactly how I envisioned my life.'

Grace was silent. Then, 'Most of the audience don't know it's a second-rate show.'

Oliver frowned, sipping his tea. 'Meaning?'

Grace smiled, slid down a step. Her bare foot brushed his leg. 'Meaning – to them, it's magic. A visit to the theatre. Sitting in velvet seats. The lights going down, the curtain going up, the players on the stage. It's an event, it's special, it's a different world. And that scene where you and Lady Evelyn are about to run off together before her husband comes in and spoils everything – that's not second-rate at all.'

Oliver shrugged, embarrassed. 'Sally West is a good actress. She makes it easy.' But inside he warmed because he too had felt the magic in that scene.

Grace's voice was soft. 'You make it easy for her. You flatter her, show off her best side. She's grateful. She'll remember you. It takes two, Oliver.'

'What do you know about it?' But his voice was gruff, not displeased.

Grace put her mug down, snuggled another step closer to him. 'My dad was an actor. Not a great one, but he kept the Pier Theatre going for thirty years. He was useful, amenable, reliable. He was a good feed for comedians, so word got around and better ones signed contracts to play here. He never upstaged, never threw a tantrum. Directors liked him, were happy to come down for the season and bring names with them. People remembered him for being easy to work with, for giving them a good season.'

'Huh.' But Oliver slipped an arm round her all the same.

She leaned against him, warm and lissom. 'There was a threat to close the theatre last year; the council wanted to put another bingo hall in. They didn't believe the outcry they got! I work there, at the theatre. Selling programmes and coffee and ice-creams. I see the faces of the audience when they come out at the end. They're all happy, all laughing. Some of them are so happy they don't even talk, they just smile. It's a wonderful gift, being able to make people happy.'

She'd caught him now. Oliver looked down into her serious, transformed face and felt some of the wonder that he and his fellow actors inspired. It reminded him of feelings that he'd once known and had thought were lost. He dropped his head in gratitude, drinking in her adoration, and without in the least meaning to, found himself kissing her.

Within the circle of his arms she ran her hands over his back, under his T-shirt, around his jeans. She angled her body so that his palm brushed her breast. He felt the nipple harden, slipped his fingers beneath the thin strap.

'Don't stop,' she breathed.

He dropped his mouth to her throat. 'We'll have to,' he said, laying an arrow of kisses down her soft, welcoming skin. 'I haven't got anything with me.'

Grace arched her back, inviting his lips to continue deliciously downwards, shivering with pleasure when they did. 'I have,' she murmured, 'and what's more, there's a nice thick picnic rug inside the hut. Guard the door, Taz.'

271

'You're late, love. The new programmes have arrived. You'll have to rush to get them folded and the flyers inserted ready for tonight.'

'No sweat, Mum.'

Getting up petitions, handing out flyers, working front of house for peanuts – all these were the mundane things that held together the fabric of the theatre and kept accountants at bay. But there were also the players themselves, the life blood of the provincial circuit. Disillusioned actors, faded divas. They were needed around the country just as desperately as were filled seats and money in the cashbox. Where would they be if no one took the trouble to tell them how much ordinary people appreciated them? Grace had learnt well the lessons entrusted to her by her father.

She and Oliver had paused in unspoken consent half-way up the cliff. He'd leant back against the railings in the same pose she had seen from the cliff top, just before she'd abruptly changed her plans for the afternoon and had raced home to fetch Taz and swap her shoes.

"Do you know?" he said. "A couple of hours ago I was ready to chuck it in and become an insurance salesman or something. Instead I'm going straight to the phone to get my agent to hustle me up some work, no matter what it is."

Grace had applauded. "That's the spirit!"

"And it's down to you." His arms had pulled her to him again in an intimate reminder of his thanks.

Now, Grace stood in the shower, her face upturned to the warm, rushing water. All right, so going all the way to the finale might not have been quite what she'd intended when she'd spotted Oliver, disenchanted and miserable, earlier on today. On the other hand, remembering how he'd looked when they'd parted, with his eyes shining and his fire rekindled, her body tingled in a lovely surge of well-being and she knew she'd been right.

Her mother's voice floated up the stairs. 'Box office receipts are up again this week. Dad would have been so proud of you, Grace, the way you've fought to keep the theatre alive.'

Grace towelled her hair dry and winked at her reflection in the bamboo-framed mirror. 'In a lot more ways than one,' she said to herself with a chuckle.

The Fox
Sally Quilford

The nursing home residents congregated on the beach, awaiting orders to enjoy themselves.

'Don't you want a wheelchair, Mrs Benson?' asked Emma.

'No thank you, dear. I'd rather like to feel the sand between my toes.' Frances was pleased that the junior care-worker had bothered to address her by her Sunday name.

'Oh you can't take your shoes off, Frances!' That was Babs, the senior care-worker. 'Health and safety reasons. We're not covered by insurance.'

'Do you think my toes might be eaten by a shark?'

'No.' The care-worker spoke slowly, as if she thought Frances might be unable to understand. 'But you might step on a broken bottle or a used syringe. Then you'll get septicaemia and die and then where will we be?'

'Well, you'd still be alive, and I'm eighty, so don't have much time left anyway. Though I could sue you for negligence before I die.' Frances winked at Emma, who blushed, but appeared to enjoy the joke.

'You don't understand the dangers out there. It's our job to keep you safe and if that means you keeping your Hush Puppies on, then by God, we'll do it. Emma, you stay with Frances and make sure she doesn't get into any mischief.'

As Babs wandered off to some of the more docile inmates, Emma saluted her behind her back.

A short time later, Frances sat on a breakwater, squidging her bare feet in to the sand.

'You'll get me shot,' said Emma, who sat on the next beam. Frances wondered how long it would take the new girl to become like Babs: as chilly as a frosty morning, with hands to match.

'You young people use such exaggerated terms nowadays,' said Frances.

'There's Babs going on daily about her passion with that mouth-breather on the moped, and you thinking you'll be shot for letting me take my shoes off. Believe me, I've been close to being shot and it's nothing like facing the ire of a care-worker.'

'You've been shot at?'

'No, well, not really.' Frances fingered the chain around her neck. It was solid gold, but the years had dulled it. At the end of a chain a small fox rested against Frances' chest, trembling as her heart beat from the exertion of the walk down the beach. 'But it was a close thing.'

'When was that? During the war? Sorry, Mrs Benson I shouldn't assume you were alive then...they taught us that in my NVQ class. It's stereotyping.'

'I *was* alive then, and near your age. I used to come to this beach once a week to meet someone.'

The tide was in when Frances arrived at the beach late one night in 1944. A faint torch flashed out the code, which her father had taught her, and she returned the answering signal. Sitting on a breakwater was the man she'd been sent to find.

"Qui êtes-vous? Où est le lapin?" His voice sounded startled.

Frances struggled to remember her grammar school French, then admitted defeat. "I do not know what you're saying. Do you speak English?"

"Oui. Yes. I speak English. Where is the rabbit?"

"He's broken his leg. He sent me instead. Oh, I'm supposed to say 'The Fox arrives at midnight?"

"And he has a bushy tail." She sensed from his tone that the Frenchman smiled, though it was too dark to make out his features. "You English with your Aesop codenames. The Germans read the fables too, you know. Comment vous appelez-vous? What is your name?"

"Frances."

"Frances?" Her named rolled off his tongue, giving it an exotic sound. "You are to take this to the rabbit. He will know what to do with it." The Fox – Frances never did learn his real name despite giving up her own too easily – handed her a bulky package. "Go, quickly."

She began to walk away then noticed that he was still sitting on the breakwater. "What are you waiting for?" she asked.

"For the tide to go out again. Now, go."

"I'll wait with you if you want."

"I do not want. We cannot be seen together, or our lives will be in danger."

Frances returned home with the package. It never occurred to her to ask her father, Jack, what it contained. Nor did she wonder about the well-dressed man who came to see her father several days later, taking the package with him. She only wanted to know about the Fox. Who was he? How old was he? Was he married? Her father could not answer, and her mother, Dora, looked worried.

The following week, she heard them arguing about sending her to meet the Fox. Her mother was vehemently opposed. Frances was pleased when Jack insisted they had no other choice.

Once out of her mother's sight she applied lipstick and rouge, loaned to her by the land army girls who worked her parents' farm. It was lucky for the Fox and for the war effort that Frances wanted to keep him all to herself. She wasn't going to share details about him with the girls.

Frances left the farm earlier than necessary. She waited on the breakwater, going over in her mind the things she could say to impress him.

"Bonsoir, Frances."

"Oh, you're here." He was good. Frances hadn't heard him approaching. "The Fox arrives at midnight."

"And has a bushy tail. This is the last package. Take it to the rabbit and tell him we are ready."

"You're not coming again?"

"Non. It is time for me to…" He didn't finish. A searchlight lit up the far end of the beach. "What is that?" He crouched down in front of the breakwater but the beam was making its way down the beach and would soon find them.

"I don't know."

"We must hide. If I am found…"

"But you're on our side."

"Tell that to all the Europeans in your prisoner of war camps."

"I know somewhere we can hide. A cave me and my brother used to play in."

Frances reached out for his hand in the dark and scrambled over the breakwater, dragging him with her. The light passed over their heads as they ducked down. Then it moved back up the beach.

Frances moved quickly, urging the Fox to follow her. A couple of times they had to throw themselves flat on the sand, hoping that the men with the light would mistake them for rocks or seaweed. They were near to the caves when they heard voices, and a shot. It ricocheted off a rock near the mouth of the cave. Frances managed to stop herself screaming.

"Frances, this is not good. They must know we are here."

"It's alright, this cave is deep. It'll be cut off when the tide comes further in, but we'll be safe."

And they were. They huddled together in a small chamber as the sea lapped around the mouth of the cave.

"That was very brave, Frances."

"My dad says I'm either brave or too stupid to know the dangers. I think he's right. I didn't realise until tonight." The gunshot had shaken her more than she wanted to admit. Her voice faltered. "We've not seen much of the war up here. Not like in London and other cities. It's all been a bit exciting, but it's not exciting really, is it? People are being shot at and dying and you're afraid of being locked up, even though you're helping us. It's not fair." The tears she'd been suppressing began to flow.

He put his arms around her, holding her while she cried. He smelled of sweat and the sea, his cheek against hers rough with a five o'clock shadow. His kiss, when it came, was urgent, warm and salty. They clung together in the cave. Her bare toes curled into the sand as her body exploded at his touch.

They lay there till the tide went out, talking quietly but not saying anything of any importance. He gave away nothing of himself and she learned very quickly not to ask.

"You must go now."

"What about you?"

"I will wait here until tonight, then leave."

"I'll bring you some food."

"No, you cannot. It is not safe."

She was about to ask if she would see him again, then realised she already knew the answer. Kissing him one last time, she left him. She thought she would cry, but she didn't.

When she got home, after ignoring disapproving glances from the people in the village who, she learned later, assumed she'd stayed out all night with a local boy, her mother was in a state of extreme distress.

"Frances! Oh my girl. Where have you been?" Dora shook her none too gently, then hugged her tight. "A man was killed on the beach last night. A prisoner of war, who escaped. I thought… I thought…"

Frances removed herself from her mother's grasp, then went to give her father the final package.

The following week she returned to the cave, not sure what she would find. Resting on a rock was a piece of paper, wrapped round an object. She pulled the paper apart and found the gold chain. Hanging from it was the fox trinket. The note said *'I knew you would return. Merci.*
'

'And then what?' Emma looked as though she might shake Frances, just as Dora had all those years before.

'Then the D-Day landings happened, and I realised that I'd had a small part in it.'

'But the Fox? Did you marry him?'

'Does Benson sound French to you?' Frances laughed. 'No, I didn't marry him. I never saw him again.'

Emma looked disappointed, as if she were hoping for a happier ending.

'Come on, Mrs Benson. I can't promise you an exciting adventure, but I can buy you a ninety-nine ice-cream.'

'Call me Frances.'

When they returned to the meeting area, they found Babs surrounded by a crowd of people from the home. It seemed, from her sobbed explanation, that the mouth-breather had dumped her by text message.

'Oh dear,' said Frances, taking over the situation. 'Come and sit with me, Babs and I'll tell you a story about how sometimes things are better if they don't last.' She winked at Emma and helped a surprisingly grateful Babs onto the coach. As they walked along the aisle, Emma held her back for a moment.

'Don't you ever wish you'd met the Fox again?'

Frances squeezed the young girl's hand, thinking there was hope for her yet.

'Why do you think I've spent the afternoon with my bare toes in the sand?'

Can't Buy Me Love
Jill Stitson

'So, will you sleep with me if I give you five thousand pounds?'

I am bending over a blocked toilet and Toby and I are surveying
the unsavoury contents and making notes about contacting the
Cleansing Department. We are Environmental Health Officers,
or the "Dirty Buggers" as one of our favourite "clients", Beryl,
calls us. As well as being a colleague, Toby is also one of my
best friends. I grunt and do not bother to answer.

'So, Gemma, will you?' Toby is peeling off his rubber
gloves and not actually looking at me.

'Aw, come on Tobe, I'm not in the mood for jokes. You
know how bloody skint I am. It's just not funny.'

Five minutes later, Toby and I are sitting in my car writing
up our notes.

'I can't face Beryl just yet,' Toby sighs. 'You know the
neighbours have sent in a petition this time? Usual story, she's
feeding the pigeons, the smell from her flat is awful, she has six
cats now, blah, blah, blah.'

We turn to each other. 'Coffee,' we say in unison.

Gino's is a quiet little coffee bar we call our "sanctuary"
and we escape there sometimes from our "life of grime" as the
TV programme put it.

'You know, I meant it, Gem, five thousand for one night of
passion. They say I'm good, you know.' His pale green eyes
behind round glasses smile at me. I decide to play the game.

'One: you haven't got the money. Two: I'm thirty-eight,
you're twenty-five. Three: I have a fifteen-year-old daughter.
Four: You're not my type. I like tall, dark and handsome.
You're even shorter than *me* and you've got ginger hair. Do you
want me to go on?'

'Jesus, Gemma. I'm not asking you to marry me, I'm asking for a shag for Christ Sakes. Also, I *do* have the money. Won a bit on the lottery. Oh, not a million or anything like, but enough.' He grins. 'Enough to pay you for a shag.'

'Would you stop using that word! I know Bridget Jones uses it all the time but, well, it doesn't exactly help your cause.' I sniff like an old maid.

Toby goes down on one knee. 'My darling Gemma,' he proclaims. 'Would you please do me the honour of becoming my lover for one glorious night?' He would say more, but we are getting some funny looks, so I kick his shin and he returns to his chair and looks at me innocently.

I narrow my eyes. There is definitely something not right about all this. Toby and I have been friends for two years and, in spite of the age difference, have loads in common. We like the same films, have the same sense of humour, we are just really good mates, but there has never been anything sexual, even at the office parties.

'You're up to something, Tobe,' I say in my best "older sister" voice. 'You've had loads of girlfriends, you don't *need* me in that way. Is this a bet or something?' I suddenly have terrible visions of being discussed in the gents.

'*Gemma!*' Toby sounds quite hurt. He takes my hand in a friend to friend way, no quivers of sexual excitement. 'Look, I like you. You know I do and I know you're hard up at the moment, Alan going off like that.' He looks away.

My husband, Alan, had suddenly left me and gone to Spain with a blonde bimbo half his age. Actually, she isn't a bimbo, just a very pretty young woman, but maintenance payments are few and far between.

'So, why not you and me?' he continues. 'I've never slept with an "older woman".' He is deliberately pricking my vanity. 'Could be fun, you know.'

'Tobe, I like you, I really do, but sex…' I shake my head. In fact, I haven't had sex for a long time. Alan and I had stopped making love a year ago and I hadn't actually missed it.

I read the articles about multiple orgasms with amazement and disbelief. I was lucky if I came every six months or so, and that was in the good times.

'All you have to do is lie back and think of England and the five thousand pounds.' Toby looks at me, then closes his eyes and makes snoring noises. I laugh as I am meant to and punch his arm.

'Let's go and see old Beryl,' I say. 'You know how much you like her tea.' It is Toby's turn to laugh. Beryl's tea, served in filthy cups, is a standing joke. We always pour it into the cats' bowls as soon as she leaves the room.

'So you'll be away just two nights?' Kim is lounging on my bed, looking at me packing, her limbs contorted, but still seeming comfortable as only a fifteen-year-old can.

'Er, yeah. Julie really needs a break and wants me to go with her. She's even paying.'

I look at Kim sideways and feel myself blushing. I've never been good at telling lies, but Kim seems oblivious to my discomfort and continues to chew the ends of her hair. I start to tell her not to, but she interrupts me.

'Seems a waste to me.'

'What do you mean? Look, I'll try and arrange for us to go away if you like.'

'Good God, no, Mother!' Kim always calls me mother if she thinks I am missing a point which to her is blindingly obvious.

'You should be going with a man. It's ages since Dad left (it isn't) and it's about time you had some sex.'

I think back to when I was fifteen and the conversations I had with *my* mother. The nearest we got to anything personal was when I said I wanted a bra.

'I don't know any men. Well, not any men I'd want to, er...' In view of what I was about to do, I needed an end to this conversation. 'So, if you'll just move, I'll get on with my packing.'

'You know who I think's really cool? Of course he's too young for you, but I think Toby's really sexy.'

'Toby! But he's short and he's got red hair and...' I run out of things to say and suddenly realise that this is my daughter I am talking to.

Kim rolls her eyes in disgust. 'Mum, you are *so* old-fashioned! I s'pose you still think Sean Connery is sexy and he's *ancient*. As old as Grandad!' She changes the subject, much to my momentary relief. 'You know, I think I'll go on the Pill soon. Jade is on it and her mum thinks it's OK so...'

She is winding me up and we both know it. I open the bedroom door and she departs without another word, just a grin, knowing she has won again.

Toby has booked us into a small hotel in Dorset overlooking the sea for a whole weekend, not one night.

'Special "beach holiday" weekend offer,' he had said. 'Might as well make the most of it.' He had leered in a "dirty old man" way which had only made me laugh.

I can't believe that I am doing this. P'raps I am having an early menopause. Women do strange things at that time, so I'm told. Or p'raps I'm just pissed off with Alan and am trying to get my own back, or rather my self-esteem back. Who knows!

'Welcome, Mrs *Smith*,' Toby smiles at his own 'wit' and takes my case. He is in the hotel lounge as arranged. We had agreed to travel separately.

'Hi, Tobe.' I feel strangely shy, but Toby appears not to notice.

'Right. The porter will see to your luggage and I'm going to take you for a brisk walk by the sea, followed by a wicked cream tea.' He sounds like an uncle taking his niece out for a treat and I start to relax. I am also glad I don't have to go to our room just yet.

Once out walking I forget everything and just enjoy Toby's company, as always. The sea is sparkling and the wind exhilarating. A few brave young girls are wearing bikinis, even though it is still quite cold for June. I look stealthily at Toby to see if he is lusting after the nubile youngsters on the beach, but he doesn't appear to be. He guides me into a cafe and we cram heavenly smelling warm scones covered in jam and cream into our mouths and talk lazily as we would at Gino's.

We are laughing as we get back to the hotel and I suddenly feel a sense of shock as Toby gets the key and we go to our room.

'OK, Gem, I'll leave you to unpack, have a shower, whatever. See you in the bar in about an hour.' He winks and leaves as if we are back at work and he is saying he'll meet me for lunch.

Stepping out on to the balcony, I look at the miles of sea and sand and wish I could really enjoy it, but returning to the room I can see nothing but the big double bed. I think about whether I should beat a hasty retreat while I still can, but decide on a shower instead. After all, Alan is enjoying himself with his young bit of stuff, why shouldn't I have some fun? Trouble is, I've forgotten how.

An hour later I descend the stairs and find Toby sitting in the bar.

'Wow! You look amazing.' He takes both my hands and looks at me with genuine admiration. I had gone to a lot of trouble and treated myself to a new outfit. My silk dress, in swirls of misty grey, cerise and palest pink, floats pleasingly around my body. The twelve-year-old sales girl had assured me that I look "minty" (whatever that is), but elegant and that it set off my dark hair.

The evening passes quickly and I find myself having fun. The food and wine are excellent and, after all, this is just my friend Toby, isn't it? And then the other diners leave and I realise that Cinderella is about to turn into a pumpkin.

We get to our room and Toby turns to me, his face serious for the first time that day.

'I'm not going to do anything you don't want, Gem.' He has taken off his glasses and his green eyes look strangely dark. He strokes my face gently while deftly unzipping the silk dress. It slips to the floor while I am still deciding whether to say a last minute 'no'.

'OK, you're all tensed up so I'll give you a massage.' He pats the bed. 'Come and lie down.' He sounds like my chiropractor and I relax and find myself doing as I'm told. 'Right, let's start with your feet.' He massages every single inch of both feet, attending to each toe separately. I start to feel a curious tingling sensation and it's not in my feet. He takes his shirt off revealing what I can only describe as a beautiful body. I knew he worked out, but neither his baggy T-shirts nor his suits had shown the toned muscles and broad shoulders.

Gently turning me onto my tummy, he works his way up my calves. When he reaches the backs of my knees and starts gently kissing and then licking, I know I am lost. He expertly unhooks my bra with one hand and turns me again onto my back. Tantalizingly avoiding my nipples, he caresses my breasts and traces their outline with his tongue. He carries on for ages, then finally relents and takes my nipples into his mouth, teasing and sucking. I feel wet and ready and hear a far-off voice saying, 'Now, Toby, now!' But he takes no notice, merely moving his mouth further up my body while still stroking my breasts. He kisses the hollow of my throat, licks my ears and eyelids and finally slides his tongue into my mouth, flicking, playing. I arch my back, thinking I can stand it no longer and only then does he thrust into me, again and again. Once more I hear my voice saying 'Yes, Toby, yes,' and I am hit by a wave of passion, realising, at last, what all the fuss is about. I collapse back on the bed and laugh in exultation. Toby is looking down at me and smiling.

'I told you it would be fun, Mrs Smith,' he smoothes my hair from my face and grasps it in both hands. 'Anybody ever tell you your hair is like black satin?' he says. But I am too sated to answer and fall asleep in his arms, only to wake two hours later when the whole delightful procedure starts again.

We don't see much of the beach or Dorset after that and in the remaining hours of our last night together I trace the outline of Toby's lips with my tongue and then start to giggle.

'You don't have five thousand pounds to give me, do you Tobe?'

'Well, not exactly, but it wasn't my fault, Miss.' He puts on his little boy act. 'It was all old Beryl's idea really. She read the tea leaves once when you weren't there. Said we belonged together, which I knew anyway, but I said you wouldn't look at me. The devious old bint said she'd seen a film where the guy got the girl by saying he'd give her a million dollars for just one night, and the idea sort of snowballed.' He squints up at me. 'I can't exactly give you the five thousand now all in one go, but I could pay in instalments over the next forty years or so.'

'I don't care about the next forty years,' I say. 'Let's just enjoy one day at a time, starting now.'

And that's exactly what we do.

Contributors' Biographies

Sheila Alcock lives in Tunbridge Wells, and is a member of her local Writers' Group. Formerly editor of the biographical section of *International Year Book* and *Statesmen's Who's Who*, she then edited *Historic Houses, Castles and Gardens*, and *Museums and Galleries in Great Britain and Ireland*. She has had a large number of short stories published and is a freelance journalist.

Lynne Barrett-Lee, though initially a short story writer, is now a full time novelist, her novels including *Julia Gets a Life, Virtual Strangers, One Day, Someday* and *Straight On Till Morning*. Her latest title, *Barefoot In The Dark*, is being published by Accent Press in October 2006, with revised and updated versions of her backlist to follow in 2007. When not writing, Lynne sometimes finds time to cook and clean for her husband and three children in Cardiff. Sadly, not often. But they cope.

Kelly Rose Bradford is a freelance journalist, newspaper columnist and fiction writer. Her short stories have been published in the UK and abroad, and her features regularly appear in the weekly and monthly women's magazines.

Tina Brown has featured in *Sexy Shorts for Christmas, Sexy Shorts for Summer, Scary Shorts for Halloween* and *Saucy Shorts for Chefs*. One of her short stories won a Mills and Boon / Woman's Day competition. Tina is a member of Romance Writers of Australia and has recently moved to Hervey Bay in Queensland.

Catrin Collier's seventeenth and eighteenth novels, *Tiger Bay Blues* and *Tiger Ragtime* will be published in April and November 2006 by Orion Books. As Katherine John, she has penned five crime novels, *By Any Name*, *Without Trace*, *Midnight Murders*, *Murder of a Dead Man* and Quick Read, *The Corpse's Tale*. All five will be published in 2006 by Accent Press.

Christine Emberson is a National Ford Fiesta Short Story Writing Competition winner. She lives in Kent with her two sons. She works part time in the City, tutors for Kent Children's University and runs her own children's party business. After success with publishing poetry, she is currently working on her first novel.

Elaine Everest is a freelance writer, Creative Writing tutor and Director of *Technology @ Home* magazine. She is thrilled to again be part of the Sexy Shorts team, especially as the chosen charity is so special to her, having been free of breast cancer for the past 26 years. Elaine lives in Swanley, Kent with her husband and her old English sheepdogs.

Penny Feeny is a former copywriter and editor and is now concentrating on fiction. Her short stories have been broadcast on Radio 4 and published widely in literary magazines in the UK and the US. Contributions to anthologies include *Her Majesty* (Tindal Street), *Naked City* (Route), *Bracket: a new generation in fiction* (Comma), *Big Voices, Small Confessions* (Spoiled Ink) and *Saucy Shorts for Chefs*. She has won several prizes for her writing and was runner-up in the recent BBC World Service Competition. Married with five children, she lives in Liverpool.

Kelly Florentia lives in North London with her husband. Her short stories have been published in women's magazines in the UK, Sweden and Australia, and she's a member of an online writers' group. She enjoys good music, fine food and wine and great conversation. Kelly plans to write a novel in the future.

Della Galton's passion is writing. She lives in a sixteenth century cottage with her husband and four dogs and works as a full time writer. She has sold hundreds of short stories to women's magazines and also writes serials and features. Her debut novel, *Passing Shadows*, published by Accent Press, is out now.

Maureen Brannigan, aka Maureen Gottfried, is a Scot who lives in Winnipeg. She has been published internationally using the pen names Kirsty Peters and Maureen Brannigan. She co-wrote the novel *Rock of Ages* with Ishbel Moore, under the pen name Alexandra Duncan. Maureen is a member of the international writers' group Wild Geese.

Zoë Griffin is a journalist, who trained at *The Daily Telegraph* before becoming deputy editor of *The Mail on Sunday*'s showbiz column. Every evening, she attends star studded parties, meeting weird and wonderful people, who provide the inspiration for the characters in her short stories. Zoë is currently working on her first novel.

Rosie Harris was born in Cardiff and grew up there and in the West Country. For some years she lived on Merseyside, before moving to Buckinghamshire. Married with three grown-up children, six grandchildren and one great grand-child she writes full time. Her Sagas have either a Cardiff or Liverpool background, and are set in the 1920s/30s; they are published in hardback by Heinemann and in Paperback by Arrow. Her most recent titles are; *Cobbler's Kids*; *Sunshine and Showers* and *Megan of Mersyside* – which was published in April 2006. The next title – *The Power of Dreams* – will be out in August 2006.

Sue Houghton lives in Nottinghamshire with her husband and two of her four grown-up children. An enthusiastic member of Wild Geese Writers, she has had over a hundred short stories published in women's magazines in the UK and abroad. Her first novel, *Nearly Dearly*, has been short-listed/runner-up in several writing competitions and she is currently working on her second.

Karen Howeld wrote 'Waiting For the Storm' after spending part of her honeymoon hiding in the closet while her beachside hotel room was trashed around her by Hurricane George. She used to be a journalist but turned to fiction because she didn't like upsetting people. She writes for children and adults.

Dawn Hudd lives in Hereford with her husband and three boys. When she's not writing short stories or working on her novel, she is a full time Teaching Assistant. She is also two thirds into a BA in Creative Writing, and is a member of the successful on-line writing group Wild Geese.

Jeannie Johnson is a full time writer who lives in the Wye Valley and Malta. She is the author of seventeen novels (some of which can be called more than sexy) and the winner of a BBC scriptwriting award. She gives sassy talks, leads workshops and will do anything for money! Her latest mainstream book is *Forgotten Faces*, paperback due in October.

Jan Jones is a member of the Romantic Novelists' Association and currently organises their annual conference. Her first novel – a romantic comedy called *Stage by Stage* – won the RNA New Writers' Award in 2005. She has had poems in the small press and many short stories printed in women's magazines.

Ruth Joseph, born in Cardiff, graduated from Glamorgan University with an M. Phil. in Creative Writing. Her memoir *Remembering Judith*, is published by Accent Press who also published her collection of prize-winning short stories entitled *Red Stilettos*. She is married with two children and two grandchildren and a rescue Labrador, who are her inspiration and comfort.

Bernardine Kennedy was born in London but spent most of her childhood in Singapore and Nigeria before settling in Essex. Her varied working life has included a career as an air hostess, a swimming instructor and a social worker. She's been a freelance writer for many years, specialising in popular travel features. Her fifth novel *Old Scores*, was published by Headline in March.

Sophie King is a pseudonym for journalist Jane Bidder. Sophie's first novel *The School Run*, published by Hodder last year, was a best seller. Her new novel *Mums@Home*, also published by Hodder, comes out in June. Sophie also writes short stories for magazines, including *Woman's Weekly* and *My Weekly*. As a journalist, she writes for several national newspapers and magazines, including *Woman*, *The Daily Telegraph* and *The Times*. She has three children and a dog.

Maggie Knutson has previously contributed to *Saucy Shorts for Chefs*. She's also had fiction published in *Quality Women's Fiction* and numerous articles in the *Hampshire Chronicle*. Maggie escaped from teaching several years ago and now concentrates on writing. Much of her fiction is inspired by visits abroad, especially Cyprus, where she used to live. Maggie now lives in Winchester with her husband and very cheeky little dog.

Heather Lister lives in Bristol. After many years teaching English, she now works to encourage reading and creative writing in groups of marginalised people. She contributed to *Saucy Shorts for Chefs,* and also writes poetry and plays. She is married, and has four large sons.

Mo McAuley has won several short story prizes and is currently working on a novel about fish, friends and family. She is also training to be a yoga teacher. Although married to an

Australian, she has never managed to fall in love with oysters and strenuously avoids young, handsome fishermen.

Colette McCormick's first literary success was second prize in a short story competition run by *Jackie* magazine in 1977. Having written for pleasure for twenty years whilst raising her family, Colette has recently decided to take writing more seriously. *Sexy Shorts for the Beach* represents her first major success.

Lauren McCrossan is the author of three novels, *Water Wings*, *Angel on Air* and *Serve Cool* and a surf magazine journalist, who divides her time between writing longhand on the beach and surfing the oceans of Europe and Hawaii with her professional surfer husband. Lauren has been known to wear sexy shorts on the beach but has hidden all photographic evidence!

Linda Michelmore lives in Torbay, just a short walk from the distractions of seaside bars and bistros. When she was awarded the Katie Fforde bursary by the Romantic Novelists' Association in 2004, Linda rather rashly gave up the day job to write full-time. Two years on and she is now able to afford the jam to go on the bread – just!

Linda Povey's short stories are regularly published in the major national women's magazines. She has contributed to the previous three of the Sexy Shorts series. Her play, *The Cat-Flap Burglar*, is to be performed this year in her home town of Bridgnorth. She has given up her teaching job to write full-time and is working on her first novel.

Sally Quilford works as an adviser in a Citizens Advice Bureau, which gives her loads of ideas for stories. She has featured in two Sexy Shorts anthologies to date, and the Bewrite Anthology *The Creature and the Rose*. She has also been published in magazines and newspapers in Britain and America.

Brenda Robb is a freelance writer and poet living in Swanley, Kent. She has won numerous competitions with her poetry and short stories and has recently had her first story accepted by a UK magazine. She is looking forward to promoting this book along with fellow students of her adult education class.

Rosemarie Rose, born in England, now lives in South Wales with her partner and two cats. She has had several short stories published in magazines, and has been placed and short-listed in various creative writing competitions. Having been part of *Saucy Shorts For Chefs*, she is thrilled to be involved with *Sexy Shorts For The Beach* and another worthy cause.

Gerry Savill has recently had her first short story published. Sexy Shorts will be her second success. Working for adult education as an exams officer, she started writing seriously two years ago by joining a creative writing class at the centre where she works.

Jill Steeples lives in Leighton Buzzard with her husband, two children and a wayward English Setter. She writes short stories for the popular women's magazines in the UK and Australia. Jill is an enthusiastic member of both her local writers' circle and the international online group, Wild Geese Writers. She is currently cogitating over her next best-selling novel.

Jill Stitson is originally from London, but now lives with her husband in Dorset. She had her first story published at the age of twelve and restarted writing six years ago after a long break. She has had articles and a short story published in women's magazines and also contributed to *Scary Shorts for Halloween* and *Saucy Shorts for Chefs*. Jill is a previous short story prize-winner in *Writers News*.

Ginny Swart lives in Cape Town, is married with three children and has been writing fiction for five years. She is a member of the 'Wild Geese' internet writing group. She was the winner of the 2003 Real Writers Fiction prize. Her stories have appeared in high school text books, anthologies and women's magazines.

Fran Tracey is married to Andrew and is Mum to Nathan, with another baby on the way. She lives in West London and is a librarian by trade, with a love of books. Having had short stories published in women's magazines in the UK and overseas, she enjoys writing saucy, hopefully funny tales.

Phil Trenfield was born and raised in Cheltenham. He now lives in Cardiff, where he works in event management. 'Trawler Trash' is Phil's third short story to be published. He is currently working on his first novel.

Nina Tucknott writes monthly gardening and cookery articles and has written hundreds of articles and short stories for magazines and anthologies. she is presently working on her first novel. Nina is a Swedish-speaking Finn who now lives in Brighton with with her husband and two teenage sons. She has taught creative writing and is the current chair of the West Sussex Writer's Club.

Jane Wenham-Jones is a novelist and journalist who has written for a wide range of women's magazines and national newspapers. She is the author of three novels – her latest *One Glass is Never Enough*, published by Accent Press, is out now in paperback. Jane has appeared on radio and television and is regularly booked as an after-dinner speaker. She writes a monthly advice column for *Writing Magazine*.

Ann West is a retired computer programmer who has never before been published. She still attends writing classes at her local Adult Education Centre. Ann lives in a tiny village in North Kent, and is owned by five cats. Her hobbies include painting, collecting and riding historic motorcycles.

Dee Williams was born in London and all her books are set in Rotherhithe, where she was born. Sixteen years ago her first manuscript was accepted by Headline. To date she has written sixteen novels, the latest of which comes out in paperback in June. Dee also gives talks about writing, donating all her fees to Breakthrough Breast Cancer, to date she has raised almost £5000.

Dawn Wingfield is a short story writer currently finishing her first novel. Her stories have been published online and in print, and she was shortlisted in the 2005 Real Writers Competition. She lives in Colorado with her four children and two mad dachshunds.

Jackie Winter writes short stories for women's magazines and also enjoys writing articles. She works in her local library, mainly for the opportunity it presents for taking home lots of lovely books and thereby feeding her other passion, which is reading. She plans to write a non-fiction book.

Lorraine Winter grew up in Northern Ireland but now lives near the sea in Sussex. Her first writing achievement was for writing the best 'book' on how she spent her summer holiday while at primary school. After a gap of many, many years, she now loves to write short stories, when she's not working as a midwife, helping her husband with his new business or enjoying the company of her four young grand-daughters. She has an idea for a novel when time allows. Lorraine is a member of the Wild Geese internet writing group.

Jan Wright had her first story published in 1999, and has since sold over one hundred stories to a variety of women's magazines. She lives in Cowes on the Isle of Wight, and has an apartment overlooking the harbour, which she shares with her husband and her trusty laptop.

Be SunSmart in the Summer Sun

Those most at risk are people with fair skin, lots of moles or freckles or a family history of skin cancer. Know your skin type and use the UV Index to find out when you need to protect yourself.

☀ Spend time in the shade between 11 and 3
The summer sun is most damaging to your skin in the middle of the day.

☀ Make sure you never burn
Sunburn can double your risk of skin cancer.

☀ Aim to cover up with a t-shirt, hat and sunglasses
When the sun is at its peak sunscreen is not enough.

☀ Remember to take extra care with children
Young skin is delicate. Keep babies out of the sun especially around midday.

☀ Then use factor 15+ sunscreen
Apply sunscreen generously and reapply often.

☀ Also...
Report mole changes or unusual skin growths promptly to your doctor.

INFORMATION ABOUT
CANCER RESEARCH UK

Who we are

Cancer Research UK is the world's leading independent organisation dedicated to cancer research. We are helping to cure cancer faster through world-class research.

What we do

As the largest independent funder of UK cancer research, we support the work of over 3,000 scientists, doctors and nurses throughout England, Scotland, Wales and Northern Ireland. Our groundbreaking work, funded overwhelmingly by donations from the general public, delivers medical advances that save thousands of lives.

How can you help us?

If you would like to support our work, please call us on 020 7009 8820, or visit our website www.cancerresearchuk.org

Registered charity no. 1089464